About the author

Ruth has dreamed of being a writer from an early age; sparked by having a poem published in an international charity newsletter at fifteen.

Her sharp wit and amusing take on life are reflected in her writing, and her second standalone novel is in production.

She spends as much time as possible writing and listening to music, juggling that with her busy life as a mum of four and director of her husband's construction company. She can be found in the Kent countryside, often drinking Shiraz.

*To Maggie
Enjoy!
Love
Ruth Brooks
x*

WRITTEN IN THE STARS

Ruth Brooks

WRITTEN IN THE STARS

Vanguard Press

VANGUARD PAPERBACK

© Copyright 2020
Ruth Brooks

The right of Ruth Brooks to be identified as author of
this work has been asserted by her in accordance with the
Copyright, Designs and Patents Act 1988.

All Rights Reserved

No reproduction, copy or transmission of this publication
may be made without written permission.
No paragraph of this publication may be reproduced,
copied or transmitted save with the written permission of the publisher,
or in accordance with the provisions
of the Copyright Act 1956 (as amended).

Any person who commits any unauthorised act in relation to
this publication may be liable to criminal
prosecution and civil claims for damages.

This is a work of fiction. Names, characters, businesses, places, events,
locales, and incidents are either the products of the author's imagination or
used in a fictitious manner. Any resemblance to actual persons, living or dead,
or actual events is purely coincidental.

A CIP catalogue record for this title is
available from the British Library.

ISBN 978 1 78465 766 6

Vanguard Press is an imprint of
Pegasus Elliot MacKenzie Publishers Ltd.
www.pegasuspublishers.com

First Published in 2020

Vanguard Press
Sheraton House Castle Park
Cambridge England

Printed & Bound in Great Britain

Dedication

For Steve and Ryan, the obsessions behind my inspiration.

One

"This is the last call for flight BA268 to London Heathrow." The tannoy echoed throughout the busy Los Angeles airport. The last of the straggling passengers made their way through the gate, the California sunshine beating in through the large windows. Aboard the plane was the usual bustle of everyone placing their bags in the overhead bins and settling into their seats for the long transatlantic flight.

Flight attendants were busy helping the passengers, all except one. Amy was at the front of the plane, enjoying the last few moments of her mobile phone being on, scrolling through her Instagram feed, looking longingly at the pictures of her favourite band, the lead singer of which she idolised. She was certainly not paying attention to the task at hand. Another attendant, her best friend, Beth, gave her a sharp elbow in the ribs. She was jolted out of her daydream and promptly got to work. Beth glared at her – Amy merely held her hands up and shrugged. Beth shook her head in exasperation.

When all the passengers were settled and the plane's engines roared into life, Amy and Beth took their places in the aisles to demonstrate the emergency procedures, as they had done so many times before, occasionally exchanging glances and grins across the thoroughfare at each other. When they finished, they made their way to the front of the plane to take their jump seats by the galley.

"Apparently, we have some VIPs on board," Beth muttered to Amy.

"Some grey humourless suits, no doubt." Amy gave her a side grin. Just as they were about to fasten their seatbelts for take-off, their supervisor appeared suddenly in front of them, frantic.

"My lovelies, Pete has been taken ill, and I need one of you to cover first class immediately," he said, at a hundred miles an hour. Lucas was a melodramatic character, but every bit as endearing as he was frenetic.

"Beth's got seniority." Amy poked her friend in the arm with her thumb.

"*I* don't want to do it." Beth looked at her. "Yes, I am senior. I delegate that you do it."

"Good enough for me." Lucas grabbed Amy's elbow. "Right, come on, Amy, we're holding up take-off. Get your sweet cheeks back downstairs poppet."

"But... I can't do first class!"

"Yes, you can. Be good experience for you," Beth said, giving her a firm shove. Before Amy could protest more, Lucas was hurrying her away. Beth waved and smiled a victor's smile. "Let me know who the Veeps are. Remember, all passengers are arseholes, just these are slightly richer!" she managed with a giggle. Amy rolled her eyes, their flamboyant supervisor hot on her heels.

She was hesitant to descend the stairs of the large plane. Lucas turned her to face him, placing his hands on her shoulders. "You can do this. You're pretty, professional and have trained for this. Own it girlfriend!" He kissed her on each cheek and sent her on her way. She breathed deep, and took each step carefully as the hubbub of economy above her ebbed away and the quiet of luxury met her ears and eyes. She found her seat without much time to glance around, and in a few moments the A380 began its slow taxi towards the runway. Amy leaned her head back and sighed. She would get into her groove down here no problem, but she enjoyed working with her best friend. The flight, and the work, was never tedious when they were on shift together.

She looked up at the lit 'fasten seatbelt' light. Any moment now it would be switched off and she would need to begin service. She carried out her business as routinely as if she were in economy still and had almost forgotten Beth's mention of VIPs, until she made her way down the wide aisles, glancing from large leather seat to large leather seat. No one of interest, no one well known, just faceless businessmen as she had expected, who ignored her presence. She moved through the cabin, and wondered which of these could be the VIP, surreptitiously scrutinising all their faces and body language. She pondered on what it might be that made them so important that their presence on this flight had reached the gossip of the cabin crew.

First class really was lovely – spacious, quiet, relaxed. She thought of Beth, and how busy she might be upstairs. Beth loved the bustle and the dramas, dealing with ordinary people, and the gratitude that usually followed. There appeared to be no drama down here, which explained why she passed this duty on to Amy. She made a mental note to scold her for giving her a boring job, and the fuss of having to prepare fancy food.

Just as this thought crossed her mind, she noticed a peal of laughter from a group of younger men she had not noticed in her previous perusal. Her eyes scanned to the rear of the cabin, where the source of the laughter appeared to be emanating from. She did a double take as she thought she saw, rather than businessmen, the familiar faces of her favourite band, Sovereign X. Had her eyes deceived her? She narrowed them and looked again, her gaze coming to rest on the lead singer – it was them for sure. She took a sharp intake of breath and slipped to the other side of the cabin partition, leaning against it, her stomach performing Olympic-level somersaults. She looked around to make sure her colleagues had not noticed her sudden unprofessional reaction. She could feel her cheeks glowing and clasped her hands to try to compose herself. She was infatuated with the lead singer, Zach Hayes, and a huge fan of their music. She had only ever seen them from afar at a concert, and although she saw famous people from time to time on flights, never anyone she admired as much as him.

OK, be cool. She smoothed her slicked hair back under her British Airways cap with the palm of her hand, took a slow breath and removed herself from the partition. Her nerves were on fire, but she did not want to miss the opportunity to serve them by one of her colleagues beating her to it. Ever the consummate professional, she made her way carefully to where they were seated. The other band members were chatting quietly and Zach had put his headphones on, seemingly engrossed in the music, nodding along. *Every bit as good-looking in real life.* Her stomach turned again and she was relieved these internal movements were not visible.

There was a pad and pen on the table in front of him; she noticed some writing on it. *Probably the genesis of some amazing new song,* she mused. Swooning inside, she attempted to be cool as ice outside. She needed to focus, and approached him directly, first. He looked up at her and her stomach backflipped. She smiled but avoided eye contact initially, fearful that if she did she would not be able to hold it together.

"Can I offer you a drink, sir?" Her voice came forth, deep and velvet, but in her head, she was screaming, 'I love you, I love you!'

"Hey… Amy…" He swiftly clocked her name badge, "Could I have a coffee, please?"

"Of course." She handed him a tray, with as steady a hand as she could muster, butterflies still swarming in her stomach.

"Thanks." He smiled benignly, and she smiled back, trying her hardest not to give away the fact that she was a massive fan. It would hardly be acceptable to start hassling him for autographs or selfies, especially in first class, plus she was sure she would get into trouble with Lucas; discretion was a matter of course. She felt herself blushing at his gaze, then swiftly moved on to serve the others, maintaining her smile as best she could.

As she turned to serve the other side of the aisle, she thought she could feel him watching her. Maybe she was just imagining it; she dared not look back to find out. She wasn't sure either outcome would have pleased her. She heard muffled chatter from his band mates, followed by a group chuckle. She wondered what had been said, she could not quite make it out, and looked up to the ceiling as she moved on to other passengers, sincerely hoping she had not made a fool of herself. This could be a long flight….

***

When the time came to serve lunch, Amy felt confident and composed. The reality of her idol being mere feet away – on her flight – was gradually sinking in. Throughout her duties, she found herself trying hard to listen to snippets of their conversation, catching glimpses of them – of him – in her peripheral vision. She loved to hear his laughter; real, and yet it was so surreal to see him, being confined with him (and several hundred other people) for ten or eleven hours in a metal tube. She had to keep snapping herself out of these musings, and on this occasion distraction came in the form of the cabin phone ringing right next to her, making her jump. She grabbed it: Beth.

"So?" came the voice from above.

"So, what?" Amy knew what she was after; she thought it worth milking, especially as Beth had put her up to it.

Beth called her on it. "Oh, I see! So, it's someone way more interesting then," she responded, matter-of-factly.

"Why do you say that?" Amy kept her cool, trying not to give the game away too soon.

"Oh, come on. I know you far too well. I can practically hear you holding back the excitement. It's a celeb, eh?"

"OK. Maybe. Maybe someone I love."

"But I'm right here!"

"Ha ha, funny. I'm serious, you gotta guess."

"Hmm…" Beth paused for a moment. "Oh! Is it? Is it really?"

"They were supposed to fly on a private jet today, but there were technical issues." Amy couldn't help letting out an excited laugh, having held it in for the flight thus far.

"Well, I don't think that's something to laugh about." Beth mockingly reproached.

"I just can't believe my luck."

"Me neither. I gave that to you! Flirt with Zach Hayes as much as you can, make my gift worthy! Gotta go, bye." She hung up. Amy placed the receiver back on its hook on the wall and continued preparation for lunch.

When she got to serving Zach, he was flicking through the calendar on his mobile phone. She took a deep breath, seizing another opportunity to talk to him, albeit through an admonishment.

"I'm sorry, sir, mobile phones should be switched off during the flight," she said, in a dulcet tone. He looked up as she spoke, startled. He had clearly not noticed her approach. He smiled, his lively blue-grey eyes brightening as he looked at her.

"Oh, I have it on airplane mode, so it's fine, right?" He drawled rhetorically, in his American accent.

"Yes, that is fine." She conceded. Of course, she could not say no to him. For anything. He could have asked her to strip naked right there; she most probably would have assented. He flies all the time, he knows the rules. She was just glad to have had another excuse to talk to him, to be near him. A little embarrassed, she was about to turn and continue serving, but to her surprise, he sparked a conversation.

"So, how long have you been a flight attendant?" he said, leaning back in his seat.

"Oh. I'm not normally in first class." She blurted, slightly high-pitched, her nerves grasping her at his sudden unexpected attention. His lips spread into a grin, at her flustering. Gone was her dulcet, velvet voice. *Don't give away that I am a fan.* She composed herself in a nano-second and brushed over her non-reply, "About two and a half years."

Professionalism had made a sharp exit, she smiled self-consciously.

"By your tone," he began quietly, she had to move closer to hear him properly, "I would hazard a guess it's not what you really want to be doing?" He looked searchingly at her, his expression playful and intrigued.

She was stunned, and more than a little alarmed, that he had come to so accurate a conclusion from her response. He flicked his mousy mop of hair back under his baseball cap. She thought she would melt, her cheeks glowed like hot embers. She looked down to her patent shoes, hoping the embarrassment she displayed would be interpreted as a result of his forward deduction, rather than her big, fat star-struck crush on him.

"No, actually, I want to be a writer," she replied discreetly, looking up to make sure none of her colleagues were in earshot.

"Cool. That's different. I like writing," he said, with a side grin. She felt her spirits rise at his apparent interest in her.

She let out a little laugh, dropping her guard completely. "I think a lot of people like your writing," she couldn't help herself retorting. He laughed and looked back down at his phone. The conversation was clearly over.

Disappointed, Amy briskly turned and moved away, so as not to outstay her welcome. She heard him melodically humming a tune, unaware that he had looked up again to watch her walk back down the aisle. Only when she reached her seat did she sneak a glance back at him. He was still looking down at his phone. She wished she had been able to engage him for longer – time was running out. But what was she hoping for? That he would ask for her number? That would be amazing, although highly unlikely. He had been attentive, but attracted to her? Probably not. Just another pleasant flight attendant, nothing special.

Amy did not get many more opportunities to speak to Zach, largely due to him sleeping. As they drew nearer to Heathrow, Amy felt her mood palpably drop. She only had moments left in his sphere, moments to try to make an impression. Wringing her hands, she tried frantically to think of an excuse to talk to him, or even just to get him to notice her. Nothing. She glanced down the aisle; he was talking animatedly to his band mates, not a single glance in her direction. She frowned in frustration and looked up expectantly at the 'fasten seatbelt' light; it would come on at any moment. She looked back at Zach one final time, before he would be out of sight when she took her seat; he smiled warmly at her. She returned the smile, just as the light came on.

When the plane landed, the crew lined up to see everyone off and Amy felt a pang of disappointment as Sovereign X neared the door for departure. Why couldn't she have been more dynamic? More sexy? Why hadn't she been able to find more excuses to talk to him? She felt her heartrate rise as they moved towards her in the line to bid thanks and goodbyes. The rest of the band passed her by, smiling and expressing gratitude, but Zach leaned in to shake her hand. As his hand slipped gently into hers, she took a deep breath and smiled, looking into his eyes.

"Good luck," he said with a wink, and exited the plane. She barely had time to thank him as he disappeared along the jet bridge.

She caught up with Beth as they clocked off their shift and made their way back to the flat they shared in their hometown. Beth was eager for all the details. Amy was happy to fill her in, albeit in a state of disappointment that she had not connected with him better.

That night after dinner, they sat down in front of the TV watching Sovereign X perform their new song on some mediocre talent show. Amy listened to Zach's soaring falsetto vocal and watched him with all his energy on stage, and sighed. How bizarre today had been. She knew that from this point onwards, rarely would a day go by when she would not think about her encounter with him.

It suddenly struck her how jet-lagged she felt. She bid Beth goodnight and made her way to bed. She grabbed the notebook she always kept close and did what she always did when she had a lot on her mind: jotted her deepest, darkest thoughts down. She sat on the edge of her bed and looked down at what she had written. She glanced through the open window at the night sky; stars glistened brightly at her, a plane's lights flashed intermittently, but steady, as it progressed out of view. She closed her eyes, her imagination sparked by her experience today – what if? What if he had asked for her number? What if he had been as attracted to her as she was to him? It was these thoughts that lay with her, at the forefront of her mind as she drifted off to sleep.

***

The memory of that flight was never far from Amy's thoughts. It haunted her, shadowed her every moment, and she placed Zach Hayes on a pedestal in her mind, so much so that no other man could get close to her. Her absorbing infatuation had been given fresh fuel and for a while she lost interest in relationships.

A few months after meeting Sovereign X on the plane, one particular man caught her eye. He was a frequent flyer, and they crossed paths several times before moving past simple pleasantries. She found out that he was an air-crash investigator, which intrigued her, and he oozed charisma. He was laid back, so she did most of the flirting. She loved a pursuit, and Will was fascinated to see how far she would push the envelope to get what she wanted. He was older than her, had an engaging sense of humour and an open demeanour – she was instantly attracted to him, and he her; with her perfect figure and quick wit, the chemistry between them was compelling. Her colleagues soon cottoned on to their relationship, and even her supervisor, Lucas, was dismissive when she would spend half her shift talking to Will.

There were plenty of times when they flew together; they spent time talking and laughing, falling in love. Their relationship was intense and passionate, and within six months, Will moved in with her. Amy discovered that the meticulousness he had in his career in engineering, he had in every other aspect of his life, especially in the bedroom. He was a perfectionist – which she found paradoxically challenging and admirable – he was particular about her pleasure though, and she came to love the quest for impeccability that he garnered in her. His methodical and stable personality was a sublime balance to her tendency for impetuousness, and sometimes volatile, emotions. But she also loved his sideways and twisted approach to problems in life; this was a great source of mirth, having acquired a chequered past, from tragedy to excess, running on the tracks.

While still at the airline, Amy completed the degree she had started before becoming a flight attendant, and she touted herself around to magazines to try to break into the career of her dreams as a writer. Will earned enough to support them both during her transition from one career to another, so she took the plunge and set herself up as a freelance journalist. She struggled at times, when there was no work, and nothing but rejections, but Will was there always, to encourage her through the dark moments of self-doubt.

Her break came when she wrote an article about nineties Britpop. Recognising she needed to make an impact somehow, she built up the courage to step into the office of *Delta*, a music magazine she had always loved. She walked through the doors, security hot on her heels, and managed to blag her way to the PA of the editor, and handed her the article, pleading with her to hand it to the editor for him to read. The PA at first looked at her with bemused curiosity – in a day and age where everything is communicated through email or other forms of faceless electronica, she was intrigued. She assured Amy her article would be seen, just before Amy was escorted from the building by security.

The editor, Paul, called her a few days later, impressed by her bold-as-brass approach to getting noticed. He thought her article was sublime, stating that, "the kids being influenced in their teens by Britpop are the artists breaking it now, these were the origins of their experimentation with music, therefore your article is current and relevant." He asked her to write another article, then another.

Finally, she felt she was on the road to success. It is somewhat ironic that providence preserves its largest blows for the times when we are enjoying the most euphoric moments of its beneficence. Or to put it another way, at a time when she felt most settled, she was utterly sideswiped one sunny June morning.

Two

Two years had passed since meeting the band on the plane. Amy had no articles to write, so was sleeping in. She was startled awake by the sound of her phone buzzing on the bedside cabinet. Her hand scrabbled around until it located the phone and she answered without looking at the caller ID.

"Hello," she croaked.

"Morning, Sleeping Beauty," came the voice of Paul from *Delta*. Ever since their first face-to-face meeting two months prior, he had been more than a little flirty with her. Amy was glad that they had not met face-to-face when he had first decided how good her work was; she did not want to get noticed because of how she looked. She was unfazed by his banter, and had decided to take it in good humour – however inappropriate it may be. She had enough mettle to enter a cut-throat profession and intended to keep hold of the favourable position she was in with this editor.

"Listen, Amy, we have a big interview booked in for Mark today. Unfortunately, he has called in sick. The rest of my team are flat out; I have no one free to cover it. I wondered if you would conduct it for me? I know it's throwing you in at the deep end, but I'm desperate... as you already know." He chuckled.

Amy's stomach turned over with nervous excitement. "I've never done an interview before, like, ever. I would love to do it, but I should prep you, Paul, just in case I cock it up completely."

"You can 'prep' me any time you want." Paul laughed again. "Amy, I have complete faith in you. Your writing's first class, let that be your guide. The questions are already set, I'm pinging them over to you now. The band are only in the country for a few days and we can't reschedule – we were lucky to get this slot."

"I mean, of course I'll do it. I'm open to trying new stuff out."

"I had heard that."

"Cheeky sod. Who's the group anyway?"

"Sovereign X. You heard of them?"

Amy's heart jumped into her throat. *Of course I've bloody heard of them, I'm probably their biggest fan!* She swallowed back down her now racing heart, before responding, "Yes, I've heard of them." This came out slightly louder and more high-pitched than she had intended. Her nerves were running riot.

"I've also put the details of where you will be meeting them in the email."

"Yes... yes, great." But she was hardly listening.

"I need the article wrapped up by midday tomorrow, please."

"Sure." Amy hung up the phone and lay staring up at the ceiling of her bedroom for a few moments.

Will was away at an investigation in America and she had been alone all week. She had gotten used to him being away, sometimes uncontactable for days on end, but she missed him badly. They always made up for it when they saw each other again though, sometimes spending all day in the bedroom. This thought crossed her mind as she sighed and checked her emails. They had not had sex for nearly two weeks, for them that was a significant drought. She had always been concerned about Will's fidelity, being away a lot, such as he was, but here she was about to conduct an interview with the most powerful infatuation she had ever had.

The details of the interview had come through from Paul, and she was to meet the band at a Mayfair hotel in just three hours.

She jumped into the shower and could not help laughing to herself. She had recently been to see them in concert, just a faceless fan in a crowd of thousands. She was nothing to Zach, just someone he had chatted to once on a flight. How many fans had encountered him in a similar way? Easily forgettable, pleasant, but no lasting impression, why should she stand out? Nevertheless, she made sure she looked her best, taking time over her appearance; not that she wouldn't normally, but the prospect of meeting one's idol for a second time added more due care and attention.

Maybe she could make an impact, especially as this time she was more than a mile-high waitress, she was in a more powerful, influential position; writing an article about them. They would be more focussed on her. *He* would notice her more and there would have to be more interaction. Maybe enough for her to switch on the charm offensive.

She decided to get to the hotel as early as she could to acquaint herself with the daunting prospect ahead of her. Half an hour before the set interview time, she found herself walking through the doors of the elegant Edwardian building, on a corner near Hyde Park. She immediately felt she had walked into somewhere she did not belong, a place dripping with money. She sat down in the lobby and glanced around at the people coming and going, musing over who they might be and what their backstory was. She loved to people-watch, fascinated with observing their behaviour. She saw an older, wealthy-looking, grey-haired businessman with a much younger, prettier girl on his arm, and smiled at a fulfilled stereotype, but she also saw an older woman with a much younger, good-looking man on her arm. She smiled at the irony of the two scenarios and watched as they went about their day, not missing the furtive but suggestive glance from a waiter towards the young man, passing them in the hallway.

"No prizes for guessing what's going on there," she muttered to herself under her breath and flicked through her phone, smiling. She was startled by a concierge appearing in front of her, blocking the sun's rays through the window. She was not dressed in keeping with a place like this, and must have looked incongruous; however, the concierge smiled and his demeanour was polite and warm.

"Can I help you at all, ma'am?" He had an accent of some sort, but Amy could not determine it.

"Oh, yes. I'm here to conduct an interview with some guests here, Sovereign X?"

"Of course, there have been other journalists here this morning. Please come with me to reception." She rose and followed him. "May I have your name, please?" he asked while checking a computer at the desk. *Polish*, she deduced, from hearing him speak some more.

"Amy Armstrong, *Delta Music Magazine*."

He frowned. "I have your magazine here, but not your name."

"Oh, it may still be under the name of Mark Steele. He's ill today and I'm filling in for him." She looked at him earnestly, willing him to believe her. Why had Paul not sorted this out?

"Please take a seat, while I check this for you."

Amy sat down again tentatively and watched as he picked up his phone, she guessed it would be to call Paul. After a very brief conversation, he smiled indicating she should approach the desk again. He told her the name of the suite, where it was located, and she headed to the lift. As she did so, her nerves stepped up a gear. Her heart was racing, beating like a distant drum, and she rubbed her increasingly sweaty palms together. She so wanted to be uber-cool seeing them again. *Hold your shit together, hold your shit together* – she repeated the mantra in her head over and over.

The lift pinged to a halt, and she took a slow breath as she exited and headed down the hall to the suite the concierge had advised her the name of. Reaching the door, she paused, closed her eyes, and knocked. A guy let her in who introduced himself as one of the management team. He led her to the lounge area.

"Take a seat, there's water on the table if you would like to help yourself. The guys will be through in a moment."

"Thank you," Amy said in as composed a voice as she could muster.

Instruments were being played in the room next door, and she could hear Zach's voice muffled through the wall. She stared at the door, and as he let out a peal of laughter, the sound stirred the butterflies in her belly. It felt so strange to be near him again, but she was determined that the awkwardness she had displayed on the plane would not overcome her this time. She read through her questions once more and sipped her water.

She felt like a different person to the one back then, older, more self-assured and confident, even her appearance had changed; gone was the bleached blonde hair, back to her natural colour; no starched, conservative British Airways uniform this time. Her outfit was much more fitting for a hip, budding freelance journalist: ripped skinny jeans and a low-cut leather-look top, obligatory heels, giving her height and heightened confidence. The adjoining room fell silent, and she braced herself for their entrance. The door opened and she stood up as they walked into the room. She felt sure that none of them, let alone Zach, would remember her. She flicked her hair and leaned across to shake all their hands, introducing her herself as Amy Armstrong from *Delta*, watching carefully to see if there was any reaction on his bandmates' faces. Nothing. She reached Zach last – detecting no recognition in his face either. *Why would he, it was a long time ago.* She tried to put it to the back of her mind that she had encountered them before in very different circumstances.

When they were all seated, she set her iPad to record, placed it on the table in front of them, and took an infinitesimal glance at Zach. *Shit, he's so hot.* She shook the thought out of her head and proceeded with the interview. She worked her way through questions about their new single, forthcoming album, tours and the like. She asked Zach about his song-writing for other artists, whether they like it here in Britain – stock questions that gave way to stock answers, with a smattering of humour. Amy felt her confidence lift with each passing moment, but just as she got into a flow and was beginning to enjoy it, she reached the end of her list of questions.

She had no choice but to draw the interview to a close, feeling a disappointment similar to what she had felt on the plane all that time ago. She gathered her iPad and notes and bade them goodbye, reluctant to be walking away from them – and especially him – once again. She rose to leave, and to her surprise, Zach rose too. He walked with her to the door.

"So, you made it into writing now then, huh?" he said. She only half-heard, the comment catching her off-guard.

"I'm sorry?" she said, as her brain frantically tried to compute what he had said.

"I hope you're not. Actually, I hope we're not, after you publish this interview." He teased with a grin. She smiled and willed her cheeks not to glow red.

"I wasn't sure if you would remember me." She ran her fingers through her hair, to flick it out of her eyes.

"Hmm. It's funny, I wasn't sure at first. You look a little different." He was looking at her hair.

"Yes, not a natural blonde, I'm afraid."

"Natural is better." He smiled with a glint in his eye. She definitely blushed now and looked away with a coy grin. She felt desire for him rise, adrenaline filled her. His obvious flirting flattered her, boosting her ego. *OK, game face on.*

"Thank you." She accepted his compliment graciously.

"I guess you remember me, then."

She couldn't help a laugh. "I think I made it pretty obvious back then that I'm a big fan." She wasn't sure she could hide her dilating pupils, and her pulse was rising with the prolonged moments of his attention. She placed her hand on the doorknob, partly to show a willingness not to outstay her welcome, partly to see if he tried to keep her there. Her test paid off; he leaned on the door to prevent her from opening it.

"Destiny is a strange thing, don't you think?" He looked at her inquisitively. She frowned at his abstruse comment. She let go of the doorknob and leaned on the door, mirroring his stance. His pale eyes were searching hers. She refused to bite and satisfy him with a predictably acquiescent response to his off-beat comment.

"I think we make our own destiny," was her simple reply.

He was obviously intrigued. "Do you? Do you not think that we have crossed paths under the most random circumstances?"

"I guess." Her aloofness was really drawing him in, like a powerful gravitational pull, and every passing moment she felt she was stealing with him in this increasingly sexually charged encounter, her nerves ebbed and calmed. The evident confirmation of his attraction fuelled her ability to allure, but she expected the moment to pass into the ether and for him to bid her goodbye imminently.

"Do you like sushi?" he blurted suddenly. It broke the spell, and she was thrown by his immediate cutting to the chase. "Erm…"

"Come try some with me tomorrow night, I know a great place. We leave the UK in a couple days."

Suddenly she was struck by the reality of her situation and an image of Will's face appeared in her mind. "I don't…" She faltered as she landed back on earth with a bump. She had fantasised about a moment like this so many times, but now it was thrust upon her, she did not quite know how to respond. Plus, she had never eaten sushi before.

As if reading her mind, he said, "It doesn't have to be sushi. Pizza?" His eyes were bright, never leaving contact with hers. He had maintained complete control of the conversation.

"You're asking me out..." The words spilled out of her mouth, barely aware that the phrase had made the journey from brain to lips. Fortunately, he laughed at her shock. "I'm..." She looked him in the eyes again, his mischievous eyes. *Man, do I fancy him so much...* He was only in London a few days, surely one dinner wouldn't hurt?

"Yeah, OK." She scribbled her number onto her notepad, tore it off and gave it to him. "This is my mobile number."

"Mobile." He mocked her posh 'Home Counties' accent.

Her feistiness made an unexpected appearance. "Taking the piss out of my accent is a strange flirting tactic." Her sharp tongue cut a path through the enormity of the situation, but she was smiling and playful. He laughed at her sudden tenacity, and seemed even more attracted to her for it.

"I just love the way you guys talk. Rad. So, I'll call you."

"Cool, bye." She grabbed the doorknob again, and this time he moved away to let her through. She looked back briefly and smiled as she strode down the hallway, full of bravado from the rush of the encounter. This time, she was aware of him watching her walk away, conscious that her figure was accentuated by her outfit. She smiled as she reached the lift, certain that he was eyeing her rear as she walked.

It was only when she heard him shut the door did the bravado subside, and she allowed herself to realise how hard her heart was thumping through her chest. *What. Just. Happened!* Not only had she met someone she idolised – twice – but they had had a flirtation, a frisson. He liked her for sure – the chemistry was unmistakable, but the whole asking her out thing? Surely that was to flatter his ego, rather than be genuine? Time would tell if he meant it. But, what about the large elephant in the room – her boyfriend, Will, whom she loved very much? She banged her head lightly on the cold steel wall of the lift. A glamourous elderly woman sharing the lift with her gave her a disdainful look. Amy smiled apologetically.

She took a slow stroll back through the lobby. As she passed reception, the concierge called to her, "Did you get what you wanted, Miss Armstrong?"

"And some," she couldn't resist replying, with a smile.

He smiled innocently in return, oblivious to her meaning. She carried on walking, mulling over what had happened, her mind filled with Zach. She tried to put it into perspective. This may have played out, but surely would fizzle and disperse into thin air. What was the point of worrying? He was unlikely to even call. She satisfied herself with this conclusion and her conscience felt lighter as she walked out of the hotel to hail a taxi. It did not stop her opening her messages to text Beth immediately she got in the cab. But before she could send her message, the phone rang. *Fuck me, that was quick!* Her stomach turned over as she looked at her phone to see that it was, in fact, not Zach, but Will. Now feeling guilty, she exhaled and feigned nonchalance.

"Hi, Babe."

"Hiya, you OK?" There was a delay, and he sounded like he had just woken up. Which, considering the time difference, he probably had.

"I'm good, how're you? I miss you."

"You too. Hate not waking up next to you." His deep voice was like nectar pouring into her ears. She closed her eyes and the bubble in her mind containing Zach's image popped instantly.

"And me. When will you be home?"

"Could be a few days, more likely a week though. What you up to?"

She hesitated. "Not much. Just kicking around really." This was her opportunity to tell him about her big break, her elevation to celebrity interviewer. Why was she holding back? *You know why....*

"Keep plugging away, it'll..." But before Will could finish, the line got cut off. Amy pointlessly looked at her phone. It read 'call failed' on the screen. She huffed. She should have been used to these unreliable long distance calls by now. She waited a moment, but he did not call back, so she went back to texting Beth. She looked at what she had already typed.

Hey lovely, is flirting cheating?

She deleted it. Maybe she could try a subtle approach to the subject.

Does Sov X lead singer have a girlf?

Did he have a girlfriend? She followed him on social media, but she could not remember his relationship status – like many celebrities, his changed frequently. She reviewed what she had typed before pressing send, then deleted the entire message. Instead, she went with:

Hiya, u OK?

WTF is up Babe?

Why should something be up?

It's ur tone

Seriously? Over a text? U crack me up

Out with it then. Oh u and Will aren't splitting? No, wait, u just shagged ZH! (several laughing emoji)

Amy dropped her phone in her lap at her friend's apparent psychic abilities.

Ur not a million miles away. Interview for Delta mag

Well, slap my arse and call me Judy! U know he just split up with his girlfriend xx

At this, Amy's stomach turned over. So, he is single. *But you're not!* Her conscience screamed in her head. She paused. Maybe she shouldn't say any more. The phone rang. Beth.

"How'd it go, then? Is he still as fit in person?"

"Oh, yeah, so hot. It went good. Really well. I behaved better than on the plane." She was not going to mention the five minutes after the interview under any circumstances. Not yet, anyway.

"Did he remember you?"

Amy screwed her face up. She did not want to tell her the whole story, now was not the time. "What do you think?" she replied rhetorically, reluctant to lie.

"Yeah, OK, fair enough. Was a long shot I guess. How did you land that gig?"

"Features Ed., Mark, was throwing up all night. Thank the Lord for stomach bugs, eh?"

Beth laughed. "That's so harsh."

"Yes, it was. Sorry not sorry, Mark."

"You should totally have nabbed his number." Beth was fishing.

"Hey, no, I'm a professional!" She could say this with veracity – she did not have his number – he had hers. "Plus, I'm in a relationship, wouldn't that be inappropriate?" She tried to be subtle, to disguise the fact that she was genuinely hoping for an answer to this question.

"Nah! It's just your average, everyday bit of celeb flirting." The sarcasm was not lost on Amy. "What about the *Friends* Laminated List? You've discussed that with Will, haven't you?" Beth had descended into full-on playful mode. Amy had no choice but to play along so as not to arouse suspicion.

"Of course we have! It's a prerequisite to any lasting relationship." Both girls laughed. Amy sat back in her seat. It was never going to happen. Of course it wasn't. *He won't call me, I'm worrying over nothing.* This call had brought her back to reality. She almost believed that she had imagined the whole episode. Her phone bleeped in her ear to let her know another call was waiting.

"Oh, hey, I have another call coming through, it'll be Will, we got cut off earlier. Talk to you later?"

"Sure. Run, Sunday?"

"Run, Sunday."

"Bye-zee-bye."

Amy switched calls without checking the caller ID. "Hi, Babe," she said, brightly.

"Hi, Amy, Zach."

"Zach?" she replied, in complete disbelief.

"Yes, Zach from Sovereign X, those dudes that sang '*Whatever I do*,'" he jibed, quoting their current hit song's title.

"Oh, shit, sorry, I was miles away." Literally, she thought – Will was in the USA. The palm of the hand holding her phone was instantly sweaty. She feared she would drop it, so gripped it tightly. "OK, start over, Amy. Hi, wow, you called me." She screwed her face up at her ridiculous comment. She was so taken aback. "Fuck," she blurted. He laughed.

"I want to arrange hooking up. How's tomorrow, Giovanni's on Mount Road, eight p.m.?"

"Sure, great, see you then." She waited for him to hang up. She could dismiss it no longer. This was a whole different ballgame. Destiny was indeed a strange thing.

Three

The next day was a blur. Will had still not called her back. She knew better than to worry, or to try to call him, his work was so consuming at times, and she would always hear from him eventually. It did not help her current mood though – she could not fully commit to the feeling of sheer euphoria at seeing Zach again, when half of her felt terribly guilty that she was now actually going on a date with a man that was not her boyfriend. Did it really count that he was her *'celebrity I'm allowed to sleep with and the other one can't get mad'* – The *Friends* Laminated List Beth had reminded her of? Had anyone in real life ever actually had to face a dilemma like this? Would she *get* to sleeping with him? It was all pretty daunting, and yet somehow the danger and excitement was incredibly alluring.

These thoughts were grossly affecting her ability to write up her interview at home. She went into her bedroom to lay on her bed and plugged her earphones in to listen to some Sovereign X. She stared up at the ceiling, thinking how wrong it felt now, lying on the bed she shared with Will, listening to their pelting anthems, his powerful soaring voice. It led to imagining how their date would unfold, what he might be like in bed... *What am I doing? I should just cancel.* But she knew there was no way she was going to. This was no ordinary date.

In no time at all, she had completed her article, emailed it to Paul, and was striding towards the restaurant Zach had suggested in her Louboutins and a bodycon dress. It was a neat little Italian, not far from the hotel where the interview had taken place. Her heart was pounding in her chest again, her mind swimming with nerves and wonder at the situation she now found herself in, the acceleration of it all. She walked into the restaurant and saw Zach with his arm around a fan while another took a photo with their phone. She stepped back into the shadows, but the maître d' spotted her and made his way over, asking if she had a table booked.

"Oh, she's with me, Giuseppe." Zach had swaggered over. He kissed Amy on the cheek as if they had known each other for a long time. She inhaled deeply. He lingered to murmur in her ear, "You look amazing." She smiled, still reeling from his kiss, resisting the urge to touch her cheek.

"Hi," was all she managed to say.

"OK, Mr Zach, I have a nice quiet table for you… away from the window," Giuseppe said discreetly, smiling at the obvious electricity between them. He led the way to a booth near the back of the restaurant – there were no other customers in the vicinity. He took their drinks order and left them with the menus. Amy watched him walk out of sight, before making eye contact with Zach across the table from her.

"So… first names with the maître d', you must know this place well." It wasn't the best line, but it was the only conversation starter that she could think of in her heightened state of bedazzlement.

He smiled. She loved his smile. She felt so privileged to be witnessing it privately directed at her. "I do. Best pizza in London, tried and tested. I always come here when we're in town. I guess some of the fans know that too, now." He gestured behind him. Fortunately, he wasn't a well-known enough face to be mobbed by crowds wherever he went. He was equally as successful as a faceless music producer as he was a member of a band, so he could travel around relatively incognito, notwithstanding the odd fan here and there, like those she had just seen him with. This worked in her favour – if he was a favourite of the paparazzi, she would surely be caught out. She subconsciously moved her tresses out of her eyes, feeling suddenly self-conscious. This had all happened so quickly perhaps she should take a reality check.

"So, what made you ask me here tonight, did you have some concerns about the interview?" she ventured, in her most professional-sounding voice while they perused the menus. It was lame, it was blarney, but trying to turn it back to work comforted her, slowed things down, especially her thudding heart.

He chuckled playfully. "Should I be concerned?" He lowered his menu and looked at her. She felt his gaze and made eye contact. He had such intriguing eyes. 'Windows to the soul' they say, and it was eyes like his they must have had in mind when the phrase was coined. He was never on the 'one hundred sexiest celebrity men' lists, but he had something. Something that got her, at least.

She smiled and looked back at her menu again after his rebuttal of her fake question.

"I don't think you need to ask me why I asked you out. Why did you say yes?"

She was not expecting that, and looked directly at him. She decided to take a chance and reply coquettishly. "Aren't you used to people saying yes to you?"

"Ouch." He grinned.

I just wish he would put that smile away for a minute, or I am going to jump him. She had a hopeless poker face, and he read the train her thoughts were running on, smiling indulgently. She knew what he wanted, and aware that she wore her heart on her sleeve, she was sure he would know that she wanted the same thing.

"So, we're gonna play rough, huh?" He leaned his elbows on the table and rested his chin on his clasped hands.

She leaned in too, unable to resist replying with a scrunch of her nose, "I like it rough."

Zach grinned, and looked down. He appeared to be getting hot under the collar too, his face was glowing. It was his turn to try to tone the conversation down. "So, apart from us, what music are you into?"

"Oh, I'm into everything."

"Are you, now?"

"Yes, I am." She replied frankly, calling his bluff on the double entendre of his response. She looked at him earnestly. The suggestive turn of their conversation had piqued her attraction to him. Amy could not quite believe how quickly their banter had gotten dirty, but the fire between them was almost too much to bare. She took a big glug of her gin and tonic that had arrived in the meantime. She had become completely impervious to their surroundings, and so, it seemed, had Zach.

"Are you ready to order?" The waiter broke their tryst.

"Wow, ya know, I haven't even looked," Zach said, with an intake of breath. "I already know what I want." He shot a sideways glance at

Amy, who was looking intently at her menu. She did not miss his look in her peripheral vision, but made out like she had.

Once their meal was ordered, Amy excused herself for the ladies' room. She rose slowly from her seat, Zach watching her every move. She was not entirely oblivious to the power of her feminine charms, her dress accentuated her curves perfectly. Zach was captivated. She walked away, his eyes not leaving her as she did.

She closed the door and exhaled the tension away. This was all so intoxicating – she had longed for this both consciously and subconsciously for an immeasurable amount of time. But Will was ever present in the back of her mind, and how inappropriate all this was. She rinsed her hands in cold water and held them against her rosy cheeks to cool them. Was this all leading to a sordid one night stand? Is that what he wanted? Would that not suit her better? Get her consuming infatuation with him out of her system once and for all? *I do not want to be some groupie, I'd better drink slowly.* She made her way back to the table, staring at the back of Zach's head as she approached. He flicked his floppy hair back and turned to watch her take her seat opposite him.

"So, how long have you been out of the flying business?" Her intermission to cool off seemed to have cooled him off too. The mention of flying caused a pang in her belly though, reminding her of Will.

"About a year. It fit in with me finishing off my degree."

The conversation flowed, she couldn't believe how at ease she was talking to him and how interesting he was. Obviously, he led a jet-set lifestyle, travelling to all sorts of places, but he was deeper and more intelligent than she had expected. She loved how his eyes sparkled when he laughed, there was an allusion to naughtiness in them every time.

He's got a great sense of humour... for an American. The thought made her grin – but it did not fit with the nature of their conversation and he noticed.

"What?" he said, bemused.

"What?" She didn't want to share her derogatory mental quip.

"Go on, something amused you – share." He cajoled. "Tell the whole group." He mocked in an English accent.

"Rumbled." She bit her bottom lip and smiled sheepishly. "I don't wanna say…"

"Come on… I can take it." His knee brushed hers under the table. Amy couldn't tell if it was deliberate or not, but it set her pulse racing again.

"Well, I was just thinking, you've got a good sense of humour." He frowned, clearly unsure as to why she would not want to share a compliment like that. "For an American."

"There it is." He looked down and laughed.

She realised the audacity of her statement, but her tongue had gotten looser with every gin and tonic she had drained. So much for drinking slowly, she was enjoying herself a little too much. "I'm sorry. That's rude and xenophobic." She instinctively placed her hand on his, on the table, feeling a surge of breath-taking electricity through her as she did.

"In truth, I don't quite know what I'm doing here. I mean to say, I can't quite *believe* I am here."

He looked inquisitively at her. "You fascinate me… I love your accent, you're so reserved and yet have such a sharp wit – a quintessential Brit. I love it. I'm a total anglophile."

"Why do you like us Brits so much? We spend half our time queuing, the other half praying for sunshine."

He laughed. "That's true."

"So, you asked me out cos you like Brits." Amy gave him a side grin. She was fishing for more, her flirt-o-meter suddenly on overdrive.

He licked his lips. "Amy, you're so damned sexy. And you don't even know it."

She blushed, not expecting such direct admiration. *OK, this is getting intense.* She shifted in her seat, the heat of the moment rising again. How many times had she looked at him from afar, on a screen, and here he was, sitting opposite her, coming on to her. What an accolade for a fan from their idol – it was a dizzying prospect for sure.

She turned the talk back to music, a subject they were both animated about, comparing favourite bands. Amy was in tune with the British music scene, as was Zach. She enjoyed the chitchat, he knew more about music than Will – naturally – being such a heavyweight in the industry; aside from his own band's success, he had written and produced songs for some big names. She revelled in their geeky two-way conversation, but there was palpable sexual tension between them, and their talk kept threatening to go down a provocative path. Amy wrenched it back each time, but that somehow made the chemistry between them fire up, not dampen down. Zach had made it clear how he wanted the evening to end, the power was now in her hands as to how it would conclude, and she felt the weight of her dilemma heavy in her heart.

At the end of the meal, he took the last sip of his beer and called the waiter for the bill. Amy tried in vain to contribute, and they rose to leave. Zach placed his hand on her back as they left the restaurant, walking out into the warmth of the summer evening.

After a moment or two walking down the quiet, salubrious London street in silence, Zach spoke. "Wanna come back to my hotel for a quick drink?" She could see the flame of desire burning in his eyes. Crunch time was upon her – high road or low road? She could let it go, have one amazing night with this unreal person so wholly unconnected to her, jeopardising her relationship, or she could just enjoy one last drink, ask for a selfie and an autograph, walking away completely unscathed.

In any other situation, she might have felt indignant at his obvious advances, but he was *him*. Maybe he had played to her badly disguised adoration of him. *Why did I fawn over him? Stupid, stupid.*

"Look I'm not really a 'groupie' one night stand kind of girl." She was reluctant.

He touched her elbow and stopped her to turn to look at him. "Hey who said anything about one night stands?" His eyes twinkled as he spoke.

She looked away awkwardly, highly embarrassed. Had she misread his signals? "Oh, I just… you've been coming on so strong all night – I mean – you must see how I feel about you. I'm sorry I guess I read it all wrong." She stumbled over the sentence, willing the ground to swallow her up.

"Amy, you haven't read it wrong. Listen, ya know, I'm totally type A. I see what I want, and I'm very focussed to get it."

She looked at his face. "And you want me?" fell out of her mouth before she could stop it.

He held her gaze in earnest, rendering it unnecessary to answer in the affirmative.

"I don't think I should come back. I don't think you'll be able to resist me. I sure as hell know I won't be able to resist you."

He laughed at her frankness. "C'mon. One drink. They do a great champagne and gin cocktail, you'll love it."

"You have no idea how much you know your audience." She relented easily and let him take her hand.

They walked down the street glancing in the boutique shops as they passed by. This was all such a world away from her life. She and Will were comfortable, but this was a cut above, his territory, Zach's – private jets and designer clothes, performing on stage to thousands of people, celebrities and travelling the world, awards ceremonies… But here he was with her, so down to earth, his Diesel jeans, Converse and easy demeanour. No one took any notice of them, but this suited Amy, she did not want any attention, she just wanted to enjoy his hand holding – those hands that were so proficient at playing the piano, what else were they proficient at…

They rounded a corner and entered double glass doors of the hotel where Amy had interviewed the band just the previous day. Such different circumstances she now found herself in.

Zach led her past reception and into the bar. Two of his bandmates were there drinking. He said 'hi' to them; Amy avoided their subtle grins and sly looks.

"Can I have two 'Under The Sheets' cocktails sent to my room please," Zach said to the bartender.

Amy raised her eyebrows at the provocative name, now expecting the evening to end up exactly where the drinks suggest. She had no opportunity to protest going to his room, as a moment after ordering, he had whisked her into the lift. He coolly flicked his hair back after pressing the button and turned to face her. He smelt amazing. They looked into each other's eyes, both thinking the same thing; the next steps, frantic kissing and removal of clothes – but these titillating, pre-emptive thoughts remained just that, while they waited to arrive at the right floor. He merely brushed her cheek with the back of his forefinger, attraction to her evident in every fibre of his being. She surreptitiously pinched her forearm firmly with her fingers, just to be certain she wasn't dreaming. Nothing happened, and she murmured 'shit' under her breath.

The lift came to a halt and he led the way down the corridor to the door at the end. He swiped his key-card and gestured she enter ahead of him. Amy looked around. It was similar to the suite she had conducted the interview in; there were several instruments strewn about in the lounge area, a couple of laptops on the table and some other technical equipment.

"Sorry, my portable studio." He began moving some items so they could sit on the couch. "Our drinks will…" He was interrupted by a knock at the door. "…Be here right now." He got up and dashed to open the door, a waiter swiftly pushed a trolley into the room. Their drinks, in martini glasses, were accompanied by an array of fancy petit fours. Zach tipped the waiter who left as promptly as he had arrived.

"Here." He handed her a glass. She took it and sipped.

It was a heady drink, very strong, but as smooth as nectar and she gulped a few more sips. "Mmm, lovely."

"Indeed." Zach placed his drink on the table and turned to her. The intensity of the situation had suddenly stepped up a notch. He took the glass out of her hand and placed it onto the table next to his. Amy's chest rose and fell with short breaths, the anticipation of his lips on hers, his body pressed against hers; she was almost overwhelmed. And then he was there, standing in front of her, face to face, merely a foot between them, and the temperature in the room seemed to be rising a degree a second. The moment felt hazy, like a soft-focus film, then she felt a jolt back to clarity as he slipped his arms around her waist, drawing her to his body, his lips gently meeting hers. He pulled back slightly and looked into her face, the face that had drawn him in, mesmerised him to act so impulsively to ask her out at the interview.

But her eyes were still closed, her mouth agape, her face frozen in position, tipped up towards his. She unconsciously mouthed the word 'wow' and opened her eyes. He was still so close, she could feel his breath, his eyes exploring hers, his pupils dilating with the thrill of a first kiss, the spark of passion between them. She wondered if she should have saved pinching herself for this moment, this, for sure, felt like a dream.

"Amy, I don't do one night stands either. I don't have 'groupies' as you put it. I really like you, and if you want to leave it here, that's fine, and we'll see each other again. I mean it," he said softly, the words resonating in her ears. Surely this was just a line, reverse psychology? Amy did not take too much store to his words; it would not have mattered if she did, much as she tried to see them as a compliment. She had decided she was not going to wait another two years to see if she bumped into him again, boyfriend or not. She knew that if she wanted to sleep with him and fulfil her ultimate fantasy, it was now or never. The realisation of this hit Amy, she was seized by a reckless daring fuelled by the surge of dopamine in her brain clouding her judgement. She could not let this pass her by, Zach standing in front of her, just the two of them, alone in a hotel suite, mutual desire magnetising their bodies.

She wound her arms around his neck, her fingers pressing into the back of his head as she kissed him with more force than he had kissed her. The embrace was so charged, she gave herself over fully to the moment, enjoying every part of his mouth, her mind filled with thoughts of wonder at her transformation from run of the mill fan to being able to do this with him; this moment that had been too seductive to walk away from, mixed with the gruesome thrill of infidelity which was morbidly arousing.

His arms enclosed her body, hands gripping her back, slowly moving lower, his fingers pressing into her contours. She staggered backwards until he had her pinned against the wall, locked in their embrace. His kissing was eager and constant, his mouth could not get enough of her full lips. She pushed him back, grabbing his top and lifting it up over his head and off; he found the zip at the back of her dress, peeling it away from her shoulders, until it dropped to the floor. She undid his belt and jeans hastily, both of them now desperate to have skin on skin. She placed her hands on his bare torso and gently pushed him so he fell back onto the couch, climbing on top of him, still in her heels. She licked his lips, before parting them with her tongue again, hungry for him, as he was hungry for her, hands pressing into flesh.

Now this was it. No turning back. She committed herself to the hedonism. She wanted to control it, savour it for all its worth, every delectable moment. Zach may be Type A, but here, now, this was her domain; she would take the driver's seat and be master over him. One place she was not shy was the bedroom, her sex life with Will had always been spicy and they were well practised in the art of maximising pleasure. She had this one chance to enjoy another man – the only other man she wanted to do any of these things with – and she was going to make damned sure she made the most of him.

Their drinks sat on the table still, hardly touched.

***

At two a.m., Amy's eyes shot open, and she inhaled a sharp breath, startled, barely aware of where she was. She looked around the room before her faculties returned. The sophisticated furnishings of the classy hotel suite jolted back the memory of the date. The heavy floor-to-ceiling curtains facing her, orange street lights grinning through the cracks, staring her down in her horizontal position, like some moral police, reminding her of her dirty deed. What an evening. Charged with passion and pleasure, she grabbed her arm for the second time in the last few hours, to be certain this wasn't some elaborate dream. Alas, nothing happened; she could still hear Zach's deep breathing in the bed next to her and she turned over. She watched his naked form rise and fall with every breath, his California sun-kissed back, smooth and perfect, their empty cocktail glasses on the bedside cabinet next to him.

She closed her eyes, recalling their antics, which had started in the lounge area and ended up here, before they had necked their drinks and fallen asleep. She felt such a mixture of emotions, remorse to euphoria, guilt to elation. *What have I done?* She had never before thought herself capable of cheating and hated it. She put both hands over her face for a moment, trying to settle the maelstrom of emotions vying for position. But this was just a one-off, right? She tried to excuse her behaviour. She glanced back at Zach. His hair had gone slightly wavy and messy on his pillow. *Was it worth it?* a small voice said in the back of her mind. They say never meet your idols, let alone sleep with them.

She got up and tiptoed to his side of the bed. She looked down at him – no stirring, sound asleep. He could no longer occupy the pedestal she had placed him on for so long, not now they had been so intimate with each other; but she had not been disappointed. Maybe they had real chemistry, maybe it was just lust. She thought about the times she had watched him in music videos, on TV, on stage. How different a scene was before her now to store in her memories. She leaned in to lightly kiss his forehead before going to the lounge to retrieve her clothes and bag. She saw no point in hanging around for the walk of shame and awkwardness in the morning. They had both got what they wanted, period.

She looked in on him once more, trying to take a mental picture of him. Her hand instinctively touched the phone in her bag, thinking she could have more than just a mental picture, but thought better of it – that would be a step too low, with him unaware, no dignity. She slipped her shoes on and left the room. The hotel was ghostly quiet as she made her way stealthily downstairs, having ordered an Uber while she dressed.

**

Amy sat in the dark of the taxi reliving the night. It all seemed totally ethereal now. She closed her eyes and replayed every moment of the evening in her mind. The libertine in her revelled in the conquest, but her conscience stung her. It was a long journey home, so she flicked through her social media pages. She noticed Zach had been tagged in a fan picture, the one from the restaurant. Looking closer at the photo, she could just about make out her blurry reflection in the obscured glass partition behind him, her red dress unmistakable. It sent a stark reality check through her bones, a modest example of his status, her undefined shape in the background. How poignant. And one thought kept playing on her mind; how could she look Will in the eyes again? It made her physically shudder.

She leaned her head back on the seat, utterly exhausted. This would be an expensive journey, but she needed the easiest way home at this time of night. Her phone suddenly buzzed, and for a fleeting moment she hoped it was Zach, begging her to come back. She looked at her phone, shame flooding through her when she saw it was a text from Will.

Hey Babe, time zone meltdown it's probably the mid of the nite there, just thinking about u. Going to be here for another few days. M Y & L U xxx

Amy felt the tears as they rolled down her face. Her night might have felt surreal, but her betrayal was certainly every bit real.

***

On Sunday, Amy didn't surface until ten a.m. She flicked through some recent photos of her and Will on her phone, before sombrely making herself some tea and breakfast. She did have a bit of a hangover – the only remnant from the night before – must have been that cocktail. She never usually suffered from hangovers and champagne was notorious for causing a bad headache. She absently checked her messages and emails – nothing. She was not entirely sure what she was looking for, but she felt expectant. Perhaps it was just wishful thinking.

Just as she placed the phone back on the table, a message buzzed through. She picked it up, the number wasn't stored to a name.

You left... I meant what I said last night (which was incredible btw) can I see u again? We go back to the US tmrw. Z x

She read it through again and again. He had kept his word – she was a little surprised, and unnerved. She had had her wicked way with him, satisfied her infatuation – should she really return to the scene of the crime? But tomorrow he would be thousands of miles away, and out of her life again. She typed quickly. She paused.

I'd like to see you too.
(sent)

When and where

She couldn't bring him home, logistics were as much an issue as the evidence of her other man, and any clues that might be left for Will to discover her dalliance when he came back. *How awful a person am I?* she thought. And yet she knew she was blatantly going to carry on regardless.

I'll come to your hotel. 4pm OK?

Yeah. See u then.

Four p.m. came around too quickly. Amy parked her Mini in the underground car park near to the hotel and walked towards the entrance feeling nervous again. After their passionate night, she felt awkward. She had only ever had nights that intense with Will, and they had been together for a long time. She may have felt like she had known Zach for years, having followed him for long enough, but how much can you really know about a person following them from afar? He certainly did not know her; but the chemistry was powerful, that was certain. And as it would appear, she stood to lose a lot more than him by pursuing this – he was single. She made her way across the foyer and passed by the concierge she had seen on the day of her interview.

"Good afternoon, Miss Armstrong, back for another interview?" he teased, with a wry smile. She smiled in return, but did not reply. He must suspect what had gone on, why she was here again. Would he have witnessed situations like this before, that he would have to be discreet about or turn a blind eye to? It was a posh hotel, she assumed there would be discretion. As she walked past reception, a text came through to her phone:

When u get here, come straight on up. Running over time a bit Z x

That must mean he has people with him. This prospect added new nerves. She made her way to the same lift they had gone in the night before, the memory giving her butterflies, and the excitement she had felt then briefly returned, but how would she feel when she saw him again? She stepped out and walked along the corridor. As she did so, the door at the end opened and a hipster-looking guy came out of the room. Embarrassed, Amy stopped in her tracks and pretended to rummage in her handbag. As he passed her, she looked up and smiled so as not to appear suspicious. He said 'hi' and carried on walking. She neared the door, and as she did, she heard voices, then Zach's vocal came belting out – just a few lines – and the sound of the odd strum or chord. Some chatter broke out and she could make out at least four or five different voices.

She stood at the door, poised to knock for several moments, plucking her courage up. *He must be rehearsing or recording with the band.* Could she face their knowing looks and grins again? She almost turned to go, when the door opened again and a beautiful girl stepped out with large sunglasses on and long dark hair. She looked familiar. It took Amy a moment, but she placed her as a former member of a girl group. Zach must have been writing with her. The girl glanced superciliously in Amy's direction and gave her a professionally practised but depthless smile, and strode away with her entourage, which consisted of a bodyguard who was as tall as he was wide, and another hipster type with the skinniest of skinny jeans on, rapidly typing on his phone. Amy walked in through the door just as it was about to shut.

Zach was sitting in front of a laptop, talking animatedly to his keyboard player, Brad, and lead guitarist, Jake, who was strumming and nodding. They did not immediately notice Amy's entrance.

She walked nearer and pretended to clear her throat. All three looked in her direction. Zach smiled upon seeing her, the others looked slightly more bemused, then recognition occurred in their faces – from the interview – and Brad had been one of the guys in the bar the previous night. He smiled, so Amy smiled back and said 'hi'.

"Grab a drink, Amy," Zach said, dismissively, and carried on talking to the guys. Amy felt a little snubbed, but shrugged it off and went to the bar in the corner of the room. She quietly poured herself a cold drink. Too early in the day – and date – for alcohol. In any case, she was driving. She perched on an armchair by the window and looked out. She saw a limo pull away, probably containing the starlet she had passed in the hallway. *He really does have a lot going on*, she thought, and momentarily wondered what she was doing there. Then, Zach stopped talking and held his hands up to the guys. Brad and Jake exchanged glances.

"Hold on a sec, guys." He got up and walked over to Amy. "Hey." He put his hands on the arms either side of her chair and leaned in to kiss her squarely and firmly on the lips, as if they had been together for years. He smiled as he pulled away.

"Hey." She grinned. "Shall I come back later?" she said in an undertone.

"No, we're nearly done, eh, guys?" They both concurred.

"I don't want to stem the flow of creative juices."

He leaned in close to her again, "There's nothing that can stem my juices when you're around," he murmured. She raised her eyebrows and licked her lips suggestively. The previous night was present in both their minds. The awkwardness that had been her companion mere moments before was suddenly non-existent.

"I mean it. I don't want to be Yoko."

He laughed. "No, no, it's fine. I don't mind any comparison to Lennon, though." He made his way back to the guys. They chatted some more and melodies were played with on the laptop, but by the time Amy had drained her drink, the guys bade her goodbye and made an exit. She got up from her seat and walked over to Zach.

"How's your songwriting going? As I got here I saw—" She was interrupted by Zach giving her a long, intense kiss. The interruption was entirely welcome, Amy was still dazzled by the fact that it was him kissing her. "Hello," she said, with a warm smile.

"Hello." He mimicked her posh accent. "I've been thinking about you all morning."

Amy's desire for him swelled. She gazed into his mischievous eyes. Will could not have been further from her thoughts as the fire of arousal rose inside her. Amy felt the rush of excitement at being with someone different.

"You're so sexy," she couldn't help whispering, as he drew her close, his body pressed up against hers and he kissed her on the neck. He picked her up, wrapping her legs around his waist, and carried her to the bedroom. Clearly, he wanted to own this encounter. No small talk, no delay, both craving to be naked together again.

***

Amy lay in his arms playing with his fingers. His hands were so different to Will's. Thin, dextrous, piano-playing, smooth. Will's were strong and rugged from his engineering days. How different they were entirely. Will had entered her mind again, having left her thoughts temporarily. Inevitably, the image of him crept back, along with waves of guilt engulfing her. She had alleviated her conscience from attacking her too badly with the whole 'he's my celebrity freebie' thing, but here she was in his bed again. And where was this going? Zach was going back to America the next day.

"I've had an amazing time with you. I keep thinking I need to pinch myself to wake up."

"It has been amazing. Meeting you again, like that… When I saw you on the plane, I thought, 'gee, she's hot', and that was it. Then all this time later we have just another interview, and *you* come into the room. Literally both times I had just gotten out of relationships. I kinda think it's fate. Can't ignore fate. Like God or karma was showing you to me, saying 'here's a girl for you'."

And all this happening while Will is conveniently on the other side of the planet.

"I really wanna see you again. I come here a lot, but do you ever come to the US?"

Amy sat up and started putting her clothes on. This was fast moving from an indulgent dip into a fantasy world to something altogether more prominent. "I don't know… I mean you have such a hectic schedule; I live here, you live there…" She had never expected him to want more, despite his earnest comments to the contrary. She had resigned herself to the vault of groupie-dom that she had so disliked the idea of originally. But surely that is all *she* had wanted anyway – passionate sex with someone she obsessively admired? Something to get out of her system? Why would someone like him stoop to be taken in by her? What a mess she had gotten herself into. And she should be flattered and elated.

He touched her shoulder to turn her to face him. "Don't you want this?" He was such a tour de force, he probably always got what he wanted. His expression was true, his hair still slicked back perfectly. But he was also still just a guy attracted to a girl. She touched his chest.

"Believe me, I have fantasised about this many times, but…"

"There's fire." His eyes were lit as they searched hers.

"Yes, there is." She had not once considered that they might click, make a connection like this. They sat for a moment looking into each other's eyes.

"C'mon." He got up suddenly. They dressed and she followed him into the lounge area. "I want you to hear what we've been working on." He grabbed his guitar and Amy sat on the sofa. He played and sang a new song to her. She felt extremely privileged and could not believe her stratospheric elevation. His lyrics were as subtle and relatable as they always were, but she read between them; they touched her, they referred to her, the way they met, long distance, across the ocean. She coloured, but could not help but melt at his serenade, his amazing voice – that voice…

"What do you think?" he said when he had finished the song.

"I'm flattered you're asking my lowly opinion."

"Music journalist? I think it's fair you can give me a valid critique."

Amy smiled. That was the first time anyone had referred to her as a music journalist. She liked how it sounded. "Maybe valid, but certainly not unbiased. Everything you do is amazing. I'm sure you don't need me to tell you that."

"That *was* biased."

"Very. I told you. I'm still just a fan."

"You're not just a fan." He could not tear his eyes off her petite features. She just flicked her long locks back and smiled.

"I found the words… moving." She was ignorant of the spell she was unwittingly casting on him with her charms.

"So you should." He smiled.

She looked down and bit her lip. "So, will this be the new single?"

"Yes, but not for us, it'll be for Olivia Sanchez."

"That's her name!"

"Huh?"

"Oh, she passed me in the hallway earlier."

"She's a good kid."

"Looks like a prima-donna."

"She's OK. Looks can be deceiving. Look at you, pretty, reserved, and yet…"

Amy was startled by her phone ringing. She grabbed it out of her bag, it was Beth. "Shit," she said. With the whirlwind that had been the last two days, she had completely forgotten she was supposed to meet her friend for a run. She hated letting people down. "I need to take this, Zach, sorry." She moved away and answered. "Hi, Babe. I'm so sorry, I forgot." Zach was putting his guitar back in its case, glancing curiously but surreptitiously Amy's way.

"Well, you're not at your place, cos that's where I am, dammit. What better offer did you get?" Beth's tone was pert.

"Oh, don't be like that, something unexpected came up, can we do tomorrow after work?"

"OK, but are you going to spill as to why you're being so fucking evasive, Mrs?"

"Of course. We'll grab a drink instead of a run, how about that?"

"Who are you with, that you're talking so damn formal?" Beth probed. Amy just laughed. "OK, I'll accept that plan, seeing as you are obviously not in a position to let on. I am really intrigued."

"You should be," Amy said, quietly. She knew she would have to tell Beth the whole sordid truth now.

"Ooh, carrot dangled! I can't wait. See ya then." She hung up and Amy walked back over to Zach who was tidying up some of his musical equipment.

"I'm sorry about that, I forgot I was supposed to see a friend today."

"But you got a better offer." He gave her a side grin.

"I guess so." She smiled back.

"All OK with her? Or him?"

"Yes, *she's* fine."

"C'mon, let's grab a drink downstairs." He took her hand.

"I can only have one, I'm driving."

"Make it a good one then."

The bar was fairly quiet, it being early evening, and they both had a large glass of six-year-old burgundy and talked and laughed. When they had finished their drinks, Zach called the barman over to order another one.

"Is your car parked somewhere it can stay, say... overnight?" He had that twinkle in his eyes again.

She looked at him, resistance was futile. "Yes."

"Wanna stay?"

"Yes."

He ordered the rest of the bottle.

Later, they ate in the hotel restaurant and headed back to his room, having had another bottle of wine between them. Amy felt more than a little half-cut and the alcohol had unleashed her raging libido. Zach had barely opened the door to the room before she was pressing him against it, kissing him, tugging at his jeans. He responded with equal passion and pulled her top up and over her head. She grabbed him by his belt and pulled him further into the room, before pushing him down to the floor, sitting astride him and pinning his hands to the ground above his head, holding him tight by the wrists. She wanted control, he was at her mercy, and he revelled in her dominance, submissive to everything she was about to do to him.

***

Afterwards, they made their way to bed, lulled by alcohol still, in a post-coital haze. They lay together spooned for some time before Zach stirred and broke the silence.

"You're amazing in the sack." Amy had her eyes closed, just enjoying her relaxed state, his naked body tucked in softly against her own. She felt his face close to the back of her head. He breathed in the scent of her hair and ran his fingers through it.

"Easy to be good with someone like you," she whispered. She grabbed her phone from beside the bed – this might be her last chance – and took a selfie, laying in his arms.

"I looked you up, ya know, this morning, on Instagram."

Her smile faded. "OK," she said, tentatively. She didn't post much about Will and she was not sure how much could be seen in public with her privacy settings, which she was always rubbish at keeping up-to-date, but there would certainly be some evidence of her boyfriend on there. Hard to hide a boyfriend in these days of narcissistic social media. She could have predicted Zach's next comment.

"Were you going to tell me you're in a relationship?" He sounded more curious than cross.

"I... I don't know." She was glad they were not facing each other in this conversation. "I never thought anything would happen between us." She paused, but in the wake of her inhibitions broken down by booze and sex, she continued, "Besides, this is probably gonna sound really stupid, but remember in *Friends*, the laminated list of celebrities you're allowed to sleep with and the other one can't get mad?"

He chuckled. "Let me guess, I'm one of them."

"Actually, I used to joke that you were in each of the five slots."

"Oh, my my. I don't know whether to laugh or roll my eyes. I mean, I'm flattered. Aren't there any other celebs you like? And there's me thinking I was pursuing you."

"What can I say? Thought I'd hit the jackpot. Two more shags and we're a full house."

"Ha, ha! I guess so. Wow, I feel used. What now though? I meant what I said before – I don't do one night stands. I don't sleep around. But I also can't afford to get in the middle of something. When I saw the pictures of you with your guy – Will, is it? I admit I was jealous. I want you... And I thought, if you wanted more, you'd find a way to see me today, despite him."

"So, you tested me."

"And here you are naked in my arms. Now I know you don't want to let go either. If you're prepared to jeopardise your relationship to see me, then an ocean between us is nothing."

Amy sat up with the bed sheet wrapped around her. "I feel so confused. I never in my wildest dreams thought I'd be faced with this situation."

He pulled her back towards him so their bodies were touching, facing each other. He looked into her eyes.

"And did it live up to your expectations?"

"No." She paused for effect, long enough to see his smile drop. "It exceeded them." She smiled, as his returned. He kissed her.

"So, what do we do about this?" His body was firm – aroused – pressed against hers.

"I think I know what I need to do about this..."

Four

Amy woke up late in the morning. She opened her eyes and was greeted with the unfamiliar surroundings of the hotel suite. She turned over in the massive bed expecting Zach to be there; this time it was he that had gone. She sat up and could hear movement from the lounge area. She grabbed his t-shirt, which was still on the floor from the night before, and walked into the room. Zach was already dressed, looking cool in black jeans, a white t-shirt and his trademark back to front baseball cap. He was busy moving his musical equipment and packing it away.

"Hey. Morning," he said brightly, without looking up.

"Morning." Amy yawned and flicked her dishevelled hair back. He glanced her way and stopped what he was doing.

"Damn, you look hot." He walked towards her. She smiled and looked away.

"I think not."

"Oh, I think so." He kissed her and put his arm around her.

"I've got a mouth like a badger's arse and I need a cuppa."

He laughed. "I can't get enough of your accent. And your Britishness." He went to the bar and made her a tea and handed it to her.

"Thank you." She took a sip. She was pleasantly surprised at how well he had made it. "That's a good cup of cha."

He moved over to her again. "My flight's at four p.m." He took her hand. "See me again?"

"I'll see you again. I need to sort out some stuff in my head though."

"I know. What's he like? Will?"

She looked at him. "He's great." She sighed. "He likes your music."

"Ha ha, that's some consolation I guess. He'd soon be off it if he knew what we've been up to."

She hung her head and leaned it into his chest. "I am a terrible human being."

He put his arms around her. "No, you're not. Some things, however bad, are unavoidable."

"Officer," she quipped. He laughed. "When are you back here?"

"Next month I think."

"OK."

"Hey, is Will not around? How come you got so much time for me on a weekend?"

"He's out of the country, he travels a lot for work."

"Like me. What's he do?"

"He works for the AAIB."

"The what?"

"Like your NTSB. He investigates air accidents."

"Oh. His job is way more important than mine then. Bastard."

"I'm sure you earn way more than him."

"Ha – there you go, one point to me."

"Listen, I should go. You have a flight later, I have to be in the office this afternoon."

"OK." He kissed her and brushed her hair away from her face. She still could not get over the fact that he was standing in front of her, touching her.

Amy had a shower and put her own clothes from the night before back on. She really was not looking forward to their goodbye, possibly forever. Did he really mean all those things he had said? Could a fling like this ever really mean anything more? Should she really be thinking this way at all with a boyfriend in place whom she loved very much?

By the time she was ready, Zach had packed and was sitting on the sofa drinking more coffee. She stood and looked at him. He looked at her. For a moment, they were still. Then Amy moved towards him and he stood up.

"Do you want some breakfast before you go?"

"No, no I'm fine. I really should get going." She touched his arm and took a deep breath. "Thank you for fulfilling my ultimate fantasy." She had to say it.

He smiled. "Don't thank me, that's weird. I'm flattered, but the way I see it is that I just met this amazing girl and we hit it off. Amazing Amy." She laughed. Just as she was about to begin a farewell, he put his fingers on her lips. She lightly kissed them. She could smell his expensive aftershave. "Don't say goodbye," he said.

"OK." She could feel a lump developing in her throat. She curled her arms around his neck. He was quite tall compared to her when she didn't have her heels on. He buried his face into her neck. She could have held onto him for much longer, but go she must. She drew back to look into his eyes once more and he kissed her hard on the lips, holding her tight. She reached up and ran her fingers through his thick hair. She realised she had not done that yet and wanted to make sure she had touched every bit of him before they parted. She pulled away and turned to leave.

"I'll text you later."

She nodded, unable to speak. She picked up her bag and left the room. He watched her walk to the lift from the door. She turned back, waved and blew him a kiss. He waited until she got in the lift and waved as she entered it. As the doors closed, tears dripped from her eyes and she could barely see the buttons. She felt immense sadness at leaving him, at her betrayal, at the dilemma before her. Her future. She had a pretty set, comfortable life right now. Her heart seemed to swell as her mind allowed Will back in. No, it wasn't ideal that he was away a lot, but maybe that would change. It'd be no different with Zach. And what if that didn't work? She would have given up everything for him. He would for sure expect her to come to America, just at a point when her career was beginning to look promising in London. And they barely knew each other – how could it work? Her life was so different to his, so normal; his so Hollywood. Was it worth pursuing? She was still infatuated by him, but she was in love with Will. Deep, know-each-other's-innermost, solid love, built up over two years. Perhaps she was just over-analysing it all and nothing would come of it.

She put it to the back of her mind, as she drove straight to the *Delta* office to check in with her editor and go over the article she had written. She was barely conscious of what was being said and tried to focus as much as she could. Straight afterwards, she headed home. She flopped onto her sofa and fell asleep for some time, exhausted. When she awoke, she absently grabbed her phone and flicked through her Instagram feed. Sovereign X had just that moment posted a photo of their Club World seats on their plane – Zach had taken the picture, his Converse just in view.

She went to her messages. She paused, then typed:

Safe journey, gorgeous boy x

She deleted gorgeous boy'. She thought for a moment with the message field still open and noticed the speech bubble with dots in that iPhones have when the other person is iMessaging. She waited. Sure enough, a message came through from Zach.

Were you texting me?

She smiled, and altered her reply:

Yes – I was just texting safe journey, just saw ur pic on Insta. Gorgeous boy xx

She typed and pressed send quickly with her eyes closed. It was a moment before he responded with a close-up selfie, baseball cap on, lips pursed, eyes closed. She smiled.

Now turn off ur phone for TO It's not in airplane mode, is it?

Ha ha, sure. Ciao, Chica xx

She smiled and put her phone down. It beeped again and she tutted. She grabbed it – and her stomach turned over – it was Will this time, not Zach.

Hi Babe – on my way back from LHR. Got a surprise for u xx

She fell off the sofa in a haste to get up. It was unlike Will to turn up suddenly without warning. Paranoia set in. She ran upstairs and got changed, putting yesterday's clothes straight in the washing machine –

they only smelt subtly of *him*, but she didn't want any trace. Will noticed *everything*. She tidied up the house and put some dinner on.

She had just sat down when she had a sudden thought. The iCloud; the photo of Zach. But she didn't want to delete it – what to do? She quickly printed a copy, folded it up and put it at the bottom of her makeup drawer. Will would never know it was there. She kept the picture on her messages that he had just sent and made sure it was nowhere else on her phone. *Stupid phones save everything*. She must not let Will get hold of her phone. Ever.

Half an hour later, she felt much more composed, just as she heard his key opening the front door. She went out into the hall and smiled as he came through. She threw her arms around him.

"Missed you," he said in his deep voice, kissing her on the lips. *Deeper than Zach's*, she thought.

"Missed you too." There was contentment with familiarity, she felt comfort and peace in his presence. She pushed Zach firmly out of her mind and allowed the elation she felt at Will's return to fill her.

"I'm starving, I could do with getting some dinner."

"I have a dinner for you – ain't I good to you?" She wasn't sure she meant it right now.

"Thanks, Babe." He kissed her on the head and squeezed her. "Oh, the surprise! I nearly forgot. Guess who I saw at the airport?" Will's face was lit with excitement. They did this frequently; he travelled a lot, often first class, so his famous sightings were a regular occurrence. Because of this, Amy did not predict what came next.

"Er… you're excited, so it must be someone big – Madonna?"

"Nope." He shook his head. They loved a guessing game.

"David Beckham?"

"No."

"Oh, I could be here all night…" She frowned, trying to think.

"It's someone you really like." Will grinned with glee. If he had been a puppy, his tail would have been wagging vociferously.

The dawn of realisation began in Amy and her mood dropped to the floor. The dots were all connecting – it had to be… the timing was just about perfect. She began wringing her hands, as she turned to go into the kitchen, relieved to get away from Will's naively excited eyes looking promptingly at hers.

"Er…" She faltered, but she had had enough. She just wanted to know for sure now. "I don't know, just tell me for fuck's sake."

"All right, all right, no need to get stroppy! Here look, I got a photo with him." He called up a picture on his phone and Amy turned to look, knowing full well who would be in it. Will thrust the phone under her nose. Sure enough, it was a photo of Will standing with his arm around Zach Hayes, against the backdrop of a busy Heathrow terminal. Her heart was racing by now. In this bizarre twist of fate – Will obviously knew who Zach was – but he had no idea who Zach had become to her, in his absence. And had Zach, who confessed to looking her up, recognised Will? If he had looked as intently at her profile as she assumed, he would have. Oh, the irony! To have met him on a plane all that time ago, then she and Will both meet him within days of each other. Now, how to react without giving anything away. *Say enough, but not too much.*

"Oh, wow! I'm so jealous. I had heard they were in the country." She had not had the courage – nor now the inclination, given what had occurred since – to tell him about the interview, it being so impromptu an arrangement. Will didn't usually look at her work, unless she offered to show him, or she wanted to go over articles with him, so there was no way of him finding out unless she told him. But here began the track covering… the elusive avoidance of being caught. She sighed.

"How good a boyfriend am I, getting a pic of my rival! Worth a cock suck I'd say." He nudged her playfully, and chuckled. "And you know I hate selfies and all that nonsense." He was obviously pleased with himself. "Your two favourite men in one photo. I'll send it to you, and you can treasure it. Keep it under your pillow." He laughed.

She gulped and smiled. "All right, don't milk it! Thank you." She kissed him. Amy had told Will early on in their relationship about meeting the band on the plane, and how she had kicked herself ever since that she never had the opportunity to get a photo and autograph. That all seemed small fry now, but she did not want to belittle Will's sweet gesture, it was well intentioned.

"Oh, that's not all. He signed his autograph too." Will began rummaging in his rucksack.

"What did you say to him… about me?" Amy said, as she dished up dinner.

"I just said my girlfriend, Amy, is your biggest fan, can I take a photo and grab your autograph for her? He was very friendly and willing," Will replied, still digging through his bag. *I'll bet he was.* Will finally pulled out one of his AAIB cards. Amy sighed and rolled her eyes, clandestine. Well, that would confirm who Will was, if there had been any doubt on Zach's part. She wondered how he had reacted to this uncanny meeting. Hoping this ordeal would end soon – putting on this front was taking its toll – she rubbed the tension from her brow. "Here." Will handed the card to her. It read:

Amy
L O V E
Zach Hayes, Sovereign X

The 'love' in spaced-out capitals did not escape her.

"He even put the 'love' in caps – I wonder if he always does that?"

Like she needed it being pointed out. She knew it was Zach's way of showing her he had clicked with the whole debacle. "I don't know," she said innocently, avoiding eye contact.

She could not help drawing comparisons in her mind, however potentially dangerous that might be. Zach was taller and slimmer; Will was stocky and strong, his aftershave muskier, he was hairier. Zach had bronze skin from living in LA, Will was paler being a Brit. How this was torture. She couldn't help wondering how their meet had gone, how did Will approach Zach? Had he been charismatic enough to him? She didn't want Zach thinking she was with some chump. Of course, Will was always charming with people, he had such a warm and open manner, it was what had attracted her to him in the first place, beside his puppy-dog brown eyes and hugely infectious laugh. And what about Zach, had he been subtle enough when he had inevitably realised who Will was? The love stunt was risky, but Will seemed to be in no way suspicious. In any case, he would not be able to begin to imagine the weekend she had had. They sat to eat and Amy changed the subject.

"How's work?" This was always a tricky question to ask, with the complex and sometimes distressing job he had. Sometimes he talked lucidly about every twist and turn of the investigation, other times he did not want to talk at all. It was on those occasions she knew not to press him, he would just want to put out of his mind the horrors he had seen or tragedies he had faced, in order to reach conclusions. This effort at a diversion from their previous conversation could go either way.

"Hard. Very little to look at. The plane pieces are few and far between…" He began to tell her all the details and describe the intricacies of the plane and the engineering of it, the possible faults that could have factored in the crash. This was clearly one of the former occasions when he wanted to offload all the details, and she did not mind hearing this at all. His job was so important to help ensure the future safety of air travel. And this is real life, someone making a real difference in the world. What was she doing – writing about musicians. Then sleeping with one of them. She tried not to let these thoughts overtake her so much that she did not hear what Will was saying.

Just as they were clearing up the dinner things, there was a knock on the door.

"Who's that?" Will traditionally said this whenever there was a random knock at the door.

"Oh, shit."

"What?"

"It's Beth."

"Oh, bloody hell, I've just got back. I want some time with you," Will said, quietly.

"To be fair, Babe, I didn't know you would be back."

"I guess so. I just wanted to surprise you."

"Well, you're a twat," Amy said with a grin, and went to the door.

"So, what's your story, deserter?" Beth exclaimed, as Amy opened the door. Amy shushed her, and gestured madly towards the kitchen.

After some signing, which consisted of Amy trying to let her know that Will was back, Amy said in as normal a tone as possible, "So I shouldn't be out too long, is that OK?"

Beth glared at her, fascinated by her flustering. "Sure…"

Will appeared behind Amy. She turned her head in Will's direction, her eyes left Amy shortly after and made their way to Will. Beth recovered herself in an instant.

"Hi, Will."

"Hi, Beth, all right?" Will leaned across Amy to kiss Beth on the cheek. "You go, Amy, I'm pretty jetlagged anyway." He kissed her.

"OK, I'll see you later." She grabbed her bag and followed Beth out into the warm evening. She looked back at Will and waved. She sighed as they walked along the road towards the local pub.

Making sure they were out of earshot and had heard Will shut the door, Beth said, "So, what's up with you?"

"I'm OK, how're you?" Amy deflected.

"Oh, come on, something weird has happened."

"Let's just get a drink first before I get into it."

They walked into the pub and Amy ordered a bottle of red. They made their way to a secluded corner to sit in.

"So, spill the beans, what was so pressing that you stood me up, and clearly don't want Will knowing about? I mean if I didn't know better I'd say you've played away from home, but I know how loved up you two are." Amy did not reply and just took a big glug of her wine, looking beyond Beth around the pub. Beth looked searchingly at her. "Have I hit the nail on the head?" Amy bit her lip and raised her eyebrows. "You told me that the only bloke in the world you would ever cheat on Will for, was Zach Hayes." Beth continued, unsuspectingly.

"Er, yes. That's exactly it." Amy broke her silence, looking sternly at Beth, nodding. Beth nearly choked on her drink.

"Shut the front door! Really? No, you're shitting me. That did not happen. Tell me the truth, go on."

"Zach asked me out at the end of the interview, we went for a meal the following day, and ended up at his hotel." She calmly watched Beth's reaction as she sipped her wine again. Beth's jaw dropped open, then she closed it.

"You're so full of shit. I don't believe you. Prove it."

"Oh, some friend you are!"

"*You* would definitely have gotten proof. You love a memento, you're a bit weird like that."

"You know me too well. You mustn't tell anyone. Look." She called up the recently deleted photos on her phone, looked around to make sure no one was looking over her shoulder, and showed Beth the picture of her with Zach, clearly in bed together.

Beth gasped. "You... you..."

"Wow. Never thought I'd be able to render *you* speechless." Amy permanently deleted the photo while she had her phone out, just to be safe.

"So, the interview went *really* well then!"

"You could say that."

Beth shook her hands in the air and screwed her eyes up, trying to work it all out. "Hold on, hold on, back up." She took a breath. "How, the flying heck, did this happen? You, Amy, have a live-in boyfriend. Now you're sitting in front of me, telling me you've actually *slept with your celebrity crush*?" She was incredulous.

"Will you keep your bloody voice down, I know half the pub." She proceeded to fill Beth in on her unbelievable weekend. "You know what amazed me? He actually remembered me from the plane! All that time I spent beating myself up that I hadn't made an impression. Wish I had asked for his number back then, I might not be in this mess right now..." She rested her head on her hand, struck by the irony. Beth watched her, fascinated.

"One day you may realise that you are a very attractive, striking person."

Amy raised her eyebrows, and sipped her drink.

"It's true, Amy." Beth sipped her drink. "Can't believe one of my friends has had sex with someone famous!" She grinned and leaned closer to Amy, enjoying the juicy details. "How many times did you do it?" She rubbed her hands together.

"Does it matter?"

"Oh, more than twice then. Have you achieved all the slots on your laminated list?" Amy couldn't help a chuckle at the reference that had come to be so poignant to her.

"But the twist in the tale really, is this: Will came home today having bumped into Zach at the airport. He got a selfie with him, and his autograph!"

"Fuck me, that's weird! Zach wouldn't know who Will was though?"

"He said he'd looked me up and saw that I had a boyfriend, so I suspected he did. Then, I was certain, when Will gave me this." She handed Beth the card with the autograph on it. "I had also told Zach that Will works for the AAIB."

Beth looked at the card. "Love in capitals. That is a bit lame. And *really* cheeky."

"I know, right?"

"What did Zach say when he discovered you've got a fella?"

"He said he was jealous, and that he didn't want to let me go."

"Yikes Amy, sounds like a smitten kitten." Beth drained her glass and poured another for them both. "Guys just fall at your feet, don't they?"

"Oh, now you're talking out of your arse." Amy waved her hand dismissively.

Beth waggled her finger at Amy with a serious look on her face. "I'll have you know my arse talks a lot of sense." Both girls giggled.

"But this must be much more agonising than you're letting on. Now, ultimately, you have cheated on your boyfriend. No matter who it was with."

Amy sighed. "Oh, believe me, I am well aware of what an awful thing I have done. Do you think I can use the whole list thing, seriously, in real life, as an excuse?"

Beth looked at her, unsure of how to approach her friend's dilemma. "Are you going to try to stay in touch with Zach?"

"That's not an answer to my question!"

"Don't avoid it – are you?"

Amy looked down and turned her glass round and round. "He wants to. But who knows if he will or not."

Beth thought for a moment. "Can you really take the list thing seriously? An idea that was on a TV show? A comedy, at that. Can you really rely on that as a defence? How would you feel if it was Will who had slept with his celeb crush?"

Amy had not looked at it from that angle before. She imagined Will 'fessing up that he had slept with Rihanna, to imagining them together. She shuddered and shook her head.

"Blimey, I can't get a relationship to stick, and there you are juggling two!"

Amy pursed her lips.

"It's true!"

Amy playfully slapped Beth's arm. "How would you feel if you were in a relationship, and I don't know… Margot Robbie walked in and made a pass at you?"

"Hang on." Beth closed her eyes and put her fingertips to her forehead. "I've got to try to imagine myself in a relationship first." She screwed her eyes up. "OK, yes of course, I would be all over her. But take it to the next step and risk damaging my relationship? I'm not sure. Depends on how strong that relationship was in the first place. Maybe you should be asking yourself that question."

"I love Will deeply, you know that. But this just seemed like one of those once in a lifetime, destiny, kind of situations. I mean, he came on to me pretty strong, and as he said, I've met him twice at exactly the time he had just broken up with someone. Both times."

"But that's his destiny, not yours."

"And I've always believed you make your own destiny anyway."

"Exactly. You wanted this."

"I did. I'm weak. And it is tough with Will away a lot. That worked OK with us both playing time zone hopscotch flying everywhere, but now… and I've been so caught up with getting my career off the ground."

"And flying isn't the same without you."

"Oh, bless you. I do miss you guys. Don't miss the jet lag." Amy smiled.

Beth looked at her, eyes bright with a sudden idea. "I have one word for you – threesome!"

Amy rolled her eyes. "Not exactly a solution though, is it?"

"Nope. Fun though. If you're into blokes that is."

Amy drained her glass and poured another. "I just could not resist him. Is that so bad?"

"And I'm sure if you say that to Will, he'll understand."

"Do you think?"

"Fuck, no! He's a bloke! He'll feel ridiculed, especially after getting the guy's autograph. Plus, you slept with someone else! He won't be able to trust you, he may not even want to be with you any more."

"OK stop, stop. That's quite a picture you've painted." Amy put her head in her hands.

"I'm sorry, that was a bit harsh."

"The way I see it is this: I can just draw a line under it as a one-off experience, a fantasy indulged. In which case, I would be better to just move on and keep my mouth shut, not rock the boat with Will unnecessarily."

"Or?" Beth implored.

"Or, what?"

"It just sounded like there was an 'or' coming after that."

Amy sighed. There was an 'or'. "Or, I could turn my life upside down and pursue Zach."

"And what about Will? Where does that leave him?"

"I have no idea. I don't want to lose him either. What a fucking mess I've got myself into."

"Just drink your wine, Babe." Beth leaned forward, pouring more into Amy's glass. "You know, you could do both options. You're a woman in the twenty-first century, I don't see why you can't have your cake and eat it too."

"By 'cake' you mean Will and by 'eat it too' you mean Zach?" They giggled.

"Yes, exactly. Don't tell Will. Just carry on as normal. See if Zach tries to contact you and if you are able to see him again – I mean it's going to be tough anyway, he lives in America, he has this hectic showbiz life. As you said, there's no point upsetting the apple cart for something that might not go anywhere. And if you're able to maintain it, make your decision then."

"I just hate the duplicity of it all."

"Whoa, Mrs big words! Look, faced with an unreal situation, I think calls for an unreal solution."

***

As they walked home, Amy felt better having unburdened her dirty little secret to her closest friend. Beth hugged Amy goodbye at the path to her house and wished her luck. Amy wandered upstairs to find Will asleep in their bed. She quietly undressed and slipped into bed next to him. He stirred and put his arm over her, his hand moving down her body. She closed her eyes and a vision of Zach appeared in her mind, what they had done together, mere hours before. It made her feel a bit sick. She moved Will's arm off her. Then she moved it back. Carry on as normal, Beth had suggested. And Will was so thorough, loving giving her pleasure intensely.

"I bought some things in the States," Will murmured. She turned to him and he kissed her sensuously. "Wanna try them out?"

"Sure," she whispered back, excitement and arousal building at the prospect. He pulled her body close to his, and she held him tight, before he got out of the bed, the warmth of love and intimacy pouring forth from her heart, but stinging her sharply as she tried to push the memory of her betrayal out of her mind. She watched him as he made his way over to the dresser. She smiled, warmed by his return. She had missed him, she really had.

Five

The next week passed by uneventfully. Amy's work had gone quiet again, and after only a few days together, Will had been called away again for two weeks. Zach had contacted her a few times, usually by text – merely a heart, kiss or flowers emoji – but the time zone difference was proving difficult and he was busy promoting their album. She had not mentioned Will and the autograph to Zach; she felt embarrassed. She texted him when he texted her and no more.

She spent her spare time trying not to think about Zach and focus on her and Will. It was so hard to try to be positive about their relationship while he was thousands of miles away with work and contact was limited. Even Beth had not been about much – she was taking on more shifts on her roster. With her quietest, most isolated moments she found herself writing again. She knew she had a book in her and she took comfort in putting ideas to paper. Inspiration came to her late most nights and she sat at her laptop for hours, sometimes till three a.m. With no freelance work currently coming in, she found her body clock adjusted and she slept in till ten a.m. most days.

As the days wore on, the memory of her time with Zach was fading; her excitement and passion at what had occurred was much more measured and she remembered their encounters as if they were a movie, or snapshots, captured in time and space, as if they had not been real after all. The separation between daydreaming and reality had always been a vice of Amy's and at times like these she found herself drifting between the conscious world of reality and the sub-conscious world of fantasy.

One stormy, clammy evening while Will was still away, she was dozing on the sofa, slumped over her laptop, and was startled awake by the bleep of a message on her phone. She came to, and picked it up. It was from Zach.

Can I FaceTime you?

This was all it said. She got up quickly, checked her hair in the mirror and put some lipstick on. The time out there would be around two p.m.

Sure

Within a few moments, the FaceTime tone rang. She took a deep breath and answered. It was lagging, not a great line.

"Hi," she said, mellifluously.

"Hey, you," he drawled. She smiled. "Have you just put some lip gloss on?"

"Maybe."

"I've got something that would like those lips round it."

"I'll bet." She smiled. She could not believe how easily she slipped back into flirting with him, having almost dismissed him in her heart entirely.

"Are you alone?"

"Yes. Will's away with work."

"He's away a lot – should I be worried about flying with how busy he is?"

She smiled. "Still the safest way to travel."

"So the saying goes. Does he know you interviewed us?"

Amy shifted uncomfortably. "No, he doesn't. After what happened between us I just didn't tell him." She looked away and thought of their meeting at Heathrow, curious again as to how it went. She dared not bring it up. But she didn't need to.

"Did you get my note?"

She knew exactly what he meant. "Yes."

"That was weird."

"I really couldn't believe it when he came home and told me that night. It was like some sort of karma, or whatever. Thank you for not letting on."

"Well, naturally. That's gotta be your call, right? Plus, he seems like a nice guy. Makes it harder to try to steal his girl."

She felt a fillip in her belly. "Is that what you want to do?"

"Don't you want me to?"

"I thought maybe you had gone off the idea."

"No – I meant it when I said I've been so busy. I'm a mess. I can't sleep, everything I write is about you."

Her heart swelled at his comment. "I miss you." She wanted to touch him, kiss him again.

"Is it late over there?"

"Not really, ten-ish."

"We got a new song dropping on Friday, I think you'll like it."

"Can't wait to hear it, I'm sure it'll be brilliant."

"I've been thinking about you a lot. And all the stuff we did together. I never thought I could be re-educated, but you've really opened me up."

Amy felt her desire for him spike. She loved that she had had dominance over him in the bedroom, when in her relationship with Will he had always had dominance over her. It added to the novelty of this. He was the same age as her too, Will was a bit older.

"How can we meet up?" The desperation of her split feelings could not hold her back.

"I'm back in London soon. Can you see me?"

"I'll try. When?"

"I'm not sure, we're trying to get a few days in the studio over there. I'll have to let you know my itinerary."

"OK."

"OK. I better go."

"OK. Bye."

"Bye." He was reluctant to go. "Amy."

"Yes?"

"… Nothing. I just wanna…"

"I know."

"I'll keep in touch."

"Cool. Bye." She hung up before he could say any more.

***

The next day, Zach texted, letting her know what he was up to and how he was thinking about her more than ever now he had seen her on FaceTime. She didn't reply straight away. It was becoming a much more agonising prospect to try to decide what to do. Will had been away so much lately, she almost felt like she didn't have a boyfriend sometimes. Maybe she should just go for it with Zach. At that very moment, her phone rang. Will.

"Hey, Babe," she said, automatically using the moniker they always used for each other.

"Hiya. You all right?"

"Yeah. Not very busy. I've been writing. I might get a book finished one day."

"That's great. I miss you loads." The line was crackly.

"I miss you, too." It felt strange saying this twice in two days to two different men. "When are you coming back?"

"Three days I should touch down."

"How are you?"

"Jaded. Just want to be back with you now."

Her heart warmed. She felt tears in her eyes; she wanted him back. How could she do this to him? He was the love of her life. "Me too." She felt choked.

"Oh, don't cry, Babe. Love you."

"Love you, too," she said, trying to stop the sobs from coming.

"I'm being called – not long now. Love you, lots." They said goodbye. She allowed herself to cry properly and laid down on the sofa. She never replied to Zach's text.

***

Over the next few days, more freelance work trickled in and Amy found the distraction more than welcome. It also meant more money coming in and so it was a good excuse for some retail therapy and a catch up over lunch with Beth. They met in town, the day Will was due back.

"Hey, Gorge, how's things?" Beth hugged her. They sat down with a coffee and sandwich.

"Complicated. Think my moral compass has been near a magnet. How's you?"

"Never better – I've met someone. In America, funnily enough."

"Really? That's funny with what I've got going on. What's she like?"

"Beautiful. Really nice. I mean, you know how over the top our cousins from across the Atlantic can be, but she's lovely."

"Well, as you know, I'm revising my opinion of Americans." She smiled.

Beth smiled back. "Zach's been in touch, hasn't he?"

"Yes. FaceTime a couple of days ago."

"Did he show you his cock?"

"Beth! No!" She paused. "Why didn't he show me his cock?"

"Ha ha, you've seen it before, anyway."

"Forgotten what it looks like."

"Surely one cock is the same as the next one." Beth sipped her drink. Amy always found their relationship chats fascinating, not least because having a best friend who was not into men always gave her such an off-the-wall viewpoint.

"Surely one pussy is the same as the next one?" They both giggled.

"Touché. And how's the other man in your life?"

"Oh, don't refer to him as the other man, it doesn't seem fair on him. Zach is the other man."

"I know, but you've already told me about him."

Amy rolled her eyes. "He's away for work."

"Finding it tough?"

"Yes. So difficult to be monogamous. The cat keeps going away, and you know what the mice do when that happens."

"Zach's not in the country, though, is he?"

"No. They've both been out of sight, out of mind."

Amy had bought Will some expensive new aftershave and she showed Beth.

"I know this is a guilt purchase, but do you like it?"

Beth sniffed it. "Hmm, yes, nice. And yes, it's a guilt purchase! When's he due back?"

"Late tonight."

"So, juggling two men – fun or not fun?"

Amy sighed. "Do you know what, I think I should stop living in a dream world and just enjoy the good thing I've got in front of me. What are the chances of being able to make a relationship with Zach work? I don't really know for sure if we could ever fall in love, or are even suited.

Part of me wishes I'd never indulged in my fantasy. Maybe fantasies are best left just that, fantasies."

Beth used her usual searching glare. "Do you really mean that?"

Amy looked at her. "No." She frowned. "I never thought I'd have to choose between the love of my life and my celeb crush. I wish he'd been an arsehole when I met him, at least then the decision would have been easy."

"Yep. One quick shag, then outta there!" Beth nudged Amy and she laughed. "Is he coming over sometime?"

"Yes, but he's busy in the States at the moment, promoting the single and the album. I didn't reply to his last text."

"Well, you know what they say: treat 'em mean, keep 'em keen. You're not going to put him off by lack of contact. If he really likes you he'll just get more desperate for you. If you don't want him, you should just let him down. You're obviously struggling with the whole thing. And besides, you love Will, you want to make a go of it. You had your fun, why not just keep that memory and let it go?"

"What happened to having my cake and eating it too?"

"I don't know. Being in a relationship has turned me soft in the head!"

"Oh yes, you said before we got distracted by my messy love life – what's her name?"

"Isabella." Beth was suddenly wistful.

"Oh, exotic! Have you seen her much?"

"Well, it's tough, long distance, as you know. I'm regularly on the planes over there, getting as many shifts as I can, so I get a day or so to see her. She's trying to make it as an actor and works in a coffee shop part time in LAX, which is mightily convenient. In fact, wanna do a ride along with me? I got a spare jump-seat to LA in a few weeks' time?"

"Oh, that won't put a cat amongst the pigeons much, will it?"

"OK, no worries."

"I mean, I'm not saying no…"

"Oh, right." Beth raised her eyebrows and smiled.

Amy stifled a smile. "Well, anyway, be nice to meet your bird."

"Sure."

"Stop it!" Amy whacked her friend on the arm. "I'll come to LA."

"Might be good to go see him on his home turf? Help you make your decision?"

"Hmm. Maybe. Maybe I'll see his massive house and fancy cars and make my decision very easily!" They giggled. "Oh, I shouldn't joke like that. I love my Will. Maybe one or both of them will have given up on me by then. Will's back today, Zach's in London soon."

"You gonna see him?"

"I've said I would. Don't know how though, he's gonna have a tight schedule when he's here."

"And what about Will?"

"I'm looking forward to seeing him. We need to see if we can reconnect having spent so much time apart."

"You're going to find it harder to juggle them both if they're in the country at the same time."

"I hadn't thought about that. They literally passed each other before. One going to America, one coming back."

"Oh, yeah! Did Zach say anything to you about that?"

"Yes – he said 'did you get my note?' Cheeky bastard. I thanked him for not giving the game away though. He said he thought Will seemed a nice guy, made it harder to try to steal his girl."

"Did he really say that?"

Amy nodded.

"Wow, you know I think he might have it quite bad."

"Hence, why I have got to choose. It's just not fair on them both." But secretly, Amy found the power having two men on the string gave her, quite addictive. And both so different; Will had always looked after her, been the one who steered their relationship. He had come along at a time when she was veering off the rails and had offered her stability and strength to ground her again. He was a dominant force in her life and in her bedroom, and for so long this had been a safety net for her. Zach, on the other hand, represented danger and vitality. He was more equal to her, and rather than her needing him as she had always needed Will, his need for her seemed greater. She did not need Zach, after all she had a relationship, but she wanted him. She had imagination in the bedroom; granted it was an imagination garnered by her experiences with Will, but the power she levied, with no reliance on her controlling boyfriend, was incredibly satisfying and emancipating. Not to say there wasn't thrill and ecstasy with Will. He had an amazing job and was someone who oozed charisma. But Amy had always felt she played second fiddle, being shy.

With Will being away so much lately she had spread her wings, and with her career prospects looking higher, she was gaining more and more confidence and desire for adventure. Perhaps Zach merely represented that. And she still could not get past the sensational aspect – the paradox of the fact that he was in a position of power and yet seemed powerless to her charms. Will had no such power, in the sense that he was a mere mortal, not part of that rich and famous league like Zach, and yet yielded so much power over Amy, a power that he never abused, he always respected her, but power still it was.

Six

Will came home as expected that night and they had the most amazing evening of passion, fuelled in part by alcohol, part by the long separation from each other. The next day, the memory of her chat to Beth about Zach felt like child's play. Here she was with a real man in front of her, devoted to her every desire, prepared to cherish and look after her.

A couple of days later, Amy came back home one afternoon having submitted another article to *Delta*. She looked at her phone while she was on the train. Zach had not texted her for a couple of days, but then she had stopped replying to him. It had been so difficult with Will being around, who was being so attentive, that Zach's presence in her mind was beginning to reduce day by day again. She walked home from the train station and saw that Will's Mercedes was parked by the house. She had not expected him to be home at that time of the day. She let herself in the front door to find him standing in the hallway, a gerbera flower between his teeth – her favourite – and his arms outstretched.

"Urgh, they taste disgusting." Will screwed his face up and took the flower out of his mouth. She giggled.

"What are you doing?" She noticed a small suitcase by his feet.

He stood up tall and puffed out his chest in preparation of his speech. "I know I've not been about much lately, so, as an early birthday treat, we're going away for a few days. I've booked a lovely quiet hotel in a quaint town. How's that sound?"

"Fabulous, Babe." She kissed him, delighted, and threw her arms around his neck. "Urgh that does taste bitter, doesn't it?" She laughed, tasting the flower on his lips. "I'll just get changed then, shall I?"

"Yep – I've packed for us both. I know I'm not great at that, but I think I did OK. Wanna check?"

She paused on her way upstairs. Her makeup drawer... the photo... "Er, no I trust you." More than she trusted herself right now. She scrabbled to open the drawer, her hands shaking. Surely if he had seen it, he would have said something? Will wasn't the type to go snooping, he trusted her implicitly, which made her feel even more guilty. Some of her essentials had been grabbed; the folded photo was unmoved, to her relief. She paused, staring at the back of it. She pulled it out. Her in the arms of her idol, both of them clearly naked. Perhaps it was time to move on. She stuffed it back in its hidey-hole, changed her outfit, and ran back downstairs to follow Will to the car.

On the way to the hotel, she leaned her head back and drifted off into a daydream. Zach's face from the photo came into her head, his handsome face. Then Will's replaced it, his features quite different, but equally as attractive in his way. The familiar face and the famous face. She was jolted back to earth from her reverie by Will speaking. He had turned the radio up.

"I like this new one from Sovereign X. You didn't say they've got a new one out, have you stopped listening to them? Haven't heard you playing their stuff at home lately."

This was not what she wanted, a conversation that alluded to *him*. "No, I still do listen to their stuff," she said, with as much nonchalance as she could manage. "I have heard this one a few times."

She had not been listening to them out loud in the house, only late at night with her earphones in. It felt like a new realm of infidelity, rubbing his nose in it, even though he was completely oblivious to the whole affair. This new one was especially difficult – it was all about her. And it was doing well, so was on the radio. A lot. Will tapped the steering wheel to the music as he drove.

"I can't stop thinking about you,
And all the things you do,
You taught me new love,
Breathing into my veins,
No ocean too big to part us,
No Will too tough to stop us...."

The words washed over her and she felt her cheeks burning, glad that the sun was bright, reflecting warm colours through the window, and hopefully camouflaging the colours in her face. It was a weird sensation to listen to a song with so private a theme on the radio, in the charts. She looked out of the window, unable to enjoy the moment, the immortalisation of oneself in a song, there forever, to be repeated often, wherever she might be. The song was going to be big, and she imagined the places she might be caught unawares in years to come, in shops, in restaurants, on MTV. Her betrayal ever to be presented to her.

Or, alternatively, if she decided to pursue things with Zach, would she be known as the girl that inspired the song, talked about by people both sides of the Atlantic? He would want her to come to America. She might have to give up her career to make it work with him – perhaps being with him wouldn't be emancipation after all. She felt him speaking the words to her, through the medium of the radio. But maybe his flame was reducing to glowing embers already, his texts had dried up.

Soon they pulled up at the hotel. It was a small, very old, pre-Tudor place, intimate, full of character. It was right up Amy's street, set back on a quiet lane just off the high street in the centre of the town. They entered and went to reception. Amy already had a smile on her face and gripped Will's strong arm as they checked in. This was just the tonic of distraction she needed.

The walls were oak-panelled, the carpets were red and threadbare in places, and it had a cobbled courtyard in the centre with a quirky fountain in the middle. It exuded all the quaint historic character that she loved. They went straight to their room and Amy flopped onto the four-poster bed.

"This is great, I love it! Thank you so much." She beamed at Will. He smiled back.

"They say it's haunted, this place. By several ghosts."

"Really? Well it is mega old – how many people must have died here? In macabre ways, too, I expect." She was ebullient.

"Yep. Nice."

"Well, it's true. Fascinating." Amy loved a bit of history.

Will smiled at her childlike enthusiasm. "C'mon, let's get some dinner. I've bought you a new dress." Will put the suitcase on the bed. Amy dutifully changed into the stunning dress – he had impeccable taste – put her heels on and they ascended the stairs, going into the small and intimate restaurant. They ate their meal and laughed and chatted like they had just started dating again. After a few glasses of wine, they decided to go for a walk through the town.

It was a lovely warm summer evening, the sun was just setting and the streets were vibrant, pubs were filling, shops and tea rooms were shut. Amy felt light and happy as they walked through the cobbled and hilly, historic streets. They walked up past the church and ambled back to the hotel arm in arm. For the entire evening, Amy had not thought of Zach at all.

As they entered the hotel and made their way past reception, a tall floppy-haired guy cut a path across them. Amy would recognise him anywhere. She gasped and he turned around. She felt her legs buckle under her. How could this have happened just as she was putting him out of her mind? Will must have felt her go and grabbed hold of her more tightly.

When Zach saw her in the arms of Will, so unexpectedly, his face noticeably dropped. Will spoke, fortunately, which covered the intense awkwardness of the situation for the two of them, otherwise he might have picked up on the sudden atmosphere.

Ever the gentleman, Will said upon recognising him, "Zach Hayes! Hi – I met you at Heathrow a little while ago. Will." He reached his hand out for Zach to shake. Zach drew his eyes reluctantly away from Amy, who was clearly squirming and trying not to make eye contact with anyone, and smiled at Will.

"Oh, hey. Hi." He shook his hand. Amy was trying to maintain a normal level of breathing and had not let go of Will.

"This is my girlfriend, Amy, you signed my business card for her. She's a big fan of yours. Aren't you, Babe? She served you once on a plane, too." He nudged her, but she had gone red and was rendered dumb. She just about managed a smile, but could not make eye contact with Zach. She felt quite literally ambushed.

"Nice to meet you, Amy." She surreptitiously rolled her eyes. Zach leaned across Will to take her hand. He lingered for a nano-second; she felt him breathe in her perfume, before drawing away and smiling to Will. "Are you guys staying here?"

"Yes, just arrived. It's Amy's birthday this week."

"Oh, really?" He looked at her as if to say, 'you never told me'. "That's great. You must join me for dinner tomorrow night then. I'm staying here too."

Amy widened her eyes and jerked her head forward in shock at this preposterous suggestion. What was he playing at?

"Oh, wow, that'd be an honour, eh, Amy? We'd love to, thank you. Well, night."

Will whisked Amy away, who chanced a glance behind her as they turned to go up the narrow rickety staircase. Zach was standing there smiling a wide smile with glee, watching them go, clearly delighted to have bumped into her in such a surprising way. He cheekily blew her a kiss and she managed to slip him 'the bird' as they disappeared. She heard him chuckle. This filled her with a dangerous concoction of rage and horniness. Her blood was boiling in more than one way when she and Will entered their room.

"That is so bizarre, we keep crossing paths!" Will seemed more taken with his own star-struck-ness than hers, which was good, because she wasn't sure she could hide her feelings that well right now. She felt like she had been side-swiped. They both began undressing for bed. Amy was distant though, she couldn't help wondering why Fate had twisted in her life so much as to throw temptation in her path again so massively. All she could think about was finding a way to sneak away from Will to shag Zach's brains out, and she loathed herself for those warped thoughts.

"You were a blithering wreck," Will said, as he sat on the bed removing his shoes.

"Thanks for that." Amy managed at his jovial, but cutting remark. "It was shock, that's all." No lies there.

"Well, we've got dinner with him tomorrow, that'll be something, hey?"

"Yes." *It certainly will be 'something'.*

"Still, enough of that, we have a four-poster bed to use." She was sitting on the edge, and he pulled her into the bed from behind her.

"I'm a bit tired, actually." She was so emotionally charged, but also so physically spent.

"Oh. OK." Disappointment was clear in his tone. She moved away to her side of the bed, and turned the light out. She was not in the mood to be coaxed tonight. "Night. Love you."

"And you."

Will was asleep in moments, marked by his heavy breathing. Amy lay there wide awake, unable to switch her mind off. Why was he here, of all obscure places? Paranoia began to set in. Did he know she would be here? But, how could he? It must just be some nasty coincidence. Had Will mentioned it when he saw him at the airport that time? She could hardly ask him, and Will was just as surprised as her, so it couldn't be that. She thought about messaging him, but that just messed with her head too. She lay in the dark, wide-eyed for what seemed like an eternity. She rolled over onto her stomach and hung her head and arm out of the bed. Her phone was on the floor and she stared at it for a moment, spinning it around. She closed her eyes, resigned to having to face the music tomorrow night. She foresaw some sort of Greek tragedy playing out and it left her feeling restless. What a tangled web she had weaved. She now wished she had told Will she had met Zach before, for the interview. Why had she not done that yet? She knew why. It would give closure to the situation, something she was not sure she was ready for just yet, and she would probably not be able to help herself from blurting the entire truth of what had gone on. Her eyes opened as the light on her phone came on, casting a bright glow in the dark room. A message – from *him*.

Hey neighbour. Can't sleep.
Bet u can't too. Fancy a nightcap?

What R u doing here?

I could ask you the same thing.

It was a birthday surprise so obvs I knew nothing about it.

Yeah, when is that?

Friday.

Rad. So, fancy a nightcap? Rm 12. I bet Will's asleep.

He was only two doors away. She felt a rush of excitement and enraged passion. She felt like a kid again, sneaking behind parents' backs.

OK. But I'm in my pyjamas.

Even better!

And no hanky panky

Who says that any more?

Seemed fitting in an old building.

Amy carefully slipped out of bed, checking that she had not disturbed Will from his slumber, and opened the door as quietly as possible. *This is a really stupid thing to do*, she thought to herself, as she locked the door behind her. She crept to room twelve and knocked quietly. Zach opened the door, bare-chested in camo trousers. He pulled her into the room and kissed her passionately, pressing her up against the wall, lifting her arms above her head, gripping her hands tightly. She uncoiled her fingers from his, and ran her nails hard down his chest, he flinched and moaned. Then she kneed him firmly between the legs – he was not expecting it, and recoiled like a scolded dog.
"What…"
"That's for putting me through the mill with this meal offer. And maybe a taste of things to come. I told you I play rough," she said, provocatively. She turned towards the door. He put a hand on it to stop her.
"You can't tease me and leave me like that."
"I said no funny business, Will's a stone's throw away, and you jump me as soon as I walk in …"

"I've missed you so bad... couldn't believe my luck earlier when I turned around and there you were." He kissed her and she grabbed him hard, but she knew she could not stay much longer.

"Damn, I wish you weren't so hot." Amy whispered as she pulled away. "I should go."

He moved his hand away from the door. His face was beaded with sweat. "I promise I'll behave at dinner. For you. But can you find some time for me while you're here?"

"How am I going to do that?"

"Find a way. I want you to show me how rough you play."

"You'll be on your knees, begging me for mercy."

"I am already." He pulled her to him for another embrace, then she left. She walked back to her room and took a deep breath. She looked at Will asleep in the bed, blissfully unaware, and screwed her face up. She contemplated waking him for sex, but thought that might make the guilt worse. She knew this could not go on much longer. Soon, she would have to make a choice.

***

The next day, when they went down to breakfast, Amy cast a furtive glance around the restaurant and saw no sign of Zach. She was part relieved and part disappointed, wondering where he could be (maybe he was still in bed). As they were just drinking their last cup of tea from the pot, Will's phone buzzed.

"It's work, I need to take this." He rose from his chair. He took the call and disappeared outside the hotel. Amy knew work calls – they could go on for some time. She decided to have a wander around. At reception, she had a look through some well-worn novels they had on a shelf to borrow – nothing of interest – then she saw a booklet describing the history of the hotel. She picked it up and sat in the lounge to read it.

At first, she did not notice there was someone else in the room sitting by the fireplace, reading the *New York Times* newspaper. She became aware after a few moments and stole a look at him without properly looking up, so she could pretend she had not noticed him. He did the same. Then they did it again.

"Hey," he said after several minutes of this to-ing and fro-ing.

"Oh, hi." She tried to sound surprised.

"Don't pretend you hadn't seen me." He spoke quietly, not looking up, turning the page of his paper.

"You did too." They fell silent. Amy shifted in her seat and started imagining herself walking over to him, sitting astride him and biting his bottom lip. She read the same sentence in her booklet three times. She bit her own bottom lip to try to distract herself. Zach kept peering at her over the top of his paper, but they remained silent for several moments more.

"Where's Bill?"

"You mean Will," she replied, even though she knew what his game was.

"Oh, that's it, 'Will'."

She pursed her lips at him. She looked down again. "Work call."

"Oh." He sat back in his chair. She glanced over at him.

"How come you're here anyway? It's a bit off the beaten track."

"I'm writing. Got some contacts here."

"Uh-huh." Amy thought she knew of one very famous musician who lived in the vicinity. She could not help noticing, looking over his physique, that Zach's skinny jeans left little to the imagination. She bit her lip again. He seemed to guess what she was thinking and smiled, shifting in his seat. She decided she was clearly not done with the novelty of him, the fire for him burned hot. The intensity of the moment was cut dead by the appearance of Will.

"Oh, there you are, I wondered where you'd gone." Amy jumped. "Oh, hi, Zach."

He noticed him quicker than I did, Amy mused.

"Hi, Will." Zach smiled. Amy tried to act normal. She got up and took Will's hand.

"Bye." Amy left with Will. They went to their room.

"What were you and him talking about?"

"Oh, I just said I love his music and asked why he was here, off the beaten track."

"And what did he say?"

"He's writing with some contacts in the area. Interesting, hey?" She tried to sound light and fascinated. Will fell quiet for a moment.

"It does feel a bit weird, him being here. You're so obsessed with him." Will was checking his emails on his phone as he said this. Amy slipped in some earrings in front of the mirror, watching Will's demeanour in the reflection intently. He said the words, but she detected no alarm in his body language.

"Oh, well, don't be silly. He's this Hollywood guy, untouchable." *That's what makes him even more irresistible*, she added mentally. Will fell silent. She did not like that. She did, however, have some minor pleasure at the prospect of him being jealous – he had never been jealous before and it made her feel he wanted her more. It certainly breathed more life into her perception of their relationship. "Are you jealous? I love *you*, Babe." She went over to him and kissed him. He put his arms around her. She felt comfort flood through her, always her sanctuary, her warmth.

They left the hotel – Zach nowhere to be seen – and wandered around town, looking in antique shops, stopping in a tea room to have a cream tea – Will's favourite. They wandered down to the harbour chatting and laughing. *How could I jack all this in for a whim?* Amy thought. *We've got such a good life, I should cherish him.*

But as they walked back to the hotel in the early evening, she found herself imagining scenarios in which she could steal some time away for Zach. They went to their room and Amy jumped in the shower. While she was in there with her eyes closed, thinking about the two men in her life – both so different, both so amazing in their way – Will opened the shower door and got in with her. He grabbed her thighs and pressed her up against the wall. They embraced and she pulled him to her, his strong body so known to her.

Seven

They both made a little extra effort with their attire. Will suggested with a glint in his eye that Amy wear no underwear to dinner. She grinned and agreed, though privately she thought that sitting with two men she found sexually attractive would make it even more of a turn on. They made their way downstairs, Zach was already waiting in the cosy restaurant. He watched Amy enter the room in her finery with delight, and rose to greet them both. He shook Will's hand and leaned across to kiss Amy, but she held back and also offered out her hand to him. She had flushed cheeks from the warmth of the evening and her nerves, but this just enhanced her features. Zach could barely tear his eyes from her.

Will, being someone who could fall into easy conversation with anybody, on any level, chatted freely with Zach. He told him about his work, which with Zach being a frequent flyer, seemed to interest him greatly. Amy was quiet, but it didn't seem to matter, and she had plenty to drink. Out of the corner of her eye, she noticed Zach's frequent glances at her, unnoticed by Will who was engrossed in their chat. Zach got onto talking about travelling the world touring and writing with some amazing people. The talk was not boring, Amy was enjoying listening, until the attention turned towards their relationship during pudding.

"So how long have you guys been together?"

Amy gulped down a mouthful and glared at Zach.

"Oh, Amy'll tell you, I'm hopeless with dates. About two years I think?" Will looked to Amy for consent and she nodded.

"Cool. It must be difficult, with you travelling for work a lot? I mean, I find it tough cos I travel a lot." Amy dropped her spoon, which startled them both. She rose from the table.

"Excuse me." She made her way to the ladies. She hung her head over the sink for a moment trying to slow her breathing. She leaned against the cold wall. 'Have it all', Beth had said. 'All' was proving hard work.

She made her way back to the table to find the men had moved on to post-dinner drinks; Will a double port, and Zach, what looked like a bourbon. They were laughing and getting on well; it could almost be deemed a 'bromance' if there wasn't the dark undertone of her affair behind it all. Amy was very tempted to excuse herself, but thought better of it and poured herself more wine.

"I could do with some fresh air, can we maybe have our drinks outside?" She stood up again. They agreed, and the triangle moved out to the courtyard garden. When Zach had finished his drink, he stood up.

"Thanks for a lovely evening, really nice to meet you both," he said, shaking their hands; Amy's with a private smile. "Dinner's on me by the way."

Will proceeded to thank him, while simultaneously Amy profusely protested the gesture.

"No, I insist. Goodnight."

"What a nice guy." Will said when Zach had gone.

"Shouldn't have let him get dinner." Amy sat back and sipped her drink. She did not want to be indebted to him.

"Why? He can afford it. Think of it as a bit of pay back from all the money you've spent on albums and concert tickets." Will chuckled. Amy whacked him playfully, but she was amused. It released some of the tension she had felt all evening. Still, it had gone without a hitch – she could almost say she had enjoyed it. "Right, let's go up too." Will got up.

"You go, I might stay out here for a bit."

"Alone?"

"Yes. Not for long. I'll be up in a bit, leave the door unlocked."

"If you're sure?" She nodded. He kissed her on the forehead and left.

The bar was quiet. Amy ordered another glass of Shiraz and sat back outside. She flipped her phone over and over in her hand. Above her, a window opened. She glanced up and Zach's face appeared, looking down at her. She looked away. Two minutes later, he appeared next to her. She looked at him. There was no one else outside. She stood up and put a finger to her lips to indicate he be silent, then took his hand and led him to the other side of the garden. It was dark, the lights from the hotel couldn't penetrate that far.

There was a ramshackle storage building by the car park, with some overgrown creepers straggling off the side, but there was enough room for two people to squeeze behind it into the gap between the building and the perimeter wall. There they stood face to face. She looked into his eyes, her desire for him at a peak. She pulled him to her and kissed him hard, biting his lip and running her tongue over his teeth. He groped roughly at her dress, and moaned with pleasure when he found she had no underwear on. She felt a sharp pang of shame that Zach was benefitting from a suggestion Will had made, but she carried on, nonetheless. She pulled hastily at his belt and bit his neck hard in the heat of the moment, the surge of alcohol and passion overtaking her. He flinched, but it fired him up and he pulled her legs around him and pressed her up against the wall. They said not a word to each other, both so buzzed by the danger of the moment, Amy intoxicated and reeling from sex with two men in one evening.

***

Amy could not help a snigger as Zach looked around the side of the building to check the coast was clear, belt and trousers still undone. She checked her hair into place and followed him out as he tidied himself up. She had some scratches on her back she was not sure she would easily be able to explain, if Will saw them; Zach had marks on his neck and arms.

Her wine was still on the table when they returned to the courtyard, so she sat down and took a big sip, as composed as she could be. Zach sat next to her. They cast sideways glances at each other and both laughed.

"I need a drink." He got up. As he was about to walk past her, she stopped him by putting her stilettoed foot out in front of him.

"Stop. You have half a tree in your hair." He bent down so she could pull the offender out and he winked as he went to the bar. He returned with another bourbon and sat next to her.

"What are we gonna do about us?" He leaned his elbows on his knees.

"I dunno. Am I really worth it?"

"Forbidden fruit. It's irresistible."

"You're unavailable to me, I'm unavailable to you."

"I don't have to be unavailable to you." He looked her way. Amy was quiet for a moment.

"You know what happens when the mortals interfere with the gods, it doesn't end well. Look at Lycius and Lamia."

"What happened to them?" He smiled at her obtuse reference.

"They both died."

He laughed. "Well, that's a bit extreme. Besides I'm no god."

"It's a worthy analogy. I'm just a normal girl."

"Amy, I'm just a normal guy, don't hold store to the whole fame thing." He looked at her and she smiled.

"I just wish Will wasn't caught up in the middle of this. He doesn't deserve it."

"So, break up with him."

"I think we both know it's not that simple."

"I want you to myself."

Amy looked at him. He was looking earnestly at her. Writing songs about her, the way he looked at her, maybe things were getting serious. She got up. Suddenly she felt stifled again. He got up too.

"We could make this work." He took her hand.

"I can't deal with this right now, I mean, I'm here with him, and look where I am? I'm just so messed up. Please give me some time. At the moment, I can't bear the thought of losing either of you. I love the new song by the way. I'm honoured." She fought back the emotion. She kissed him tenderly on the lips and walked back inside. The more time she spent with him, the more complex her feelings became. She looked back as she went to turn through the doorway and they held eye contact for a moment, before she disappeared upstairs with a heavy heart.

To her surprise, Will was awake and looking at his phone. "Hiya. Did I hear you talking to Zach outside?" Amy's heavy heart dropped into her shoes. What exactly *had* he heard? Her mouth went dry. "I did see him briefly, he came back down and got a drink at the bar."

"Oh." Will fell silent. "Goodnight." And he turned away from her. This was not good, but she thought better of pursuing it.

***

The next day was Amy's birthday. She did not feel much like celebrating it and stayed in bed longer than usual. Will was up bright and early.

"Come on, get up, get dressed, breakfast!"

"I don't think I want any." Came the pillow muffled reply. Will climbed onto the bed to lean over her. She turned her head to him.

"Happy birthday, Babe." He kissed her. Last night's suspicion seemed to have abated.

"Thank you." He had placed a little blue bag on her shoulder. She sat up and opened it. It was a Tiffany heart necklace. "Wow, it's beautiful. Thank you so much." She kissed him on the lips.

"Now, come down to breakfast."

"I really don't want any. You go. I'm quite happy crashed out up here."

"All right. See you in a bit." And he was gone. She fiddled with the necklace, it was lovely. She felt tears. Why was she unable to decide what to do? She could not kiss goodbye to what she had with Will, so why didn't she stop what she was doing with Zach? It was still so delicious. Why then did she not let Will go and go for it with Zach? She had so many doubts about it lasting or anything stable coming out of it, their random meeting, twice – should she ignore Fate if that was in fact what this was? It was such an unrealistic proposition.

She lay in bed mulling these thoughts over and over, when a text came through.

Happy birthday, got u a present not much at short notice. I'll send it to you Z xx

She frowned, this seemed a bit cryptic – send it to her? He was staying in the same hotel. She began to worry it would be a big gesture – something like flowers would be hard to explain to Will. As the thought crossed her mind, an audio file came through to her messages. She plugged her earphones in and pressed play. It was just him with a guitar, a short ballad to her, a love song, or half of one at least. His falsetto was flawless, full of emotion, the words so touching. Her eyes welled up at such a personal and unique gift. She was truly blown away and the gravity of the situation hit her with the force of a thousand bullets. She ripped the earphones from her ears and threw them down.

Two very different gifts from two very different men, both utterly special in their own ways – the gifts and the men. How should she get out of this? The sensible and safe thing to do would be to end things with Zach and make it work with Will. Every time Amy moved towards this conclusion, she felt herself drawing away from it. The novelty of Zach had not yet worn off. But surely that *would* wear off? Was there really a happy ever after for a scenario like theirs?

At this moment of deep contemplation, her phone rang: Beth.

"Hiya." She answered. Maybe she should talk to Beth about her woes anyway.

"Happy birthday to you, happy birthday to you, happy birthday dear shit-face, happy birthday to you." Beth was laughing as she finished her song.

Amy laughed in spite of herself. "That's the second time I've been serenaded on my birthday."

"What? It's only nine o'clock in the morning!"

"Oh, that's the important point to focus on!"

"Yeah, I guess. Are you enjoying your naughty mini break?"

"…Er, 'enjoy' might be the wrong word. Quandary or awkward or triangle might all be more appropriate words."

"Why, has Zach been in touch?"

"Yes, I should say he has been, *in touch*." There was certainly double entendre in her words. "And I dare add, you knew all about this surprise, clearly!"

"Yes of course! Will told me to keep it from you! I thought it might be a good thing for you guys to reconnect, but sounds like that hasn't gone according to plan?"

"Zach's here."

"What the actual FUCK?"

"Indeed!"

"But you're in the arse end of nowhere!"

"I know!"

"That's like some sort of karma or something, isn't it? Have you shagged him again?"

"What, on my special birthday break with my wonderful boyfriend?" Amy replied with melodramatic incredulity.

"Have you?" Beth virtually squealed.

"Yes."

"How?"

"Oh, for fuck's sake woman. Up against a shed in the hotel grounds."

"Where the hell was Will?"

"In bed, in our room." Amy grabbed her face as she said this. She was ashamed of her behaviour. It was not acceptable doing what she had done. "I shall have to pay penance for my evil doings one day."

"Oh, shan't we all! Might as well enjoy it while it lasts!"

These flippant words hit Amy harder than they were meant. She was messing with people's emotions, including her own, it would not do.

"I need to stop this. Zach sent me a song. He says he wants me to himself."

"Oh dear. Do you love him?"

Amy paused. She tried to un-cloud her mind from the infatuation, the obsession, the prize she had effortlessly won, the dizzy heights of her crowned position as Zach Hayes' favourite fan. It was a hedonist's wet dream. But was it love?

"Can you be in love with two people at the same time?"

"You're asking the wrong person, mate." Just as Beth said this, Will came into the room and Amy changed tack completely.

"Thanks for the birthday wishes. We'll catch up when we get back."

"I'm guessing Will just appeared," Beth said, in an undertone, even though Will could not possibly hear her.

"Yes." Amy tried to give nothing away.

"This isn't over – we'll talk again when you're back."

"Great thanks. Bye!" Amy hung up.

"Who was that, Babe? Oh, I know. Beth. She all right?"

"Yeah, she sung me happy birthday down the phone, silly cow." Amy forced a chuckle.

"Zach asked after you at breakfast. Said to say happy birthday." His voice was uncharacteristically monotone. Amy picked up on it.

"Oh, OK." She felt this non-response would be the only acceptable way of answering. Will was certainly becoming prickly about Zach's presence. *So he should be*, said the small voice in the back of her head.

She decided a change of subject would be advisable. "So, what we doing today?"

Will perked up as he told her he was taking her to the beach then dinner at a nice pub on the way back. Amy got up and put her arms around him, kissing him on the lips.

"What?" He smiled.

"I love you." She hugged him.

"Love you, too." He paused and drew away slightly. "Not gonna leave me for him, then? Cos I think he fancies you." Amy's stomach turned over. He always thought guys liked her – she always refuted it – but this time, being right on the money, Amy just let out a nervous laugh. Maybe this was an opportunity to test the water. She pulled away from his clasp.

"Well, he is on my list." She looked at him through her long lashes, gauging his reaction.

"I know. Guess I can't say anything if you shag him." He was blasé, but Amy detected stiltedness. Was he suspicious? She had been careless at times. She now did not know where to take this conversation.

"Well, I'll bear that in mind." She tapped him jovially on the shoulder and walked into the en suite. She jumped in the shower and they did not discuss it again. Amy felt the fragility of the situation she found herself in, as the bubbles from the shampoo slid from her hair down her back, and she felt the series of scratches across her shoulder blades from the previous night's frisson. She was torn. Torn between the magnetism of her moral compass, what was right and wrong, and the thrill of having two men besotted by her. It was a massive boost to her ego and she could not help feeling exhilarated by it as she got herself ready to go out.

They left the hotel and had a quiet relaxed day at the beach. Amy decided to put all thoughts of the quandary out of her mind. Maybe she would see the wood for the trees, maybe switching off from it all would lead to clarity.

In the early evening, Will drove them to a small, posh and intimate pub, just outside of town. There was already a bottle of Prosecco in an ice bucket waiting for them when they sat down. There was also a bunch of white roses on her side of the table. Amy smiled at his attention to detail.

"This is lovely, Babe." She sat down. He sat opposite and smiled. The place was dimly lit by candles, very romantic. They were both glowing from the day in the sun on the beach. They ordered their meal and Will poured the prosecco into their glasses.

"I'm just so glad we've had some quality time together – I know it's tough when I'm away a lot, and you're trying to get your new career off the ground." Amy let him take her hands.

"This goes a long way to getting you back in my good books. And I love my necklace," she said, touching it as she spoke. Zach was diminishing in her mind again. Tonight was all about her and Will. They had a lovely meal and made their way back to their hotel, going straight up to their room.

They went to bed and Will initiated foreplay, something he loved. He pulled some restraints out of his case and attached them to the four-poster bed, grinning at her. She removed her top and as he put his arms around her, he ran his fingers over her scratches.

"Hey, what have you done to your back?"

"Oh, nothing, I slipped in the shower this morning." Will frowned, but Amy kissed him hard on the lips to stop him asking any more questions. She lay back spread-eagled on the bed and allowed herself to be immersed in pleasure. She closed her eyes and Zach's face appeared. She opened them again with a start – this would not do – she had to put it out of her mind that he was only two doors away. She leaned back to focus on Will and his exceptional attention, his fingers pressing into her flesh as he lavished her body with his mouth and hands. *He's too good at this to be thinking about another man.*

***

The next morning, they were due to leave. Amy woke early and got up before Will, starting to pack their stuff away. Before Will awoke, she decided to message Zach. She sat in the bathroom and opened her messages.

Hey you, just letting you know we leave today. I really loved your 'gift.' Wow, just wow. I will treasure it. I need to go away and think everything thru. When u get to LDN get in touch and we'll meet.

She was not sure how to close the text off. 'Love Amy' seemed too leading. She decided on merely:

Amy xxx
(Sent)

In the meantime, Will had stirred. He got up and came into the bathroom. She stood up with a start.
"You're up already."
"Yes. Morning." He kissed the back of her neck. She gasped. Even a small gesture of affection like that sent tingles throughout her body. He knew exactly what spot to kiss to titillate her.
She smiled, still in awe of his sexual savvy, but moved out of his way. She wandered over to the window and looked at her phone to see if Zach responded, making sure her phone was on silent. Sure enough, he texted back.

Hi Honey, I need to check our schedule, I wanna make a big gap in it 4 u. Will let u know. Prob best we say bye now, like this hey?

Yes. Bye xx

Bye, Gorgeous xx

Having dealt with this, she deleted all the messages and put her phone down. She got dressed, put her makeup on, and by the time she had finished, Will was dressed and ready too. They made their way down to breakfast, and to her alarm, Zach was there. She tried not to look too confused, having just said her farewell, and chose a table at a distance from him, hoping Will would not notice the scratches on Zach's neck, that matched those on her back.
He walked over to them, "Nice meeting you."

Amy shook her head almost imperceptibly, wide-eyed, and Zach cast a brief furtive glance at her. He was about to give the game away – how would he know they were leaving today? It was certainly not mentioned at their meal together. Will looked a little confused. Zach jumped in straight away.

"Oh, I'm leaving today," Zach said, quickly. Amy breathed again.

"Oh, us too," Will said. He was frosty. Amy felt tense. She had suddenly lost her appetite.

"Well, bye, then." Will shook Zach's hand. Zach leaned over to kiss Amy on the cheek. She watched Will's reaction as he did, and saw his back stiffen and eyes darken. Zach smiled and left the breakfast room to Amy's – and Will's – relief. They sat down in silence.

"Has he got a girlfriend?" Will asked, without making eye contact with her. Amy was not sure how best to deal with this – if she said yes it highlighted the fact that she followed him intently, and was also a lie, if she said no, this would make Will even more hostile.

"I don't know." This felt like the safest option. Will was not convinced.

"Well, it's good to be going our separate ways."

He was taciturn all through breakfast.

The journey home was very quiet and the radio was kept off.

Eight

The very next day, Will was called away again, much to Amy's chagrin. It had been an emergency in Malaysia and he wasn't sure if she would be able to get hold of him or how long he would be away, but it would probably be at least four days. Zach had been in touch to say he had arrived in London, but would be busy in the studio for a couple of days. Amy mentioned that she would be up town the following night, clubbing with friends.

It was a long-planned night out with some of her former colleagues from British Airways, a bit of a late birthday bash with her old mates. She met Beth at the local pub for a quick drink before they got on the train to take them into town to meet the others.

Amy looked less than happy, pensive. Beth asked her how things were.

"I just need this night out to not think about either of them, and let my hair down. They're currently both out of sight, out of mind."

"Well, tonight you must keep them both that way and enjoy our night with some old buddies."

They met up with the others, including Lucas, in a bar in Covent Garden. They were a fun bunch and all up for a wild night out, greeting each other loudly. Amy and Beth were quick to join in the fray and ordered double gin and tonics. Beth clinked her glass for everyone to be quiet.

"OK – thank you for coming everyone," Lucas, Amy's former supervisor said. "I just wanted to propose a toast and to say what an honour it is to have our dear sweet Amy amongst us again; belated happy birthday, old girl!" They all cheered and Amy smiled and held her glass up.

"And I wanted to congratulate her on following her dream of becoming a journalist. I have here a copy of *Delta Music Magazine* in which features a whole interview with Sovereign X, written by the lady herself!" He held up the mag and everyone whooped. She laughed humbly.

She had not seen a copy of the interview yet in print; it held very strong feelings every time she thought of it. A few of them asked her about the interview and they passed around the magazine. She glanced at it and drifted off for a moment. Her interview had come just before the release of their current single, which was gaining massive attention. Some of those gathered were asking questions about the band, which she answered as best she could without gushing too much about how great Zach was, or giving away how intimately she had gotten to know him. They all knew Will and doted on him. Beth glanced Amy's way and saw that she was putting a face on with all the talk about the interview and the band.

"Champagne!" Lucas shouted and plonked several ice buckets down on the table. As he did this, Beth made her way over to Amy, who felt peripheral, standing on the edge of the crowd.

"Are you OK?"

"Yes. Need to get used to the attention of it all I guess."

"Are you referring to being a published writer, or on the arm of someone famous?"

Amy looked at her with one raised eyebrow, and sipped her drink. "Both, I suppose," she said grimly, sipping her champagne.

"So, have you made a choice then?" Beth leaned against the wall.

Amy looked at her. "Every time I come down on one side, I want the other. What is wrong with me?"

"You love it, don't you?" Beth smiled and flicked her cropped blonde hair back.

"What do you mean?"

"It's like a power kick, running two guys at once. One is the love of your life and the other is your ultimate celebrity crush. It's no wonder you haven't let go." Beth gave her a hug unexpectedly. Amy felt her emotions swell at the tender gesture from her friend.

"It *is* a kick. I mean, like the sort of kick you and I used to get from drugs. I thought the novelty would have worn off by now, but it hasn't. I love Will deeply, but there's so much animal magnetism with Zach, and the danger of him being the other man just adds to it. Word to the wise –

never indulge in your ultimate fantasy. You might enjoy it so much it ruins your life." As she said this, Lucas wandered over and stood between them, his arms around them both.

"So, what are you bevy of beauties talking so intensely about? Come, come, I don't want to miss the goss!" he said, jovially.

"Nothing." The girls chorused in unison. Lucas looked from one to the other; they were maintaining eye contact with each other, then Amy looked away and sipped her drink. Lucas dropped his arms.

"OK, are you two having an affair? What the fuck is going on? Lucas must know immediately!" he exclaimed, melodramatically.

"Taxi for Lucas DeMontfort!" came a shout from the bar. Beth sniggered and Amy theatrically wiped her brow, and mouthed 'phew!' at her unexpected escape from the inquisition of Lucas.

"Right. That's us. This is not over you two." He pointed his fingers from his eyes to Amy's, narrowing his own. "C'mon. Let's par-tay!" And he strutted like a peacock out of the bar, miming a flick of long hair.

They bowled into two people carrier cabs, which took them to a night club up town. Classy, trendy music, but not too fancy.

Amy and Beth both had a gin and tonic as they got there – straight up no whistles and bells – while the others ordered mojitos. Soon they both were leading the way to the dancefloor.

They had both done their fair share of partying in the past, but it was more of a rare thing these days (Will was not really into nightlife). Amy loved letting loose when she had the opportunity and having a good dance. Now she needed it more than ever. She was in her element, singing and dancing with her best mate, letting go of her cares and worries, just enjoying the moment, seizing the carefree feeling, shedding the world and its complications.

She moved to the beat, the alcohol releasing her of inhibitions; she fell into rhythm with Beth, feeling the music flow through her veins and became one with it, as her friend did the same by her side. Her hair flicked from side to side on the hot, crowded dancefloor. Slower funky tunes played and she moved her hips and arms to the music, closing her eyes as she did so.

She became aware of hands resting on her hips from behind. She assumed it was Beth mucking about – it wouldn't have been the first time she had gotten rambunctious with her after a drink. She smiled and grabbed them, as she continued to move to the music, and she was startled when she realised they were a man's hands. Pianist's hands. She turned her head with a jolt to see Zach standing there behind her, moving with her to the beat of the music. Her jaw dropped and she smiled, but turned back and carried on dancing, with his body close behind her, their hips moving in rhythm together. He discreetly kissed her on the neck as their dancing was getting hot and heavy. Amy glanced towards Beth who looked shocked, but she smiled at Amy and raised her eyebrows. As the song came to an end and another started, Amy turned to face Zach.

"We must stop meeting like this!" she yelled in his ear to be heard over the music.

"Am I stalking you, or are you stalking me?" He grinned. "How many more chance meetings are we gonna have before you give up and let me have you?"

"Come on – you knew I was clubbing up-town, tonight." She smiled and pinched his bum.

"True. Struck gold with the same venue though." She put her arms around him and gave him a quick peck on the lips. They hugged for a moment in the middle of the dancefloor. Lucas had clocked the apparently random behaviour and drew Beth away from the dancefloor.

"Hey, Amy looks awfully flirty with that guy, who is he?" It was too dark to see properly. "Does she know him? He looks familiar…"

Beth didn't know what to say, it was not her place. "Yes, he does, doesn't he?" She watched Lucas as he frowned in the darkness to look at Amy and Zach, who had moved to a quiet and darker corner of the dancefloor.

"He's fit too, I must say. I wouldn't turn him down." Lucas sipped his champagne flute.

"I would."

"Well of course you would, he hasn't got a vag. How can you not love a cock?" Lucas looked at Beth. This was not the first time they had had this kind of conversation. Beth shrugged and screwed her nose up. Lucas returned to looking in Amy's direction. "They do look awfully intimate."

Beth looked down and did not respond. Lucas looked at her. "Beth? You're uncharacteristically quiet all of a sudden. Is Amy screwing around? Is that what you were discussing so secretively earlier? Who *is* that guy?"

Beth maintained her silence. Lucas frowned again, narrowed his eyes and moved a little nearer. His face changed as he had sudden comprehension. He moved back to Beth and stood square in front of her. "You know what, he looks a lot like the lead singer of Sovereign X. And isn't it a coincidence that she has just done an interview with them?" He was looking sternly at Beth to gauge her reaction. None of what he said caused any surprise. She averted his gaze and was looking at Amy and Zach. She awkwardly looked away and Lucas shot a look at them – they were locked in a passionate embrace. Lucas' jaw dropped and he grabbed Beth's arm. He was shocked, but also loved a bit of drama.

"You know all about this? Has she split up with our dearest Will?" Finally, Beth looked at him and shook her head guiltily. "That is him, isn't it, the guy from Sovereign X?"

Beth nodded.

"How weird that all that time ago I shove her in first class to serve them and here she is making out with him!"

Amy walked over to them at this point, unaware that her tête à tête had been spotted. She smiled at Beth and Lucas. Beth was still looking very sheepish and Lucas looked enraged. Amy's smile dropped as she guessed she must have been rumbled. They had not been discreet, in the heat of the moment.

"What are you playing at, young lady?" Lucas said maternally, pursing his lips, hands on his hips.

"Oh, shit."

"Oh, shit, indeed. What's going on with you and him? Is this how you got that interview?"

Amy bristled at the insinuation. She was not someone to sleep her way to the top. "No! It's not like that at all. He asked for my number at the *end* of the interview and I saw him once or twice, that's all." She kept the details brief. Tongues would wag enough if more of their friends had seen her.

"Oh, that's all. So, Will knows, does he?"

"No, of course not. Look, you've got to let me sort it out, OK? And I will, I promise."

Zach walked over to them at this point. He was there with his band mates and had made his excuses to them, intent to join Amy. They all composed themselves and Amy made the introduction.

"Lucas, Beth, this is Zach. Zach, this is Lucas and Beth."

Lucas shook Zach's hand vigorously. His disdain at the revelation of their dalliance had dissipated. "I love your music!"

Beth also shook his hand, "I've heard so much about you."

"All good, I hope. Nice to meet y'all." He grabbed a handful of peanuts from the table next to them.

"I really love your current song." Lucas was practically swooning.

"Thanks. Have you guys got drinks? Let me get you one."

"Well, we're actually drinking champagne," Lucas said, holding up his glass.

"I'll get another bottle." Zach went over to the bar and Lucas' jaw dropped again.

"Amy! What the fuck?"

"Don't, just… don't."

"I mean, I hate that you're doing whatever you're doing behind darling Will's back, but a little bit of me is also like, impressed. This guy has won *Grammys*!"

"You're so flaky." Amy laughed.

Beth laughed too. "Yes, you've changed your tune – star-struck, are we?" she said with palpable sarcasm. "Get over it. I have."

"Yes, but I mean, I know what you're struggling with. Aside from the fame thing, he is F.I.T. Have you shagged him?" he said casually, sipping his drink, looking at Amy.

Amy smiled, "A lady never divulges things like that."

"No, a lady doesn't," Lucas replied. "So… have you?"

Amy laughed, but did not answer.

"OK, so that right there, is a yes. Has he got a massive cock?"

"For crying out loud!"

"Also, a yes!"

They were all three laughing by the time Zach re-joined them. Amy had quite a loud laugh, especially when loosened by drinking, and Zach tilted his head and smiled at her.

"What did I miss?" They all looked from one to the other.

Lucas stepped in, lightning fast. "We were just discussing which Sovereign X song was our favourite."

Amy smiled at how effortlessly he lied and with such an obsequious comment.

"Rad. Oh, you've never told me yours, Amy?"

"Oh, the current one I think."

Zach got close and whispered into her hair, "Is that cos it's about us?"

She looked into his eyes and nodded. Meanwhile, Lucas was watching them with fascination; Beth was watching Lucas watch them. He widened his eyes at Beth, who smiled.

Amy drank another glass of champagne from the bottle Zach had bought.

"I'm going back for another dance." She grabbed Zach's hand, leading him back to the dancefloor. Will had never been much of a dancer, so this was a novelty for her. Soon Lucas and Beth and a few of the others joined them. To start with, Amy made sure the others with them did not notice the flirtation with Zach, but by the end of the night; and the champagne, they were all over each other and the group began murmuring. A couple of them had gotten autographs and selfies with him as they left to make their way to the taxis for home. Zach was about to leave to go back to his hotel.

"There's space in our taxi," Amy said to him, in an inebriated slur. "Come back to mine."

"You sure?" He looked earnestly at her. "I've totally gate-crashed your night with your friends."

Amy shrugged her shoulders, "Given them gossip fodder."

Amy quietly informed Beth that Zach was coming with them.

"Really? Are you sure?"

"Yes. If you don't mind."

"Course not. It's your life. I don't mind playing gooseberry."

They got into the cab and began the long journey home. They were all quiet apart from Beth making occasional chit-chat with Zach. They dropped Beth off first and Amy kissed her as always on the lips.

When Beth got out, Zach turned to Amy, his face lit with lust. "Kissing your friend on the lips, that was a massive turn on."

"Was it? We've always done it. How much of a turn on was it?" She whispered, discreetly grabbing the bulge in his trousers. He gasped, her grip was bordering on uncomfortably firm, but his body responded to her.

The car rounded the corner and pulled up outside Amy's house. She paid the driver who gave her a Cheshire grin and a wink – he must have picked up on their antics.

They got out and she led him into the house. This was a huge step, taking him into her world, her modest home, for the first time. They barely closed the door before Amy had pinned him against the wall in the hallway and was kissing him, tearing at his t shirt and belt.

Zach stopped her, he wasn't as drunk as she was. "Wait, wait. Will's away, right?"

"Yes." She was impatient, completely governed by booze and desire.

"Amy, I want you to myself…" She kissed his neck and undid his trousers. She dropped to her knees.

"You have me."

He moaned as pleasure overtook him and threw his head back. "No. Exclusively." He managed in a half whisper. Amy did not reply but carried on pleasuring him with her mouth. Just as he was at the point of climax, she drew away, leaving him in agonies, and she turned away. He kicked off his jeans hastily and followed her, as she slipped off her dress and strode slowly up the stairs ahead of him, leaving her in just her heels and underwear. Zach caught her up on the landing and tried to grab her, but she evaded him, teasing him further, and pushed the door to her bedroom open. She felt in complete control and powerful in her own domain, enough that she could push the boundaries further. Maybe that was an attraction as much as other things, the power she exuded when she was with him. She was much more experimental and it was an existential indulgence to be master of him. Like dipping your hand in a box of chocolates way too expensive and opulent for you to handle, but dip you must. And keep dipping, because it is just too delectable. It is going to make you feel bad, but oh, you are going to enjoy your moment of assuagement.

"On your knees," she commanded.

He did as he was told and she handcuffed him. "Whoa, Amy." He hesitated, as she produced a blindfold.

"Just go with me." She reassured him, getting him ready. She stood in front of him and guided his head to lick her. She kicked him gently with her heels and he gasped. She pulled away, placing a gag on him, and stood back looking down at him, her idol, that she had made her submissive. The power swelled her arousal and she sat astride his trembling body.

After their intense encounter, Amy released him and he kissed her hard on the mouth.

"Consider yourself fucked."

"I do. That was something else. But you're not normal." He dropped, exhausted, onto her bed.

"Good. I don't want to be normal. Normal is boring."

He looked at her admiringly. She flopped down next to him, feeling that she would be asleep imminently.

Just as she felt her consciousness waning, he leaned over and said in her ear, "Come to the US with me."

She had passed out before she could respond.

She did not wake until nine a.m. the following morning, when the sound of a car pulling up outside the front of the house made her sit up in bed with the biggest start of her life. It was the familiar quiet, steady engine of a Mercedes.

Nine

Amy's eyes shot open as she heard the car door slam shut. Her heart fell to the floor and she felt sick. It couldn't be... he wasn't due back for at least two days! She shook Zach, laying stark naked next to her in bed, in *their* bed. He wouldn't stir. She tapped his cheek lightly, then slightly harder; he groaned and opened one eye.

"Morning... what?" She put a finger to her lips. He lifted his head. "What's up?"

"Get dressed." She shot out of bed and started throwing his clothes at him. "Will's back."

"What? Did you know?"

"Course I didn't fucking know! We wouldn't be here now if I did, I'm not a sado-masochist."

"You sure about that?" He gave her a wry smile. She was in no mood for quips at a moment of potential catastrophe like this. Just as he spoke, keys could be heard opening the front door. She wasn't quite sure how this could be rescued, how she could get out of the predicament she was in, but she had to at least try. "Where's my pants?"

"Shit, they're at the bottom of the stairs!" Amy slapped her face with her hands in despair. Zach had just got his underwear and t-shirt on as Amy heard Will's steady footsteps on the stairs. It was futile with the trousers abandoned downstairs, but before she could make any moves to hide any further evidence of Zach, or the man himself, Will had opened the door to the bedroom.

The situation seemed to move in slow motion to Amy, from the confused look on Will's face rapidly turning to shock, Zach's trousers in one hand, a beautiful bunch of flowers in the other hand, that fell away from him to the floor as he saw Zach standing behind her, half-dressed. Amy was overcome by numbness and extreme shame as her sordid secret was exposed in so sudden and humiliating a way as could be. She did not know where to turn. Or look. Each second that passed by with the three of them standing there in stasis seemed like an eternity. She could not bear to make eye contact with Will and the many emotions that were passing through his face like a flick-book, and she could not look at Zach in his compromised state, for fear of how he would deal with this – would he use it as an opportunity to expose her and attempt to completely alienate his rival, thus claiming her as his prize? She put her hands over her face, unable to come to terms with whatever fall-out faced her.

Will spoke after what seemed like a lifetime, flowers looking pathetic at his feet.

"So. You've fucked him. Are you happy? Can we get on with our lives now?" his words cold and jarring.

Amy was unsure how to respond. She had pondered frequently how Will would react if he found out about her affair. Finally, here was his initial response and she wasn't sure she would ever have second guessed what he had just said. She was dumbfounded. He stood in the doorway glaring at her, not even glancing at Zach, the charm that had blossomed during their meal at the hotel that night, completely obliterated. Zach remained silent.

Amy tried to formulate some words but nothing would emanate from her mouth.

"I'll wait in the kitchen," Will said calmly, throwing the trousers at Zach, kicking the flowers as he left the room.

Amy's eyes welled up as she looked towards the door, the diminishing sound of Will's footsteps as he descended the stairs. Zach walked nearer to her.

"Now's your chance to make a choice once and for all." He gently rubbed her arm. "I'm sorry it happened like this." He kissed her cheek lovingly. He finished getting dressed, made his way downstairs and swiftly left the house. She heard him on his phone outside, calling someone for a car to pick him up. She looked out of her bedroom window. He glanced up.

She mouthed, 'I'm sorry.'

He mouthed back, 'Make it right.' She nodded. She wasn't sure what right was any more, or how to make it there.

She put some clothes on and slowly and morosely made her way to the kitchen. Will was pacing backwards and forwards. He barely noticed her enter the room and sit at the table. She felt physically dishevelled from a bad hangover and mentally dishevelled from the mess she now found herself in. She felt it best to wait for Will to speak first. At length, he broke the silence.

"I thought you were out with the BA lot last night?"

Again, he came in from an angle she was not expecting and was not wholly satisfied with. It complicated the explanation that was now inevitably expected from her. She would have to – at the very least – allude to the fact that the crowd she was with would certainly suspect her level of intimacy with Zach. Will would find that particularly humiliating.

"I was. Zach just happened to be at the same club as us." She said the words, but knew that if she was in Will's shoes, she would not believe yet another random meeting, and indeed, would question the randomness of the previous times they had 'bumped into him'. This frustrated her immensely as it was probably the most honest part of whatever she would decide – or he pushed her – to tell him.

"Of course he was." He sneered. "You know, I thought something was going on at the hotel. But I thought, no, that's ridiculous, you've never met before, apart from the time you served him on the plane, which he wouldn't remember. And anyway, he's this big shot musician, totally not in our sphere... then I come home to this." He threw his hands up.

It stung her that he dismissed Zach remembering her from the plane. It did her an injustice, he disparaged the power of her charms and she felt the full force of the unintended insult.

"I'm so sorry." Her voice came out small and unrecognisable.

Will appeared to not be listening. "And I'm torn. I stupidly gave you license to shag him because he was your celebrity freebie, never in a million years believing it would be a threat – how could it be? This is *real* life. Only to come home and find you have taken me at my word. Then, I come into our kitchen, and what do I find?"

Amy looked up at this comment, perplexed. Maybe he had found her photo... but no, it was not that at all. He picked up the copy of *Delta* magazine she had been sent and tossed it under her nose. The front cover mentioned the interview with Sovereign X, but not her name. Will aggressively turned the pages in front of her, halting at the article, and pointed to the name under the title.

"That's the same Amy Armstrong as the one sitting in front of me, right?" he said, snidely. "It all makes sense now. I thought, I just need to get my head straight, so here I am flicking through this magazine, while I'm waiting for *him to* get THE FUCK out of our house; then I see this! And I'm thinking, why wouldn't she tell me about a massive accolade like this? Unless this interview – which must have happened a while ago – was the start of this affair, or whatever you want to call it. I can't believe how naïve I have been. What a mug! The meal with him at the hotel… you two must have had a good laugh at my expense. I knew I heard you two talking in the garden that night." He was incandescent, his voice strained with rage and hurt.

"Please stop. I'm so sorry. I never meant to mess things up like this."

"Am I right then, what I just said?"

Amy looked at him through her tearstained hair. The truth was no longer relevant. He would probably not believe anything she tried to explain away. "I guess so."

"And did you hook up with him at the hotel? No, do you know what? I don't want to know. I'm sure I can fill in the gaps pretty accurately myself." Will put his hands on his hips. He was still pacing the kitchen, but remained perfectly calm through this. He suddenly seemed to come to a realisation, "The autograph… he knew you then didn't he, he'd guessed who I was – the love in capitals – it all makes sense now. What a fucking idiot this makes me look."

It aggravated Amy how concerned Will was with what people thought of him. But every word he uttered, she could feel the last two years or so of her life fragmenting before her, unable to see any way back – he was too damaged by her betrayal. She was seized by a nothing-to-lose mentality and felt the urge to defend herself.

She spoke quietly. "I kind of let myself off, cos he was on my list."

"What?"

"I said, I kind of let myself off, cos he was on my list."

Will fell quiet. "How long have you been doing him?" It was more a statement than a question. "It's not just last night, is it? This has happened before."

"Yes. Yes. I'm having an affair with him." She looked at him, shame eating her up. Will smashed a cup into the sink which made Amy jump. He leaned his hands on the edge of the sink and without looking at her, said, "Do you love him?"

"I don't know." She was at least being honest about that.

"Of course you do. He's your idol. What a kick that must be, getting off with him." There was malice in every word he spoke. And unfortunately, truth. It *was* a massive buzz. She had mustered the courage to get up and walk over to him. She stood behind him, put her hands on his biceps and leaned her head into his back. He was rigid at her touch, she hated that. He drew away from her.

"I'm so sorry, I never wanted to hurt you. I love you, I just became addicted to the thrill of… of him, who he is…"

"OK, I need some space. I need to think. And I can't do that with jet lag. I'm going to bed." And he left the room. She went upstairs into the bathroom after a few moments and closed the door. After she had showered, she peered through the gap in the door to the spare bedroom to see that Will had already gone to sleep. She stood there for a moment, unsure of what to do. Then she grabbed her phone and bag and decided to do what anyone would do when they are in a dire situation.

***

She was on autopilot for the entire drive to Beth's house. She knocked on the door feeling exhausted and ill. Beth opened it, quite surprised to see her, but surprise turned to alarm as Amy virtually fell through the doorway.

"Hey, I didn't expect to see you surface today – where's Zach?"

"I don't know." Amy sat down on the sofa.

"What's happened? Tell me." Beth sat next to her and put a sympathetic hand on her back.

Amy's mouth went dry and she struggled to speak. "Will came home."

"Oh, shit – did he… catch you?"

Amy nodded. "Not in the act, but certainly 'in flagrante.'" Amy started sobbing. Beth put her arms around her.

"Has he broken up with you?"

Amy pulled herself together so she could speak to her friend. "You know, I don't know. He said he needed to think. The list thing came up. I'm clutching at straws, but I hope he considers it."

Beth looked at her with pity. She did not like to suggest to her at a time like this that an affair is an affair, no matter how much you dress it up. Amy looked at her and guessed what she was thinking.

"You think I'm screwed, don't you?"

"Amy, the whole list thing is sleeping with a celebrity and the other one can't get mad. Once. You've slept with him numerous times, been texting and FaceTiming – it's more than the list thing now."

"I know. You're right. I was caught up by the novelty of it, I was dazzled by him. I guess I still am."

"Are you dazzled by him enough to turn your life upside down for him?"

"I don't want to lose Will. I love him."

"That may not be your decision now."

"I know that too. I think I should call Zach. He was thrown out on the street, nowhere near his hotel or anywhere that would be familiar to him." Amy grabbed her phone and called him.

Beth got up. "I'll make some tea." She went into the kitchen.

"Hey, you."

"Hi."

"How's things?"

"To be expected." Amy sighed. "I'm really sorry you got chucked out the house. I really had no idea he'd be back. Did you get back to your hotel OK?"

"Sure, don't worry about me. Just pulling up now."

"OK." Amy fell silent, but she did not want to go.

"We go back to the States tonight." It was a leading statement.

"Can I see you?" she said, almost as a reflex.

"Anytime. You know that."

"I'll be there within an hour."

"OK."

***

Beth came back in and handed Amy a tea. "I feel culpable in what's gone on. I told you to have your cake and eat it too. I'm sorry."

"Don't be silly – I made my choices, I and only I, have to face the consequences." She touched Beth's arm affectionately and smiled. "Thank you for always being there for me."

"You're always there for me too. S'what friends are for, to pick each other up when they're in deep shite."

Amy smiled. "I'm going to see him." She guzzled her tea.

"Will?"

"No."

"So, pledging your allegiance to the star-spangled banner then?" Beth gave her a wry smile.

"I don't know. I need to see him again, now it's all exposed. See how I feel. I think half the allure was the rush of doing something I shouldn't. Plus, I can't leave it the way it is, he flies home tonight." She finished her tea and gave Beth a big hug. "Can I come back and see you later?"

"You must. I want to know what happens! What if Will calls here?"

Amy sighed. "Tell him I'm off clearing my head, but I'm coming back."

"OK."

Amy left and got in her car. She drove all the way to the hotel Sovereign X had stayed in before – the hotel where it had all begun, from the rush of adrenaline of a fan meeting their idol, the sexual chemistry that was obvious after the interview, to the date where it all became real to her; their first encounter, that charged night, the sneaking around on her and Will's mini-break... What an epicurean buzz the whole experience had been. Now she felt the cold, stark dawn of reality descending upon her. The fantasy could no longer be deemed just that. It had passed into actuality and the gloss and ephemeral vision of the past month or so was disintegrating fast, to become mere dust.

She must face the real world, no matter how painful and how tough she found it. She needed to see him – the other man, her idol, her ultimate guilty pleasure. He had known almost from the beginning that she was unavailable, and she feared that part of the beguile he had for her had been because of that. Now that she was potentially free, would the excitement be gone? Where did it leave Will if it was not gone?

She pulled up in the car park behind the hotel and made her way through reception. The concierge from before noticed her and smiled. She realised she was not sure of Zach's room number, so she called him.

"Hi, Amy."

"Hi. I'm here."

"Come on up. Room 406."

She got in the lift, reminiscing about the time she had gone into that same lift with him. She found his room and knocked on the door. He opened it and had clearly just had a shower, just a towel round his waist, his skin and hair still wet. This did not make it easy for her, she found him irresistible with clothes *on*. He did not go to kiss her, which she was grateful for – it did not seem right in the circumstances. But still, the cloud of sexual thoughts filled her mind as she looked at him in his compromised attire. *Just one sleight of hand and he would be naked*, she thought. She wondered if she would be able to curb her insatiable libido, especially if she was reduced to one man in her life. Having two men to satisfy her had certainly given her an increased appetite.

He sat down on the bed and rubbed his hair dry with a hand towel. She tried to push the lecherous thoughts from her mind, especially after her altercation with Will mere hours before. She bit her lip and avoided eye contact with Zach for a moment.

"You OK, Amy?" Amy was pale and red-eyed.

"Not really." Now that she was here, she wasn't sure what to say. She wandered to the window and glanced out. She turned back and looked at him, he was looking at her with concern. She walked back over to him and kissed him, then turned away again.

She felt all kinds of hell in her mind and watched Zach as he dressed. She really did lust for him – there was no doubt – but could she move past these clandestine trysts to formulate a proper relationship? She hardly knew him in truth, and still had more respect for Will – they were so in tune with each other, ultimately so compatible, her soul mate. She sat on the chair by the window. *What am I doing?* she asked herself. Enchanted by Zach she was though, and in the vestiges of break-up mode in her mind, she clung to the one phoenix she might be able to raise from the flames, a possible proper relationship with Zach.

"I'm coming to the States in a week or so. I could stay for a bit."

He shot a look at her. "Really? Has that just happened?"

"Beth asked me to come, meet her girlfriend in LA. She had a seat going on one of her shifts, I said yes."

Zach looked delighted. "So, come see me. Be my girl." He kissed her, cupping her face in his hands. She touched his hands and moved them away. "I'll come see you. Let's just take it from there." As she said this, her phone rang. It was Will. She picked it up.

"Hello," she said, tentatively.

"Hi. Where are you?"

"Um, just out, thinking." Zach kissed her neck; she tried to move away and glared at him lest he make a noise and it would be completely over. She was on a knife-edge – why did she answer her phone? If Zach wanted to get rid of Will once and for all, he could just murmur something right now and that would be it. Game over. But she hoped he respected her enough to not ruin everything – it would certainly not raise him in her estimation. Instead, he took the phone out of her hand and hung up.

"What the fuck?"

"There's nothing you can say to him from here. If you still want him, then go and get him back. I'm going back home tonight; if you still think we can give it a shot, come out like you planned. I'll wait for you." He gave her a lingering kiss on the lips.

"I want you both."

"But that's no good for anyone, is it?"

"I know. I just… can't help fucking you every time I see you." She smiled half-heartedly.

He smiled back. "Ya know, I'm not complaining. I'm just so irresistible."

She laughed. "I should go. I'll call you." He still had her phone in his hand and he typed into it.

"This is my address in LA. Call me when you land. I'll be in the studio a lot over the next few weeks."

"OK." She kissed him again and left.

Ten

On her drive home, Amy felt sadness again. She had played roulette with her relationships and the ball seemed to have stopped on Zach, but it did not fill her with the elation that being the girlfriend of someone high profile should have – she felt empty, with a massive chasm of uncertainty ahead of her. And where was she heading right now? Should she go home to Will, or should she go straight to Beth's? She really should go home to finish the conversation with Will – she did not want to call him back and do it all again on the phone. She headed down her street and saw that his car was gone. She rushed into the house, checking her phone for messages as she opened the door – nothing. She went into the kitchen and found a note on the table, with a printout of a screenshot on top of it. It was a picture from Find My Iphone, of her phone at Zach's hotel. She dropped the paper on the table and picked up the note. She almost dared not read it.

Amy,
I really thought we could get past this – I would have done – if you had been prepared to never see him again, or play his music or have anything to do with him and his band, but having just called you and lost the call, I was worried. So, as you can see I checked where you were and I can only assume you are at his hotel. You have run straight back into his arms.
I think this is the end of the line. I am heartbroken and I still love you, even thinking about proposing to you as I was on the red-eye last night.
I'll be at Matt's place, please don't call me or try to see me today, I don't think I can handle any more.
Love always
Will x

Amy dropped to her knees, the flood of regret, what she had sacrificed for her obsession; it pierced her like a knife in the chest, and she buckled as the sobs took hold of her body. Damn phones! Why had they got a joint Apple account? Because of their commitment to each other, that was why. He was the love of her life, Will, the man she wanted to be with forever, and she had blown it for the infatuation of a celebrity. But had it become more than that? Zach had persistently made his feelings clear. Amy pulled herself up and made her way upstairs. The bunch of flowers still lay limp and dank in the doorway of her bedroom, damaged and lifeless. She stepped over them, finding herself incapable of getting rid of them. It felt like the last nail in the coffin of her life with Will, to throw them away.

She threw herself face down onto the bed and drifted off into a disturbed and restless sleep, her dreams filled with argument and anguish, Will's face morphing into Zach's, Zach's morphing into Will's, through images of torment, to intense sex with them both. She awoke as the sun was going down, to the sound of banging on her front door. She lifted her head up, feeling rough, and slowly got off the bed and went downstairs. The knocking on the door was getting faster and more persistent.

"All right, I'm coming!" Her tone was impatient. She opened the door to see Beth standing there, frowning and white as a sheet.

"Amy!" She threw her arms around her. "I was so worried! I thought you were coming back to mine – I've tried calling and texting you a thousand times! I thought, fuck me, that's it, she's dead in a ditch somewhere! I even rang Will – he was unsure where you'd be, so, as he said he was at Matt's, I thought I'd drive straight over here." She babbled quickly in a panic.

"I'm sorry, I was just so bereft and lifeless, I must have fallen into a deep sleep."

Beth followed Amy into the house.

"You really should consider getting a landline. You couldn't have slept through if *that* had been ringing all afternoon."

"True. Yes, I should. Probably be cheaper for transatlantic calls too." They sat down in the kitchen.

"Think you'll be making a lot of those now, do you?" Beth looked searchingly at her.

Amy nodded.

"You know, you may think you have lost Will, and maybe you have, but that doesn't mean you have to go running into Zach's arms. You could just walk away."

Amy looked at her friend's imploring face. She considered what she had said for a moment. "I've got nothing to lose any more. I feel it's only fair that the thing that cost me my relationship is given a chance to see if it can grow into something more. The true test will be when I go to LA with you."

"You should at least talk to Will before you kiss goodbye to your relationship with him."

"I will. But he doesn't want me to contact him today, he's hurting too much." She felt a lump in her throat. "And to be honest, I'm a wreck too. Look what I came home to." She showed Beth the note and the picture.

"Oh, shit…" She looked at Amy, who held her head in her hands. "I told you not to get a pissing joint Apple ID!" She exclaimed, and got up. "Hair of the dog?" She picked up Amy's bottle of Brockman's from the sideboard.

"Go on, then."

Beth poured them both a double gin and tonic. Amy allowed the alcohol to wash through her and relax her, and she felt some comfort and temporary relief as her clarity ebbed away. They talked through the evening and ordered a takeaway together. Late on, Beth's FaceTime tone rang. She answered it – it was Isabella.

"Hi, Babe, how're you?"

"I'm good – missing you," Beth said. Amy stayed out of the way so they could talk. She took their glasses to the kitchen.

"You too." Isabella was saying, blowing her a kiss, as Amy came back into the room. It made her smile to see her closest friend so happy. It lessened her heartbreak a little.

"Remember me telling you about my friend, Amy?" Amy walked over to Beth.

"Yes, the hottie you showed me a photo of?"

"Hi." Amy spoke from behind Beth's chair, and waved.

"Hi! Nice to, kind of, meet you!" Isabella waved back.

"You can properly meet when I come over. She's coming with me."

"Oh, cool – can't wait to see you. Listen, I can't be long I'm at work."

"OK. Looking forward to hooking up."

"Me too. Oh hey, famous spot alert – look who's just walked in!" She turned the phone around and there were three members of Sovereign X, including Zach, walking in. Amy's jaw dropped, she could not believe the quantity and diversity of chance encounters she and Zach had had, so random and yet perhaps so destined. Maybe she should accept what appeared to be fate – as Zach had said, they keep being presented to each other.

"Oh, hey, Isabella?" she said.

"Yes?"

"Stay on till they come to be served."

"Are you a Sovereign X fan, Amy?"

"You could say that." Amy looked at Beth, who was incredulous – wide-eyed and open-mouthed, clearly also stunned by another chance meeting.

"I love their new song," Isabella said, still oblivious to the looks on Beth's and Amy's faces.

"Can I tell her?" Beth whispered to Amy. She shrugged. *No need for secrecy any more*, she thought grimly.

"Izzy, she and Zach Hayes have a thing going!"

"Seriously? That's so cool! When you told me Amy had a boyfriend you didn't say he was famous."

Beth looked at Amy for consent to fill her in properly. Amy shook her head.

"Cool, huh?" she replied, instead.

"This is so exciting! Here he comes." She spoke away from the phone. Beth gave her phone to Amy. She watched as Isabella spoke, and heard Zach respond. He was ordering an espresso.

"I love your music, you guys! Would you mind, please, just saying hello to my friend? She's a big fan and just happened to be FaceTiming me when you guys walked in here." She turned the phone around and

Zach's face appeared. He was smiling, but he laughed when he saw Amy's face.

"Hi." She waved, grinning.

"Hey…" He laughed again, "How…what…"

"The lady serving you is my friend, Beth's new girlfriend. How weird is that?"

"Not weird. Destiny. I told you."

"So it would seem."

"You OK? You look happier than earlier."

"I'm OK. Got my bestie here, plying me with gin."

"Miss you, already," he said, quietly. "See you soon though, hey?" He clearly did not want a public conversation.

"Yes. Bye."

He handed the phone back to Isabella. Amy sat down in the lounge, a distance from Beth while she talked and laughed with Isabella. It made her miss Will more than Zach – he was the one who she would have been giggling and joking with like they were. She waited for Beth to finish the call. Beth looked at her introspective expression.

"How many random meetings are you going to have? It is just bizarre. You couldn't make this stuff up!"

Amy rested her head in her hand, "It is weird. Perhaps it is destiny and I should just accept it and go with it." She yawned.

"Want me to kip over?"

Amy nodded. "That'd be grand."

She struggled to get to sleep that night. The long nap she had had in the day did not help matters. She lay in her bed, looking at the empty space beside her – twenty-four hours ago, it had been Zach's perfect form lying next to her. A number of nights before, it had been Will's rugged body, just there sleeping peacefully next to her. She stared at the pillow for what seemed like hours. Zach… Will… Now that she had apparently lost Will, her heart yearned for him more than ever, and she wept. This continued for quite some time and she was not aware the next day of when the weeping ceased and sleep gradually claimed her.

***

She woke up the following day with a fug of a heavy head and a raging sore throat.

"Morning, my dear." Beth breezily came into her room and handed her a cup of tea. "Good grief, you look like crap."

"Thanks." Amy's tone was sarcastic. "Don't feel good today."

"See – men. They just make you ill." Beth smiled and brushed Amy's hair away from her face affectionately. Amy smiled and sipped her tea, but then grimaced, pained by her throat.

"Think I'll stay in bed today." She put the drink on her bedside cabinet and laid back down.

"Sounds like it might be best. I can stay here for a bit, but I'm working tonight."

"Where you off to?"

"Singapore."

"Bring back some orchids, if you can."

"I'll try. Talk to Will today."

"I will, if my voice holds up." Amy touched Beth's arm. "Thank you. For everything."

Beth just smiled. "Get yourself well again. I'll get you some breakfast." She stood up.

"Just a slice of marmite on toast will do." Amy's voice was croaky.

She ate her breakfast and shortly after, Beth left. Amy grabbed her laptop and checked her emails. There were three from Paul at *Delta* asking for articles from her. She could not face it today and emailed him to say that she was off sick and would call him in the morning. She laid back in bed and considered her fate for some time. Was she meant to be with Zach? Is that why everything had unfolded the way it had? If so, why did she feel so unnerved by the prospect?

She fell back into a deep sleep for most of the morning, feeling unwell. When she woke up in the early afternoon, she found that her voice was virtually non-existent. She decided to text Will.

Hi, I would have called but I have lost my voice today. I am a mess. I know I've treated you like shit, and I wouldn't blame you if you never spoke to me again, but I am begging your forgiveness and a 2nd chance. I love you and always will. A xxx

She put her phone on the bed not expecting a response straight away. To her surprise, the phone rang. She picked it up – it was Will. Her heart rose and she answered.

"Hello." Her whisper was raspy.

"Oh, you do sound rough. I wasn't sure you were telling the truth."

"I've got a bad throat, woke up with it."

"I'm sorry to hear that, I hope you feel better soon."

"Don't say it like that, sounds so formal."

"I think any informality between us is gone, now."

Amy closed her eyes as tears came thick and fast. "I'm so sorry. There's no excuses, I never wanted to hurt you."

"Because you never intended me to find out."

"No, you're right. What can I say… what do you want from me?"

Will sighed. "I don't know any more. I just don't. I need some space. Everywhere I go I hear their bloody song and see *him* on MTV or whatever. It sickens me. I had considered how I would feel if you ever got it on with him, and I thought I'd be OK with it; turns out it's a more bitter pill to swallow than I envisaged."

"I don't want to lose you."

Will paused. "I don't want to lose you, either. Look, I'm away again next week, let's talk after that. Get yourself well. Do you need anything?"

She smiled at his altruistic concern. "No, I'm OK. Beth stayed last night. I'm due to go with her to the States next week, meet her new girlfriend, can we meet up when we're both back?"

"OK." He paused. "Are you going to see him while you're out there?"

Amy screwed her face up and did not know how to respond. *No more lies*. "Yes, he wants to see me."

"How can I compete with him and his riches and fame?"

"None of that means anything to me, you know that."

"You say you love me, and yet you're going to see him. You need to make a choice."

"Yesterday I thought that was the *only* choice."

"What you did doesn't stop me loving you, I just… can't be with you, right now."

"You know, with him, I feel more in control of my life. With you, you control everything. Even now, it's you calling the shots."

"I never meant to be like that, it's just my personality. If you felt unhappy, you should have said so before you slept with someone else," he said, sharply.

"I don't think I realised, until there *was* someone else." Amy was starting to feel confused, stressed. And her throat was hurting so bad. "Can we talk again soon? I'm really struggling."

"OK. Just look after yourself." They ended the call and Amy fell back to sleep.

Eleven

Amy was quite unwell. Having visited the doctor, it was confirmed that she had tonsillitis and was prescribed antibiotics. She moped around the house for a couple of days. She spoke to Paul at *Delta* and managed to write two of the articles he had asked for, but it wasn't easy. Zach had called her early in the week to see how she was, but she couldn't talk for long.

On the Saturday, he sent her a text to say that he had caught her bad throat. She felt awful, she knew that they had a few performances planned and assumed they would not go ahead. They were due to perform on a popular American chat show, one she and Will used to watch together on a Sunday. She sat down to watch it as usual, and it was announced at the start that Zach had tonsillitis and was unable to perform. Amy closed her eyes. If Will was watching it at Matt's house, she imagined his reaction. The reminder wherever he went of her betrayal, and now this. She pondered if he had joined the dots with the lyrics in the current single yet. It was everywhere and it devastated her that he was out there having his nose rubbed in it persistently, but he wasn't one to look into things like that. She liked that about him – being someone who read into everything herself – it was a nice balance to be with someone who did not hold store to that kind of thing. He was the Yin to her Yang. This thought pained her. How can Yang survive without Yin?

She began thinking about their time together, reminiscing – maybe she had come to rely on him for her happiness a little bit too much? In fact, she felt incredibly frustrated by the whole situation. She was ill and stuck in, Will was only a few streets away, sickened by the sight and sound of Sovereign X... and his nemesis.

The following week, she was much better. On the Wednesday, she managed to get to the *Delta* office to have a meeting with Paul.

"Amy! How's the throat?" Paul kissed her on the cheek.

"Much better thanks." Amy sat opposite him.

"You know, obviously, it's a coincidence, but Sovereign X had to cancel a couple of performances last week because Zach Hayes had tonsillitis." Paul took his seat. He was looking at her. She avoided eye contact.

"Isn't that strange?" She deflected his insinuation. He was still staring at her. He paused for a moment.

"Right. Loved the articles. How're you fixed for the next couple of weeks?"

"Well, I'm going to America for a week, in two days' time."

"America... Hmm." He narrowed his eyes at her, smiling.

"What?" Dare he suggest anything? He had thrown her directly in the path of Zach anyway. They had never really had a boss and employee relationship, especially as she was freelance, it was much more informal.

"How's the boyfriend?" he said brashly. He had always flirted with her in any case.

"He's OK, I understand." She was evasive.

"I see. So, America then? LA?"

"Yes. My friend, the air hostess, has a ride-along seat available and she wants me to meet her new partner."

"Cool. In fact, better than cool, perfect timing. Can you go along to the Radio Music Awards while you're there and do a report on the evening? Zach Hayes is up for a song-writing award. Perhaps you could, you know, *hook up* with him and get some comments? He'll probably remember you from the interview you did last month, don't you think?" Paul was probing her, teasing her, she could see that. She wondered if or how the rumour mill had made its way back to him. It was alarming, but he was someone who connected with anyone or anything if it made good newsworthy material.

"He'll remember me," she said with alacrity. Paul flicked a biro between his teeth, making an annoying clicking sound, and watched her intently for a moment before saying anything.

"Think you've bewitched him?"

She was taken aback by his sudden directness. "That's an odd turn of phrase. I'll get what I need out of him," she concluded, standing up.

"Oh, I've no doubt about that." Paul raised his eyebrows, with innuendo, also standing to see her out. She looked him in the eyes.

"I know how to get what I want," she said with determination. She wasn't going to let his jealousy or whatever it was scare her. She could handle Zach; and the mess of her love life for that matter.

"Just watch yourself. Hollywood is a whole different ball game. You're moving in another sphere now. Little fish. Big pond."

"I'm only there for a week, for one article. Don't be so over-dramatic." Amy turned to go. Paul touched her arm to stop her.

"I think we both know what I'm talking about."

"I'll go to the awards, I'll get what you need. Do I need a press pass or something?"

"You tell me?"

Amy huffed. She was sick of his games. "Just give me the bloody pass." She held out her hand.

"It'll be ready for you when you get there." He turned to go sit behind his desk again. "I'll be interested to know if you used it."

"I'll let you know, I promise." She left, with a side glance back at him. He grinned at her feistiness.

"Check in when you get back," he called after her exit.

"Will do," she called back.

***

The day arrived for Amy to go with Beth to America. She packed light; she was well practised at that from her flight attendant days and was just loading her case into the back of a taxi, when a black Mercedes pulled up behind her. Will stepped out looking dapper in a smart suit and her heart swelled at the sight of him and the spontaneous nature of his visit. She smiled and turned to walk towards him; she checked herself before she went to kiss and hug him.

"All right?" he said, in his typically casual way. He looked like he hadn't been getting much sleep.

"Yes. You?" They were both very guarded with one another and it made her feel sad, she didn't like feeling like that around him, they had always had such a strong bond. She smiled and just wanted to throw her arms around him. He seemed unsure as to whether to do the same.

"Just wanted to say, safe trip."

"Thank you. I'll be doing a bit of work for *Delta* while I'm there, so that's good. And you're off, too aren't you?"

"Germany, tomorrow, for a few days, for a conference."

"OK." She hated the stilted conversation. He looked at her, but she could not read his expression. He pulled her towards him for a tender cuddle. She wound her arms around him and fought back the tears. She had missed him greatly, and this intimate moment of affection opened a flood gate. She clung to his strong, stocky frame and breathed in his aftershave. It felt like home. She could no longer hold back and the tears rolled down her face, soaking into his jacket. He pulled away as he heard her sniff.

"Hey, don't cry." He pulled her back to him. "I hope you find your way back from there." What he said had a cryptic slant, but she understood.

"Will you be here when I get back?"

"Call me. We'll see." He gave her a lingering kiss on the cheek and turned to walk back to his car. As he opened the door, he looked back at her. "Bye," he said, with a little wave.

"Bye." She waved back. She felt deflated as she got into the back of the cab and had a sudden regret that she was going to America at all.

She dismissed these thoughts as they pulled up outside Beth's house to pick her up. She came bounding out of the house with a big grin on her face. She was immaculately dressed in her British Airways uniform, and Amy got out. It felt nostalgic to be going to Heathrow with Beth again.

"Yo, bitches!" Beth said loudly with her arms in the air. "Just like old times!"

Amy laughed and grabbed her bag. The cab driver put it into the boot and they got into the back of the cab together. Beth looked at Amy who had a smile on her face, but it was not hiding the remnants of a frown, and her eyes showed signs of previous tears.

"What's eating Gilbert Grape?" Beth tilted her head at her.

"What? Oh, nothing. Well, not nothing. Will just turned up as I was leaving."

"Oh, shit, are you OK?" Beth touched her arm, her joviality dissipating.

"Yes, he just wished me a safe trip and gave me a hug."

Beth looked at Amy, who was fiddling with the strap of her handbag. "Well that's a big mind-fuck for you before you go and see how you feel about your mistress!"

Amy laughed, in spite of herself. "Mistress?"

"Well, I don't know! What would you say? It's incredibly sexist that when you say a man has a mistress, we all know what is meant, but what about when a woman has one – is he called a mister?"

Amy thought for a moment. "Do you know what, you're absolutely right. Another example of masculinity dictating idioms." Beth looked at her.

"Yeah, all right love, you don't have to go all 'Freud' on me. I'm not as intelligent as you!"

"Well, you're not that thick to know who Freud is, and use it in the right context!"

Their silly banter had completely distracted Amy from her confusion and Beth was pleased. She didn't like to see her friend suffering – she had been side by side with her when she had lost her mother and saw the torturous state she went through in the years that superseded it. Their conversation was animated for the rest of the journey and they made their way to the plane they were flying on. Amy knew most of Beth's colleagues, all of whom welcomed her with open arms; even Lucas, who was flapping around everyone like a mother hen, came bounding over to Amy.

"My darling! Mwah, mwah." He air kissed her in his over-the-top way and then gave her a big hug. "How's things?" he said, gently. "Beth told me *everything*."

"I'm OK. I'm not sure where I am with either of them right now, but I'm gonna just try to have fun in the States."

"And you're going to hook up with your hot piece of ass while you're there?"

Amy tutted and shook her head. "I expect so. Need to see how I feel about it all, really."

"Well, I love Will dearly, but when I saw you and him in that club, like dirty fucking dancing – I mean, the fireworks between you two were immense." Beth came over to them.

"He's right. I love Will too, but… it's Zach Hayes!"

"Yes, and I'm infatuated with him and have been since before Will, but what if that just fizzles out to nothing and Will doesn't want to take me back?"

"But that's a chance you just have to take. Go to Zach. It'll be an amazing experience if nothing else, seeing how the other half live. Fuck his brains out," Lucas said softly to her.

Beth giggled. Amy rolled her eyes. She tapped him on the arm. "Some things just don't change, do they Lucas?" she mocked.

He held his hands up. "What?" he said, innocently, as he backed out of their seating area into the plane, to help the passengers settle.

Amy took her seat. She felt the dark cloud of self-doubt creep over her again. Should she have stayed home and tried to win Will back? But he was going away – again – anyway. Plus, she had promised Beth she would come and meet her girlfriend, and she was working for *Delta* while she was there. She need not even see Zach if she didn't want to. They had not had much contact over the last few days, he was much better and was behind on the band's commitments, which she felt to blame for, so had limited her contact.

Just as she was about to switch her phone off, she noticed a message had come through. Zach.

Hey sexy girl, I think u said u were flying out today. Can't wait to see u, call me when you land. U should come stay at my place, leave ur friend to get it on with her girlf and I can get it on with u…

He had implored her previously that she should come and stay with him, but she had flatly refused – Beth wanted her to stay with her at Isabella's house, and if that did not work out she certainly had the means to get herself into a hotel. Or even better, she could call Paul and get him to sort one out on *Delta*'s purse.

Hey you, on plane now. Call u when I land. We'll have to see about the rest… xxx

Have u gone cold on me? having infected me with ur disease? ;-)

I feel awful about that, were ur bandmates cursing me?

I was cursing u! Felt like shit. Nothing a BJ wouldn't fix tho…

I've heard that licking pussy is a great throat healer…

OK need to stop, getting a semi and we're in rehearsals. Not a good look.

LOL. Gotta go anyway, about to take off. Xx

Safe flight. Xx

Beth sat down next to Amy, who was smiling from her messages. Beth sat back and sighed.
"You are not allowed to sleep all the way there, missus."
"I won't. Much."
"You got to keep me company, I'm working. And you wouldn't be here, gratis, if it wasn't for me, so my rules."
Amy pretended to close her eyes and snore. "I can't seem to find any fucks to give." She kept her eyes closed. Beth elbowed her in the ribs and they both giggled.
They were going to have a lot of laughs on this flight.

Twelve

It was nine p.m. local time when the plane touched down at LAX. Beth and Amy strode through the gate chatting and laughing, and nearly walked past all the people waiting for loved ones to come through, or taxi drivers, or chauffeurs with name boards, but one person at the end of the line leaning his foot against the wall caught Amy's eye. He had a fedora hat on, almost completely covering his face and was holding a placard that said simply, 'AMY GET YOUR ASS OVER HERE'. She nudged Beth in the ribs to look.

"Is that...?" Beth began.

Amy nodded. "Shall we pretend we haven't seen him?"

"That's a bit mean, he's obviously trying not to get noticed by other people."

"I told him I'd call him when we landed," she said, truculent. Some people milling around had noticed his placard too and were murmuring. Amy couldn't tell if they were just amused by the wording or whether they might recognise him – he was more famous on his own turf. She decided to go over to him. He lifted his hat slightly and smiled that smile.

She played it cool. "Hi, I'm Amy Get-your-ass-over-here."

He laughed. "Good. C'mon then."

"But I'm with Beth." She looked back at Beth, who was already distracted by the appearance of Isabella, who had run over and jumped on her, amidst squeals of joy from them both. Zach and Amy saw them as they hugged and shared a passionate embrace. Zach looked back at her.

"Are you?"

"Let me talk to her."

"Don't interrupt them." He grabbed her arm as she walked towards them.

"Hey – hi, Isabella."

"Amy! You're even prettier in real life! And please call me Izzy!" She gave her a hug. "I see your boyfriend is here," she said quietly, gesturing towards Zach who was walking up behind her to join them. She was still under the illusion he was the boyfriend Beth had told her about.

"Er…" Amy started.

"Amy, if you want to go with Zach, don't mind me. As long as we meet up for dinner tomorrow like we said, it's fine, honestly. I thought it might go this way when I asked you to come along. Just don't be a stranger while you're here." Beth leaned in so no one else could hear her say, "Especially as you'll be staying somewhere a whole lot posher!"

Zach caught them up at this point. "Hi, girls."

"Hi, Zach." Isabella and Beth chorused in unison, then looked at each other lovingly and giggled. Amy thought that maybe Beth was right – she should go with Zach.

"OK, OK. I'll come with you Zach." Amy relented.

"Great."

Amy hugged Beth and Isabella, and they exchanged more pleasantries.

"If we don't catch up in the day tomorrow, the meal is booked for seven, OK?"

"Sure," Amy said. "We'll speak before then."

"OK." Beth went off arm in arm with Isabella, canoodling as they went.

Amy watched them walk away, so pleased to see her bestie in love. She paused for a moment to bask in the warmth of their simplistic, unadulterated affection, and meditated on her complicated situation. Did she want Zach or did she want Will? Would Will even want her still? He gave her renewed hope, turning up before she went away… to see him, her other man. How much damage would that have done knowing she was going to him, again? She had to stop hedging her bets, with both of them. It was all so screwed up. She frowned.

"Amy?" Zach's voice bought her back to the present. She glanced at him. He was still so alluring to her, his impish eyes and radiant smile. "Let me take that." He grabbed the handle of her small case. "Wow, you travel light."

"Years of experience."

"Course. Me too. Just not used to a girl being like that." He led the way out of the airport and into the car park. Amy didn't even know what car he had. She imagined something ostentatious and American. She could hardly expect him to be completely perfect and own her favourite car.

He held his key up and pressed the button, a car blipped, she saw the indicators flash just beyond the row of cars they were walking past, and there it was, an Aston Martin DB11, in black. She laughed under her breath. Will would want to kill him if he knew he had this. Never mind the fact that he's sleeping with his girlfriend.

"Get in." He put her tiny case in the tiny boot of the car. She got in and looked around and touched the car. It was beautiful, but she must not be blinded by these material things.

"You like the wheels then, huh?" Zach got in the driver's seat and looked at Amy who was practically salivating.

"You keep surprising me. I didn't expect something as refined as an Aston. Just my absolute favourite car."

"Is it?"

"Shit, yeah. That's not so hard to believe?"

"I guess not. Wanna make out in it?"

She smiled, feeling like a teenager again. He turned to kiss her hard on the lips. It had been too many days since she had been kissed like that. By anyone. Her thirst for some physical satisfaction suddenly took hold of her. He drew back, looking into each of her eyes, his face still close to hers, he knew what she was thinking.

"Let's get back to my place first."

It wasn't a long drive to his trendy modern house in an exclusive part of town. The automatic gates opened and he parked near the front door. They went into the house: it had a large, tiled hallway, tastefully decorated, with steps leading down to an open plan living area. It was very Hollywood, but classy all the same. And it was huge. They went into the minimalistic kitchen.

"Nice place. How long have you been here?"

"'Bout two years. Drink?"

"Please."

"I don't have gin – glass of red?"

"Yes. Thank you." She took the large glass from him.

"Here's to… getting my girl to come back to my place, finally." She smiled and clinked his glass with hers. She took a few big sips and watched him take off his hat and flick his hair back. She put her glass down and pulled him close to her, pressing her body against his. Without speaking, she slipped her jeans off and hopped up onto the worktop. She leaned back and lifted her thin shirt up so he could see she was braless. He kissed her chest then her belly, before moving further south. She had that insatiable feeling seeing him again, to have him, to get what she wanted. She arched her back as his mouth ravished her, and all thoughts of Will gave way to the infatuation of the current environment, and the novelty of the glamour, from him, the star, to his lifestyle here in Beverly Hills. Something she told herself she would never sink into, being taken over by the superficial, albeit sublime clasps of celebrityhood. This was not what had attracted her to him, Zach, but it was hard to ignore now she was in the lion's den.

His tongue traced its way up her body. "Fuck me, Amy. Fuck me hard, like before," he said, pulling her down off the sideboard. He took her hand and led her down the hall to his bedroom – all modernist art, the room dominated by the massive low slung bed, with a large grey-quilted headboard.

He kissed her on the neck and whispered, "I've missed you."

"You too. Take your clothes off."

He obeyed. "No more sneaking…" he said, and drew her close, pressing his body against hers. She pushed him back onto the bed. She loved being the master over him.

Zach laid back and was passive under her control, in fact, he seemed to relish it. He had so much control in his life, it was refreshing for Amy to take over, and she was so hot, such an amazing body and she knew how to use it, she was so much in tune with her sexuality, he found their sex incredibly intense and overwhelming, he could not get enough. He loved her on his body, just irresistible, mouth-watering pleasure.

She kissed him and pulled him close to her. But the danger was gone. No more fear to fire the passion, the thrill that she was doing something wrong. It felt strange to be here, in a place she had never been in before, his place, his life. Quite different to their other encounters, on her grounds, in her home country. But here she was, his hands all over her body, his perfect body, naked and expectant before her.

She stopped him. "Wait here." She walked back down the hall to where her suitcase was still standing, abandoned, and pulled some rope and handcuffs out. She went back to the bedroom; Zach was sitting on the bed waiting for her. She dangled the rope at him to get his assent.

"I'll do anything, I'm at your mercy." He held his hands up.

"Lay back." He did as he was told. She tied his hands and feet to the bed legs, so he was spread-eagled. "Can we put some music on?"

"Yeah, my phone's in my pocket, grab it." She pulled his phone out of his pocket – he had so much to choose from. "Hurry, Amy, I'm so horny." He was breathless with anticipation.

"Slowly, slowly, catchy monkey," she said, teasingly. "You have so much music on here! Have you got a sex playlist?"

"What?"

"A sex playlist! Hasn't everyone got one?" Mine's called 'chill out'." She did air quotes with her fingers. He laughed.

"Yeah, I guess I do. Look for 'late night'." She found it and connected to his speaker system. As she came out of the music app, she tapped on Twitter – he had loads of direct messages. Curious, she went into them. There were lots of girls' names in there, all asking him out with their phone numbers, some with naughty photos attached. She wondered why he was keeping them, but strangely she did not feel jealous.

"You're popular." She went back to the bed, showing him the extensive list.

"Oh, I don't even look at them any more."

"Not even a little bit?"

"Once or twice."

She kissed him. He tugged at his restraints.

"If you do that, you'll hurt yourself," she said, running her finger lightly down his chest, stopping just before his nether regions, revelling in her dominance. He wriggled in frustration. "Half the fun is the anticipation." She moved down his body with her mouth. Now it was his turn to arch his back, as much as he could within his restraints.

She stopped again and got up. "I'm going to get my drink. Stay there!" She laughed.

"Amy…" He was trembling with arousal. She walked away, got their glasses and came back. She took a big sip from hers, and put them down beside the bed. She slowly unbuttoned her shirt. He watched her as she took her time, desperate to be inside her. Her shirt dropped to the floor – she was savouring every sadistic moment of his frustration. He tugged roughly at his shackles; twisting his hands, he drew blood slightly at his wrists. She leaned over him, her body barely brushing his and kissed him, before submitting to the final act, intense and rapturous.

***

She released him and he rubbed his ankles and wrists. He had quite prominent marks on them.

"I should wear longs sleeves for a bit." She couldn't help giggling.

"In LA, in July? I think I'd rather face the curious looks from people. You know that 'sex sent me to the ER' programme? I reckon I'll see you on one of those one day." He reached across her and grabbed his wine glass and handed her hers.

"You love it. I'm sorry, I think I may have tied them up too tight." She sipped her wine. "This is nice wine."

"Should be. It's two hundred dollars a bottle."

She nearly choked "It… what? Fuck me."

"Not yet, you killed me just now." He sipped his own glass nonchalantly.

"What's that in real money, like a hundred and fifty quid?"

"Real money." He laughed. "That's a matter of opinion."

"I can't get used to your notes. They all look the same. We have blue ones, brown ones, purple ones – and my personal favourite – red ones. Yours are all green!" She was very animated. He was laughing at her passion over a silly thing.

"You're funny," he said, affectionately.

"I'm serious!"

He grabbed her and kissed her. "I'm so glad you're here. And free."

She pulled back a little. "I'm not entirely free."

"I thought things were through with you and Will? I feel sorry for the guy really, he seems nice enough."

His comment stung her. She still could not let go of him as dismissively as that. "Well, I don't know. He turned up as I was about to leave for the airport."

Zach bristled. "Did he now? Does he know you were coming here to see me?"

"Well, that's not entirely why I came here." She pulled away fully, narked by his arrogance. She could be arrogant and was brazen about it at times, but she did not like it in those near to her. She felt that arrogance was such a masculine-dominated attribute, it was a little more palatable in a woman than a man, and quite often termed differently – self-confidence or assertiveness.

"C'mon. You couldn't wait to jump on me when you saw me at the airport." His American, slightly southern drawl was irritating all of a sudden. She would not allow him to have the upper hand. She sat up, poised for battle.

"Actually, I suggested to Beth that we ignore you. But she stopped me."

"Why would you do that?"

Amy shrugged. "Cos I'm evil? Or I just thought it would be funny? I wanted to see how you'd react."

He was bemused. "You still couldn't wait to fuck me though."

"A girl's gotta eat." She ginned. He pulled her back down onto the bed. "I have to do some work while I'm here." She kissed him, then pulled away and got up to go to the bathroom.

"Work?"

"Yes, I've got to do a report on some awards thing."

"The Radio Music Awards?"

"That's it."

"I'm going to that."

"I heard."

"Was going to ask you to come along as my date."

"So, ask me then." She climbed back onto the bed.

Zach was suddenly cold with her. "What sort of report is it? If you come as my date, you can't write down everything you hear me talking about or people I talk to." His tone was sharp.

"I know that. I shall keep the professional apart from the social, I can do that. Don't you trust me?"

He looked away. "You're a journalist, Amy, I'm just being cautious. You can understand it, given our start."

She sat up and turned away from him, she knew he would have trust issues, being who he was, but she bristled at the insinuation. "You pursued me! And my interview with you was good – did you even read it? I never strayed from my points, I could easily have written how flirty you were. But I didn't, cos that's part of my personal life, just as it is yours. And I only ever told my best friend about us."

"Because we were going behind your boyfriend's back. Not exactly trust inducing is it?"

"I don't really see what that has got to do with it," she snapped. "You knew I was taken pretty much from the get-go. You didn't let it hold you back. Where are *your* morals?"

"I'm sorry. That was a low blow. I don't want to fight."

"Neither do I, after a long, tiring flight. Maybe we should just get some sleep." She laid down, facing away from him. She did feel incredibly weary – the flight, the sex, the wine.

"Sure." He got up. "I'll get your case in here." Amy watched him walk down the hall, naked, but couldn't help feeling that the novelty and honeymoon period might be over before it had all begun.

Thirteen

Amy woke very early the next day. She looked around the room expecting to see familiar surroundings before her faculties returned and she remembered where she was. Zach was fast asleep next to her. The sun was streaming in through the massive windows and she could not help but admire the Californian climate. She decided to get up, quietly went into the bathroom and closed the door to have a shower without waking Zach. It was barely six a.m.

She got dressed and had a wander around. She made her way into the lounge area and looked out of the window. She had not gotten a proper grasp of the place when she arrived last night – it was dark, she had been tired and rather preoccupied.

The lawn, perfectly manicured, led to a huge patio area with lots of sun loungers, a barbecue area, and, of course, a lovely aquamarine swimming pool. She wandered into the kitchen and started rummaging through cupboards to try to find some tea or coffee. There was a very fancy, complicated-looking coffee machine on the counter. She took one look at it and got herself a glass of water. This was a lad's pad, but he had taste. She wandered down the hall, looking inside rooms. She came to a heavy door and opened it – it was his state-of-the-art home studio. She closed the door again and made her way to the living room and put the TV on quietly. She flicked for a while – nothing. Just like home.

She switched it off – the beautiful weather, even at this time of the day, was too enticing. She opened one of the patio doors and wandered out into the garden. She made her way over to the pool and dipped her toe in. It was covered, so that's all she could do, but it was very inviting. She looked back at the house. The car, the house, the beautiful life he had – all the trappings of glamour and wealth – it was all incredibly attractive and hard to ignore.

She wandered around more. The property was nestled in the Hills and looked out onto downtown LA. Very private, you couldn't even see the neighbouring properties on either side. She mused as to who might reside in them. Unbeknown to her, Zach had risen and noticed her, watching her from the open patio door, taking her surroundings in. He smiled and left her to it.

She sat down on one of the sun loungers for a while. Such a far cry from her humble life in England. Could she see herself here? She eventually wandered back into the house to see if Zach was up and found the coffee machine was on. She saw no sign of Zach, so she wandered back to the bedroom; he wasn't there. Puzzled, she made her way back down the hall. Just as she was about to pass the studio door, it opened and Zach walked out.

"Jeez, you scared the crap out of me!" He started.

"Sorry."

"What ya creeping around the house for? I thought you were outside."

"I wasn't creeping, I was looking for you."

He put his arms around her waist and drew her near for a lingering kiss. "Let's start over. Morning, Honey."

"Morning." She did so love kissing him. "I was just looking around. I couldn't work out the coffee machine."

They walked into the kitchen.

"It's OK, it's ready now. Sorry, I don't have any tea."

"No tea, no gin. I'd have been no worse off in a hotel." She smiled. "It's almost like you didn't plan this at all."

"I didn't. Just wanted to turn up when your plane was due to land, see if I could surprise you. Thought it could be another one of our crossing paths in bizarre ways."

"True. Kind of weird isn't it."

"Meant to be." He spoke with surety. She noticed he had sportswear on.

"Are you going to the gym?"

"A morning run. It's my routine."

"OK, no problem. I need some breakfast."

"Ah, yes, I may not have tea and gin," he said. "But I do have bacon and eggs," he continued, putting on an English accent. She laughed.

"You're quite good at that accent you know." He poured them both a coffee.

"Thank you very much." He maintained the accent and got the breakfast things out.

"You love cooking."

"I do."

"I read that about you. Your other great love in life apart from music is food, right?"

He laughed. "You have done your homework on me."

"I'm like your biggest fan. Which seems like a weird thing to say now." She sighed and looked around her again. "I definitely know a hell of a lot more about you than you know about me."

"Don't believe all you read. The Internet says I'm five-foot-nine when I'm six-foot! That few extra inches mean a lot to a guy!"

"A few extra inches mean a lot to a girl too."

He laughed.

"And yep, I knew that too."

"Really?"

"Well, aside from the obvious – how tall you are compared to me, a short-arse – I heard you say that in an interview." At this point, Zach's phone rang. It appeared to be one of his bandmates. They were arranging to get together in the studio later that day. He finished the call.

"I'm sorry. I've got to spend most of the day in the studio," he said. "Hey, how're you for driving on the 'wrong side of the road'?"

"Er… not great." She spoke apprehensively.

"You'll get used to it." She was looking at him as if he was mad. "You're not getting the Aston, I'm not that stupid! I've got a nice easy SUV you can use. Why don't you go have a look round town or meet Beth? We'll catch up later. Wait, you've got a meal with them, haven't you?"

"I think Beth will expect me to bring you along to that."

"You sure?"

"Yes, of course. Saves me playing gooseberry to those two as well. Plus, it's sushi, your favourite." She smiled. Something else she had learned as a fan.

"Ya know, I don't need to know your fifth-grade teacher or the name of your first pet to know that I wanna be with you."

"I know." But deep down, she still felt that he should know her a little better than he did. She had a messed up past and some full-on personality traits, none of which he knew about or seemed bothered about knowing. Will knew it all; he knew she struggled to maintain her grip on reality at times and needed grounding. Would Zach be man enough to stabilise her? Would he even want that responsibility? They were both impetuous – were they too similar to work?

As she watched him humming a tune while he cooked her breakfast, she suddenly felt like a fish out of water. It was all well and good being dazzled by the high life and victorious that she had bagged him, but she was struggling to give in to the whole thing completely.

He served a nicely presented plate of breakfast, clearly pleased with himself, and placed it in front of her, seated at the breakfast bar.

"There, enjoy. I'm off for my run."

"Are you not eating?" She called after him as he made his way to the front door.

"When I get back. See you in a half-hour or so."

"OK." She answered quietly, but he would not have heard her. She looked around at the large empty house, quiet again. She ate her breakfast, stripped to her bikini, grabbed her phone and headphones and sat out in the sun listening to her music, with a hat and sunglasses on. She lay back and tried to enjoy the rest at least. What a few weeks, or even months, it had been. She breathed a deep breath in and out. Just as she was drifting off into sleep, the phone ringing interrupted her music. She answered it through her headphones, without looking at who it was.

"Let me guess, you are laying in the sun, and I bet you are in the Hollywood hills somewhere." It was Paul from *Delta*. She sat up and looked around, as if she was being spied on, the accuracy of his statement startling to the point of sinister. She was so taken unawares, she did not have chance to think of a smart retort.

"Uh… Hi, Paul," she said simply.

He chuckled down the phone. "I haven't interrupted anything I shouldn't have, have I? What time is it out there? Oh, it's only like eight or nine a.m., right?"

"Yes, it's about that. And yes, I am sitting in the sun."

"In Beverly Hills, right?"

"Did you need something?"

"Yes, of course! I wouldn't be ringing you just to gossip now, would I?"

"Yes." Her retort was fast, before he could continue.

"Amy, Amy, Amy. I emailed you the details for the press pass and the itinerary for the awards, just wanted to make sure you got it. That's if you need the press pass."

"Hold on." She checked her emails. It was there. "Yep, I've got it."

"Well, your ID pass will be there, if you need it." He was fishing for an answer. She was not going to satisfy him with one.

"OK, thank you."

"Amy, just remember, first you're a journalist," he said, seriously.

"No. First, I am a woman, who does have a personal life," she shot back.

"OK, I know that. Just looking out for you." He was desperate for some gossip, she could tell.

"Thanks. I'll be fine. I'm here with a friend, don't forget. We're getting sushi later," was all she dare say.

"Well, enjoy. And enjoy the awards. Drop me a line the day after, can you, with your notes?"

"Of course. Bye." She was relieved the call was over with. It had rattled her; she did not like the interest in her personal life. She feared that it was only going to get worse if she and Zach got serious. She called Beth.

"Hey, Babe." Beth answered brightly.

"Hiya, how's you?"

"Great. How beautiful is the LA weather? Me and Izzy are walking along Venice Beach near her flat with her dopey dog."

"Ah, sounds idyllic."

"And how's things with you? How many times have you two shagged?"

Amy laughed.

"Come on. Bet it's not more than us."

Amy giggled. "Dirty bitches," she said, jokingly. "No. But he has battle wounds."

"Who's the dirty bitch then?"

Amy laughed. "Is it OK if I bring him to our meal tonight?"

"I expect you to bring him! Izzy is all star-struck anyway, so she would be upset if you didn't."

"Cool, thanks. I don't think I'm going to see much of him today. He's gone for a run and got the guys coming to record in his studio for most of the day."

"Bummer. He could have cleared his schedule for you."

"I don't mind. He's lent me one of his cars. Thought I might have a look round, fancy meeting up?"

"One of his cars, for fuck's sake! Go on, what's he got."

"Well, he picked me up in an Aston yesterday."

"Bastard's got taste too!"

"Well, you know that from him liking me!"

"Oh, well of course! You know who would be livid don't you?"

"Yes, I had already thought that."

"He's not lending you *that* car though."

"No and I wouldn't accept it – what if I smashed it up?"

"And *you* probably would."

"Thanks for that. He's got some SUV or something."

"OK. Well, you can pick us up. *My* other half has this week off." She mock-boasted.

"Lucky you. Well, I'll probably be there in an hour. You better give me the zip code or address for sat-nav or I will get lost."

"Will do. I'll text it to you. Oh, what's his house like, by the way?"

"Oh, hang up I'll FaceTime you, you can see it." They hung up and Amy FaceTimed her straight back.

"Hello." Beth's face was very close to the screen.

Amy laughed. "Twat. Show me where you are." Beth held out the phone – the beach was beautiful, no one there, Isabella was walking ahead of her with a Labrador on a lead.

"Isn't this gorgeous?"

"Stunning scenery."

"Oh, I meant Izzy's ass," Beth said, in a mock American accent. They both laughed. "No, seriously, I could get used to this life."

"Well, don't get any ideas. I need you in Blighty."

"And what if you end up over here?"

"Oh, I doubt that will happen."

"Really?"

"I don't know. I can't let go of Will."

"Hmm. Aston Martin, Mercedes. LA, London. I guess it is tough. Not!"

"It's not the things, it's the men."

"I know."

"Zach is amazing and I'm besotted by him and all this, but he's not Will."

"Show me all this, then."

"Oh yeah, before Zach gets back and wonders what the hell I'm doing." She held the phone up and scanned around the extensive garden.

She heard Beth talk to Isabella. "Wow, hey, Izzy come look at this, Zach's place." Amy turned the phone around.

"Hi, Izzy." She waved.

"Hi, Amy."

"Amy, show us the house too." Amy walked into the house with the phone up and wandered round the lounge and kitchen. She looked out the front window.

"There's sex on wheels." She showed them the car. Then she turned the camera on the phone around. Both girls were peering into it with great interest. "Ha ha, you two look so funny!" she said, giggling.

They both smiled. She wandered back out and sat down on the sun lounger.

"So, I'll pick you up in about an hour or so?"

"Great – I'll text you the address," Beth replied. "See ya." She hung up. She put her tunes back on loud and started dancing around. She closed her eyes again thinking about the two phone calls she had just had. As she settled into being absorbed by the music, she became aware of a shadow cast over the sun. She opened her eyes; Zach was standing in front of her watching her lost in the groove. She halted her moves immediately and lifted her sunglasses.

"Hey." She smiled.

"Hey. What are you listening to?" He was amused.

"Just some favourites," she said, pulling her earphones out. There were some of his tunes on her playlist. He was looking at her perfectly formed body in her bikini. Her innocent smile twisted lasciviously. "Music is so connected to sex, don't you think? The rhythm, the beat, the way your body wants to move…"

She dropped her sunglasses back over her eyes so she could see exactly how delighted he was in looking at her body. She saw that he was certainly semi-delighted.

"What time are the guys getting here?"

He was sweaty from his run, earphones round his neck, phone strapped to his arm. She walked towards him.

"'Bout half an hour. I need a shower." He kissed her. "Sorry, I'm sweaty."

"I don't care," she replied, kissing him back, tugging at his shorts.

"The gardener and the cleaner will be here any minute." He spoke with little physical protest.

"Well, this will give them something to talk about," she said, naughtily. He pulled her bikini bottoms down and she slipped his shorts off. She laid back down on the sun lounger, pulling him with her. He pushed the lounger so that it fell flat, so sharply, they both fell back and giggled as it went. They were not interrupted by cleaner or gardener.

Fourteen

Amy jumped in the shower with Zach – it was plenty big enough for them both – as he had made her sweaty. They could easily have done it all again, but the sound of the doorbell interrupted any notions they might both have had. She sniggered as he slipped trying to dive out of the shower and dry off as quick as he could.

"Just coming!"

"Well, you could have been."

He gave her a look. "Hurry up!" he said to her, chucking her a towel.

"If you're in the middle of a booty call, we'll come back in ooh, two minutes!" one of the guys shouted through the door.

Zach sniggered at the insinuation. "Fuck you!"

Amy got out of the shower with the towel around her. "Did they know I was staying here?"

"I mentioned that you might be here."

"Man, I hate being predictable."

He looked at her, his fascination for her at a peak. "That's one thing you're not."

By now, he had gotten dressed and left the room to go to the door. She closed the bedroom door after him and dressed. She did her hair and makeup and took a deep breath as she knocked on the studio door.

"Come in!" She opened the door and about four faces all turned to look at her.

"Perfection at last!" Zach was saying, bent over the laptop and mixing desk with his producer, neither of whom had noticed her entrance.

"That's what God said when he made me," Amy quipped. They both looked around as the others chuckled.

"Hi," she said, to a chorus of 'Hi, Amy'. "I was… going to go out, Zach." She needed the car key, but was too embarrassed to state that in front of all these guys.

"Oh yeah, back in a sec," he said to the others, getting up. He came out of the room with her. "Keys." He went into the kitchen; she followed him. He gave her a set of keys to a Land Rover. "Press this button to open the garage; the front gate will open when you drive up to it, OK?" He kissed her on the cheek and disappeared back into the studio.

She grabbed her handbag and went out of the front door. She didn't even know where the garage was. She walked down the drive and saw a building round the side of the house. Two double garage doors. She pressed the button and one door opened, revealing a smart SUV. She got in and familiarised herself with everything being on the other side of the car. She had not really driven much abroad and when she had it had been a right-hand-drive car. Still, she was not going to let it beat her and she got herself started. She checked the address Beth had texted her and put it into the sat-nav. She headed out onto the road and found that Isabella's place was only twenty minutes away.

She drove down the freeway and headed towards the beach. Isabella was in a decidedly poorer part of LA, in a five-storey building off the beaten track. She was not sure about parking Zach's fancy vehicle outside – the building opposite looked like a crack den. She got out and pressed the bell for Isabella's flat, looking back at the car, totally out of place on a street like this. She could not help being relieved at where she was staying. How different her start to this week in America had been. Beth and Isabella came bounding out, all smiles. Beth hugged Amy, Isabella kissed her on the cheek.

"I can't believe I'm going in Zach Hayes car!" Isabella gushed. She got in the front with Amy to direct her, Beth got in the back. Isabella led them to the Sunset Strip, up Sunset Boulevard.

Amy had flown to LA many times in her British Airways days, but she had never really gotten much further than the airport. They parked up and spent the morning window shopping, dreaming about the designer stuff and hopefully being able to afford it one day. Amy did buy herself a modest clutch bag in Gucci, and they stopped in Starbucks for a light lunch. They all had a laugh and Amy was enjoying their company.

They wandered around, sightseeing all the typical places. Isabella led them round to see The Chinese Theatre, Hollywood Walk of Fame; they took pictures in front of the Hollywood sign. In the afternoon, they picked up Isabella's dog, Gizmo, with a blanket for the car, and drove down to Santa Monica and sat on the beach. Amy sat down with Beth while Isabella threw a ball with Gizmo. Amy looked at Beth watching Isabella.

"So nice to see you in love."

Beth looked at her. "Who says I'm in love?" she said, but without any conviction. She smiled. "And what about you? You're not sure are you."

"No. Don't even go there. I just want to shag Zach all the time – how can I go back to Will and try to fight for him with this insatiable thing in me? The road to hell is paved with good intentions," she said, philosophically.

"But that's natural. He's new, he's different, he's very inviting – all the showbizzy stuff. That novelty will wear off, and you need to have a relationship left."

"I know. I mean, he's a lovely guy."

"But..."

"Yes, *but* indeed."

***

They spent the afternoon at the Pacific Park before Amy dropped Beth and Isabella back at Isabella's apartment. Amy made her way to Zach's place, the sun glowing low in the Western sky, beautiful colours behind a back-drop of tall palm trees, Amy drove back admiring the beauty. The gates were open and the guys were just leaving in various luxury cars. They waved as she made her way back into the drive and parked the car in the garage. She walked back to the house and opened the door. She put her new bag in the bedroom and noticed the patio door was open and the sound of splashing water. *Zach must be in the pool.* She looked out and saw him swimming, so she put her bikini back on and went out.

"Hi."

"Oh, hey, you're back – good day?"

"Tourist day. Yes, we had a great time." She jumped in near him and he pulled her close to him.

"And what time is our reservation tonight?"

"Seven."

"So, we have, what, a couple hours?"

"Yes."

"What can we do for a couple of hours…" He looked at her suggestively.

"Talk?" She ventured half-heartedly. She moved away from him to do a few laps of the pool. He swam after her. He got close quick – he was a stronger swimmer than her.

"Amy, tie me up again. I'm enjoying my recent conversion to BDSM," he murmured in her ear. She felt herself salivating at the prospect and the yearning build in her belly. She thought about the other props she had bought with her.

"I have some other toys too."

His eyes lit up. He immediately pulled himself out of the pool, and reached down to pull her out by the hand. They made their way back to the bedroom, Zach almost bouncing as he went, like an excited puppy.

***

Amy had her third shower of the day. They got dressed and Zach made them both a smoothie.

"Hey, come listen to what we've been writing today." He led the way to his studio room and Amy followed, sitting down on the sofa. This was it, she was being allowed in to the inner sanctum, his new material. He played her some demo-type recordings of several songs.

"What do you think?"

"Bit different listening to the songs before they've been finished. Play that last one again." He played it. "Seems a bit slow, maybe better more up-tempo?"

"Yep. That's what I was thinking." Her pride swelled that she had judged right. What did she know in comparison to him?

The time came for them to leave to go to the restaurant; they made their way there in the Aston. He parked out the front, and they saw Beth and Isabella walking down the street towards them. They were smiling and chatting avidly, both looking towards the car and its passengers, who were disembarking. They all greeted each other, entered the restaurant and sat down.

"Ya know, I asked Amy to go for sushi when I first asked her out. She wasn't sure, so we went for pizza instead."

"Ha ha, that sounds like Amy." Beth chuckled. "Sushi virgin."

"Yeah, well, I'm getting my education now, aren't I?"

"Baptism of fire more like." Isabella joined in.

"Just look after me, don't get me anything too fancy," Amy said.

"I'll look after you." Zach leaned across to kiss her. Beth observed them both. She could see quite clearly from the way Zach looked at her that he was smitten by Amy. She looked at Isabella who had clearly noticed it as well.

"By the way, Zach, I know it's fangirling, but could you sign my copy of your album please?" Isabella said, getting a CD and pen out of her handbag. He laughed.

"OK." He scribbled on it and gave it back to her.

"Thank you! I swear I'll behave now and treat you like an ordinary human being."

"I am an ordinary human being." He leaned his elbow on the table, resting his chin on his hand, and glancing at Amy as he said it. She looked at him and smiled. His wrist was on display for the first time and Beth noticed the red marks.

"Oh!" she exclaimed suddenly, putting two and two together with the battle wound comment from Amy on the phone. She didn't realise she had exclaimed out loud and all three of them looked at her.

"What?" Amy and Isabella chorused in unison. Beth looked at them with wide eyes.

"Oh, nothing, sorry. Just thought of something." She rubbed her own wrist unconsciously. She knew what Amy was like in the bedroom and guessed this must be partly why Zach was so on the hook. Amy clocked Beth rubbing her wrist and knew exactly at that moment why she had exclaimed. She chuckled to herself and made eye contact with Beth. They had a knowing glance and giggle.

"Have I missed something?" Zach glanced from one to the other.

At this critical moment, their drinks arrived, which broke the awkwardness of the conversation. They chatted freely after that and laughed the evening through. What a different ambience this was for Amy – strange food, strange surroundings, strange people, apart from one.

After they had eaten their meal, they decided to head to a local bar down the street. Zach held the door open for Beth and Isabella to go through first, then he put his arm across Amy's shoulders as they walked through the door. As they reached the main path, there was a flash from the doorway of a closed shop near the restaurant. Amy was startled, noticing a long lens camera and a man with long dark hair holding it. The camera flashed again as they walked past. Zach tucked Amy into his body more and they walked quicker; with his free hand, he shielded his face from view of the lens. Beth and Isabella had also realised they were being 'papped' and started jogging down the street towards the bar. They were laughing by the time they got to the bar; Zach and Amy were not.

Zach had not really suffered from paparazzi following him and he had never courted nor done anything to warrant their interest, and he liked it that way – his private life had remained just that. Until Amy – the journalist – had arrived. He had a dark look on his face; Amy was puzzled. She thought she had recognised the photographer. This was more than a little alarming to her. She thought she had passed him in the *Delta* offices before. She felt sick as she recalled with bitter regret mentioning to Paul that she was getting sushi that evening with Beth. He had clearly put two and two together and must have tipped the guy off. They had gone to one of the most well-known sushi restaurants in LA. Easy prey.

Isabella's smile faded as they reached the bar and Zach and Amy caught them up looking grim. Beth though, still out of breath, had not noticed.

"Well, that was a bit of fun, running away from a pap! We won't get to do that too often," she said, laughing. Her laughter soon stopped when she saw the serious look on Amy's face.

"Right. Not funny. Drinks!" She turned towards the bar. She set up a tab and the others told her their drink order. Zach and Amy meanwhile found somewhere to sit. Zach was quiet.

"How annoying that was, hey? They're bastards really," Amy said.

"You're a journalist, thought you'd be on their side."

"No! I hate that invasion of privacy, it's not fair when you are trying to have a private life."

"They never normally bother with me. They must have been tipped off that we'd be there." His tone was cold. Amy felt her cheeks glow. She felt guilty, she was sure this was all Paul's doing.

"I hope you're not insinuating that I had something to do with this?" She felt she had to defend herself, even if it was Paul's doing; she had certainly not wanted it. She dare not tell Zach she had spoken to her editor that morning.

"So, you're saying you didn't?"

"No! I don't want to be papped, just as much as you! If not more so – how do you think Will would feel if he saw our picture emblazoned all over the tabloids?"

"Oh, for fuck's sake, let go of him already. He's gone, it's over, it's us now."

Amy turned her head away and fought the emotion of his blunt remark. She did not want the evening to end like this. Beth and Isabella came over to the table with drinks and noticed the frosty body language; the air could be cut with a knife between them. Amy grabbed her gin and tonic and downed half of it in one hit. Isabella was first to break the tension.

"Hey, come on you two, don't fall out over it, it happens. The paps are always outside places like that hoping to get a star falling over drunk or with someone they shouldn't be. Or, to be the first to break a new relationship with a mystery British girl." She said the last bit pointing to them both. "I should have thought and booked somewhere more off the beaten track. I wasn't sure Zach would be coming with us and I wanted you to have a good virgin sushi experience, Amy." Isabella's words dissipated the bad feeling and Amy smiled at her kindness.

"I'm sorry, Amy," Zach said. "I just hate all that."

"So do I."

He gave her a peck on the lips.

She couldn't wait to get back to London and wring Paul's neck. And what to do when the pictures got published, possibly tomorrow? Maybe they would be a non-event and just as Isabella had said, mention his date with a 'mystery girl'. She knew journalism well enough, although she was quite new to it, to know that there would be more of an angle to it than that. But what dirt could be slung at her? She was fortunately old enough that her chequered past all took place before social media had really taken off. Time would tell. She made a mental note to check the tabloids this side of the Atlantic and back home tomorrow. She also made a note to check *Delta*'s Twitter feed and news page. If it was Paul's doing, it would surely appear there first.

Fortunately, the evening became more relaxed as the three girls drank more drinks. Their talk and laughter got more raucous. Zach participated but in a more measured, sober way as he was driving. Just before closing, they left. Beth and Isabella, already all over each other, bade them goodbye and hailed a taxi. They drunkenly bundled in and Amy heard Beth's loud laughter and whooping as the taxi went off down the street, arms waving out of the window. Zach put his arm around her and they strolled back up the street to where his car was parked. He opened her door and stopped her before she got in. He glanced around to check for photographers again.

"Not ashamed of me, are you?" she slurred slightly, as he leaned in to kiss her.

"Of course not. Just want my private life to be just that. Private."

"Contrary to the fact that I am a journalist, I want that too. So just trust me now, already." She was firm, albeit drunkenly.

They got in the car and sped back to his house. Amy was dozing by the time they pulled up outside the front door. Zach got out and opened her door. He undid her seatbelt and tried to lift her out. She stirred as he did so.

"Are we home, Will? It's OK, I can walk upstairs," she said, still virtually asleep. Zach bristled at the mix-up with names, and he certainly had no stairs in his single-storey home. She came to enough to allow him to help her over the threshold. "I'm sorry. I'm not *really* drunk, Babe." She staggered into the house. She had never referred to him as 'Babe' before.

"I think you are a bit, Amy." Zach picked her up and carried her to the bedroom, placing her on the bed. She kicked off her shoes and put her arms around his neck.

"Fuck me. Bend me over and fuck me."

"Not like this. Not when you can't get my name right." He kissed her anyway.

She frowned at him. "Zach," she said, matter-of-factly. "Fuck me, Zach. I didn't get your name wrong… when did I get your name wrong? What did I say? I know your name… I love you… my idol…" She was babbling. He looked at her with disdain.

"Just get some sleep." He lifted her back onto the bed and brushed the hair away from her eyes. "I'll get you some water. And maybe a bucket." He disappeared and Amy drifted into sleep again, hardly conscious of what she had been saying.

She did not wake again until about four a.m. when a raging thirst woke her and she was cold. She looked over at Zach's place in the bed and noticed he wasn't there. She still felt wobbly and went to the bathroom. She came back out and looked down the hall. One of the spare bedroom doors was open and Zach was fast asleep in a bed half the size of his. Her heart was touched by his care for her. She considered waking him for some early morning sex, but he was sleeping so peacefully, she decided to leave him and go back to bed.

Fifteen

Zach woke her late the next morning. He bought her a coffee in bed and she sat up. She felt weary – not a great start to the day. She screwed her eyes up at the bright sunlight.

"Exactly how much did I drink last night?"

"Well, that bar is probably completely out of gin, you drunk it dry."

"Shit. Don't do doubles, Amy, when will you learn?"

"I think they were more like triples the girls were getting."

"Fucking Beth. Typical. I'm really sorry. I do like a drink, but I never get like that normally."

"It's OK. I know you Brits have a reputation. And you think you can drink us Americans under the table." He smiled.

"Well yes, but that *is* true."

"You nearly drunk yourself under the table last night."

She put her hand over her eyes. "I'm sorry, was I really embarrassing? There are bits I don't remember. Like getting from the bar to the bed."

"You're a lot louder than I thought. And you called me Will."

Amy looked at him. "I did? I'm sorry."

"No matter. Can do it all again tonight. It's the awards."

"Oh, yeah. No, it's OK, I'll drive if you like."

He looked at her, smiling at her naiveté. "I have a car coming," he said, gently.

"Of course you do." She closed her eyes at her stupidity. "You're nominated. I forgot to congratulate you on that, you thoroughly deserve it."

"Thanks. Have you got something to wear?"

She looked at him – she *did* have something to wear, but it was not exactly limo-exiting, red carpet-treading quality. "I have a dress."

"I hope you don't mind, but I took the liberty of getting a dress sent over here. Just one – wanna take a look?"

"Does a bear shit in the woods?"

"What?"

"I mean, hell yes!" she said, excitedly. She could hold her own and be independent in every way, but there was a princess deep inside her like any other girl, that would not let her be a complete feminist and be affronted by or refuse his kind gesture. Besides, it was double-edged. If she was going as his – a nominee's – date, she needed to look the part. She understood that. He got up and left the room returning with a large dress box, placing it gently on the bed.

"You open it."

She slipped out of bed and excitedly lifted the lid. Inside was a beautiful blue, sparkly Calvin Klein gown.

"I'll leave you to try it on." He smiled, and left the room. She was overtaken by the beauty of the dress and barely noticed him leave.

She put on some fresh underwear and carefully slipped the heavy sequinned dress on. There was no way she could wear a bra under this dress – it had a daringly plunging neckline, shoestring straps, and sexy side cut-outs. The back plunged to just above her bottom and had criss-cross straps across her back. She fiddled with it slightly to make sure the straps were in the right place and that it fit – which it did – perfectly. It complimented her figure and she lifted her chest; it made her feel amazing. She shuffled over to the mirror on the wardrobe door and stood on tiptoes. She turned around and saw the Jimmy Choo sandals she had worn to dinner the previous night strewn on the floor. She sat gently on the bed and slipped them on. She stood up and swished the dress so the deep side slit revealed her slender legs and a flash of her five inch heels. It was nothing short of perfect. She smoothed her hair down and straightened the bust of the dress.

"Zach!"

He opened the door immediately. He must have been virtually pressed up against it, waiting for her to try it on. She looked over to him and did a twirl with a laugh, putting her hand on her hip and throwing her head back as if she was a model.

"Slay!" He couldn't take his eyes off her. "I do have good taste."

"Which is why you are with me," she said, pointing to herself and laughing.

"You know it could look better." Her smile dropped. "On the bedroom floor." He walked over to her.

She smiled again, and rolled her eyes.

"You like it then. It looks so good on you. But then what doesn't."

"Thank you." She kissed him.

He went to touch her, but she moved away.

"Don't, you might crumple it before tonight."

"Crumple?" He chuckled. "Well, you need to take it off anyways. We're off for a massage before tonight."

"Really?" She could not hide her surprise and excitement.

"Let me help you out of the dress." He carefully slipped the straps off her shoulders. She watched him as he carefully slid the dress away from her body, and placed it in the box, leaving her standing there in just her underwear and shoes. She breathed a deep breath as he turned towards her and looked at her stood there, topless and wanton. She did not move and let him look at her, up and down, her imposed vulnerability causing an involuntary shiver through her body, hardening her nipples.

She had never allowed him to take control in the bedroom and now she felt her prowess diminish under the spell of the dress, her femininity brought back into sharp focus. He kissed her, putting his arms around her, his fingers travelling down the small of her back, slipping between her underwear and her skin. He flicked them down in a sharp motion and they slid down her legs and she kicked them off. She succumbed to him, let him lay her back on the bed, and he lifted both her arms above her head, ran his fingers down them and over her breasts. He leaned over her, still fully dressed and kissed her belly. He pulled her towards him and slid his arm under her back to get her to turn over onto her front. She was submissive and flipped over, resting on her forearms, lifting her knees up so she was on all fours. He hastily undid his belt and dropped his trousers and could not get his underwear down quick enough. He thrust deep and hard inside her so suddenly she let out a moan of pain. He reached round the front of her to get to her with his fingers.

Amy closed her eyes and Will's face appeared in her mind. He was unrivalled in the bedroom, no holds barred, always intent on her pleasure. She opened her eyes again and glanced across at the full-length mirror on the wardrobe to be able to watch what Zach was doing to her. His physique was a huge turn on, bronze skin, more muscly than Will. She needed this visual aid to help her come, watching him take control of her from behind. He came quickly after her and withdrew, moving the dress box away, and he lay on the bed next to her.

"I'll get some breakfast on." He got up, did his trousers back up and left the room. Amy lay there for a moment. It was the first time the sex between them had been less than incredible, bordering on mediocre. She sighed, got up and got dressed. She would have her shower later.

She grabbed her phone and had a sudden thought: the photographer last night… She knew how quickly these things could be published these days and thought it was worth checking to see if it had hit anywhere yet. First stop was *Delta*. To her relief, there appeared to be nothing on there. Perhaps she had misjudged Paul, perhaps he had nothing to do with it. Surely it would all have been too much of a coincidence to *not* have been his handiwork? She scrolled through other outlets, including the trashier gossip magazine pages and ones popular in America. Sure enough, there was a photo of her tucked in to Zach's side, with a red circle placed on the picture around the restraint marks on his wrists, on full display, one arm swung forward as he was mid-stride in the photo; the other was wrapped around her shoulder, the flash of the camera highlighting the marks perfectly. The headline read:

'ZACH HAYES AND MYSTERY GIRL – AND WHAT HAVE THEY BEEN UP TO?'

Amy clicked onto the article. It was top of the magazine's list of articles on their website. It was only short, with the one picture, plus a zoomed in shot of Zach's wrist. It read:

"Sovereign X front man and mega songwriter Zach Hayes was spotted with a mystery girl on his arm leaving Nobu late last night, Gloss *magazine can exclusively reveal. Never single for long, the much sought after musician, who could be described as one of the most eligible bachelors in showbiz, was seen leaving the popular sushi restaurant with three unknown women, one of whom he had his arm around. Even more intriguing are the red marks that can*

clearly be seen on his wrists, that look distinctly like handcuff wounds! Kinky! We shall never look at the otherwise clean cut songwriter the same way again! Zach is up for a song-writing award at tonight's Radio Music Awards, for a song he penned for Olivia Sanchez, and is expected to be at the ceremony. Gloss *will keep you informed of the night's event and fashions. Let's see if Zach takes his mystery girl as his date!"*

Amy swayed as she finished reading the piece. What would Zach's reaction be when he found out, and should she be the one to inform him? By the time the awards take place that night, her identity will surely be known – that she was a journalist; and how many questions would now be asked about his sore wrists? He was a serious songwriter, not tabloid fodder. She foresaw the damage this could do to his reputation and probably, in turn, their relationship. She felt entirely to blame. She was certain Paul would have anonymously tipped the photographer off. She imagined his fury when he found out the pictures had appeared in some trashy gossip mag in the States first. But maybe he wouldn't care… if the dots were connected as she felt sure they would be, her name, linked to Zach, would surely also be connected to *Delta*. That was the subtle, but very clever way of getting *Delta* well and truly on the map, through her sensational affair with the frontman she had interviewed mere weeks before. She had simply added to the story with her noticeable bedroom escapades. She sat on the bed and glanced at the dress. Perhaps she should not go. But with Will out of the picture, she needed to make rent. She needed the awards article. She suddenly felt trapped and a little sick. Being hungover didn't help matters.

"Amy!" Her stomach turned over. She got up and wandered into the kitchen. "Pancakes!" he said cheerfully, serving her food. He was concerned when he looked at her face. She was white as a sheet. "Are you OK? You look like you're going to pass out. Here." He put the plate in front of her. She sat at the breakfast bar.

"A plague on both our houses…" she whispered, staring into space.

"What was that?" Zach said. He put a hand on her shoulder. "You're worrying me, do you feel ill? What's wrong?"

She had to tell him. She handed him her phone.

He took it and looked at the article and pictures. His face grew dark very quickly. "Here." He handed her phone back to her. "Well, this won't do *your* career any harm," he said, bitterly. He walked away from her and headed outside through the open sliding door. He carried on walking, clearly fuming. Amy chased after him.

"Zach! It's just a trashy mag, please don't worry about it." Her optimism for this statement was empty. He had his hands on his hips and was shaking his head.

"I don't know what to think. In this town, a squeaky-clean reputation is paramount. If it spreads around that I'm into bondage or whatever they want to throw at me, I can see it'll tarnish me for ages."

She walked towards him. "I'm so sorry." She rubbed his arms. He looked at his wrists, the marks had faded, the wounds were barely visible now.

"Ya know, you're nothing but trouble, Amy Armstrong." He looked down at her. She was looking up into his eyes, fear all over her face, still very pale. "And those injuries were so worth it." He allowed himself a small smile. She felt slight relief that he wasn't as mad at her as she thought he would have been.

"So, do you still want me to be your date tonight?" she said, timidly.

"Of course I do. Let's be open and show the world that we're together." He kissed her. "C'mon, let's go get pampered." They went back indoors and got ready.

He drove them the short distance to Wilshire Boulevard and they entered the spa. It was incredibly posh. Amy was trying her hardest to be cool and nonplussed, but inside she was jumping up and down with glee. They had a back massage, next to each other, which was much more titillating than she anticipated. She looked across at him and he at her as they lay on parallel massage tables. Amy started giggling, which in turn set Zach off.

"Stop it," he whispered. "We're supposed to be relaxing."

"Can't help it."

They both had a facial and Amy felt amused again. She looked at him as the masseuse rubbed his face, he had his eyes closed. He opened them as he heard her snigger.

"What?"

"I've never been with a bloke that has facials. Not many Brit blokes do that."

"Well, I don't do it regularly. I'm just here for you," he said, closing his eyes again, clearly enjoying himself.

"Yeah, right."

Amy felt all soppy and relaxed as they left the spa and got in Zach's car to head back. They stopped at a hotdog vendor off the beaten track, for a late lunch, before making their way to Zach's place. Amy's phone rang as they got through the front door. It was Beth.

"Hey, how're you today?"

"Not too bad, bit rough this morning from all the triples you were buying, you bastard."

"Thought you needed it after photographer-gate. Have you seen it?" Beth asked tentatively.

"Yes."

"Has he?"

"Yes."

"It wouldn't have been half as bad if they hadn't pointed out those bloody marks! You really should consider going easier on your men."

Amy could hardly respond too explicitly in Zach's company. It rankled her though, she had *told* him to cover his arms.

"Hmm. Don't knock it till you've tried it."

"Maybe I will now with Izzy. She's game for anything. Oops, she just gave me a look."

"I'm not surprised."

"How did he take it anyway? I suppose you can't say."

"Not easily."

"Well, it's your thing, tonight isn't it?"

"Yes, he took me for a fancy spa treatment today. And I've got a dress."

"Lucky bitch – talk about A-list treatment!"

"Indeed."

"Hope it goes well. I look forward to seeing a more official photo of the two of you on the red carpet!"

"Oh, shit, yeah, I've got all that to face. I think I prefer being incognito."

"Amy, you're a gorgeous girl, it will suit you."

"That's very kind. Bullshit, but kind."

"It is not bullshit, my love. You can shine as bright as the other stars."

"Bless you, you're so sweet. I'll catch up with you two tomorrow, shall I?"

"Yep, that'll be great. Bye."

"Bye."

Meanwhile, Zach had also taken a call, from one of his bandmates, Amy deduced. From the tone of the conversation they were ribbing him about the photo. He was good-humoured, but she feared if they took it too far he would get cross – he was saying 'no' an awful lot and sounded evasive. She decided to take a shower and start getting ready. They were due to be picked up in two hours, but she wanted to look her absolute best.

Sixteen

Zach got ready in half the time it took Amy, and he was suited and booted before her, looking dapper in a smart grey suit and a slim black tie. He went into the kitchen to pour them both a glass of wine before they left, while Amy finished getting ready. When she was done, she looked at herself in the mirror before carefully walking into the kitchen. Zach turned at the sound of her heels across the hall.

He was dazzled, and walked over to her. "You look stunning. Just stunning." He kissed her gently on the cheek. She could not stop smiling.

"Thank you. You scrub up pretty good yourself." She had her new Gucci clutch in her hand. "I feel like a movie star."

"You look like one, too." He checked his watch. "The car will be here in a minute." He handed her the glass.

"I don't want to spill anything on this dress." She held the glass very carefully. She knocked it back anyway, starting to feel a little nervous. He clocked her nerves.

"Just relax. You'll be fine."

"OK," she said, with no conviction whatsoever. This was a big deal. She tried to put her professional head on but that was proving difficult dressed as she was.

The car soon arrived, Zach and Amy got in the Lincoln Continental. Amy sat on the seat, wild-eyed at her situation once again. She checked her makeup in a compact mirror and glanced at Zach next to her. He was taking a selfie and posting it on Instagram. She contemplated her present reality. Had none of this happened, she would possibly have still been going tonight, under her own steam as a reporter, not in a dress like this, sat with someone as influential as him. She watched Zach as he posted his photo with a comment, and felt her phone buzz as it was notifying her of his post. At one time, she would have jumped to see it, as a fan, but she made no such movement now, she was capturing it all live, real, here with him, such as she was. She smiled benignly and sat back in her seat. She felt a little dazed by it all. Zach's hand touched her leg.

"OK?" he said, smiling at her.

"Yes." She picked up her phone to make some notes to formulate for her article. The car set off on the half-hour or so journey from Zach's house to the theatre where the ceremony was being held. Amy kept herself in the clear and present, despite feeling that this was all part of some dream she was having, and she would wake in her bed back home at any moment.

The car stopped and she was faced with something that any girl could fantasise about, stepping out of a limousine onto a red carpet. She tried to relish, savour the moments, from the chauffeur opening her door and lending a hand to help her out, to the cameras and people waiting outside poised and looking her way, seeing she was unknown and not looking twice at her. She glanced at the press pack – she could so easily have been the other side of the barrier there with them. How differently her article would be angled to theirs. She had ideas already and did not care what Paul thought; this was going to be her edge.

Zach got out behind her and quickly gripped her hand tightly. Now the interest in them began. The cameras flashed and he was being called by several people waiting along the walkway to the entrance of the building. He was unfazed, this was all stuff he had faced many times before. Amy followed his lead and smiled as naturally as she could. They stood and posed for the gaggle of cameras; Amy did her best, having briefly looked at the way the stars posed on the red carpet, feigning to project as much confidence as she could muster. Zach had placed a protective arm around her waist, smiled and did his trademark two fingers in a V-sign to the photographers.

"Zach! What's your new girlfriend's name?" One of them yelled.

"Amy," he replied, simply.

"Give her a kiss, Zach!" another called. Amy felt embarrassed, *he wouldn't want to do that*, she thought. Therefore, he caught her unawares as he turned towards her and planted a kiss square on her lips. She managed to close her eyes and not look too taken aback, as many flash bulbs went off to catch the money shot.

"How are your wrists?" One called. "How did you hurt them?" There were a few sniggers, but Zach completely blanked the comments and they walked down the line. Amy breathed a sigh of relief that he did not seem to react to them.

There were other famous faces there, milling around, talking and posing for pictures and interviews. They all looked utterly glamourous and Amy felt she was not outstanding at all, in fact she blended in, and perhaps more, paled into insignificance. She was an anonymous face, dressed up and on the arm of someone far more important. She did enjoy being in the same sphere as some of the people she admired; she could walk past them and feel that she was one amongst them. Some of them were shorter than she had imagined in real life, others not so good-looking up close. This amused her and she smiled to herself. Zach glanced at her, saw her smile, which satisfied him she was OK, but his gaze remained with her for a moment – if it wasn't so crowded and such a hubbub of noise, he would have been curious to know what had amused her so. She was never one to take things – especially herself – seriously and she had been particularly quiet in the car. Much as these evenings were a necessary part of a career in this industry, they were sycophantic at best, two-faced at worst.

Several very famous people stopped Zach, as they walked along the red carpet, to greet him and ask him how he was, and to mention hooking up to maybe write some music together again. All the while the cameras were snapping, Amy stayed out of the way for some of the pictures, and most of those people completely ignored her presence at Zach's side. One, however, a well-known singer-songwriter from Britain, came over and spoke to Zach, giving him a big hug.

"Hey, man, good to see you," he said to Zach. Amy loved his music and her eyes lit up at the sight of him. She grinned and he noticed her.

"Hi," Tom said.

"Hey, Tom," Zach said, grabbing his hand to shake, and patting him on the back.

"Are you going to introduce me?" Tom was looking at Amy, smiling.

"Sure – Tom, this is Amy; Amy I'm sure you know this is Tom Murphy." Tom shook her hand.

"Hi. I just love your music, Tom, I'm a massive fan; I love your current album!" Amy gushed.

"She's a Brit, Zach!" he exclaimed with glee.

"Yeah." Zach laughed. "And a journalist, so watch your mouth," he warned. Amy shot him a look.

"I'm only a freelance music journalist, I'm no tabloid hack," she said, defensively, but Zach appeared to not be listening.

"How long you been with this guy?"

"Not long, a few weeks I guess."

"He's a great guy, for a Hollywood type I mean." Tom was renowned for being down to earth, even though his star had well and truly risen, and his music was explosively successful all over the world. Amy was pleased that this rumour about him appeared to be true and was appreciative of his attention to her.

"He is great."

"He loves Brits too, which means he has taste. We've spent a few recording sessions together. I remember him once telling me that he'd love to go out with a British girl, ever since this one time he met an air hostess he liked once, and regretted not getting her number, but he hadn't met the right one yet. I'm pleased to see he has found someone great!"

Amy looked at him and smiled. She debated briefly whether to tell him the truth of the matter. Zach had been collared by some young presenter of some sort with a microphone, so was not party to their conversation.

"I *am* that air hostess. We met on a flight briefly about two years ago. Then I happened to fill in for someone doing an interview for *Delta* magazine and we just hit it off."

"You obviously made an impression! I read *Delta* a fair bit. It's a good mag."

"Yes, I need to get an article done from tonight."

"Well, you can say you spoke to me and I'm working on some new material, should have something out in the next two weeks. There you go, exclusive right there," Tom said.

"Wow, that's really kind of you, I don't know what to say!"

"Got to help someone from Blighty, there's not many of us at this particular awards."

In the meantime, Zach had finished his brief interview and had walked back over to them, to see Amy and Tom talking animatedly. He did not look best pleased.

"Thank you, Tom, I hope you have a good night, and I hope you win."

"Thanks Amy, enjoy the night. Later, Zach," he said, tapping Zach on the arm.

"See ya, Tom," Zach said.

"I'm sorry, we got talking." Amy picked up on his frostiness, assuming he was jealous.

"Oh, Tom is a great guy. Me, I get probed about these damned wrist photos. I managed to brush it off." He fell silent, but still smiled as they neared the doors. Amy felt it best she stayed quiet and smiled sweetly. As they entered, they were handed a goody bag each. Amy had heard about these luxury goody bags and the sort of things they contained, but dare not take a peek, to appear too keen.

They made their way to their seats in the auditorium, about eight rows from the front, not far from where Olivia Sanchez was seated, who looked back and waved at Zach with a more genuine smile than the one she had given Amy when they passed in the hallway of the hotel less than two months ago. He gave her the thumbs up.

The evening passed in a slow way, but it intrigued Amy to be there all the same. She watched as the famous faces seated in front of her rose to either present awards, perform or receive awards. Some used their acceptance speech as a forum to put across political views, others to try to be as cool as possible by saying very little. The time came for the People's Choice Best Song award – this was the award Zach was involved in as it was Olivia Sanchez's song that was one of the nominations. Tom Murphy was also nominated in this category, amongst many others, having won several on the night.

The winner was announced: it went to Olivia Sanchez. Zach, plus Olivia and a team of people rose, to applause. Tom shook Zach's hand as he passed him and went to the stage to accept the award. Zach stayed in the background, but Amy had to own that it was a huge turn on that the guy she was sleeping with was up there. Having tried so hard not to get caught up and blinded by the big lights of Hollywood and the fame, the money, the lifestyle, she found that the memories of Will, of their intimate knowledge of each other, were fading into insignificance compared to this. Did it even matter that she probably wasn't in love with Zach? He glanced down at her and winked. Amy felt her phone buzz and discreetly opened her bag to check it – it was a text from Beth.

Ha ha – I saw you on TV when Zach got up to accept the award! You look amazing. Own the night. Forget everything else RN. L U Beth & Izzy xxxx

Thanks, lovely. Quite an experience anyway! I chatted to Tom Murphy a bit – bet ur well jel!!

Oh, Bitch – I love him! Is he as nice as he seems?

Lovely. Really down to earth. Zach got awks Qs about wrists

Don't worry, it'll blow over. Smart move him taking u 2nite, makes u two credible to the press don't u think?

Yes, ur right. Speak to u tmrw xx

By this time, Zach had returned to his seat and he kissed Amy as he sat down.

"Congratulations, you. Hashtag goals!" She began thinking about getting him home again. The beast inside her was awake and needed feeding. "Wait till I get you home," she said, quietly.

He smiled. "Let's go as soon as possible."

***

Zach had many invites to after-parties when the ceremony was over. He declined most of them – he only had eyes for Amy and what they might get up to when they were alone together. The time came for some official photos with the award gong and Amy stayed well out of the way. He posed with Olivia and the production team, and Olivia implored him to join her at the party she was going to at The Gravity Club just off the Sunset Strip. He spoke to Amy.

"What do you think? I'll do what you want to do."

Amy was desperate to go to an after-party; she was also keen to get Zach home and do all sorts of things to him. "Shall we just go for an hour or so? Seems a bit mean to not join the celebrations."

"OK. Rad." They got in their limo and it took them to the club, which was halfway to Zach's place anyway. The place was buzzing already by the time they got there, and Amy wished she had a more nightclub friendly dress on, but they entered… and the place was full of stars. Olivia was already there, so they headed to her table and Zach chatted to the guys. Amy looked around – there was literally no one she could talk to. Who would be relatable at a party like this? Someone handed her a glass of champagne; she turned and Olivia was there.

"So, you're Zach's new girlfriend, I assume?" she said to Amy over the loud music.

"Yes, I'm Amy." She instantly felt on guard.

"Have I seen you somewhere before?" Olivia ignored her introduction.

"Yes, we passed in the hallway of The Winchester a month or so ago."

"Right. Zach's a great guy." She looked at Amy. "Wouldn't want to see him hurt. Or taken advantage of."

Amy looked at her, affronted. "No. There's nothing worse than a girl that uses a guy to further herself." She could not help replying with a stern look at her, sipping her drink. Olivia turned and moved away. Zach looked back as he saw Olivia walk away with a disgruntled look on her face. He turned and looked at Amy who was standing by the table knocking the champagne back. He walked over to her.

"OK? Not causing trouble again, are you?" he reproved.

"You know me." She polished off the last dregs of her drink.

"That's what I'm afraid of," he said, into her ear.

"Nothing like a bit of fear to keep you on your toes." She looked at him and grabbed him suddenly, pulling him close.

"Just behave."

"Do you really mean that?"

He looked at her and smiled. "Till I get you home." He turned and talked to some more people. Amy knew she would have to find her own amusement at this place. The music was thumping and the dancefloor was half-full, so she made her way over to it. She joined in the dancing, this was where she felt she could relax and enjoy the night. Zach watched her move on the dancefloor and really let her hair down. He thought to join her, just as he saw Tom Murphy approach her. They greeted like long lost pals and chatted animatedly, as much as they could against the music. Tom had a girlfriend, Zach wasn't usually the jealous type, but something made him go over to the dancefloor to join Amy.

"Hi, Zach." Tom said. Then he spoke close to his ear. "She's lovely. A real keeper."

Zach smiled. "Do you think?"

Meanwhile, Amy was dancing away, every now and then glancing at the plethora of celebrities in the club. Zach moved over to her and kissed her neck. She smiled and turned to him. They danced for a while then went back to the table with Tom and his girlfriend who had joined them in the meantime, also a British girl. Amy finally had someone to chat to she had things in common with.

"Shots?" Tom said.

"Go on then!" The four of them did a few tequila slammers and Zach was still drinking champagne. Amy had not really seen him very drunk, but tonight was going to be the night. He got very feely with her and was laughing and mucking about with Tom. After their third slammer, Amy was about ready to go home.

"Zach, I think we should go," she said discreetly in his ear.

"Thought you were a party animal?"

"Yeah, come on, Amy, the night is just beginning," Tom piped up.

"I wanna get out of this dress."

"She wants to fuck me," Zach slurred. Amy gave him a stern look.

"You better get home then, mate." Tom smiled and tapped him on the shoulder. "Or you won't be getting some." Tom kissed Amy, Amy kissed Tom's girlfriend goodbye, and they made their way through the club to the exit. There were a lot of photographers outside, and Amy held tight onto Zach's hand, concerned that he was in a state similar to the one she had been in the previous night.

They managed to stride past the flashing cameras to their car. They got in and the car drove away. The quiet hit Amy, the contrast to the club made her realise how much she had had to drink and her ears were ringing. Zach leaned across and kissed her, his tongue deep in her mouth, his hands all over her. They got back to his place quite quickly and made their way inside. Amy slid herself out of her dress. Zach's fingers were immediately pushing into her flesh and he pressed her up against the wall as they embraced. She flicked his jacket off, and it fell in a heap to the floor onto her dress.

He kissed her hard, but she stopped him and pulled him into the bedroom. He took his tie and his shirt off as he walked, kicking off his shoes. Amy took his hands and put them on the full-length mirror on the wardrobe above his head, as if he was being frisked. She stood behind him, kissing his back as she undid his trousers, and pushed them with his underwear so they dropped to the floor.

He watched in the mirror. She dug her nails into his backside, he flinched. She moved her hand around to his front, his hands slid down the mirror, but she pushed them back up. Amy grabbed her set of handcuffs out of her case and put them on his wrists, careful not to do them up too tight this time. She moved him back slightly so she could pleasure him with her mouth. He watched her in the mirror, the stimulation heightened by the novelty of the different visual experience, seeing what she was doing to him. She pulled away desperate to get on his body, and she took off her underwear; he dropped his handcuffed hands and tried in vain to touch her, but she pushed him backwards onto the bed. He laid back and she put his arms above his head, running her nails down his arms and chest, as she sat on top of him. He gasped; she was tight and dry, but not for long. She looked down at his body, such a turn on it was to her, sitting on him getting her rocks off.

When she had come, she undid his handcuffs so he could touch her body, and he knelt over her, laying on the bed, and flicked her legs up so they were hanging over his shoulders to go deeper inside her until he came too. He let her legs down and flopped onto the bed next to her, his arm draped over her body. He was quiet for a moment, then his breathing became heavier, as he seemed to have gone straight to sleep. Amy lifted herself out from beneath his arm, and looked at him for a moment. She touched his face. His small but perfectly formed mouth, nicely shaped jaw. She pulled the covers over him and went to get some water. She got into bed next to Zach and glanced at him again.

What an amazing few days she had had with him. The idea of waking up to find herself back in England in the arms of Will seemed at present to be a million miles away. Will. Her heart was pained when she thought of him. He would still be in Germany right now. She lay in the dark trying to work out the time difference from Los Angeles to Berlin when the light flashed on her phone. She grabbed it and saw a text message had come through. From Will. *Spooky.*

Hi you. Been thinking a lot. especially now, here, alone in another foreign hotel room. I'm sure you're having an amazing time out there, probably with Him, but if you think of me at all, consider this. I do not have his wealth, or talent, (or physique) but I do love you. And I know you love me. So, I will fight to keep you when you get home, if I haven't lost you to Hollywood already. Will xxx

She put her phone down and looked across at the fantasy made real next to her. She closed her eyes, turmoil engulfing her entirely again.

She dreamt she was drowning, sinking deeper into the abyss; hands touched her body and grabbed at her from all angles. She saw again the flash of camera bulbs, several at once, and holding on to Zach's hand, he turned towards her in the dream and morphed into Will, the red carpet, the gloss of the place, dissolved and she was in rainy London.

She awoke, soaking from sweat, her heart racing, her body trembling. There was a storm progressing outside, lightning was flashing and thunder rumbling through the hills, rain came beating down, a rarity in these parts. She leaned her legs off the bed to get up, but found herself very wobbly. She looked around the vast bedroom, but suddenly felt claustrophobic, stifled, surrounded by the memories of the last few days in this consumeristic town of dreams, both broken and realised. The place of image-obsession and wealth. Zach was not weaned on these ways, but he had certainly bought into the ethos, the culture. She got out of bed and rinsed her face in the bathroom. She looked at her reflection in the mirror, contemplating the evolution of her recent past; she had gone from a student on a shoestring with a hardworking boyfriend, to celebrity's WAG in a matter of months. Her life had suddenly lost its direction again and she felt the gyroscope of her emotional state spinning off its axis. She left the bathroom and headed to the kitchen to get a strong drink to knock her back to sleep. She found a bottle of not-too-expensive-looking Bourbon and poured herself a double. She knocked it back and poured another. She sat down and leaned against the cupboards. She held the glass to her head and began to feel sleepy. She sipped more and put it on the floor beside her, not seeing the bottom of the glass.

Seventeen

"Amy... Amy..." She heard the voice as if it was from a distance. She slowly opened her eyes and saw Zach's face close to hers; he was shaking her shoulder to wake her. Why did she ache so bad? Oh yes, she had fallen asleep on the wooden kitchen floor, bourbon bottle and glass extant beside her.

"What happened? How come you're here?" Zach looked concerned. Amy could barely speak; her mouth was so dry.

"I... had a bad dream in the night." She sat up, flicked her hair back and got up. Zach helped steady her on her feet. She did hurt so.

"Scared the shit out of me when I woke up and you were nowhere to be seen. I saw you slumped on the floor in here and I thought... well anyway, you're OK, that's all that matters." She looked at his face again, now she was more focused. He looked pasty and a lot more worried than she had first realised. She smiled to indicate that she was fine.

"I'm OK, really I am, I just ache from laying on the floor." She drew away from him and wandered back to the bedroom to freshen up. She looked back and he was following her. "I'm fine, Zach."

"I know. Kiss me," he said, catching her up and pulling her to him. She put her arms around his neck and kissed him softly on the lips. "OK, I can get on with the day now." He smiled at her. "I just love those lips. Especially when they're wrapped around my cock." She smiled and looked away.

"I love your neck. Especially when my legs are wrapped around it." She grabbed his crotch.

"Listen, I've got the guys coming in later, are you OK with that? Don't feel like you've got to go out. Get Beth and Isabella to come here for a swim or something."

"OK. I need to have a bit of time writing my article anyway."

"Oh? You still doing that?"

"I've got to pay rent. It'll go some way to covering that."

"I'll pay your rent, then you won't have to write it."

Amy held her hands up and walked away from him. "Whoa, whoa, whoa. We do not have that kind of relationship. Besides, why are you so anti me doing this?"

"It's just press crap."

"This is a legitimate music magazine. And I would have been writing the article anyway, had I gone with you or not, if that's what you're worried about." She put her bikini on and put some loose clothes over the top. She walked over to him. "You should trust me." She looked into his clear eyes.

"I do, I do. You're sure you're OK?"

"Yes, I am. I think the storm woke me."

"Storm?"

"Yes. You were too tequila-d up to be woken by it."

"We never have storms here."

"Well, you did last night."

"Weird. Anyway, I'll get breakfast, but the guys will be here soon. I'm sorry."

"Oh, please don't be. It's fine." She smiled and grabbed her phone to text Beth. Zach went back to the kitchen.

Hey Babe, come over for a swim with Izzy, Zach's in the studio with the guys. He suggested it xxx

She waited a moment for a response. Sure enough, a typical Beth-like response ensued.

Argh! Izzy just wet herself at this idea!

Amy smiled and another text landed.

Do I need to say yes, or do u get that?

Yeah, I got that lol. Come over in an hour or so.

An hour or so soon arrived and the Sovereign X band members – who had already arrived – seemed keen to see Amy and her two friends. She guessed Zach may have told them they were a couple. As they made their way out to the pool and all three stripped to their bikinis, she noticed faces at the window that disappeared when she made eye contact. She smiled, they were probably hoping to see Beth and Isabella make out.

And little wonder at their interest; Amy worked hard at keeping her figure trim, but Beth was slightly taller and more athletic and Isabella was slim with long legs – all in skimpy bikinis – cut a pretty landscape for six hot-blooded men to be curious about. Just as Amy sat on her lounger, she heard Zach's sliders head their way, a tray with three coffees on, in his hands.

"Hey!" he said cheerfully. He had mirrored sunglasses on, but Amy glanced up at him and deduced he was checking the three of them out.

She got up and grabbed a mug from the tray. "Thanks. Perv," she said, sotto voce, smiling a lopsided grin at him. He grinned back and waited for the other girls to grab their drinks before leaving them to it.

"Laters." He turned and went back to the house, swinging the tray as he went.

Beth sat on the end of Amy's lounger and sipped her drink; Isabella sat on the one next to her.

"So, fill us in on last night properly, then." Beth was eager.

Amy told them everything from the dress, to the limo, to meeting Tom Murphy and her rebuttal of Olivia Sanchez. "What an experience. Seriously. An eye-opener."

"Have you been online at all this morning?" Isabella said, gently.

"No I haven't actually. Why?"

"There are a lot of pictures. A lot of interest in you and who you are," Beth said. "You must remember, Amy, that you have bagged one of this town's most eligible bachelors. Not everyone is going to be overjoyed by some unknown Brit nabbing him." They were both looking at her. She grabbed her phone and scrolled through the pictures from the awards. There were several versions of the kiss shot. She was disappointed to see that her surprise did, in fact, come across in the picture. It looked like Zach was planting a kiss on someone much less enthusiastic than he was. Some of the tag-lines read things like: 'Zach

Hayes and new girlfriend, body language says they won't last.' And, 'At least try to look like you want to be on the red carpet – Zach Hayes shows off new girlfriend, British journalist Amy Armstrong, and ignores questions about restraint marks on wrists.' And, 'Songwriter, multi-instrumentalist and frontman of Sovereign X, Zach Hayes, collects award for penning Olivia Sanchez song with new girlfriend on his arm.'

"Wow. We've garnered plenty of interest." She continued to look through the pictures and brief anecdotes that accompanied them. Some less interested, some negative. Amy was thick-skinned; she knew the press enough to not take much notice of the interest, it would soon lose steam. But how could she pursue her article now with everyone knowing who she was? Did it even matter? She was more concerned about the effect all of this would have on Zach. And Will, for that matter.

"Are you OK?" Beth asked tentatively.

Amy looked at her. "You know, I am. I don't really care. They can say what they want. Zach is not a media darling anyway. We've made a big statement by going on the red carpet together. Like you said, Beth, it makes us credible. They'll soon lose interest I'm sure."

Beth and Isabella looked at each other. "Look, I'm just concerned for you. I know you want your career to be taken seriously, I just worry that it will all get swallowed up in a media furore and eclipsed by this relationship. I know you wouldn't want that."

"I just… I don't know what I want any more." Amy stared listlessly down at the still pool in front of them.

"That's not like you. You used to be so focused and driven," Beth said. "Has Hollywood gone to your head?" She tilted her head and looked at Amy.

Amy tutted. "Don't be ridiculous."

"I could understand if it has. Look around you, Beth." Isabella was in awe looking around the massive private garden. "Perfection. I'd do anything to keep hold of this if it were me." They fell silent.

"Right. For proving that Americans are superficial, you're in the drink." Beth got up suddenly and grabbed Isabella round the waist, who squealed and fought laughing, as Beth dove sideways into the pool with her. There was a massive splash and Amy laughed at their shenanigans. Beth resurfaced and pulled herself up slightly on the side of the pool.

"Come on, get in."

Amy got up and jumped in, much more daintily than their entrance. She swam a few laps while the others mucked about and exchanged kisses and hugs. Isabella swam a few laps under water and Beth swam over to Amy.

"Can you believe we go home the day after tomorrow?" She watched Isabella swim.

"I know. What a whirlwind it's been." Amy stared into space for a moment.

"And what's next for you and the two men in your life?"

Amy sighed a big sigh. "I think I will arrange to see Will when I get back, see how I feel."

"And your novelty fling? Has it worn off?" Beth smiled. "Is it ready to be *flung*?"

Amy looked at her. "Not really. All this doesn't help, does it? I mean, I'm not blinded by this Hollywood stuff, but it does cast a much more romantic, rose-tinted light on it all."

"And what about Zach? How does he feel about you?"

"You know, we never talk feelings. That's a failing. But I think he's pretty keen."

"You know, you have the guy on a string, or should I say handcuffs?" She grinned. "Keep him on that leash, and he'll be at your mercy forever more."

"Yes, but when the excitement of sex wears off, which it inevitably will, what am I left with? A relationship founded on what? My obsession with him."

"I think you underestimate yourself – *he* is obsessed with *you*."

"Do you think?"

"Yes, I do."

Amy had not considered Zach's feelings and this struck her. Beth was right. She had dominated him – something she had relished – and had made herself indispensable to him. She had been selfish, all this time considering her own position, and all the while Zach was getting in deeper emotionally. She got out of the pool and laid back on the lounger, thinking it all through. How did she really feel about Zach? Maybe she should just seize the day and go for it. She lay back in the perfect

California sunshine and slipped her sunglasses on. Beth soon flopped onto the lounger next to her. Amy glanced at her then glanced back at the palm trees towering above them.

"I think I'm gonna go for it with Zach," Amy said to the sky. Beth leaned herself up on her elbow.

"Are you?"

"We're practically in a relationship anyway. I shall still see Will when I get back – guess we'll have to end it properly." It pained her greatly to say these things out loud, having mulled it over so frequently of late.

"Wow. OK." Beth looked over to Isabella who had also just exited the pool. "You owe me twenty dollars." She pointed to her girlfriend.

"Shit," Isabella said, and produced a twenty dollar note from her purse, handing it begrudgingly to Beth. Amy watched with a mixture of disdain and amusement at the transaction passing before her, at her expense.

"*You bet against me and Will?*"

"You're upset about that, rather than the wager itself? What does that say?"

"Careful, I'll change my mind just to spite you and you'll have to pay your twenty dollars back to your girlfriend! I can't believe you two bet on me! What made you think I would choose Zach?"

Beth looked at her, eyes stifling a grin. "I thought you wouldn't be able to resist him when you came here."

"Well, just to say, I hate that I've proved you right. That really annoys me."

"Hmph. Well, I'm always right."

"So, tell me, will it last between me and Zach then, if you're always right?"

"Hmm. I think that is going to depend on *you*."

"So you say. You think he's more obsessed with me than I am with him."

"I do." Beth nodded and lay back on her lounger, having put her twenty dollar note in her bag. Isabella went back to the pool.

"What about you, how's your love life doing? Looks like it's hunky dory."

"Definitely. More *Dory* than Hunky." Beth and Amy laughed at the connotation.

"So, you gonna move to the Golden State?"

"Maybe. I love her so much. We'll see. I'm not making any concrete plans till we know where her career is going."

"We could both end up other-halves to famous Americans."

"True!" Beth laid back on her arms and watched Isabella swimming. Amy's phone rang. It was Paul. Amy looked at it ringing for a moment before answering hesitantly.

"Hello."

"Hey, gorgeous."

"Inappropriate as always. Must be middle of the night over there."

"It's late. Got some lovely pictures here in front of me: Zach Hayes and his new girlfriend, allegedly. Care to comment?"

"Why, am I on the record?" At Amy's comment, Beth looked over at her.

"That's up to you," Paul said, and paused for a response. "How's the article coming? Could do with it by close today."

"What photos are you going to run with it?"

"Well, that will depend on its content."

Amy was torn. Part of her would rather have written this article under a pseudonym, now that her relationship was public, but that also would not do her career any good.

"I don't want my private life entirely public property. And at the present, I'm losing that battle. I will only say this to you: yes, I am in a relationship with Zach, but that is all. If you need to confirm that, fine. What I did not appreciate was being papped on my own time with my friends when our relationship was still unknown."

"And you had your ex-boyfriend to consider. I know. News is news however, and the paps always find a way. If you're going to enter into a high-profile situation you need to develop a thick skin."

"So, you sent that photographer chasing us to teach me a lesson? That pap was definitely tipped off." She called him on it.

"Maybe. Maybe not. Ways and means, Amy, ways and means." Paul was evasive.

"Well, we were not impressed. Caused me to have an awkward conversation, I can tell you. Do it again and I'm through."

Paul laughed lightly and sighed. "Yes. Well, now you know the interest in you both. Get me my article by tomorrow morning your time. I'm sure you'll put a kitsch, Amy-style slant on it that will melt my stone heart and make me fall in love with you all over again."

"Creep. Flattery will get you everywhere." She spoke partly tongue in cheek, partly charmed by his brazen conceit. "I'll email you later."

"Be sure that you do. When you back, by the way?"

"Tomorrow night. Or the following morning. I haven't checked with the flight and time difference."

"Well, safe flight. Stop by the office next week. Try and get a scoop."

"Stop it! Bye!" Amy put her phone on the table and heaved a big sigh.

"Let me guess – Paul," Beth said, without looking across to Amy.

"Yep. Wanker."

"He's another bloke under your spell." Beth was matter-of-fact.

"Oh, would you stop? I'm not some witch, going around giving guys love potions. I think you over-estimate my feminine prowess."

"I really don't. It takes a girl who's into girls to know these things."

"You know jack about blokes though."

"I don't need to – I can see the sex appeal. You ooze it."

"Oh, fuck off." Amy batted a dismissive hand towards Beth.

"See, and that adds to the attraction, that down to earth, I-don't-see-my-own-appeal attitude. It's irresistible. To men. And women for that matter. Izzy said she'd shag you any day of the week. With a little too much enthusiasm, I might add. I'm glad you're straight."

Amy couldn't help laughing at this. "Really?"

"Yes. And I know you – a fiend in the sack, right? I've seen the way Zach looks at you, and Will before him. They can't wait to get you alone. You're a very sexual person."

"Ha ha!" Amy laughed out loud. "I guess you're right. I love it. But you know it was all Will. He was the experimenter."

"Yes, I see that much. But we all learn our expertise in whatever, from someone, in the first place."

"And for you it was… Jodie in year twelve." They said the last bit together in stereo, Beth's first lesbian encounter being a much-covered subject by them both.

"So, where are you with your article and your life after Hollywood?"

"My article will be done today. My life after Hollywood? I don't know. I might feel different when I get back to Blighty. But I have this… this itch for him, for Zach. No amount of scratching seems to satisfy it. It may all blow away in the wind, who knows. But what's done is done. I think I need to be a bit more laissez-faire about it all."

"Well, fuck a duck, I agree. Now get in the pool, bitch!" Beth shot up and dove head first into the pool. Amy smiled and followed.

Eighteen

Beth and Isabella left just before lunch, both giggly and not wanting to outstay their welcome at what they had jokingly through the day referred to as the 'rockstar's house', part serious, part tongue in cheek to wind Amy up. She refused to bite though, just laughing it all off. The band members all poked their heads through the door of the studio when they took their leave, and grinned at the girls as they went through the front door.

Amy slipped away into Zach's bedroom as quick as she could so as not to be in the way. She closed the door and took up her laptop to write her article. It was finished within an hour and a half and she was happy as she re-read her take on the night, sure to mention the nuggets from Tom Murphy, who was arguably a bigger scoop than Zach, particularly her side of the pond. She lay on the bed, after emailing the article to Paul.

She tossed her laptop to one side and could just about hear the music being created next door. It truly was a special position to be in, and she listened carefully through the sound-deadened walls, to hear Zach's vocal. Sure enough, it came and she closed her eyes. All those times she had lain on her own bed with her headphones full bore, eyes closed listening to their music, envisaging his face. And here she was in the next room. Her hand travelled down her own body and she sighed.

She grabbed her phone and took off her clothes. She took a naked selfie and sent it to Zach with the invisible ink feature on the iPhone; meant surely for this sort of message. She lay on the bed, hardly able to stifle a giggle at her naughtiness. She tossed the phone to one side; it landed with a slide across the laptop. Within moments, the music next door had halted and a message came through to her phone.

Do not move. I want u just like that... shit. I'm coming...

She could not help herself responding –

Well don't waste it, get ur arse in here right now.

In middle of recording…

And he sent about ten eggplant emoji. Amy loved this, the not wanting to, but wanting to. So, she replied with:

Can't wait to have that in me.

With several tongue emoji.

Within ten minutes, she heard the guys disembark from the room and bid their goodbyes to Zach. She began to feel a bit guilty at her selfishness, wanting Zach to herself – he had said that they were due to be in the studio all day, it was barely two o'clock. She lay there all the same, naked, draping herself provocatively half in covers, half out, scrolling, or pretending to scroll, through the social media on her phone. She heard the front door close and silence. Zach's footsteps came at almost a run towards the shut door of the bedroom and he burst through with an urgency unrivalled.

Amy did not look away from her phone. There was a tension released in her from deciding to go for it with Zach, that made her feel more at ease, more relaxed. She wondered if it would affect the balance of power in their relationship. She hoped not, it worked for her in its present guise. She pondered on this for a moment before closing her eyes as she felt Zach's hands on her legs, then his lips. He pressed his fingertips into the skin of her exposed thigh and sighed.

"So sexy…" he breathed. She smiled and rolled onto her back to face him. He was crouched over her on all fours and she pulled at his top; he lifted his arms as she slipped it off. He leaned in to kiss her and she pulled away not allowing him to. Instead, she bit at his neck. She pulled back and tugged at his trousers, undoing them with her hands, slipping them down with her toes. He looked down at her.

"When you text me… no, when I left you at the pool in your bikini… I haven't stopped wanting to get you… you just keep me wanting more, all the time. You're gonna be my downfall, Amy. My song-writing is at its best but most distracted for ages. What a paradox."

Amy listened to what he said, but now was the time for sex not talk. Talk could happen later. "Shut up and fuck me." She looked at him seductively through her half-shut lashes. Her hands were directive on his hips and he obeyed his orders.

***

She lay next to him and wiped her brow before looking at him and mopping his considerably sweatier brow. They lay still in post-coital chill for some time. Then Amy leaned her arms across his chest and rested her chin on them. She looked at him with a small contented grin on her face.

"What?" He had curiosity on his.

Her smile widened. "I don't know." She put her head on his chest and could hear his heart rate, still fast, beneath.

"No, tell me, there's something on your mind."

"Well… a couple of things. Beth made me laugh earlier. She thinks I put something like a spell on guys and they can't get enough, or something." She petered out almost dismissive, not wanting him to think she was being big-headed .

"Ah, is that what it is? Black magic? I had been wondering myself." He grinned. She lifted her head up and leaned on him again.

"Are you under my spell then?" She continued the analogy.

He looked at her in earnest. "Yes. Completely. Just wish I could put you under the same spell and stop you thinking of the past. I know that's what upset you last night, I'm not stupid."

By the past, Amy knew he was referring to Will. She took a deep breath and resolved to tell him what she had told Beth.

"I want us to make a go of it, Zach." She pushed the words to tumble out of her mouth. With each one, she felt the memory of Will and their love dissolve a little bit. It was not a comfortable feeling. It unnerved her, but her resolve was steadfast.

His eyes had new sparkle, he smiled broadly. "So… I've no need to fear Will in the background any more?"

She hesitated, but covered it with a stroke of his cheek. "No."

His arms curled around her body and he kissed her so fully on the lips she thought he would take her breath away.

"Back in a sec." Zach suddenly jumped up, nearly knocking Amy over. He grabbed his boxer shorts, slung them on and darted out of the room. He was gone a good twenty minutes and when he returned he had a pot of cookie dough ice cream in his hand and two spoons.

He was gone quite a while to just have been getting a pot of ice cream... He gave her a spoon. She dipped into it; soft, creamy, fluid. She licked it off the spoon and looked at him, still just in his boxers, his spoon sank into the oozy pot and he put a large mouthful past his lips. She made eye contact.

"How erotic is this?" she said, slipping her spoon into his pot once again. She pushed the spoon deeper; he watched her do this, withdrawing the spoon, moving closer to him to put the spoon directly into her pursed mouth and suck the creamy liquid off. He bit his bottom lip as she did this, maintaining eye contact at all times. His eyes drooped slightly as he became aroused and fidgeted where he was sitting. Amy took the pot of ice cream from him and he lay back waiting for her to do whatever she was going to do. He watched her all the time, his body temperature rising. She sat astride his legs and dipped her spoon into the pot again slowly. He lay waiting, his body writhing under her. She took a slow mouthful, letting the cold, creamy residue drip off her lip onto his chest. She put her spoon down and pulled his boxers down. She dipped her fingers in the ice cream pot and smeared some of it onto him. He gasped as the cold hit this, his hottest of body parts, especially just now, but he groaned with pleasure – he knew what would surely happen next – but she paused to add to the arousal, putting her fingers into the pot again, this time putting a lump of ice cream in her mouth and holding it there, making her mouth so cold. He lifted his head to look at her, waiting, wanting, and sure enough her tongue and mouth engulfed him, ice-cold, making him gasp once more at this new sensation, as she licked every bit off. She felt her own arousal kick in and did the same again to him before covering her fingers with more, wiping it on and in herself, before thrusting the same fingers into his mouth, which he took with pleasure. He sat up and leaned her back to lick the rest...

***

She lay back next to him on the bed quite tired now, a morning in the sun, sex twice in an hour, in the middle of the day. She mused silently on how this was no normal life. Back home on a week day like this she would be working. In the rain. She also mused on how less complex Zach's needs were in comparison to Will's. Will needed lots of foreplay and games to get off; Zach seemed content to just roll with whatever Amy wanted to do. But maybe all this was still the honeymoon period. It left her feeling apprehensive.

Zach seemed worn out too. He lay breathless for a while. Amy thought he may nod off, but suddenly he perked up and sat up. He looked back at her smiling. "Get dressed. We're going out. Pack some overnight things." He got up and dressed. He disappeared into the en suite before she could ask questions. He came back some moments later with a sports holdall. Amy chucked a few things in and stared at him for a moment. She had no idea what scheme he had in mind.

"Just don't ask questions," he said, noticing her looks.

"Zach, you know I'm on Beth's flight tomorrow night."

"Don't worry about it." He drawled. Within about an hour they were freshened up and ready, and a taxi pulled up outside the gates to his house. They jumped in and it took them to Van Nuys, a much smaller, less commercial airport than LAX. She was intrigued at what he had managed to pull together, at such short notice. They went into the airport – Amy had never been to it before. It was mainly set up for private flights, she guessed, and they made their way to a charter gate. He led her down the tunnel and out onto a quiet part of the runway where a Bombardier Challenger was waiting with its steps down. Amy looked at Zach, her mouth agape.

"Seriously?"

He nodded. "We're going to dinner back where I come from."

She knew he was from Colorado, as any die-hard fan would. A three-hour flight away. She went up the steps, Zach a few paces behind speaking to the crew before boarding behind her. She was lost for words. He chucked their bag on a seat and went over to her.

She barely moved. She had flown hundreds, probably thousands of times, on different planes, but never something like this.

"This... isn't... yours?"

He chuckled. "Shit, no! I called in a favour."

She noted the embroidered initials on the seats – it was easy to guess who they might belong to.

"Is this...?" She started. "You know, I don't need to know. It'll put me on edge that I might damage something." He smiled without looking at her and sat in a seat. He patted the one next to him, so she sat and fastened her seatbelt. She was looking all around the plane still taking it all in.

"Welcome Mr Hayes and Miss Armstrong." The pilot's voice spoke to them. "We're cleared for take-off in twenty minutes; wind speed running north-easterly, so we should make Centennial Airport, Denver in good time, hopefully before seven p.m."

Before take-off, Amy took a selfie of her and Zach, then sat back as the small jet taxied. The plane's engines roared and before she knew it, they were in the air. She looked out of the window, the sun was just beginning to show signs of wanting to begin its departure from the sky and the surround had a beautiful glow. They flew over downtown LA and they both looked out of the window at the amazing views. She was mesmerised for a moment before Zach turned her head to him and kissed her. He looked into her eyes.

"Don't go tomorrow. Stay a couple more days."

"I don't know. I'd have to try to get on another flight... speak to Beth... then there's work..."

"Stop making excuses. Come on. My manager will sort a flight out for you. He does ours all the time."

"I don't want to put anyone out."

"You'd be putting me out – in the cold – if you don't stay. Just till our tour starts next week. I won't have much time then."

"OK. I'll see what I can do." She relented. Zach poured her a drink from the bar when they were at cruising altitude.

"Happy glass." She always said this instead of cheers.

He chuckled. "Well, that's a new one on me. Happy glass." He clinked hers.

The plane travelled over more barren landscape before the lights of Las Vegas were just visible. Amy peered through the window again at the spectacle beneath.

In just over three hours, Denver came into view, just beyond the beautiful stretch of Rockies that it resided next to. Amy was pleased with what she saw. She had never flown or been to this city before, or Colorado at all for that matter. Much greener than California, and she loved the mountains. Yes, this was more her sort of place – mountain biking and skiing rather than sunshine and celebrities.

"You like?"

"I do."

Nineteen

They landed smoothly and Zach got a taxi sorted to take them across the city to his house. The car took them through town to an upmarket area, along a neat and private, tree-lined avenue with large gated properties hidden from the road. They pulled up to large wooden gates at the end of the avenue, Zach paid the cab and they got out with their small bag. He pointed a key fob remote at the gates as the cab pulled away, and as the gates slowly parted, Zach took Amy's hand. The house came into view. It was a large property, seemed bigger than the Beverly Hills villa, and much more traditionally constructed: brick walls, two-storey, pseudo-period design, with pillars standing sentry either side of the front door. It was a property that would not have looked out of place in Sevenoaks or Weybridge. As Zach opened the front door and put a lengthy code into the alarm, he switched the lights on. Oak dominated the hall, from panelling to the beautifully polished floor. Steps led down to a lounge with smart Chesterfield sofas and Amy was struck with a much more cosy, old-world feel to the place. It felt homely. Zach led the way to the kitchen, which was ultra-modern. There seemed to be doors everywhere leading in any direction, so Amy stayed close to Zach, not wanting to get lost in this enormous mansion.

"I'm sure I've got a decent bottle of red here somewhere. My mom normally checks in to make sure I'm stocked up with all sorts of things. Ah, here it is." He produced a bottle and two large glasses with fine stems. He filled them both and handed Amy one, for the first time catching her expression and reaction. "Amy." He diverted her from her awe. "This is my place."

"It's lovely, Zach. Truly lovely. It's a wonder you're not here more."

"Oh, I get here a lot. But my work dictates that LA is more convenient. And that's no hardship really, let's be honest."

"I guess. I like this though. Denver looks a great city."

"One day when no one wants my songs any more, maybe I'll come back for good." He said it so devil-may-care, she wondered if there was any truth in it.

"That will be a decision you make, not the populous, the no-more-songs thing."

"Maybe. Maybe one day I'll have had enough. Or maybe anyone that wants me must come here, and I'll just sit in my studio and get fat."

"I don't think so. Mr Adrenalin Junkie."

"Oh, I guess I'll still ski. And run. What gets your adrenalin pumping?"

She looked at him, sipping her wine. "I think you know what."

He gave her a wry smile. "What about sports?"

"OK, running is my thing. And I really love tennis. It's funny, these seem like parts of a conversation we should have had some time ago." She smiled.

"I know. I think we just got off to a strange start. Nothing was normal about it, was it, random meetings, interviews, hotels…"

"Clandestine trysts behind my boyfriend's back." Amy sipped her drink again but struggled to suppress a shudder at the thought of her behaviour.

"Are you going to see him when you get back?" Zach asked tentatively. He seemed edgy about her response and she wondered if he had wanted to ask this question for a while.

"Yes. I need to. If nothing else, to sort out living arrangements." Amy did not particularly wish to discuss with him (the reason for their break-up) all the finer details. Will lived at her place and had sub-let his flat. He would effectively be losing the roof over his head *and* his girlfriend if it was finished for good. She couldn't bear that double whammy of grief for him. Not that he did not have the means to get a place sorted; Will earned good money. Though it was good money by ordinary people's definition; in comparison to this lifestyle, it seemed a world away.

Zach fell quiet and Amy was happy not to discuss it any further. She drained her glass and placed it on the counter.

"Right. I've made a reservation; we need to leave in half hour, is that OK?"

"Yep, great – can I change and freshen up somewhere?"

"Sure, I'll show you around." He took her through the hall downstairs and showed her some of the rooms and his studio before leading the way upstairs along the galleried landing to the master bedroom.

Zach went into the dressing room and came out moments later with a new top; Amy changed into an outfit suitable for a meal out. They made their way downstairs and through the front door to the garages. He opened one of the double doors, revealing a custom 4×4. They got in and he drove into town. They parked outside a proper all-American-looking restaurant, all steaks and burgers and dry rub, and they went inside. They made their way to the bar to get drinks.

"Zach! Hey, man, how're you doing?" The bartender, a portly man of about sixty with a kind face, beamed a friendly smile and reached across the bar to shake Zach's hand.

"I'm good, man, how're you?"

"Great. Good to see you – how long are you back in town?"

"Oh, only a day." The bartender glanced at Amy standing at Zach's side. "Oh, Bill, this is Amy; Amy, this is Bill." She reached across to shake his hand too.

"Pleased to meet you," she said, her Home Counties accent conspicuous.

"Hi, Amy. The accent, Australian? British?"

Amy smiled, he obviously had not seen their recent press. "British," she replied.

"Hey, great! I love London, but we've also been to Wales – Snowdonia? Great place, lovely people, but way too much rain!"

Amy laughed. "Yes, that's an epidemic in Britain I'm afraid. I love Snowdonia too. Not quite the Rockies though."

"Epidemic rain! I like that. Living near the Rockies is great, we are blessed. So, you guys eating here tonight?"

"Yep," Zach said.

Bill handed them their drinks.

"Well, go through, Judy's round in the restaurant somewhere, she'll be delighted. Nice seeing you. Nice to meet you, Amy."

"See you later, Bill," Zach said and led the way through to the restaurant area. Amy noticed the place was relaxed; the atmosphere was lively, much like a gastro-pub back home. This was not a fancy place – she guessed it was all about the food – clearly owned by Bill and Judy, who, it seemed, had known Zach for a long time, certainly pre-fame, and treated him so... so normal. She was probably over-dressed, but that was something that never really bothered her – she did not mind standing out from the crowd, which was fortunate now she was dating someone well known. The restaurant was busy, and Judy came over to greet them.

"Zach!" She kissed him on the cheek. "Nice to see you! Your dad was in here just a couple days ago."

"Hey, Judy, how're you doing?" Zach said.

"I'm fine, as always. I see you won another award, congratulations!" Judy said, like a proud aunt.

"Thank you. Judy, this is Amy." She was standing slightly behind him and he moved so she could see her. Judy looked pleased and Amy smiled.

"Hello," she said quietly, as Judy smiled at her, in an appraising way.

"I saw you at those awards with our Zach, you looked beautiful in that blue dress." She seemed to approve, to Amy's relief.

"That's so kind, thank you. It was an amazing dress." Amy looked at Zach. She meant it as a compliment to him; after all, he had chosen it. He smiled in acknowledgement.

"It reached its potential on the person wearing it." Zach spoke quietly to her and they shared a smile. Judy observed all of this.

"Nice to meet you, Amy," she said, and showed them to their table in a quiet corner away from everyone. They sat down and looked at the menus. Zach started chatting animatedly at what the best things on the menu were. She looked at him and smiled. He seemed more relaxed, more down to earth here. Or maybe it was just her perception of him. She watched him and for the first time, she felt on a level with him; she was just a girl, he was just a guy, they were on an ordinary date, in an ordinary restaurant, with ordinary people around them, taking no notice of them.

Notwithstanding the massive compound they would be going back to tonight, and the fact that less than an hour ago they had arrived in the city by private jet. She put that and Hollywood, and his career, to the back of her mind and set herself to just enjoy his company: Zach, her boyfriend. She knew she would have to get used to a certain amount of interest, but she knew Zach had style and was clever not to let the media intrude on his life when he wasn't working. They ordered their meal and Zach steered the conversation more to getting to know her. They talked and talked and Amy began to forget the difference in their lives – the chasm between them seemed to be closing. She didn't even notice the Americanisms much any more, like his accent and terminology. It was starting to feel magical, like a holiday romance.

After they had eaten, they left and walked around town for a bit, arm in arm. He explained some of the places he'd known since he was a teenager, which was when he had moved to the area. They went into a bar for a drink, where there were more people that knew Zach – old high school acquaintances – and they greeted each other warmly. As they drank their drinks at the bar, Amy smiled at him.

"What?" His lips curled into a smile to match hers.

"Nothing," she said, looking away to sip her drink. His gaze stayed on her for a moment. Her eyes were brighter than usual and the dimmer light made her complexion glow. Her hair was more wavy tonight, from less attention, but it suited her. He had never been more attracted to her than right now. And he didn't know it, but she felt the same about him. For her, it was his attitude rather than looks – he was a different person, he had become very real to her. There was probably no design in whisking her here, away from Hollywood, other than an acknowledgement, an appreciation of her declaration of commitment to him being the prompt, but Amy could not help privately congratulating him on his smart move and its success. She looked at him again then leaned her head up to give him a slow lingering kiss on the lips. His small pert mouth gently pressed against hers; he reciprocated, putting his non-beer holding arm about her shoulders. There was a 'whoop' from the direction of his old school friends. Zach pulled away and smiled.

"C'mon, let's get back." They drank up and made their way to his car. The drive back was silent, but it was contented silence.

When they arrived, they had another glass of wine, but Amy was tired. *What a day.*

"I think I wanna call it a night." At this, Zach succumbed to a long yawn and nodded. "I just want to text Beth."

"OK. Ask her about staying, won't you? I'm going up. Don't be long." He kissed her and went upstairs.

"I won't."

Amy grabbed her phone and sat on the sofa in the lounge. She went into her messages and clicked 'Share My Location', sending it to Beth, and waiting for what she knew would be an immediate response. She giggled to herself in lieu of what Beth might say. Sure enough, a text landed nano-seconds later.

OK, so how did u get ur phone to put ur location as DENVER FFS?

I am, in fact, in Denver.

With Zach? Or did u 2 have a bust up? That's a monumental storm off if so!

Ha ha! Yeah it would be. U ready for this story?

Hell yeah!

He arranged a friend's private jet and no more than 4 hrs after u left, we were flying over Vegas! Just had dinner in town, back at his lovely house. Be back tmrw, but he's asking me to stay longer.

After this message, Amy's phone rang.
"Hiya."
"Hey you. Fucking hell, you really have had the Hollywood treatment while you've been here!"
"Ha, I know. But here seems different. *He's* different. I think I am starting to… you know."
"Well, stay then. Don't worry 'bout me. In fact, if you don't take my spare seat, Izzy will have it. She wants to try her luck in the West End, see if she can get some auditions. Might work out well."

"OK, that's settled then – I'll get myself on another flight, Izzy can take my place. What about visas and stuff at short notice?"

"She was sorted anyway, thinking about coming over, plus she's got dual nationality – her mum is from Scotland!"

"Great, well, I'll see you before you head back, catch up with you tomorrow."

"See ya then, Babe."

"Bye, Hun."

Amy ended the call and made her way upstairs to join Zach, who was listening to music on his headphones in bed, eyes closed. She undressed and got into bed next to him. He pulled one headphone away from his ear.

"OK, Honey?"

She liked him calling her that. And was pleased it was a different pet-name to the one Will had for her. "Yes, cool."

"Rad."

"Zach?"

"Yeah?"

"I'll stay a few more days." She smiled. His face broke into a wide smile and he took off his headphones and put them by the bed to give her a hug. She breathed in his scent and put her arms around him. She closed her eyes and felt herself drifting into sleep. His slower, deeper breathing indicated he was drifting off too. This would be the first time they had not had sex before going to sleep. They lay in this clench for most of the night before Amy found herself getting too hot and rolled away early in the morning.

She had strange dreams from then on: Will appeared – angry and heartbroken – then Zach appeared, begging her for sex. She found herself flying too fast on a private jet, then she was on a commercial flight, back in her flight attendant uniform, serving drinks, walking down the gangway. She saw the back of Will's head, as she had so many times before on the plane, but as he turned, it was Zach's face, smiling, but the plane was going too fast, through turbulence, then it all dissolved – darkness, thick engulfing darkness…

Amy shot bolt upright in bed with a sharp intake of breath, cold sweat over her whole body. Her breathing was shallow and short. She carefully got out of bed in the dark room and found her way, fumbling, into the bathroom – it was not in the same place as the one in Zach's LA house. She splashed cold water on her face and went back to bed. Why was she having such bad dreams lately? Was it just her conscience pricking her after what she had done? It did not sit well, cheating on Will, even despite all the allowances she had made for her actions.

Zach stirred as she got into bed next to him and he put his arm lazily across her, sleepily muttering, "OK?" She rubbed his arm in assent but lay staring into the large dark room. *Funny how creepy everything looks at night*. Something was filling her with a dread she could not explain and it unnerved her to know what it was; it was more than her situation, more sinister, she was certain. She was tempted to get up and get a strong drink to knock her back to sleep, but she resisted and tried to take comfort from the loving clasp of the man lying next to her.

Twenty

Zach woke first in the morning, his arm still draped over Amy. He noticed her skin was cold to touch, but clammy. He leaned up on one elbow to look closer at her and swept her hair away from her face; she looked paler than normal, but her beauty was enhanced by the pallor – it defined her features more starkly. She opened her eyes to be met with his, peering down at her.

"Hey, are you OK?"

"Yes. Just didn't have a good night." She rubbed her face. Some colour flooded it again.

"You feel sweaty."

"Just… bad dream." She yawned.

"Again?"

"Yeah." She glanced at him; he looked worried. She smiled and took his chin in her hand. "You're so sweet." She kissed him and got out of bed. He watched her naked form wander to the bathroom. She was dismissive to Zach, but she had not had bad dreams like this since her mother had passed away. Certainly, none while she was with Will. She pushed these feelings of foreboding out of her mind as she made her way towards the shower, turning it on and closing the door while the water heated up. Zach appeared behind her and pressed his body up against hers. He put his arms around her and kissed her neck. She accepted his advances, thinking some morning sex might just be the tonic she needed to pick her thoughts up. She opened the door and beckoned he follow her into the huge shower. As flesh pressed against flesh, Amy cleared her mind of all her negative thoughts.

***

Shortly after they had got dressed and had a coffee, Zach told her they had to get on the plane soon. They packed their things and ordered an

Uber. They got to the airport and had something to eat before making their way to the jet. Zach glanced at her and smiled as they boarded the plane. They sat down and Amy leaned over for a kiss.

"These twenty-four hours have been insane but amazing," she said. "Thank you."

"It was a bit mad. You make me want to do crazy things, like throw off a day. I just wanted to show you my other life before you go home. I know you have had a lot of thinking to do and I respect that."

"I think my thinking is over." Their eyes met. He smiled and grabbed her leg affectionately as the plane began its ascent into the air.

They touched down in LA just after two p.m. Amy wanted to head straight to Isabella's apartment to say goodbye to them both, so they got the cab to take them straight there. Amy wondered what Zach might think of the place where Isabella lived, but he never let on and followed her to the door. She buzzed, but there was no answer. She buzzed again, just as they heard shrill voices behind them down the street and turned to see both girls and Gizmo the dog bounding towards them.

"The jetsetters return!" Beth said, throwing her arms around Amy. "Hello you."

"Hello. I wanted to catch you before you go. Everything sorted for the flight?"

"Yep. Hi, Zach." Beth shook Zach's hand.

"Hey, Beth. Hey, Isabella."

"Hi." Isabella had a big beaming smile on her face, Gizmo jumping up at her.

Zach stroked the dog. "Listen, Isabella, I know a good acting agency. Not a big concern, but they might help you get somewhere. I'll call them and give them your details if you like?"

Isabella's jaw dropped and her face lit up. "Really? You could do that? That's fantastic! How can I thank you!"

"Tell your friend to tell her friend to move to the States?" He was part jesting, part serious.

"That is amazing, Zach, so kind of you, thank you." Beth kissed him on the cheek. Amy looked over to him and smiled proudly. She knew the extent of it being all about connections in this world and how influential he could be. She wondered if he had pre-planned this move, or whether he had done it on the spur of the moment, perhaps after having seen where she was living.

"Thank you," Amy said, quietly. He smiled at her.

"Hey, guys, dump your bag in my place and we can wander down to the beach again," Isabella said excitedly, opening the door. Amy looked uncertainly at Zach, but he unhesitatingly followed Isabella through the door and dropped his bag in her modest apartment. As they came back, Beth was struggling with the lead of the dopey dog. Isabella and Zach were chatting and fell into step in front of them; Amy was pleased as it gave her a chance to talk to Beth. They followed on after Beth had handed the lead to Isabella.

"So, you're taking her home? Gonna take her to see Mum and Dad?" Amy ventured, tongue in cheek.

Beth snorted derisively. "Yeah sure. That's just after they finally accept my lifestyle choice."

"They're OK with it."

"Hmph. Well they say they are, but I think if I bring a girl back, you'll be able to cut the air with a knife."

"You need to rip off the band aid. I could come with you. They love me." Amy smiled.

"Ha ha, yes, well they did. But I'm afraid they know about you leaving Will for Zach. My mum reads all the trashy mags; she rang me yesterday in utter shock, seeing you on the red carpet with Zach."

"Oh, shit. Maybe I won't come with you then! They don't hate me, do they? I love your mum and dad."

"No, they'll get over it. By the end of my conversation with Mum, she was almost impressed at your 'networking prowess' I think she called it. She's so bloody flaky, it's unreal."

Amy laughed. "I'm not networking." She watched Zach striding in front of her. He flicked his hair and glanced back at her. She smiled, so he smiled back. Beth observed it all.

She smiled at Amy. "Wow. What happened in the last twenty-four hours? I'm gonna call it 'the Denver effect' I think."

Amy laughed again. "I don't know. Something happened." They reached the beach and Isabella let Gizmo off his lead. He bounded through the waves and Beth joined Isabella, walking along the shore.

Zach fell back into step with Amy further up the sand. He put his arm around her.

"This is pleasant."

"Oh yes, very pleasant," he said, mocking her accent. She playfully tapped him on the chest.

"Stop taking the piss out of my accent! I so wish I could do a Yank accent." He squeezed her.

"Hey, less of the yank. Limey."

"Redneck." He stopped and began tickling her until she lost her footing and her legs buckled. They fell into the sand tickling each other. Amy yelled "Stop," laughing hard. He was on top of her looking down at her, his hair flopping forward. She looked into his eyes and smiled. He looked like he might say something, but didn't.

Instead he kissed her fully on the lips.

"Oi! Get a room!" Beth yelled as they approached them. Before they could get up from the sand, Gizmo had wandered over and shook himself next to them, soaking them. They got up fast and laughed.

"Gizmo! Naughty boy!" Isabella yelled at him and put him back on the lead. "I'm so sorry, guys."

Amy and Zach were arm in arm again, laughing still, sandy and wet. "It's OK," Amy said. Just then, Zach's phone rang.

"Excuse me." He pulled away from Amy and answered it.

Beth and Isabella sat down, so Amy sat next to them dusting herself off.

"We need to get back in a minute. We're all packed, but I've got to get into my uniform, and we have to get Gizmo to the dog-sitters."

"Sure. When Zach's finished, we'll make our way back."

"How much longer are you planning to stay for, Amy?" Isabella asked.

"I don't know, probably no more than three days – Zach has to rehearse for the tour after that."

Amy's attention was caught by the tone of Zach's voice just a few feet away – he seemed to be having a heated conversation. Beth caught it too, but tried not to listen, whereas Amy leaned in slightly to try to eavesdrop.

"... I don't care. I know that. Listen, I'm doing this and I don't care. Just get her a seat on a flight for Sunday to England. The next three days I'm incommunicado. That's it. I'll be there for rehearsals at the studio Monday morning. Speak to you later."

He re-joined the girls, Beth and Isabella got up. "We have to head back, Zach," Beth said.

"OK, cool." He had a darkened expression on his face but shifted it when he went back to Amy. She looked at him, concerned. Should she let on that she had heard most of his conversation, his part of it, at least?

"OK?" She looked at him as they walked back along the beach behind Beth and Isabella.

"Yep." He fell silent. They did not talk the rest of the walk back. He ordered an Uber before they turned into the block Isabella lived on. Amy hugged Beth and Isabella goodbye and felt quite sad that she would not have them here in this strange place. As they said their last few words of farewell, Zach had another phone call. He moved further away this time so Amy could not hear. Beth handed her their overnight bag from the apartment.

"You gonna be OK?"

"Absolutely," Amy said, smiling. The nature of Zach's phone call unnerved her. She did not want to be the cause of him being distracted from his career. He had obviously cleared his diary to be with her for the next few days.

"Yoko." Beth nudged her playfully on the side.

"Piss off," Amy said playfully back. They could joke, but it worried her.

"You two insult each other a lot considering you're best friends," Isabella said, bemused by their humour.

"Bless. Ignore her, she's an American." Beth leaned into Amy and patted Isabella on the arm, mock-condescendingly.

"Hey!" she said, but smiling. "Bye, Amy, lovely to meet you. Maybe we'll see you when you get home?" She hugged Amy.

"Yes, I expect to see you! Lovely to meet you too." Amy looked across at Beth who threw her arms around her. She suddenly felt very emotional.

"Oh, this is silly, I'll probably see you next week. Safe flight."

"Yep, and you. Enjoy these next few days; sounds like it's just going to be you two. You won't be able to sit down for a week from all the shagging you'll be doing," Beth said.

"Neither will he," Amy replied, smiling. She could always rely on their humour to break the tension of any situation.

"Err, too much information!" Beth hugged Amy tightly again.

"Our ride's here." Zach had returned. He said goodbye to both girls.

"Look after my Amy," Beth said, sternly.

"Oh, I will." He smiled. "I'll get that agency sorted."

"Thanks!" said Isabella. Amy and Zach got into the cab. Amy turned and waved as the girls waved them down the street, arm in arm. Amy felt tears in her eyes. Zach pulled her close to him.

"Just you and me for the next few days. Bliss." Amy looked at him and smiled through her tears.

"Yes." He interlocked her fingers in his and squeezed her hand. He kissed her on the head. Amy decided she could not rest until she had cleared up something that was bothering her. "I haven't caused a great big problem for you by staying more days, have I?"

"No, of course not! Plus, it's my bad – I asked you to stay."

This answer did not satisfy Amy. "Look, I don't want your bandmates or management, or whatever, thinking I'm taking you away from your music." She had an anxiety frown on her face.

Zach laughed. "You're adorable. And I love that you care like that, but honestly there's just a couple things I reorganised. Nothing important, I promise. I love my work too much to be intoxicated to that level by you."

"OK. And I really appreciate your help with Izzy's career. That will mean a lot to her and Beth."

"Well, I did it all for you. I hadn't planned it, but I saw the look of sympathy on your face when we turned up at that dive she lives in. I know too keenly what it's like to give up everything to follow your dream, even if that means slumming it and taking on shit jobs till you make it."

"And ten thousand hours of work, you can be an expert in anything." Amy knew this was a theory he believed in.

"It's weird how well you know me," he said, smiling.

They arrived back at Zach's house just after four and Amy was eyeing up the pool. They got into their swimwear and had a swim for an hour. Just after five, they ordered take-out pizzas and sat in front of a movie. Amy had been interested to see how she would feel now they were back in La-La Land; she found she felt the same as in Denver. She concluded that the inhibitions she had felt must have been all her own issues. Zach was Zach; he had not changed. He was the same live-wire, the same big personality that people gravitated towards. But he was also just a guy, a guy who was with her, Amy. Just Amy, a girl in the right place at the right time. But maybe they were meant to be together? Zach had said that very early on – destiny. And how many chance meetings had they had? Like the forces of nature or whatever you wanted to believe in had made them cross paths so many times. And yet there was still Will... and the fact that she wanted her career so bad. How would Paul react when she informed him she would not be back for a few more days? She had emailed her article and had not checked her messages since – her phone had been on airplane mode since just after her call to Beth last night. Perhaps she should just check.

She got up to go to the bathroom and checked her emails and messages. There was one voicemail from yesterday; she clicked onto it.

"Hi, Amy, it's Will. I've just arrived back from Germany. I guess you'll be back tomorrow night – I can pick you up from the airport if you like. Talk soon, bye." Amy closed her eyes and sighed. How to deal with this – she needed to call him and at least break it to him that she was not coming back when he thought. That would probably speak more volumes to him than anything else. That would be final. And it hurt her. She had decided to make a go of it with Zach, but she still loved Will so much. She would call him in the morning. But then, he might try to go to the airport anyway... No, she had to let him know, but it was two or three in the morning over in England. She decided she must text him.

Hi Babe, (should she still use that?) I'm just letting you know I'm not on Beth's flight, I'm taking another one on Sunday. We will meet up and talk when I get back. Sorry if this text wakes u, I know it's middle of the night back home. A xx

She read and re-read the message a few times before sending. She waited a moment, there was no response.

"Hurry up, Honey!" Zach called from the other room – he had paused the movie for her.

"Just a sec!" she yelled back, going into her emails. There were loads, notably one from Paul.

Amy,

Thanks for the article – tasteful and edgy writing as always. Great scoop on Tom Murphy – we're the first to get that nugget of gold. I'll let you off for not getting me much inside gossip, especially on a certain Mr H we both know you are intimate with, and I know he must be planning on working with some big names – he's so in demand after the Olivia Sanchez award.

Come into the office when you're back. I want to talk about a permanent position for you here. How does that sound? I want to pin you down before someone else grabs you.

Paul

She read and re-read the email. This was what she wanted. She questioned his morals at times and she did not like his occasionally unethical approach, but these were things you had to overlook in journalism. She had to be more sly if things with Zach were going to get serious and she was going to have a career as a music journalist. She was not blind to the conflict of interests. She knew she would have to put Zach's mind at rest. She did not want to lose this opportunity because of this relationship, surely Zach would understand that, with his high-level work ethic? She replied very simply.

Paul

Sounds good. I'm back Sunday, so I'll stop by the office Monday.

Amy.

She went back to the lounge buoyant. Zach noticed her altered attitude.

"You look happy – what exactly *were* you doing in there?" he said with a lopsided grin, obviously thinking naughty things. He had not noticed she had surreptitiously taken her phone with her.

"I've had a job offer." She sat next to him. He sat up and comically looked in the direction of the toilet.

"What?"

She waved her phone at him. "I was just checking my messages."

"So, I paused the movie for you to check your emails?" He was incredulous.

"Well, just while I went to the loo. I was multi-tasking – it's a girl thing."

He rolled his eyes. "What's the job then."

"*Delta* – they want me to permanently join the team."

"Reporter… for a music mag."

"Yes. I know you're not keen, but I can keep work and private life separate. I'm confident of that."

"Look, you gotta do what you gotta do. I just don't want us to clash over work – we're on opposite sides of the fence."

"I know. But I need this right now." She looked at him. He seemed calmer since they had displayed themselves as a couple at the awards, and more relaxed since Denver. He was sitting back on the sofa rotating the TV remote between his fingers. She licked her lips and climbed onto his lap. "You know what else I need right now?" She sat up, taking her top over her head and throwing it on the floor. He looked from the TV to her sitting on top of him. She unclipped her bra and he watched as she threw that on the floor too.

"What do you need right now?" he said rhetorically, touching her body.

"This." She undid his belt and slipped his trousers down.

Twenty-One

The next three days passed quickly. Amy was enjoying Zach's attention. When he was busy at times with his music, she was happy writing, or swimming. She even went out for a run – Zach told her a route he used. It was tough, quite hilly. She saw one or two of Zach's famous neighbours – an actress from a drama series she had liked and an American comedy actor she recognised but could not remember his name. She tried not to stare and was glad she had her darkest sunglasses on.

They went out sightseeing together one afternoon. Amy had done most things with Beth, but Zach wanted to do some of it with her; he had said it was a novelty doing the tourist thing in the city where he lived. She went grocery shopping with him – that felt so domesticated, like they were already living together. It was like their relationship had skipped several stages. She had to keep her head though, she was worried that was a vulnerable position to be in – they still had a lot of ground to make up. But she was enjoying the novelties of a new relationship, like stopping to have a kiss in the empty cereal aisle of the supermarket and sex several times a day. That had not dampened at all – she was still enjoying the games and dominance and Zach was loving it. He was distracted from his music, only a little, but with the intense nature of her stay with him, he seemed eager to spend as much time with her – and in her – as he could while she was still in the States. The band were going on a long nationwide tour, and it was unclear when they could catch up again. He would disappear into his studio for some time most days and she did her best to leave him to it when he went.

One of these times, on Amy's last full day, he had been in his studio for about two hours. Amy was sunbathing – it was a particularly hot sunny day – listening to her music and making some notes. A text came through to her phone.

Hey you. Sitting at my mixing desk, all I can think about is u in that bikini. Can I take it off with my teeth?

She grinned and glanced over at Ken, the gardener, as he trimmed the bushes, imagining what his reaction would be if Zach came out now and tried to do that. It made her giggle.

U're supposed to be writing! and so am I. Plus, wd prob give Ken a cardiac arrest, I don't want that on my rap sheet. Why don't u go over to Jake's if ur struggling to concentrate with me here?

And leave Ken to enjoy the view? No way. Besides u leave tmrw. Gonna miss u

U too. I don't know why but i keep thinking about biting ur arse.

Only if I can bite yours

OK, serious Ladywood now. Good job Ken can't see what we're texting each other lol

Good job ur Ladywood is not obvious to those around like when a guy gets wood.

Have u? Got wood, I mean?

Talk dirty some more

So... we haven't used my handcuffs much, do it to me... Handcuff me, gag me and blindfold me, then put ur cock in me really hard...

Ur so naughty, I love it.

Has Ken fucked off yet?

Amy looked around, the gardener was nowhere to be seen.

I think so

She was just texting this, lying on her belly, when a shadow appeared over her. Zach was there, his shorts protruding next to her. He was smiling down at her and she rolled onto her back and put her hand up to her forehead to shield her eyes from the sun to be able to look at him properly.

"Look what you've done to me." He pointed unnecessarily at his crotch.

"Shall we do something about that?" she responded in an official-sounding way. He leaned over to kiss her, wrapping her legs around his body. He picked her up, and still kissing her hard, he walked back to the house, carrying her to the bedroom. He threw her on the bed and took her bikini bottoms between his teeth, pulling them down as best he could. His mouth was all over her and she rolled onto her front and up into all fours, flicking her bikini top off in a flash.

"Spank me, Zach." He tapped her on the bottom. "No, harder."

"Seriously?" He was hesitant.

"Yes. Go on, do it." He hit her hard and she recoiled.

"Sorry, was that too hard?"

"You're not supposed to say sorry!" She laughed. "Now, bite me. Hard."

He sank his teeth into her and she whimpered, but pleasurably, feeling his breath on her skin. He did it again.

"Pain gets the blood pumping, heightening the intensity of the pleasure." She got up. "Let me do it to you."

"I'm not sure, now – don't be too rough with me," he said, dropping his shorts.

"I want you to have a strong memory of me when I go tomorrow, something that will stay with you on your lonely nights on tour." She kissed him on the lips, biting his bottom lip gently as she pulled away. She got him to bend over and spanked him hard. Then she sank her teeth into his rump. He flinched, so she pulled away and ran her fingers in a feather-light touch down his back and bottom as a contrast. He turned around and grabbed her wrists tightly, laying her down on the bed – the rough play had charged him up; he was desperate for her now. He held her wrists wide and pressed them into the bed.

She looked at him, fire in her eyes. "What are you gonna do to me?" From her position of seeming submission, but he was under her control, he would do what she had given him instructions to do. She lifted her head to him. She whispered, close to his ear. "Let's do stuff we both remember for ages."

***

Afterwards, they both lay on the bed, spooned, getting their breath back. He put his arm across hers and traced patterns over her fingers. She reached her hand back and rubbed his thigh, tucked in behind her own.

"When can I see you again?" His voice was part muffled in the pillow.

"You tell me. Have you any free time in the tour?"

"No more than two days together." They both fell silent.

"We'll find a way," Amy said, optimistically. She wasn't sure she believed it herself though. "It will be our first true test."

"Well, second really. Will was the first."

It still cut her like a knife to talk about Will like this, in past tense and as a hurdle to be got over. She sat up, grabbing her summer dress from the seat by the bed. She threw it on.

"I'll get a drink." In reality, in the cold light of day, she still wasn't sure how, or if, this relationship could work.

***

That night, they ate at Nobu again. It was Zach's favourite and they enjoyed a private meal, just the two of them, albeit both subdued by Amy's looming departure. There was no paparazzi to contend with at the end of the night and they went home early. Amy's flight was at ten a.m. the following morning. She had scolded Zach that the flight was not with British Airways, who she could not help still having allegiance to and ultimate trust in. He told her not to be so ungrateful – his manager had arranged it and he had upgraded her to business class. Zach had insisted it was all on his purse too. She apologised and made sure she was all packed just after they got home from the meal. They sat cuddling in the lounge with a large glass of red each. He did not seem to want to be more than a few inches away from her.

"We really should get to bed," she said. Both were reluctant; it meant their parting would come around all too soon. "I want to be at the airport early. Old habits and all that."

"Sure." Zach slowly got up. They made their way to the bedroom, undressed and got into bed. Amy snuggled up to Zach and he kissed her.

"Can you just leave your lips here," he said. "Both sets."

She laughed. "Is that all you want me for?"

"You make me want it. You're just so… delicious."

She laughed again. "I've been called many things in my life… never been called delicious."

"It felt right."

"So does this…" She stared dreamily into his pale eyes. She thrust her tongue into his mouth as they groped each other, desperate to be joined again, probably for the last time on her stay.

***

In the middle of the night, Amy woke with cold sweats again, nightmares and dark feelings. She got up and got a strong drink to get herself back to sleep. She wished she knew why this kept happening – was it just her conscience coming alive at night or was there more to it than that?

The time came quicker than it should have for Amy to go to the airport. Zach put her case in the back of his Aston and opened Amy's door. It seemed to her like only yesterday they were making these moves in exact reverse. They were both subdued and the journey to the airport was fairly quiet, apart from Zach occasionally asking her if she had her passport and ticket to hand, or if she had got everything. He took her to the gate and they had a long goodbye hug.

"Call me when you land."

"I will."

"Miss you already."

She had a lump in her throat and fought the tears. Why did it feel like this would be the last time she ever saw him? Her sense of foreboding crept back in and she let the tears flow.

"And you," she said, through the tears.

"Hey, angel, don't cry." He wiped her tears with his thumb. "I'll see you as soon as I can."

She nodded. "I need to go." She started to walk away, her heart struggling to allow her feet to move forward.

"Bye, Amy." He waved, and as she walked, she kept turning back to wave. He stayed until she was out of sight, at least that's how long she assumed he stayed for. In fact, he stayed until he saw her plane in the air, before heading back home, dejected and pining. He went straight to his studio and called Jake, his closest bandmate, the one he wrote most songs with, and they spent some productive hours writing, Zach drawing on his high emotional state, his anguish at Amy going away for an indeterminable amount of time providing a succulent source of writing material.

Amy, meanwhile, found her seat on an unfamiliar aircraft, with unfamiliar staff helping everyone out. She was so disappointed not to be on a British Airways flight, she felt slightly uneasy. She often knew at least one member of staff on British Airways flights she had taken before, it was all so familiar, so nostalgic. This was not. She sat and wept again, her hair falling over her face to cover her distress. She thought about lying by the pool at Zach's, lying next to him in bed, his face, his body, his voice, coming prominently into her thoughts.

"Are you OK, ma'am?" A young American flight attendant spoke to her. She looked up.

"Yes, I'm OK, thank you. I just said goodbye to my boyfriend. Long-distance relationships are tough."

"Does he live in LA, ma'am?"

"Yes, yes he does. And please." She looked at the girl's name tag. "Chloe, it's Amy, not ma'am. I used to do your job. For nearly four years. I loved it."

The girl smiled as she checked the overhead bins were shut properly. She seemed to relax at Amy's comments. "I've only been doing it for three months. I still get so nervous."

"That will go… till you meet someone famous on your flight." Amy reminisced about her first encounter with Zach. She felt emotional again.

"Who did you meet?" Chloe asked intrigued.

"Lots. I met my favourite band, that was intense."

"Well, I love Sovereign X. I would love to see them on a flight."

Amy laughed at the irony. "Maybe one day you will." She smiled. "Go, do your duties or your supervisor will tell you off."

"Can we talk again?"

"Absolutely." Amy found the diversion more than welcome.

***

Halfway through the flight, Chloe found a moment to come back to Amy. Amy ordered drinks from her periodically so they could chat for longer – no one was seated next to Amy, so they could chat relatively undisturbed. She told her how she had left flying to follow her dream of writing and becoming a journalist. She also told her some of the names of famous people she had seen on flights, some of the antics the staff got up to, and how she had met both her current and previous boyfriends flying with the airline.

"So, your previous boyfriend was an air-crash investigator? That's cool; what a meaningful job. What does your current boyfriend do?" Chloe enquired. Thus far, Amy had skirted around elaborating on who Zach was. She considered the eager innocence of the girl before her, much like her when she had started out. And a fellow fan, like she had been. What harm could it do to tell her?

"He's a musician, a songwriter."

"Wow, cool, is he well known?" She had not connected the dots with Amy's hints.

Amy paused. "Yes, as a matter of fact he is." She pulled out her phone and showed Chloe a decent picture of her and Zach together. Chloe threw her hands over her mouth, possibly to stop herself screaming with glee.

"Oh my gosh! He's currently dating a British journalist…" she said, as if quoting words from an article she had read. Which she probably had. "That's you!" Amy nodded with a smile at Chloe's excitement.

"See, now, maybe I'm destined to meet the people *dating* famous people."

Amy laughed. "No, you'll meet loads, I guarantee it."

Chloe did not seem to want to leave her now she knew the juicy details.

"So… you were upset earlier because you just said goodbye to Zach Hayes? And you're dating him?"

"Yes." Amy sighed. She did not want to say too much. She was not even sure Zach would take too kindly to her talking about them to a perfect stranger. In her defence, she held a certain affinity with flight attendants and this one was sweet and nervous and young. She showed her a couple more pictures of the two of them.

"He's going on tour in a week around the States."

"I know, I'm going to see them!"

"Wow, that's cool! I was a fan you know. Then I became a journalist, interviewed them and we just hit it off. The rest, as they say, is history."

"That is just amazing." Chloe was in awe of Amy more than ever now. She looked like she wanted to ask her more questions but she held back. Amy was relieved. She did not particularly want to tell her any more. She asked Chloe which concert she was going to and told her she would get Zach to do a shout out to her on that evening. Chloe was over the moon, Amy wished she could promise more than that, but as his new girlfriend she felt she was hardly in any position to guarantee anything more impressive. At that moment, Chloe's supervisor appeared and asked her to serve drinks to some irritated-looking businessmen on the other side of the aisle. Amy apologised and Chloe moved away.

Amy was left alone with her thoughts again and tried, unsuccessfully, to get into the in-flight movie. She fingered the Tiffany necklace that still hung about her neck from Will. Now she was going home to face the music and, she supposed, to end it for good. It still did not sit well, and with Zach on tour, it would leave her completely alone – a rather selfish thought, but still, she could not help herself.

Twenty-Two

"Ladies and Gentlemen, we will be experiencing some turbulence; please fasten your seatbelts, we should be through it shortly." The captain's voice sounded throughout the plane. Amy reckoned that at this juncture they were probably no more than an hour away from Heathrow. They must have hit some sort of storm and she fastened her seatbelt as advised. The turbulence buffeted the plane as it hit air pockets, some of the passengers gasped as the plane seemed to drop suddenly and shake. She knew that this was normal; however, it was a particularly bad episode. After about fifteen minutes or so, the storm seemed to pass and the plane was smooth once again, much to the relief of most of the passengers. The seatbelt light went off and the atmosphere was relaxed again. Amy noticed Chloe checking that passengers were OK as she made her way towards Amy's row.

"I still hate those air pockets," she said to Amy, rolling her eyes.

"They are unnerving. I had them a fair bit. The Asian flights are the worst. I had a really bad one to the Philippines, it really worried me. Never had anything as severe as that again, so I suppose anything less I'm unfazed by. You'll get used to it."

"I hope so," Chloe sighed in relief, before moving away.

As they neared the approach to Heathrow, Amy noticed that the plane must have been stacked, as it rose and began a wide circle above the airport. She glanced across at the window and surmised that the airport was busy. The plane circled for quite some time and Amy noticed several planes seemed to have gone ahead of them and landed, but their position remained. She looked down the end of the gangway to see if she could catch Chloe's attention. Their supervisor was talking very intensely to several of the cabin crew. Amy was curious; their body language and facial expressions were very serious. She knew at once that something was not right. As the crew dispersed, Chloe strode down her aisle. Amy put her hand out to stop her.

"Chloe, what's happened?" Chloe looked at her, concern creasing her brow.

"I can't talk, Amy, I'm sorry." But she held eye contact, as if trying to telekinetically inform her.

All Amy could surmise was that there was a technical problem, the likeliest culprit would be the landing gear.

The plane continued its circling for another half-an-hour at least, other passengers were also starting to notice and become curious. Amy sat back and thought of all the things Will had told her about issues that planes can have. She knew that there were few with this, an old jumbo seven-four-seven – any that had caused serious crashes had been put right. Maybe it wasn't as bad as it seemed; Chloe was obviously a little nervous and may have over-responded to whatever had happened. All the same, she was uneasy. Her recurring bad dreams had always featured flying, natural really, she had thought, considering her former employ. She had had more dreams about flying since leaving than she had ever had while still working for the airline. Strange. She closed her eyes. With Heathrow just below them, she began to feel agonising frustration. *We are so close, what's the hold-up?*

Just at that moment, the captain's voice came through the tannoy again.

"Ladies and gentlemen, we are having a technical issue with the landing gear; we hope to land shortly. Apologies for the delay." He was calm, but Amy was unsure. The landing gear was not engaging. This could be caused by several things, and was it not working or was it just that the computer was telling them it was not working? She wished sorely that Will was on the plane. Not only could he have reassured or explained things to her (she wished she had retained more of his technical knowledge), but he could, critically, have been some assistance to the crew. She threw her head back. Damn whim and fancy; if she had come back with Beth she would be home right now.

Just three days – that is all she had gained. And now here she was, unable to land. Some other passengers were starting to ask questions of the cabin crew, who all remained calm and professional, even Chloe. Amy knew they would not have a great deal of fuel left and they could only continue like this for a short while longer. The plane continued its circle and Amy glanced across at the runway beneath. She could just about see through the pre-dawn darkness the flashing lights of several fire engines. Foam would be sprayed on the runway, she knew that much. She inhaled deeply.

Chloe appeared and Amy grabbed her arm this time. Suddenly her mouth was dry and she was nervous. She did not need to ask this – she knew the answer – but she asked anyway.

"Chloe, they're going to try to land the plane without the landing gear, aren't they?"

Chloe nodded slowly.

"They're not sure if one or both has engaged." Amy could see the fear in her face. Amy held her arm still.

"It's been done before." Amy tried to reassure both Chloe and herself. She smiled; Chloe forced a smile back and placed her hand on Amy's that still gripped her arm. Amy let go and Chloe was gone.

The captain's voice was heard again. This time he was more forceful, more direct.

"Ladies and gentlemen, we are experiencing severe difficulties with the landing gear mechanism. We are unsure as to whether one or both have engaged and as we are low on fuel, we will be attempting to land shortly." Passengers gasped and several started to panic. The cabin crew did their best to keep everyone calm and seated. "You will be required to assume the brace position – which the cabin crew are demonstrating – as a precaution. When we land, the emergency procedure will take place and please exit as quickly and calmly as possible."

As the captain's voice ended, the plane erupted into chatter; people's voices were strained and stressed. Amy closed her eyes. Planes had landed without landing gear, she knew that from Will's job. Most of the time, the plane would be quite damaged, and most of the time people walked away with nothing more than minor injuries. Particularly with prior warning like in their situation. But they had been smaller planes – a jumbo? The biggest risk to them as passengers – if the plane did not break up when it hit the runway – was fire. Amy felt tears in her eyes. This was one moment anyone could dread. All the flights she had flown for work… and here she was on a pleasure flight, facing a serious issue with their plane – something few people lived to tell the tale about. In a moment of sheer panic, she grabbed her phone and switched it on. She hastily sent two texts, one to Will, the other to Zach.

Many others were doing the same, or praying. Several people were upset; the atmosphere was incredibly tense, yet remarkably quiet. As the plane began its descent, an eerie calm fell. Everyone had their seatbelts tightly fastened and were poised ready for a crash landing.

Amy sat back, remembering her training, remembering practising for a moment exactly like this one. She waited, her heart racing beneath her chest. The plane approached the runway smoothly and perfectly. The angle they came in at was a strange one, one that the pilots would have deliberately taken to ensure the safest way to land the plane on its belly. Any moment now, impact would occur.

The voice seemed to echo around the plane: "Brace! Brace! Brace!"

Amy, along with everyone else, put her head down to her knees and put her arms over her head to protect it. She closed her eyes, images passing through her head, and fear, just pure fear, gripping her tightly about the chest. She said a little prayer too, in her head. *If I get through this, I must value things more, I must be better.* She had looked so selfishly inward these last few months, and in the last week or two had been caught up in the allure of material wealth and extravagance and physical pleasures. She also could not stop her mind from savagely pointing out the irony of her situation: just as she had decided to let Will go – the air-crash investigator – she is involved in an air accident. *Life is twisted,* she mused briefly before the panic of the situation crept over her and the rest of the passengers like a fuggy black cloud.

She gritted her teeth as the plane impacted with a judder and a bang, making contact with the tarmac, skewed at a strange, lopsided angle. It shook terribly and people screamed as they hurtled forward. The unmistakable sound of metal scraping along the runway blocked out the sound of cries across the cabin and Amy glanced out of the window. There was a sinister glow increasing on her side of the plane. She closed her eyes and tried hard to maintain her position, wedging her head against the seat in front. The large plane creaked and moaned as it struggled to come to a halt. People gasped as the plane's engines grinded loudly under them, vibrating the overhead bins to the point where bags came tumbling out and flew about the plane. Then suddenly, the plane lurched dramatically over to the right – Amy's side. People fell against each other, the plane banking at a forty-five-degree angle as it continued its drag along the runway, metal flying off the two large jet engines on that side. The oxygen masks flew down from above everyone's heads, but all the passengers, including Amy, were still bracing themselves.

Amy's eyes caught open as the light of flames engulfed one of the engines on her side. She saw it breaking up and prayed – begged – for the plane to stop. It still seemed to be travelling at a rate of knots – it was a massive plane; how much longer could it stand this force before it exploded or was overtaken by the fire? It was a ticking time bomb and there were still over four hundred passengers plus crew to evacuate. The plane felt like it was cracking; heat in the cabin was rising rapidly, but the velocity was slowing, the plane was coming to a stop, not before both engines on her side of the plane were on fire. Amy looked up and around her as the plane skidded, but stop it did, the plane lit in an eerie glow by the engines on fire, the wing severely gnarled and damaged and limp against the tarmac. The cabin crew were immediately out of their seats as smoke began to seep into the gangway.

"Get off the plane! Get off the plane!" Yelled the flight attendants. Amy struggled to get up and climb out of her seat, with the plane at such an angle. She had some cuts and bruises and a nagging pain in her neck, but she had to help them. They would be the last off, making sure all passengers were safely off the plane.

People shot out of their seats and made their way to the exits. One was unobtainable due to the fire that had spread from one right wing engine to the other. The heat was almost unbearable on Amy's side. Everyone began to cough and Amy was sweating profusely. She helped everyone seated near her and directed them to the nearest exit where the inflatable slides had already been deployed. She spotted Chloe on the other side of the aisle helping an elderly couple leave their seats. She glanced forward sharply and noticed the plane had twisted and tilted, but was remarkably intact, aside from the right wing. However, the smoke and heat was increasing fast. They had not a minute to lose. Amy moved behind her and helped people get out fast and orderly so no one was left. The hazards of luggage throughout the walkways caused many people to trip. Amy grabbed as many as she could and threw them into the now virtually empty central seating area. As she did, she tripped over a large bag and fell awkwardly on her leg. The pain was excruciating, but her adrenaline was pumping so hard, she limped on to help some other elderly people who were nervously trying to get out of their aisle.

"Miss, you must exit the plane!" A flight attendant called to Amy.

"No, I must help!" she called back. The smoke was now obscuring vision of the path and the electricity had just failed. Amy coughed her way to the front of the plane, fighting the smoke. She could hear the sirens outside and the blasting of foam onto the burning aeroplane. The heat was still rising in the cabin, and Amy did the same as the other flight attendants in checking that there were no passengers left, her training all those years ago, coming back in a heartbeat, instinctive. She looked across the aisle. Chloe was there, struggling in the smoke. She was rubbing her arm. Amy limped through the aisle to her.

"Everyone's off, let's go!" Amy yelled at her. She nodded, but she looked lulled by smoke inhalation.

They made their way with the other crew to the nearest exit as the plane seemed to creak, buckle and bend beneath them. Amy, still holding Chloe's hand, tumbled awkwardly, her leg felt twisted and the dull pain was increasing. Both coughing, she pulled Chloe towards the emergency slide and looked at the precipice. The plane jolted to the right again dangerously; the flimsy slide wobbled, barely in contact with the ground beneath. Amy took a deep breath and bravely threw herself and Chloe down, the last two to leave the plane from the main cabin. They fell awkwardly.

Amy looked up at the melee from the heap she had landed in; the cloud in her head and the relief at getting off the plane, not to mention the shock of the crash overwhelmed her. Her eyes were blurry, her ears fuzzy. She was aware that someone grabbed her arms, helping her up and moving her swiftly away from the aircraft, asking her questions. She glanced back and saw that Chloe had been taken by another paramedic – they were both being led to ambulances at a safe distance from the wreck. Amy looked back at the mess, barely able to put one foot in front of the other. It could have been so much worse; it seemed there were only minor injuries and smoke inhalation related issues amongst the passengers. Everywhere was covered in foam… and people, people everywhere getting passengers and crew to safety. Amy became aware that it was tears that were blurring her eyes – she could barely take in the scene before her. *Had they definitely got everyone off the plane?* She kept repeating in her mind. Was the fire out in those two burning engines? She was made to sit down on the ambulance steps by the paramedic and was asked questions again.

"What's your name, love?" She placed a blanket around her shoulders. Amy coughed.

"Amy," she replied, croakily.

"I'm going to give you this oxygen mask to help you breathe a little easier , OK?" The paramedic put the mask over Amy's face and Amy leaned her head back. She was aware of her eyes rolling and she thought she would lose consciousness, largely from pain in her leg and neck, partly overtaken by shock. She stared unbelievingly at the spectacle before her. The plane wreckage, the people, wrapped in blankets, some limping, crying, mostly with relief at being back on terra firma.

Then something caught her eye; two men were wandering around with purpose, talking frantically. As they turned their backs on her, she saw letters on the backs of their high-viz jackets – AAIB. She felt too weak to call out. She made a move to get up and nearly collapsed on her leg – *it must be broken*. The paramedic caught her as she fell and made her lay on the stretcher, examining her ankle. Amy lay there reaching out her arm. She watched as the AAIB men turned towards the light of the ambulance – it was dark still, dawn not quite breaking through. She tried to sit up again, but the paramedic stopped her. She lifted her head as best she could with the mask on, just as he turned; a pinched, worried look on his face. He saw her and ran towards the ambulance.

Will climbed in, unquestioned by the paramedic – he was an official here as far as she would be concerned.

"Amy!" His voice was full of emotion. She cried, tears streaking over the mask. She grabbed his strong hand as he stroked her grubby forehead. He had tears running down his cheeks and for a moment they just looked at each other. She took her mask off, her head felt clearer. Will was explaining to the paramedic that he had been looking for Amy.

"I thought I was never going to see you again," she half whispered in a croaky voice, sobbing.

"I'm here," he said simply. "Always here." He would not let go of her hand.

"I suspect that apart from the smoke, she has whiplash and a broken ankle," the paramedic said to Will. "We will need to get her to the hospital to get an X-ray."

The other AAIB guy had appeared by the ambulance doors. "Will."

Amy looked up at Will. He did not take his eyes off her. "I'm going to the hospital with Amy." He was still looking at her. Amy smiled in relief.

"OK. Call me later."

"Will do."

The ambulance door closed and Will sat down next to Amy. They did not speak, the awkwardness of the situation, of their relationship, completely overshadowed by this disaster. Amy glanced at him wondering if he had got to the scene specifically quickly because he knew she had been on the flight. Or was it just chance, being there in a professional capacity? He would have received the message she had sent before their harrowing landing. She lay still; Will was watching her all the time, stroking her head occasionally. She felt herself shaking with the shock of it all and briefly glanced at Will's face and the paramedic's face above her, talking, but she wasn't listening. She closed her eyes for a moment, the abatement of adrenaline leaving her bereft of energy.

She wondered how Chloe was. Poor girl, so new to what was otherwise a great job and safe mode of travel. She hoped she would find out how she was doing, she had coped so well. The other thought creeping into her mind was the two messages she had sent to the men in her life. She was obviously not in her right mind, but she was wondering how she could explain the fact that she had told them both that she loved them very much. It was this thought that was carved into her mind as the ambulance seemed to go dark, she knew no more and oblivion engulfed her.

Twenty-Three

"She's fine."

"Are you sure?"

"Yes. She was given a sedative in the ambulance, for shock."

"But the smoke… she's asthmatic…"

"She's fine."

"And her leg?"

"Not so good, they think the ankle, for sure, is broken, but possibly trapped a nerve as well. Hence the morphine drip."

Amy heard two very familiar voices, talking in lowered tones. There was a general bustle of noise around, but she felt queer, soppy and high – *must be the morphine they're talking about…* Then she realised that she could open her eyes and see what was going on. Sure enough, she was in a ward of a hospital, Beth on one side of her, Will the other.

"Amy." Beth noticed her open her eyes. She looked at Beth, who was incredibly concerned, and grabbed her hand. "Shit, girl, if you want fame, this ain't the way to go about it!"

Amy smiled. "Never free of dramas, am I?" she struggled, good-humouredly. She could not feel her left foot. She looked down to make sure it was still there. It was.

"You're a hero. I saw one of the crew on my way in, said a female passenger helped the crew get everyone off the plane. I thought, that'll be Amy! Once a crew member, always a crew member." Beth's pride was clear in her voice. Amy tried to sit up, but her leg was too painful.

"Did we get everyone out? Is everyone OK?" Amy was unable to forget the images of those last few minutes on the plane.

"Yes. Everyone. And only minor injuries. Just stay there," Will said. "I'll leave you girls to chat for a moment." Will kissed her forehead and left them. Amy watched him go.

Beth was still looking at her. "Zach called."

"Did he? Did you speak to him? Where is my phone?" Amy looked around her.

"I didn't speak to him. Will did." Beth was tentative. Amy looked at her. What a strange turn of events today had been. Aside from the trauma of the landing, her emotions were thrown as well. Maybe it would be as well not to think about it.

"How was it?" Amy asked, managing to raise the bed so she was more upright. Beth puffed her pillow under her.

"I wasn't here, but Will told me briefly that he had been ringing your phone incessantly since you were knocked out in the ambulance. He had managed to retrieve your phone from your back pocket and spoke to him just to tell him that you were safe and relatively unscathed."

"Was anything else said?"

"That's all he told me. You mustn't think about all that now, Hun. You must just get better. Don't liven up your mind."

"I want to speak to him," she said. Her mind was fine right now. She knew what Beth was getting at – the last time she had experienced trauma, she had gone right off the rails. And this will probably haunt her for a long time. The feeling of foreboding she had had, those recurring dreams in America; she had never believed in a sixth sense, nor did she now, but she was sure that maybe even just her conscience had led to this – bad karma or whatever you might want to see it as.

"I think Will has your phone."

"Can you get it back, please?" The urgency was sure and the fear, fear that Will would look at her messages and see that she sent virtually identical messages to him and Zach. She was not sure she could determine right now exactly what she meant or what she wanted. From either of them. She could not begin to describe the feelings she had when she saw the back of Will's head on the foamy runway. Relief – her comfort, her stay. Her rescuer. There at her side in her time of need, albeit through convenience or coincidence. But then there was Zach. The man she had idolised.

"Please get my phone," she said, feeling drowsy again.

"Sure." Beth went off to find Will. She came back a few moments later, phone in hand. The screen was badly cracked in one corner. She handed it to Amy, who called Zach's mobile.

"Will?" He answered straight away.

"Hi, Zach."

"Amy! How're you…? I was so worried when I got your message… I watched the plane on the news – I couldn't believe it… I've been a mess, then I got through to Will, and he told me he had not left your side, then that threw up a whole mess of crap in my head – I should be with you, not him, but then I suppose it's his job…" Zach rambled.

"Zach, I'm fine, just a bad ankle. Will was just there, cos it was a… you know." She found she could not say the words 'plane crash' or 'air accident'. And her reassurance was empty; she had been so delighted to see Will, it had thrown up a whole mess of crap in *her* head too. She felt tears welling again.

"I feel totally shit – capital A, capital F. I got you to stay longer, I got you on that flight…"

"Don't be silly. It could have happened at any time." She thought to add that it must be destiny, but it hurt too much to admit it.

"I just want to be there with you."

"I want you here too."

"Are you in hospital?"

"Yes – they think I've broken my ankle and maybe have a trapped nerve. I tripped over some baggage, would you believe. Clumsy as always."

Beth yelled out from the corner of the room, "She's a hero, helping everyone off the plane!"

"Of course. Bet you fell into cabin crew mode. You're amazing, Amy."

"Rubbish. I did what anyone would have done."

"And broke your foot in the process. I don't think so. You are a hero. When will you be home?"

"Oh, I don't know – Beth, when do they say I can go home?"

"They want to X-ray and plaster your leg, then I think they will turf you out. Unless they need to operate."

"Later today, I guess," Amy said to Zach.

"FaceTime me when you do."

"Sure."

"I can't believe… I thought you were gonna…" He couldn't finish any of the sentences.

"It didn't happen though. I'm still here."

"Get some rest, we'll talk."

"Bye." She put her phone on the table by the bed and sighed, staring up at the ceiling. Beth was leaning up against the wall opposite scrolling down her phone. She glanced at Amy without looking up. She frowned.

"You OK?"

"Yeah. Tired. You sure everyone got off the plane and they're all OK?"

"Yes, absolutely, I promise. Don't worry. Emotionally, are you OK?"

Amy sighed. "I don't know. I feel weird. But then I am high on morphine."

"Enjoy it while it lasts!" Beth smiled. Amy smiled too, but Beth noticed her lips were pale and she was ill at ease in her mind. Of course, she would be after what she had just been through. But she also saw the difficulty she was thrown back into with Will and Zach. "Don't think about them right now, Amy."

"Who?"

"You know full well who. It doesn't matter just yet. You've got to recover, and I don't just mean your foot."

Amy looked away. She had been fighting off the mental image of the broken plane, the mechanical voice shouting 'brace', the distress on all those passengers' faces, the burning engines. Being part of a disaster, or potential disaster, changes you, it puts a different perspective on life and what's important. It can become the very thing that defines you and you must learn to live with it. Amy was aware of all this and she wondered if she would ever be able to get back to normal and not relive this day, time and again, like she had when her mother had died. That had taken years, but this was different; that was a loss, this was something that had actually happened to her – would that be harder or easier to recover from?

At that moment, a face appeared round the curtain.

"Knock knock," a young American girl said, with a smile on her face. Beth looked up.

"Chloe," Amy said. "Come in."

"I've been wondering where you were, if you were even here. Wanted to see you were OK."

"I'm fine, just a dodgy foot. Are there many from the plane here? Are there any serious injuries?"

"I don't think so; there's quite a few people with smoke inhalation – I think one elderly lady broke her arm on the emergency slide. Then you. I wanted to thank you for your help and support, it meant so much to me. Even before all this began."

Amy smiled. "I hope it hasn't put you off flying?" It had put *her* off flying.

"It shouldn't, I guess – I'm flying back to LA tonight."

"Surely not on a shift?"

"Are you a trolley dolly too?" Beth piped up.

"Sorry, Beth, this is Chloe; Chloe, my best friend, Beth. And yes, we chatted a lot on the flight."

"Amy was amazing when the plane came down."

"*You* were amazing. Considering you are new to it all as well."

Chloe smiled. Amy noticed that she had been crying too. This was an experience that only those involved could really relate to. They all had a strange bond now; they would all be damaged in different ways mentally. Amy was inclined to try to stay in contact with Chloe.

"Me and the other crew that are here are going back to Heathrow to wait for our flight home. I really want to stay in touch if that's OK?" Chloe said. She must have read Amy's mind. "My name is Chloe Maskowicz; I thought I could friend you on Facebook?"

"Of course. Amy Armstrong. Look me up."

"I will. I hope your leg recovers."

"Thank you." Amy smiled. She put her arms out to give Chloe a hug. "Keep flying. You're a fabulous flight attendant."

Chloe smiled as she moved away. Amy wasn't sure if she would.

"And I haven't forgotten my promise about the shout-out. All the more important now, you're part of a heroic team who got us all to safety."

"Thank you. Tell him 'hi' from me and I love them," Chloe said, choked. "Bye, Amy."

"Bye, Chloe." And she left. As she did so, Will came back.
"They want to send you for an X-ray if you're up to it?" he said.
"Yes, I'm ready. I just want to go home now."

***

The X-ray showed that Amy had sustained a lateral ankle fracture, but they were happy that it was minor enough to just be plastered and monitored; the nerve was not trapped. Her foot and leg were put in plaster up to her knee and she was given crutches and pain killers and discharged. The hospital also advised her to arrange some counselling. Will and Beth helped her to her feet and the hospital porter provided her with a wheelchair to get her to the car park before giving her the crutches.

Dawn was giving way to the brighter light of early morning. It was misty in the busy hospital car park. They must have been on overdrive with many of her fellow passengers. She found the pain starting to return with her clarity as the morphine was gradually leaving her body. Beth and Will helped her get into the back of Beth's car. Will got in the front with Beth. Amy was quiet and leaned her head back gently, the pain in her neck more a dull ache now. She was utterly exhausted – jet-lagged, in shock still. She could not close her eyes to sleep though; natural sleep would probably be a long time coming.

"You OK, Hun?" Beth said, looking at Amy in her rear view mirror.

"Yes." Will looked back and smiled sympathetically. Amy made eye contact and smiled back. He knew. He knew all about this kind of thing. He was the closest she could get in her own sphere to someone being able to relate to her harrowing experience. He leaned his arm back and touched her knee affectionately, and she put her hand on his. He seemed slightly surprised, and left it there for as long as he could comfortably do so. Zach was not in her thoughts now and momentarily she wondered why she had done something so stupid to have ended up losing Will.

The journey was quiet and quick, being so early in the morning. Within an hour, they pulled up outside Amy's house. Will helped her out of the car and got her crutches ready. Beth looked at her, full of emotion.

She wanted to say several things, but found she could not find the right words.

"I love you," she simply said instead, and hugged Amy carefully.

"I love you, too."

"Want me to stay?"

"No, I'll be fine. I'll give you a call later." They kissed and Beth got in her car and drove away. Amy looked at Will who had gotten his key out and was opening the front door. It could almost have been as if nothing had happened between them and she hopped gently on her crutches over the threshold.

"Go put your feet up, I'll make a cuppa." Will opened the lounge door for her. She smiled at him as he saw her to the sofa. She put her feet up and lay back. Will put several cushions under her bad leg and several behind her back. His dark eyes met hers and she touched his cheek.

"Thank you," she whispered. "All the hurt I've caused and yet here you are, looking after me," she said, with a lump in her throat.

He looked at her. "I would do anything for you, Amy." He got up and went to the kitchen to avoid any awkward response to this. He came back with a cup of tea for them both and sat opposite her. He sighed. Amy realised that he must have been up all night too. He looked tired. But she liked that he was here. She liked seeing him again.

"What do you think went wrong with the landing gear?"

Will raised his eyebrows in thought. "Without any information other than what we know already, I would say that the turbulence you experienced possibly had something to do with it. The left side engaged, the right collapsed on landing – it hadn't engaged properly. I shall have to get into it." He sounded professional, sipping his tea and clearly deep in thought at the mention of the accident, his mind computing all the details and possible reasons. She wondered if it would affect the way he carried out his investigation, being so emotionally invested in this particular incident. Amy watched him. Strange how they had been thrown back together like this. She refrained from voicing that thought though.

"Strange how you'll be investigating an accident where you know someone involved," she said, instead.

"Yes. Yes, it is." He looked at her. "Why don't you try to get some sleep?"

"I think I just need to watch some telly for a bit." She grabbed the remote and put the TV on. The news was on and it was reporting the plane and its dramatic landing. She stared at the smoky mass being filmed from above, then turned the channel over to something trashier, less emotionally taxing.

"Can I get you something to eat?" Will said, brushing over the scenes that Amy had hastily switched over.

"No, I'm fine thanks. Thank you for being here with me." She did not look at him.

"Of course. Listen, I have got to go out for a few hours, but do you want me to come back later? Are you going to be OK if I go?"

She looked at him. She dearly wanted him to stay. "Why? Where are you going?" she said, disappointed.

He got up and moved over to her. He took her hand in his. "I have to be back at the airport."

She looked at him. Of course, he was going to be busy now. She felt bad that he had come all this way back home with her from the hospital when he was only five minutes away. "You should have said, Beth could have brought me home."

"I wanted to be with you, to see that you're OK. I would not have done it any other way. Now, I want you to stay put – can I get you anything before I go? If you really want me to stay I will, Amy."

Amy kept her eyes on him, quite taken aback that despite all they had been through, here he was. She wasn't even sure how he was going to get back to the airport, his car wasn't there. Of course, she would not stop him going. She was eager to see what his investigation would find as well. He was needed, he had to go. She only had a broken ankle after all. But she found she did want him to stay.

"No, no, I'll be fine. Perhaps I should have some food and some more drinks." Immediately, Will put together some provisions from the kitchen and a charger for her phone, which was almost dead.

A car beeped outside. "Well, I think that's my ride," Will said. He leaned down hesitantly to kiss Amy on the forehead and she lifted her head at the last minute, so he caught her nose. They looked into each other's eyes, their faces close, and it was like the last two years came flooding back into their consciousness. Amy put her arms round his neck and they shared a lingering kiss on the lips.

"Come home later," Amy said as they pulled away.

"OK." And he left.

Twenty-Four

Amy popped a couple of co-codamol when Will left, partly for the pain, partly to see if it would relax her enough to sleep. After half-an-hour or so, she nodded off on the sofa where Will had left her. But she was unsettled in her mind. She part dreamed, part woke to thoughts of the plane, the images etched into her brain. The feelings of fear, the relief of making it home, the relief of seeing Will, who had been elevated in her mind to some sort of knight in shining armour. Then there was Zach, who she had said a tearful goodbye to just the day before. She had felt that dread then… should she be reading into it as a sign? Or was that just a load of nonsense?

She tried to evaluate her feelings for both men again. They had gotten so confused so suddenly. It did not help that there was such a distance, geographically as well as lifestyle. The thought of getting on a plane to go see Zach right now filled her with a shudder. That would not do. But maybe he would be able to come see her? Not with this tour starting imminently. And what of Will? She could not escape the fact that deep down, beyond this ridiculous obsession made real, she still held Will in her heart. But the time had come to make a choice – it was not fair to mess with both of them like this. Her dream-state mind tried to reach the decision, her emotions yo-yoed from one to the other… She was startled awake, several hours later by her phone ringing in her lap.

"Hello," she said, sleepily.

"Hey, lovely. Sorry, did I wake you?"

"Yes. Bitch." Amy attempted to joke. Beth chuckled.

"Sorry, love."

"It's fine, I was restless anyway and should try to stay awake so I sleep tonight, I guess. Wanna come over? Is Izzy still here, by the way?"

"Yes, just for a few more days. She sent her love, but she's at auditions all day today. Is Will there?"

"No. He went to… work."

"Oh. Of course," Beth said, realising what Amy meant. "I'll be there in ten."

"Bring that spare key I gave you, then I don't have to get up and muck about with these bloody crutches."

"Course. See ya."

She was letting herself in within ten minutes and went into the lounge.

"All right, Hoppy?" Amy was sipping her water and flicked the bird at her. "Do you need anything?"

"Yes, I need my best friend to sit down and let me bend her ear." She felt a little better having had some sleep.

"And there's me worried about you getting PTSD or something. I think you're gonna be fine." Beth assessed her with her eyes as she said this. She was light-hearted, but she was still determined to keep an eye on her friend's mental health for some time.

"I will be fine. I always bounce back, eh? Can't bring Amy Armstrong down that easily." Amy smiled. It was all bravado, but it helped her push herself, not to be broken by what life threw at her. "My love life on the other hand, is a mess."

"Kinda weird, how when you were with Will, Zach was the spanner in the works. Now you're with Zach, Will is the spanner in the works."

"Yes, thank you for that," Amy said, sarcastically. "I really needed that being pointed out."

"I really don't think you should even be worrying about it right now."

"I know, but I can't help it."

"Look, let Will look after you and see how you feel when you're stronger. Zach is not about now anyway with this tour kicking off."

"I guess so. I'm back to stringing them both along, though."

"Tough. Do it. You've just been through a hell of an…. experience, we shall call it. Now, let's just see what we can do to cheer you up and distract you." Beth got up and fished through Amy's DVD collection, hooking out *Notting Hill* and a comedy. "I recommend these for the convalescent."

They put the film on. Beth hilariously drawing comparisons between Amy and Zach's relationship and the one portrayed in the film, then they laughed till they cried at the comedy DVD.

"This is just the sort of therapy I needed," Amy said. "How have things been with Izzy?"

"Great. She's spoken to that agency that Zach put forward – they sound keen; she's meeting them when she goes back to LA next week. She trotted off to the West End this morning, so we'll see."

"Bet you're hoping she'll land the West End gig."

"Hmm, maybe a little bit." Beth smiled. "It all seemed so trivial to us when we heard what had happened to you." Beth looked at Amy to gauge a response. Amy stared at her plastered foot.

"Just makes you appreciate life and the ones you love. And to not let silly things hold you back." They fell silent for a moment. "I think I should call Paul. He was expecting me in this week." She grabbed her phone and dialled him up.

"Yello, Amy Armstrong," he said, in his arrogant manner.

"Hello, Paul Finkley."

"Back in Blighty?"

"Yes. Just." She meant the 'just' in two ways.

"I was just thinking about you actually – that plane crash-landing at Heathrow last night, saw it was from LA. Did you see it?"

"I was on it."

"What the *fuck*? Are you OK? I saw everyone made it out with minor injuries. Looked bloody scary though. I can't believe you were on that! Tell me are you OK? Can I do anything for you?"

"Letting me get a word in edgeways would be a start! I have a broken ankle and feel a bit emosh, but apart from that, I'm fine."

"Oh, I'm so glad you're OK, it must have been terrifying."

"So, he does have a heart after all."

"I do – who'd a thought it? Always, when it comes to you, Amy. You're so special." He sounded genuine. She smiled.

"I was actually just calling to say I won't be in this week, I don't think. I hope the offer still stands?"

"Absolutely and absolutely. Take all the time you need."

"I could do with some work. I'll be bored out of my mind otherwise. I can't drive, but I might be able to get up to the office by train."

"No, I won't hear of it, get up here when you can, but do not rush. I'll email some stuff over, but only if you're sure you're up to it?"

"Definitely. Will keep my mind off other things."

"I understand. Keep in touch. And all the best, you gorgeous thing."

Amy rolled her eyes, she didn't know how he got away with it, but somehow, he did. "Bye, Paul."

***

Beth left Amy around six p.m. and within ten minutes of her leaving, Will's Mercedes pulled up outside the house. Amy mused how it was just like old times, the sound of his car pulling up, hearing his key in the lock. He came in to see how she was – he looked exhausted – then he got them some dinner.

"Have you got anywhere with the investigation?" she asked, as they ate.

"Can't get anywhere at the moment. The crew have had interviews, but the plane won't be accessible till tomorrow. I still think the turbulence… I wondered if there had been lightning… maybe issues with the maintenance. We'll have to see. I'll let you know as soon as it's conclusive," Will said. "How're you?"

"I'm OK. Bit frustrated at the lack of mobility. Beth came over today."

"Oh, good." They fell silent. Will glanced at her, she glanced at him. There seemed to be so much to say to each other and yet neither wanted to broach the subject. Amy wanted him to stay over, but how could she ask him? They would have to talk about their situation, their future, but today was not the day for that. She dare not drop the Z-bomb in front of Will, but he was likely to want to FaceTime later. That could potentially be awkward. Will cleared up the dinner things and Amy twiddled her hair anxiously.

When he came back into the room, she declared, "I want you to stay the night." She thought better of just asking him, she wanted him unable to refuse.

"OK," he said. She looked at him, searching his face. He was having an inner battle, she could see that much. She was facing a similar battle herself. But she would need help getting up the stairs – she did not want to sleep on the sofa – and she just could not bear the thought of being alone in this vulnerable state. She decided to text Zach. There was no way she wanted to subject Will to witnessing her talking to him – that would be below the belt.

Hey you, I'm home, but I can't talk tonight, so exhausted. I'll try to call you tmrw morn ur time. Miss u xxx

There was no reply straightaway. Amy checked the time; it would be about eleven a.m. over there – he would be in rehearsals and probably could not hear his phone. Will came back into the room with a cup of tea for Amy and handed it to her.

"I thought about getting you a glass of wine, but thought it might be better not to with the drugs you've had today."

"Bless you. Yes, I don't really feel like drinking."

"Oh, you must be under the weather then," Will said, with a smile, Amy smiled back. How well he knew her. Her phone buzzed as a text came through. Will's smile disintegrated and he sat down. He clearly could guess who the message was from. But how could he be upset in Amy's time of need? She opened the message in silence.

Hi you – no prob get some rest. No bad dreams. Speak tmrw Z xxx

Amy put her phone down. There was silence for some time.

"How was America?" Will said, carefully.

Amy hesitated to reply. She thought about her time over there, the awards ceremony, the private jet, the sex… "Interesting."

"I saw the pictures of the awards thing you went to." He avoided looking at her. Amy did not know how to respond. He looked directly at her suddenly. "You looked amazing. I won't let you go without a fight, Amy," he said, with determination. She avoided eye contact and shifted her plastered leg uncomfortably.

"I'd be disappointed if you did."

"I'm sure he wowed you over there."

"I don't think we should talk about it, especially not today."

"I know, and nor will we." And with that, the conversation ended.

They watched TV together and at about ten-thirty, Amy was ready to go to bed. She swung her legs off the sofa carefully and grabbed her crutches. Will helped her stand and followed her to the stairs. He stood behind her as she contemplated the summit. There was no way she could easily do this alone.

"Here." He turned her to him, put one arm about her shoulders and scooped her up under the knees with the other arm. She put her arms around his neck and he carried her upstairs. She marvelled at his unquestioning commitment. Her heart panged and she leaned her head onto his strong broad shoulder. He pushed the door to the bedroom open and placed her carefully onto the bed.

"Thank you, Babe," she said, without thinking.

"Do you need help getting changed?" he said, innocently.

"No, it's OK, I'll be fine." She was glad she had worn a skirt – jeans might have been tricky.

"Well, I'm going in the spare room." Will kissed her head. He brushed her hair back and went to the door. "Call me if you need me. Night."

"Night."

Twenty-Five

Will stayed for the next two nights. Amy was trying hard to get used to her decreased mobility, but it was frustrating. She spent most of the day writing – Paul had sent her plenty to do – and on the second night, Beth and Isabella came over with a takeaway for the four of them. Fortunately, Beth had filled Isabella in on Amy's complicated love life and the evening was very pleasant. There were no Freudian slips mentioning Zach at all. At around nine-thirty they left. Will saw them off, just as it was starting to rain hard. Amy was sitting in the lounge. She checked her phone; she had not heard from Zach at all. Will clocked her looking at her phone but was silent on the matter. Both had been indirectly avoiding the elephant in the room for two days now.

Just as Will sat down, the doorbell rang. He looked at Amy with a puzzled expression. She shrugged. "Maybe Beth's left something here."

He got back up and went to the door. Amy took a big sip of her glass of wine and nearly sprayed the living room with it when she heard the voice from the doorstep. She tried to hear what was being said and looked down at her shabby outfit.

Will came back into the room with a dark look on his face. "Amy, you have a visitor," he said, starchily, before revealing a bedraggled Zach.

"Hey." Ironically, Zach was holding a bunch of flowers, much like Will had on that fateful morning.

She felt caught in a Greek tragedy again. Zach smiled his sparkly smile. He was markedly awkward – she had not told him Will had been staying with her. Will stood next to him stiff as a board, clearly suspecting that Amy must have known of this visit and clearly not prepared to give them any time alone. He folded his arms and Amy did not know what to say. To either of them.

"Hi," she said. Zach handed her the flowers. "Thank you." She put them on the table next to her.

"Wow, this is beyond awkward," Zach said, laughing nervously. Will stood his ground, not looking at Zach, but glaring at Amy with his hands in his pockets.

"Babe, would you be so kind as to get me a painkiller?" Amy said sweetly to Will. She certainly needed one right now and thought it the only possible method that would work to break this intense situation. Will brushed past Zach and went silently to the kitchen.

"'Babe' again, is it?" Zach whispered, sitting on the end of Amy's sofa. Amy looked at him. She felt an urge to throw her arms around him, but it was not as overpowering as it might have been three days ago.

"Don't. Just don't. I can't believe you're here, why didn't you tell me?"

"Warn you, you mean, so you could lose him?" Zach gestured towards the door with his thumb.

"Zach, please, I can't do this right now." They spoke in undertones. Amy was not sure how long Will would give them. At that very moment, he entered the room, handing Amy her painkillers and a drink, giving Zach a sideways evil look.

"I'll be upstairs if you need me, Amy." Will gave her a possessive kiss on the forehead and left the room.

"Thank you," she said, as he went. Her eyes followed him as he left the room, not glancing back. Zach's gaze followed Amy's with interest.

He rubbed his forehead with the palm of his hand. "This is so messed up. All I could think about was you all alone here, trying to cope. Of course you're not alone. I shouldn't have come, I'm sorry." He made to stand up, but she stopped him with her plastered leg. She winced at the movement.

"Are you OK?"

"Yes. Do not make me move like that! I'm not equipped for getaways right now. I'm really pleased to see you, I've been wondering why I hadn't heard from you." She carefully swung her legs off the sofa.

"Amy, I had to come see you. I can't believe what you've been through." He put his hand behind her head and leaned his forehead against hers. She breathed him in.

"I thought that was it. I thought I'd never see you again," she whispered.

"Me too, when I got that message. It felt like… a goodbye." He had tears in his eyes. He kissed her again. "What's the deal with Will? Should I be worried?" Amy's stomach turned over. How the tables had turned.

"I'm not sleeping with him, if that's what you mean. He's been more like my… carer." This made Amy laugh in spite of herself. Zach laughed too.

"He was fucking grumpy with me. I thought, well, I should be the grumpy one now, him opening your door to me! And shouldn't he be off finding out what was wrong with your plane?"

"That's a bit harsh, Zach."

"Sorry. I want to be so angry that he's back here. But I can see that he's being good to you. I hate that. I should be here looking after you."

"What about rehearsals, your tour? How have you managed to swing this?"

"I can't be here too long, two days, tops."

Amy's brain went into overdrive. "How did you get here? Where are you gonna stay?"

"Hire car from the airport, and I was thinking I'd stay here, but then at the last minute I booked that hotel type place around the corner from your place as a back-up. Glad I did. I'm sorted."

At that moment, Will opened the door to the lounge suddenly. "I'm going up the pub with Matt," he said, bluntly.

"Will…" Amy began, but he left as quick as he spoke and they heard the front door slam. Amy looked down at her leg. "Well, I can't exactly chase after him." Zach looked down and smiled. "I'm sorry I look a mess. If I'd known you were coming, I would have made more of an effort."

"Don't do that. You're relaxed enough in *his* company not to worry about making an effort, I want you to feel like that around me, always." Zach leaned forward to kiss her again.

"Charmer." She still felt a burn of physical desire towards him, but it was more measured now, she noticed.

He looked down at her leg. "I don't think I've ever done a girl with a broken leg before."

"Yes, well, not tonight, Josephine."

"Is that another one of your obtuse, colloquial British-isms?"

"Have you not heard that before? It was supposedly a quote from Napoleon declining sex with his wife."

Zach laughed and shook his head. "You're funny."

"I'm in touch with my inner nerd." She touched his hand, which was resting on her leg. "It's good to see you."

"You too. You have no idea. Do you think we can have some time together while I'm here?"

Amy looked at him. How on earth was she going to manage this again? She sighed. Having intimated a commitment to Zach in America, she was beginning to get cold feet. The first person she thought of on those fateful moments on the plane had been Will. But here was Zach, still so attractive, so magnetic… throwing everything off track. She thought when she met Will that was it, game over, this is the person she wanted to be with forever. Zach really was the spanner in the works, her guilty pleasure.

"Will's working tomorrow."

"OK. Well, I'll go now. I'll come back in the morning."

"OK. Might be best. He'll only have one drink at the pub and then come back."

Zach looked at Amy. He seemed to want to say more. He looked like he was going to take a pop at Will. Amy wouldn't have blamed him, but she was also glad he refrained. Her harrowing experience had left her in a spin emotionally. She still had the fire burning for Zach, but all she wanted was to be looked after. And Will was there for her. Full stop.

"Can I do anything for you?"

"No, I'm good, honestly. I'm well looked after."

"I'm sure you are. At what cost I wonder." He seemed to be thinking out loud. He looked down at the floor as he said this. Amy was too careworn to respond. She was getting drowsy, part from tiredness, part from the painkillers kicking in. Zach glanced at her. "You look tired."

"I am. I need my bed."

"Can I at least help you do that?" He looked her in the eyes, his captivating blue-grey eyes searching hers.

"Sure." She shifted to the edge of her seat and grabbed her crutches, standing up. She hopped with his help to the steep staircase of her Victorian terraced house and leaned the crutches against the wall. Will had carried her up; Zach put her arm across his shoulders and walked her up clumsily next to him – like a couple of drunks – on the narrow stairs. He opened her bedroom door and helped her limp through. He turned her to him and kissed her firmly on the lips. She still felt a rush from kissing him, but something in her had changed, had perhaps died on the plane. The parting message she had sent from the crashing plane began to hold more meaning and resonance.

This was all very exciting, but in the stark, cold light of day, of life and its future and all it could behold, Will was there, her stay, her crutch, the one she turned to in time of need. Zach was an unrealistic schoolgirl infatuation, an ethereal experience caught on the breeze of her zeitgeist. Will was every bit real and present and adult, the person she could sit with silently in a room for hours, doing nothing, just being there, company, existing together. When the thrill of all things dies down, surely that will be what is craved for, the tranquillity of someone to relax with. She could not see Zach as that. Sure, he had shown her a more relaxed version of his life in Denver for twenty-four hours, but his star was still rising; he was still so full on with tours and show business and fame – how would she fit in with all that?

She smiled a benign smile and touched his chest gently. "Thank you." She sat down carefully on the bed.

"Need help getting undressed?" His voice was dry. She detected an undertone despite the honest inflection of his comment. She looked at him standing above her.

"No, I'm good." He knelt in front of her and kissed her again, longer this time, more passion, less tenderness. She pushed her fingers through his hair; his hands grasped her body hungrily, but she pulled away whispering, "I'll see you tomorrow."

He got to his feet. "I'm so glad you're OK. You have no idea," he said, and walked to the door. "Bye, Amy."

"Bye, Zach."

He paused to look at her, then turned and walked down the stairs. She heard the front door close and a small car's engine start up. She lay back on the bed and sighed. She shifted her way up the pillow and pulled the cover over herself.

Had she not still felt in the throes of some sort of post-traumatic psychosis that she feared was clouding all her judgments and emotions – not to mention the fact that he had taken the trouble to fly nine hours across the globe to surprise her with his visit – she would have ended it with Zach there and then.

***

She fell asleep quickly and was roused from her slumber by the sound of Will fumbling his key into the front door, after last orders time, but probably before closing. Judging by how long it took him to open the door, Amy assumed that he had certainly had more than his usual one drink, and she heard him go through to the kitchen. A few minutes later, she heard his footsteps on the stairs, slow and deliberately steady. He pushed her door open slowly and peered in. Her light was still on, she turned to look at him.

"Hey. You OK?" Her voice was croaky.

"Yeah, you?"

She nodded. He was clearly trying to act sober. Amy was reminded of some of their drunken sex encounters when they had been together. *So much fun.* He hesitated, then walked into the room and sat on the bed. He was looking at her with a mixed expression. She wondered if he had expected to see Zach lying in the bed next to her, stirring up bad memories of a few weeks ago. She was not disappointed to have proved his suspicion wrong. As if she could have allowed something that callous to have happened with him staying there. She hoped he realised she had more mettle than that. She put her hand on his, and he gripped her fingers. She marvelled at his stoicism, not questioning her about Zach's sudden visit, or what had gone on between them while he was at the pub.

"Been a mad few months, hasn't it?" she said, quietly. He looked down at her. She smiled serenely.

"Mad…" He continued to look at her. He still had love in his eyes and her attentiveness to him had not gone unnoticed. He was cautious, but conscious of her apparent rekindling of affection. He leaned forward and kissed her softly on the mouth, his lips just barely touching hers. She closed her eyes as he moved to her, leaving them closed for a moment after his lips moved a few inches away from hers. She opened them to look at his face. His eyes were bright and alert. Perhaps he wasn't as inebriated as she had thought. There was clarity in his expression and she felt like she was seeing him in a renewed light. She pulled him to her to kiss him again; he put his arms around her drawing her close to him, but he pulled away after a moment.

"Get some sleep," he whispered, not regaining eye contact and standing up.

"Will…"

"Night." Will left the room. Amy sighed heavily and switched her light off. It took her some time to get back to sleep.

***

Amy got up the next day with the distinct feeling of purpose. She made her way to the bathroom, and nearly bumped into Will as he was making his way there as well.

"Sorry," they both said, at the same time. Will smiled and looked down. "You go first," he said, ever the gentleman.

"Are you working today?"

"Yes."

"Then you go in first." She hopped back and gestured her arm for him to go into the bathroom. He looked at her with affection. She smiled. "There was a time, not so long ago, when we would have just gone in together."

"Hmm. Yes." He continued looking into her eyes for a moment longer, raised his eyebrows and sighed a big sigh. "I'll try not to be too long."

"It's OK." She watched as he went into the bathroom and glanced furtively at her as he closed the door. Her comment was the first time she had properly mentioned their relationship since the plane. He was cautious, she knew it, and little wonder at it. She had led him a merry dance before, and once bitten twice shy. She would have to win him over if she wanted him back, she knew it. He may have stated that he would do anything for her and would not give up without a fight, but she would need to prove herself worthy after betraying his trust so badly. That would be tough to win back. She limped back to her bedroom and sat on her bed. A text message had come through to her phone. She grabbed it.

Hey you, can I see you today? xx

Sure. Come around about 10?

OK, see u then

Amy sat and stared into space for a moment. She had awoken with a firm resolve. She felt clarity had returned enough to trust her own judgements and decisions. She knew what she must do, but the execution of it was going to be so much harder. A wicked thought passed through her mind and she saw the morning events play out before the actuality of them. *Why shouldn't I have my cake and eat it too?* Having been through what she had been through she had been given a new vision to life itself. All the usual clichés had a resounding meaning to her – *que sera sera, laissez-faire, carpe diem…* she would have what she wanted and refused to feel guilty for it.

Life was too short, too fragile to worry. Her dalliance was not going to last – maybe deep down she had always known it, but pleasure and thrill and bedazzlement had blinded her; the fantasy had engulfed her, eclipsed her better judgement, jeopardised her future. But so what? She was so glad to be alive right now. Relieved to be safe, to be here, at home. Relieved to be with Will. Who was to say that they could make it work anyhow? Nothing was certain. But her intentions were clear as the light of day, as was the devil on her shoulder, giving her ideas – just one last play with her toy…

Twenty-Six

Will left the house within half an hour and Amy watched as his car sped down the street and out of sight. He must have seen her standing at the door because he flashed his hazard lights as he rounded the corner. She waved and went back into the house. She had put on her most seductive lingerie after her fumbled shower – leg hanging out in all its plastered glory. She did not feel at her sexiest, but she made up for that with her hair and makeup. She put on a dress – she had been wearing a dress most of the time anyway as it was still warm and more practical with her leg the way it was.

At ten-past-ten, there was a knock at the door. Amy paused before getting up carefully and grabbing her crutches. She bit her lip as her resolve solidified. A cold shiver ran through her and she momentarily closed her eyes. It was one thing making a decision about someone in your life while they are not with you, another thing entirely when you see them again. She briefly ran through all their encounters in her head – the hotels, her house, her time in LA, Denver… She felt herself wobble. But she loved Will. Loved him. Wanted to marry him, have babies with him. She could not let this dangerous obsession get in the way of that. But one more dip in the water was too enticing to ignore and pass up . She made her way to the front door and opened it. Zach was facing the road and turned as she opened the door. He had a khaki jacket on and jeans ripped at the knees; his trademark back-to-front baseball cap. *Damn he's still so irresistible.*

"Hey, you."

"Hi."

"Are you on your own?" he asked, tentatively glancing around as she led him into the house.

"Yes." She closed the front door. As she turned around, he kissed her on the lips with so much force and pent up passion, she fell back against the wall and dropped one of the crutches. She pulled away. "Zach…" She wobbled on her bad leg.

"I'm so sorry, let me get it." He bent down to get the crutch for her. "I've been restless all night, thinking about seeing you again, and doing that."

"Do it again," she said. "Without knocking the crutches out of my hand this time." She smiled. He smiled too and slipped his arm around her waist, gently pulling her near him. She breathed him in as he placed his lips on hers. It felt so good; it felt so good to be bad again. She knew she had reached a conclusion, although she was probably still in the midst of some sort of shock – she would end it with Zach and patch things up with Will. She felt in control again. It was not an ethical way to end things, but her recent experience had made her feel justified in dispensing with ethics, at least for a little while longer. Was she worried about hurting Zach? Yes. That was the only thing nagging her in the back of her mind. But how much did he feel for her anyway? It was a big deal him coming to visit her now, for sure.

He put his hands under her thighs and lifted her up carefully, wrapping her legs around his waist as best he could with the plaster cast in the way. She drew her lips away from his to speak.

"I was gonna offer you a drink first."

"I'm not thirsty."

"Not for a drink, anyway," she huskily whispered. He carried her into the lounge and laid her back carefully onto the sofa. She wriggled her way out of her dress and dropped it on the floor. Zach hastily took his jacket and t-shirt off and leaned over her.

"No games today, just your body against mine." He kissed her lips, then her chin.

Amy would normally have closed her eyes and lost herself in these moments of pleasure, but she wanted to savour them, watch as this, her last indulgence, played out, Zach blissfully unaware of what was going through her mind. She watched as his head moved down her body, kissing her cleavage, hugged tightly by the lavish Agent Provocateur underwear she had purposely chosen. His hands held her by the small of her back, warm and soft, his floppy hair tickled her belly as his mouth left a trail of kisses on her skin as he moved downwards. Her skin tingled with goose bumps as the light touch of his lips excited her. She watched as his fingertips tantalisingly pulled her underwear down.

She lifted her hips slightly, desperate for him to get his mouth on her. He looked up at her from where he was and smiled with a devilish look on his face, moving up to kiss her on the lips, leaving her expectant for any other sort of oral pleasure. Instead he slipped his fingers into her, moaning as he felt how wet she was. Her back arched and she gasped.

Unable to keep her eyes open any longer, she gave way to the sensations. He drew away and kissed his way down her body again. She was squirming for him now; his journey was quicker and his mouth engulfed her. Back arching again, she groaned. This was not how she liked to play – she liked control, dominance, but her leg rendered her subject to practicality. She had to lay there and let him lead, let him do what he wanted. And she so desperately wanted to be on top... She held back as much as she could, and just at the point of climax, he drew away and undid his belt and trousers, gliding easily into her. She gripped his rear hard; he flinched slightly and pushed deep.

She bit his neck, as thoughts of Will and his unconquerable prowess in the bedroom flooded her mind, threatening to propel her far from the climax she had been so tantalisingly close to just moments before. . She screwed her eyes shut and tried not to think of him, tried to focus on Zach, her last wild oat to sow before she threw in the towel. It was no good. She opened her eyes and placed her hands on Zach's face.

"Talk to me," she whispered, eye to eye.

He obeyed. "You're so fucking sexy, Amy, I love being inside your tight, wet pussy..." he whispered back, kissing her neck, murmuring dirty things in her ear.

She turned his head to kiss him hard on the lips. As his tongue explored her mouth, her breathing became quick and shallow and she came. As she was in the peak, so did he, and he leaned his body against hers, both clammy and breathless. She put her arms around him, feeling his back and hair once again, trying to relish these moments. She felt a tear in her eye, it crept upon her unawares, and she pondered on why it had appeared. Sadness at this, her planned, last encounter with him, her deviant contrivance of how she intended things to play out, her feeling of betrayal towards Will, something she had never quite shifted away from at any point during her fling with Zach, her fear that things with Will would not be salvageable, had too much damage been done… and last but not least, the consciousness of the heartbreak she was to inflict on Zach, however large or small, she dared not determine. She believed all his professions of feelings for her, but she had such a humble opinion of her own dominion over men that she struggled to accept that he would be truly distraught. Plus, he was still this highflyer, with women throwing themselves at him, women much better looking and with bigger personalities than her, she concluded.

Zach got up and went to the bathroom to freshen up, helping Amy up the stairs to do the same. By the time she limped down the stairs, he already had the coffee machine on. She smiled at the simple differences between her two men. Will would have had the kettle on to make a cup of tea; Zach was coffee. Will liked suits; Zach wore hats. Will liked Indian food, Zach Japanese. Will was into movies, Zach music. The torture of these snapshot comparisons must have reached her facial expressions, as Zach glanced curiously at her with a bemused frown.

"You OK? You look pensive." He was aware of the fragility of her mind after the plane.

She looked at him, lost in thought still, trying to switch her overactive brain off. "Yes, yes, I'm fine." She hopped with her crutches towards the table and he came over to pull out a chair. As he did, he put a finger under her chin and tilted her face up towards his.

"Come here." He put his arms around her and hugged her tightly, but tender, protective, and he breathed in the scent of her hair, which was always coconutty. He placed a hand on the side of her head and kissed her hair. Her face was pressed into his strong chest. She felt her resolve to break it off dissipate inside her and she hated herself for her weakening. She closed her eyes and allowed him to hold her. Out of the blue, tears proceeded forth, and she wept into his crisp white t-shirt, leaving mascara stains front and centre. She tried to hide her emotion, but one sob gave the game away and Zach drew back, realising.

"Hey, why the tears?" he said, surprised. He sat her down on the seat and knelt in front of her. She felt so childlike right now, so needy physically. She hated that. She was such a together person since her off-the-rail teenage days. She smiled and rubbed his chest where her black mascara had run.

"Sorry."

He looked at his top. "Oh, don't worry about that. Are you OK? Tell me the truth."

She took a deep breath. This was a chance, an opening. "Oh... I just... I'm emotional right now." She bottled it. Looking at the concerned eyes in front of her, she just could not bring herself to be honest.

"Of course you are. You're bound to be. I was a bit nervous flying over here, and I'm on and off planes like buses." He stood up. "After one of my coffees, you'll feel loads better, I guarantee it."

She smiled at his simplistic, albeit tongue-in-cheek answer to her complicated woes.

"Of course." She played along. The mention of the plane sparked her memory of something important she had almost forgotten. "Oh, Zach, I just remembered, there was a flight attendant I met on..." She gulped the words out, "The plane. She's going to one of your gigs – the one in LA – and I said you'd give her a shout-out. I probably shouldn't have promised it, but she was so sweet and young and I felt an affinity with her; then she was so brave at... at the end of it all. Is that OK?"

"Of course, what's her name?"

"Chloe Maskowicz."

He handed her a mug of coffee. "What did you tell her about us then?"

This was tricky. She had not wanted to discuss this with him, unsure of how he would react, and whether she was justified in describing him as her boyfriend to a perfect stranger. Even more awkward knowing what she was planning now.

"I, well, at first I told her I had just said goodbye to my, erm, boyfriend. I was upset, you see, when I got on the plane, and I guess in conversation she just put two and two together. She's a big fan of Sovereign X, so I said I would do that for her." Not strictly the full story, but again, after what she had been through, what did it matter?

"Absolutely, she will get a shout-out. That's no problem." He walked over to her and kissed her again. She shifted in her seat, keen to change the subject.

"How's rehearsals going?"

"Good, well they were going good. Writing some new material too; should be dropping a new song within a few weeks." As he said this, the doorbell sounded. "I'll get it," he said, before she could do or say anything.

She was not expecting any visitors, or parcels, but if it was someone she knew, they would certainly have a shock with Zach opening the door to them. She heard a familiar shriek and peals of laughter, which indicated the arrival of Beth, and by the sound of the jovial and friendly chatter, Isabella too. Zach led the way into the kitchen and proceeded to make more coffee. Beth's eyes were out on stalks behind his back. Amy just raised her eyebrows briefly and sipped her coffee.

"All right, mate?" Beth said, hugging Amy.

"Yes, you?" Amy replied, conversationally. She knew Beth would be burning with questions and equally be totally shocked by Zach's appearance. She wished she had been at the front door with him, to see her response first hand.

"Hi, Izzy." Amy got up carefully and greeted her.

"Oh please, don't get up on my account."

"Oh well, I sort of was, but sort of also wanted to move into the lounge," Amy said, awkwardly.

Isabella laughed. "OK."

"I'll bring the coffee through," Zach piped up.

Isabella grabbed Amy's coffee for her and Beth led the way to the lounge. Beth started to giggle.

She moved close to Amy and whispered hurriedly, "You know, it's weird," she said, pointing with her thumb over her shoulder in the direction of the kitchen. "But Will is really starting to look like Zach these days." They all giggled despite themselves. "You clearly have a type."

"Clearly." Amy was relieved at a moment of humour amidst the complexity of her situation.

"I was like, what the fuck? When he opened the door."

"Trouble with her is that where most normal people would have just thought 'what the fuck' she actually allows it to come pelting out of her mouth at full speed and full volume," Isabella jibed, affectionately.

Amy laughed. "I don't doubt it."

"I offer no excuses," Beth said, holding her hands up. "Last night we had a nice dinner with you and Will, Zach was thousands of miles away; this very morning, Will's absent, and here Zach is!" Any further conversation on the matter was stymied by the appearance of the man himself with the drinks. He sat next to Amy and put his hand on her knee.

He asked Isabella about her auditions and the agency he had put forward, and they chatted animatedly for a little while. Amy was subdued and Beth allowed the conversation to bypass her occasionally to observe Amy. She was not comfortable, Beth could see, she deduced that the reason for it was her warmth to Will the previous night. Zach had obviously surprised her with this visit, at a time when she was wavering on her intention to make a go of it with him. Beth caught eye contact and gave her an imploring look.

"Beth love, help me get to the bathroom, will you?" Amy spoke almost in an undertone.

"Oh hey, I can help you." Zach offered.

"No, it's OK, Beth will help." She got up and Beth briskly followed her to the stairs.

"I meant it when I said 'what the fuck', too. As in, what the fuck is going to happen? Are the three of you going to shack up together and they just share you?" Beth whispered conspiratorially, part jokingly, as she helped her get upstairs. "I know you could do without all this right now, but it's all so messy."

"I know. You ever get the feeling you've had your ass handed to you?"

Beth sniggered. "Indeed."

They reached the top of the stairs and Amy limped to her bedroom. Beth stopped.

"I thought you needed the loo?"

"What? No! I just used that as an excuse to talk, away from Zach."

"Oh, good stuff, great plan. So, he just turned up?" Beth sat on the bed next to Amy, clearly eager for the juicy details.

"Yes, last night, after you left."

Beth sucked her breath in through pursed lips. "Ouch. Awks. Bet that went down like a lead balloon with Will."

"I've been in less awkward situations. And more awkward, to be fair, with the same players." Amy sighed and looked up to the ceiling.

Beth suddenly grabbed her arm. "Wait – have you two shagged already? I bet you have, you dirty bastard." She got up from the bed quickly, looking back at it with disgust.

Amy watched her, amused, and looked down. "I just can't help myself. Anyway. It wasn't in here."

"Errr, you did it in the lounge where my Izzy is sitting, didn't you?"

"Hmm, maybe not *exactly* where she's sitting."

Beth sat back down. "So, what now then, Amy Armstrong? Girlfriend of a singer-songwriter or air-crash investigator? Both sound pretty cool to be fair."

Amy smiled. She loved how Beth could make any situation light-hearted, without losing sight of the real issue that needed sorting out. "You know, I feel like I've been a yo-yo. Do you think it wrong that I've let the plane incident cast clarity over my life and future?"

"You use it however you need to. If you're sure it's clarity that it's casting, not clouds. But if you want to make changes and put it down to that, then do it." Beth was looking searchingly at her. Amy looked over to her, absentmindedly rubbing the knee of her broken leg.

"I had all these dreams, bad dreams, in America. I feel like I was ignoring an omen. The first person I thought of as that plane came down was Will, but then I sent them both the same sort of 'goodbye, I love you' message before landing."

"So? You were bound to. Will was (and probably still is) the love of your life, and you'd just spent the maddest, most intense week with Zach, with an emotionally charged parting of the ways." Beth spoke so matter-of-factly, that Amy felt a load lifting off her shoulders.

"Do you think I've been worrying over nothing then?"

"Sounds like it." Beth got up. They had already absented themselves a little too long. "The only question is, who do you love the most?" Beth put her hand on the door handle ready to leave the room. "And I think you already know the answer to that." She gestured Amy to get up so she could help her downstairs.

They entered the lounge to find Zach talking to Isabella about the tour. They looked up as Beth and Amy came into the room.

"Sorry. Pisses like a man, this one." Beth rolled her eyes, nodding her head back towards Amy.

"Fuck off. Least I don't act like one." Amy retorted in their usual way of bantering insults at each other. Neither of the Americans entirely got this method of humour. Isabella laughed nervously.

"Well, Amy, we wouldn't want to keep you too long from your surprise guest, especially as he was just telling me he's only here for another day. We just came to say, well, I wanted to say, goodbye. My flight home is later today."

"Oh, I see." Amy wished to ask her if she had heard back about any of the auditions yet, but was unsure if she should. Isabella had risen from her seat to kiss and hug Amy. "See you again soon?" Amy asked.

"Oh yes, for sure! I got a part, offered just this morning! Only a small one, but in the West End at least, running for three months over the fall! I should be back in a month."

"Yay, that's fab news, I'm so pleased for you!"

"I'm hoping to have a few cameos in a TV series back in the States too, thanks to Zach."

Amy's heartstrings gave a twang. He had done that for her. She glanced at him. He was looking directly at her.

After they had said their goodbyes to Zach, Amy saw them both to the door. Beth hugged her and murmured in her ear, "We'll talk again."

Amy nodded and waved them both off. She shut the door and hopped back to Zach in the lounge. He was by the door and put his arms around her, kissing her softly on the lips.

"Hey, let's make the most of this twenty-four hours together."

His words had more of a resonance with her than he could have imagined. He kissed her again and she felt a jolt in her stomach. She had to do it. She had to break it off. This was it, as Beth had said – so simply – who do you love the most? And she had been right: she did know the answer.

"Zach, sit down. I think we should talk." She hopped to the sofa and he sat opposite.

"Uh-oh. I know those words... I've *said* those words."

Amy avoided his eyes, which were boring into her. "You know, these past few months have been like a weird dream for me."

"Amy..."

"No, Zach, please let me finish. I never thought I would have had this time I've had with you. Not just because you're my celebrity fantasy or whatever, but because my relationship with Will was my forever one, the person I wanted to spend the rest of my life with."

"But what we have, it's amazing, you can't deny it. You just... you keep me wanting more..."

"I know, and I just can't keep my hands off you. But that's almost the point: in spite of all that, Will is still there in my heart." Amy touched her chest and looked at Zach sadly. She almost couldn't believe she had managed to get the words out – her attraction to him, the electricity between them, still ever present and strong, but she did not regret her statement, it felt right, in her gut, it felt proper and true.

Zach had his elbows on his knees and was looking down to the ground. He got up suddenly and flicked his hair back. She looked away, still so drawn to him – this was tough. In the beginning, she had been in awe of him, but very soon it was clear that she had control of the relationship, he was putty in her hands. He had all the status, but the power was hers. It had been fun and she was delighted that meeting her idol had not been a disappointment, in fact, it would have made her situation much more tenable if it had been, but he was a lovely person. Nevertheless, there was no depth, her soulmate was someone else. It had taken her brush with her own mortality to realise that while the rush of feeling like naughty teenagers had been fun, sooner or later she had to grow up and look to the future.

She plucked up the courage to look Zach in the eyes. Those eyes...

"I don't think we should do this right now. You're still recovering from the plane, you're not thinking straight." Sadness was clear in his tone.

Amy sighed. "I know it looks like that, and maybe a day or two ago it was, but it did get me thinking, and I have been thinking a lot, stuck indoors such as I am. The first person in my mind when that plane came hurtling to the ground, was him. I wanted him when I got off the plane."

"Of course you did, he's an air-crash investigator! He was nowhere near your mind when we were having sex earlier, I know that. And what was that? A goodbye fuck?" He began pacing, his temper rising.

Amy rubbed her forehead with her palm. "I'm sorry. I'm sorry you came all the way over here to see me, and now I'm saying this stuff to you."

Zach turned away. "Do not apologise. Never apologise for sex, or anything we have done. Life is life, what happens, happens. I knew that him staying here, he would silently manipulate his way back into your affections," he said, glumly.

"That's the thing though. He could not have succeeded – if that was in fact his intention – had those affections not still been there dormant in me anyway. I hate doing this Zach, it kills me, honestly. I wish I could keep you both." This last bit slipped out without Amy really thinking. Zach turned around and moved closer to her. She looked up but could not make eye contact.

"I don't want to lose you."

She stood up carefully, wobbling on her good leg. She grabbed his arms to steady herself; he held her by hers. She looked into his eyes, tears forming in her own. He kissed her and her tears fell as she closed her eyes.

"Don't, Zach," she said, pulling away, but he pressed his lips on hers again, slipping his hand under her dress, his dextrous fingers gently feeling all of her. She gasped.

"You sure you want to let me go…?" he murmured.

"No… but I've got to," she whispered, softly moving his hand away.

"Amy, I want you. I know you want me." Zach took her chin in his hand so she had to look him in the eyes again.

Amy looked him directly in the eyes and took a deep breath. "But I want him more."

Zach closed his eyes, his head dropped. "I think I should go." He was dejected. Amy felt terrible as he walked past her towards the front door. She grabbed her crutches and followed him.

"Zach." He looked at her. "I never dreamed it would end like this. It's just destiny, I guess."

"Destiny…" He looked down at his feet and smiled. "I thought our destiny had collided. And so many times… I thought we were meant to be, I thought it was written in the stars…"

It was Amy's turn to look down. It was devastating to be breaking up with your ultimate fantasy.

"I can't go on like this, I've made my choice. I've had an amazing time with you and I'm so glad you allowed me into your life, I really am."

"And you. Damn that air-crash investigator!" Zach said, with a slight smile. He looked Amy in the eyes, her sincerity clear on her face. "Amy." He brushed her cheek with his hand. She moved in to kiss him on the lips, savouring his taste, his breath, how close he was to her. This was her final goodbye.

"I think we were fooling ourselves to think that we could make it work."

"What does he have that I don't?"

"My heart. That's all. You're lovely, Zach," she whispered, close to him. He closed his eyes and leaned his forehead on hers.

"You too," he whispered back. "I've had a blast. And I'm glad you're safe."

"Thanks." Amy touched his bicep. "I'll always buy your music. Always." She smiled, but her eyes belied the sadness.

"Little consolation," he said, with the smallest of smiles.

The goodbye was prolonging the agony for both, but neither were in a hurry to conclude.

"We'll always have the songs you wrote… about me. I shall hold those in my heart forever."

"I guess they will always be there, indelible, for eternity. I'll think of you every time I perform them. Expect a few more now. Bye, Amy." He smiled sadly.

"Bye, Zach." They shared another lingering kiss and hug and Amy watched him leave. He turned back to wave as he got in the hire car and drove away down the road and out of her life. Amy closed the front door and leaned against it, sobbing. She made her way sombrely into the lounge and grabbed her phone to text Beth.

It is done.

Twenty-Seven

Amy spent most of the rest of the day coming to terms with what she had done. Not only had she had an affair with her celebrity crush, she had dumped him under the auspices that she could salvage her much-damaged relationship, a relationship she could not be entirely certain was still eligible for salvage. Inevitably, regret began to sink in. What had she done – was it the wrong decision? Beth's replies to her text helped.

So now you must move on. win Will back – that won't be difficult. You made the right decision. It's what u really want I can see that. Love u Babe

Having a major wobble… What have I done, have I actually just dumped Zach Hayes???

Don't do that. Want me to come over?

No, it's OK. Thank u lovely. Need to think about what I'm gonna say to Will… wish me luck xx

You don't need luck, sweet xx

Amy cooked a meal ready for Will's return home. An hour past the time she expected him home, and he still hadn't arrived. The dinner was almost ruined, dried out, and she was just about to throw it in the bin when she heard his key in the front door. He walked through to the kitchen with a bag in his hand.

"Oh, hiya – you've cooked! I didn't expect that, I picked up an Indian." Will smiled.

Amy laughed. "You know, I think it's ruined anyway. I'm up for a curry. I thought you'd be home earlier."

Will placed the bag on the table and started to get the containers out. He smiled. "I'm not sure you should keep referring to it as home for me," he said, without looking at her.

She looked up at his face. His dark eyes were reserved, but his smile still firmly playing the corners of his mouth. She so wanted to blurt everything out, but did not know where to start. She wondered if he wished to ask her if she had seen Zach today and wasn't saying. She felt a pang of guilt that she had had sex with him, guilt towards Zach that she had done it knowing full well that she was going to end it, but also guilt for Will's sake. She wanted him back... perhaps she should not have indulged herself. *Oh well, too late for regret now.*

"You've gone rather quiet." Will looked quizzically at her.

She sighed and looked away, her chin in her hand. "Remember our first date?"

Will smiled, knowingly. "Yes, we had a lovely lunch."

Amy looked at him, waiting for him to meet her eyes. She crunched on a poppadum. "Followed by the police chasing us on your motorbike for speeding."

Will laughed. "Yes, that did add a bit of a memorable twist to it." He glanced at her with a frown. "Why suddenly think about that?" he said, sitting down opposite her.

"I dunno. Got a lot of thinking time stuck in on my own all day."

"Have you not had any visitors today?" His question was loaded. She shifted uncomfortably in her seat.

"Beth and Izzy stopped by to say bye."

"Oh yes, didn't she go back to America today?"

"Yes. Back in a month though, she got a part in the West End."

"Oh, cool, I bet Beth is over the moon."

"I'll say." Amy felt relieved that for the first time since her return, conversation was flowing freely and warmly between them. She also felt she may have side stepped the Zach landmine. They fell silent for a moment while they ate.

"Have you not seen anyone else today?" Will said, more statement-like than questioning. Apparently, she had not side-stepped the landmine after all.

Amy made out she was eating to buy herself time to consider her response. "Um." Her quick wit was failing her badly when she needed it most. Typical.

Will looked at her across the table. "Come on, Amy. You must take me for a fool if you don't think I'd guess he's been here. I can smell him." He took a mouthful of his dinner and looked at her expectantly for a squirming response. "It's OK, we're not together anymore." It bit him, she knew it.

She turned her knife over and over in her hand and looked him square-on. Perhaps blatant, carte-blanche honesty was the best way forward. She put her game face on and drew a deep breath.

"Yes, Zach was here. We had sex in the lounge."

Will dropped his fork onto his plate which made Amy jump. He nearly choked and took a big swig of the Cobra he had bought with the food. "Fuck's sake. I wasn't expecting that." He coughed.

"Clearly." She took a big sip of her wine. She looked at him, his sensitive brown eyes and interesting bow-shaped lips were busy, displaying the thoughts going ten to the dozen in his mind.

Before he could respond, she spoke again.

"But he's gone now." She looked away.

"Right. When shall I move out?" he said, sullenly.

"Will, when I say he's gone, I mean, he's gone. For good. I ended it."

Will looked at her. He took another swig of beer and set it down on the table. "So what?"

Amy looked down. He was not going to make this easy for her. She did not blame him for that.

"So... you were fishing for it and I'm being honest with you. For the first time in a long time. I ended it with him, because I am not, nor do I want to be, over you." She tried hard to leave emotion and sentiment out of her speech, to guarantee maximum impact with him.

"But you had sex with him anyway."

"Yes. I'm not going to apologise for that. You know, and have always known, since we got together, that I have an itch for him. I had to indulge my fantasy one last time before I shut it down. I have been seized by a don't-give-a-shit, need-to-live-life kind of attitude since... well, since the plane. But it also made me realise how much I love you and don't want to lose you. Ever again."

Will looked at her, astonished by the bluntness of her statement. It T-boned him emotionally. He truly did not know how to react. He remained silent, computing the information that had been launched at him, and got up, clearing the dinner things away.

He turned towards her and sighed. "We've got a lot of ground to make up, Amy. I just don't know."

"I don't expect miracles. Just give me another chance. No more celebrity flings, I promise." She smiled a cheeky grin. He smiled back, in spite of himself.

"You're incorrigible, Amy Armstrong."

"Is that a yes?"

Will looked at her. "Not yet." He paused. "But there's a glimmer," he said, as he topped her wine glass up. He picked the glass and his beer up and took them into the lounge, before coming back to help Amy get up.

"Making good progress with the investigation, by the way. Thought you'd like to know."

Amy looked at him. "Really? What do you think happened?"

Will proceeded to tell her about hydraulics and maintenance and the flight recorder, but her mind had drifted. She really did want to know about the plane, but there was so much else to think about. She knew Will – patient, methodical, meticulous – he wouldn't throw caution to the wind and just passionately accept her back. But when he did, if he did, he would totally devote himself to her and forget the past. He was so different to her. She was not patient – act first, think later, spontaneous and headstrong. But maybe that was why they worked so succinctly, yin and yang, black and white. Amy looked at Will, nodding, wondering if he was thinking about her, like she was thinking about him.

"… Anyway, we shall know a little bit more tomorrow. I still need to look through the maintenance logs and speak to some of the guys."

"And do you think you'll be able to put it right so it doesn't happen again?"

"I just said that, have you been listening to me at all?"

"Of course! I really want you to get to the bottom of it. It was so frightening, I wouldn't want it to happen again, or worse."

Will looked at her and smiled benevolently. "I don't either. I could not have borne it had anything happened to you…"

Amy looked over to him, unconsciously rubbing her plastered leg. She did it every time the plane was talked about. "All I thought about was you, as we landed," she said, quietly. She knew he wouldn't believe it.

"Are you sure?" He looked away. She gritted her teeth, cross with herself that she had caused him so much pain, but also cross that despite that, she could not regret one single thing.

"I can't take back the past, Will. And in truth, nor do I want to. But experiencing what I have made me think about the future and how important that is. He and I never had a future, but more importantly, I realised I didn't want it to include him. It's you, it's always been you; my future, it's you. But I want a better balance in our relationship, you know, no more controlling; we must be a partnership – I need that. I want things to be different this time."

He looked at her intently as she spoke, his brow furrowed with the complexity of his feelings, taking in everything she said.

"Look, I think I'm going to go to bed. We'll talk more in the morning." Amy hiked herself off the sofa and grabbed her crutches. Will automatically got up and followed her to the stairs. She leaned her crutches against the wall and turned to him. She looked into his eyes, those eyes so full of love when they had looked at her before her betrayal, had been so closed off to her since, but now, now they had a spark, an ignition of former feelings, locked away behind the pain and bitterness of the break-up; she saw the shadow of warmth returning in him. He placed his arms gently round her and picked her up. She curled her arms around his neck and nestled her head onto his shoulder, his familiar scent a solace to her, his secure, strong arms holding her tightly as he ascended the stairs to her bedroom.

He put her down carefully as they went into the room.

"Thank you," she said, smiling at him. He held her eye contact for a moment before brushing her hair back from her face and pulling her to him for a lingering kiss. His lips were soft and warm as they always had been and she wound her arms back around his neck. She moved backwards towards the bed, but he hesitated. "Come to bed with me."

"I just…"

Amy put her finger to his lips. "Let me take control… you must learn to let me take control. Lose yourself." She began undoing the buttons of his shirt; he gave little resistance.

***

Amy woke the next morning to the sun beating into the room through her pale curtains. She opened her eyes. The window was wide open and the curtain was being twisted and blown by the incoming breeze. She looked across at Will lying next to her, sound asleep. She felt content, happy, in a place she should be. She smiled and closed her eyes again. Will opened his to see her with her eyes closed, smile on her face.

"Hey, Babe. I know you're awake," he said, croakily.

She opened her eyes straightaway. "I only wake up with a smile on my face when you're next to me."

"Oh, that's very corny." He smiled.

"Corny or horny?" she said, devilishly. He pulled her to him and kissed her nose.

"You've always been both."

"It feels so good to be back here."

"In England?"

"Well, yes, but, *here*." She touched his face and kissed him. "Love you," she said with ease, not fully expecting him to say it back.

"Love you, too." He returned the kiss.

Amy closed her eyes. All the memories from the past few months – her whirlwind, sensational fling, her dabble in celebrity lifestyle, the plane – all these images and experiences were set in her mind like a string of images on Instagram, captured and preserved forever. And then there was Will, so real. Will was always there, always constant, and yet complex – his job, his petrol-head, adrenaline for speed and yet a consummate professional, wild and imaginative in the bedroom… He was a paradox in his own way.

"Tell me all about Hollywood sometime."

"OK." She was under no illusion that this, her indiscretion, would just be brushed aside, there was still so much ground to be made up. But make it up they would and could, because the basis of it all was a knowledge in them both that they were truly in love and meant for each other.

***

Will drove to work at the airport with Amy waving him goodbye from the doorstep. She went back into the house and set herself down to finish an article Paul had asked her to write, happy that things looked like they were going to move on.

She thought for a moment about her time with Zach, about him flying home today. She hoped she had not damaged him too much. But he was a free spirit, he would bounce back fast, she knew it. Fulfilling a fantasy like she had, and to have given it so much airtime, had impacted her greatly. She could not regret it, it was a special thing, encapsulated into her memories. An anecdote for the grandchildren. She mused as to whether Will would ever let her listen to their music again or watch them on TV. She smiled to herself and called Beth to tell her that it looked like things were going to be good between her and Will again.

Meanwhile, Will arrived at the airport and made his way through the main entrance. As he did, he almost ran into someone rushing through the doors.

"Sorry, mate," Will said, as they collided. He looked at the back-to-front baseball cap and wayfarer Ray Bans and recognition struck both men at the same time. "Zach."

"Will." For a moment, they stared at each other, stilted. Will was not the type of person to gloat over someone at his success, he was too kindly-natured for that. Likewise, Zach had too open a personality to begrudge what had gone on.

"Hey, man, listen. No hard feelings." Zach took his sunglasses off. Will noticed that he looked like he had not gotten much sleep.

Will offered to shake his hand. "Thanks for looking after Amy in America." Was all he could muster.

"Ya know, she don't need looking after. Taming, maybe, but not looking after. She wants a partner. And I guess that guy is you. She never looked at me the way she looks at you, never saw me in the way she sees you. Go make her happy. She's one special girl. You should get her to marry you as quick as you can, or I might try to steal her again." Zach winked and squeezed Will's shoulder. "Bye," he said, walking away.

Will stood watching him dash towards Departures and out of their lives. He could see why Amy liked him: he was younger than Will, taller, slimmer, good-looking, oozed charisma – a natural threat. He could understand her bedazzlement and found that he could come to terms with her infidelity through that understanding. He was her celebrity fantasy, right? This was not some normal affair with Joe Bloggs. Will stood in stasis for some moments, the bustle of people in the airport all happening around him. His resolve became clear in his mind and he made a quick phone call before dashing off to get on with some work.

Before he left work, Will texted Amy:

Hey, Babe – get yourself ready, I'm taking you out for a meal xx

When he arrived home, he opened the door to find Amy as dressed up as she could be, one high heel on. She looked at him and started laughing.

"Do I look ridiculous?" she said, giggling still.

"No! Well, maybe a little bit." He smiled. "I'll just go freshen up." Within ten minutes, he was helping her get into the car.

"Where are we going then? Please don't say I've dressed up just for McDonald's."

"No, no." He drove the half an hour or so to their favourite restaurant, a gastro-pub out in the countryside. Will helped Amy get out and could see the look on her face, so pleased to be out, despite her lack of mobility. They were shown to their seats and the waiter brought out an ice bucket and champagne to them. Amy grinned.

"This is all lovely and so unexpected. So out of character for you, Will," Amy said, smiling. "You don't have to woo me or make big gestures. It's I that should be doing that for you, with what I put you through."

"Well, you know, it did hurt. But what hurt the most, even in spite of seeing you with him, was the fact that I thought I had lost you. So, here's to finding each other again." He clinked her glass. "I've always known you liked him and I can see why. He's a great guy. Most people don't get a shot at indulging their celebrity fantasy and, you know, he was always going to fall for you: you're so beautiful and have such a wicked sense of humour."

"You're so sweet. Just remember how much above your weight you're punching!" she joked, wagging a finger at him.

He smiled his beaming smile. "I mean it. And I'm made up that you came back to me. You know, something happened to me today and it made me think, why am I hanging around? Why don't I just get on and do the thing that I have had on my mind since before all of this?"

"What happened? What's on your mind?" Amy frowned at him.

"I had an epiphany, brought on by the unlikeliest of sources." Will sipped his champagne and looked across at Amy, wide-eyed and interested. "Maybe one day I'll tell you the whole story. But not now." He rummaged in his jacket pocket and produced a small, shiny box. "Now, all I want to say is… marry me?"

Amy's jaw dropped and she looked down at the box he had placed in front of her.

"Really?" She was in shock; she really had not expected such an acceleration from last night. But then, why shouldn't she? It was not like they had just met, and of course, she had no hesitation at all – she was delighted.

"Yes! Yes, definitely." She opened the box to see a shiny, dainty solitaire diamond ring glistening up at her. Tears filled her eyes and Will got up and put the ring on her finger, kissing her softly on the lips. She looked into his dark eyes, all their former affection flooding back to them both, and felt that everything was as it should, and was meant, to be, written in the stars, her stars, blissfully unaware of the part that Zach had played in this, their eternal union.

Twenty-Eight

EPILOGUE

Amy checked the time on her diamond-studded Omega watch. Will should have been home by now – she so wanted to see him before she left. She put her earrings in and fingered serum through her long hair once again. Jon and Anna would be there any moment now to pick her up. She looked at her reflection in the mirror one more time before dashing downstairs. As she did, the front door opened and Will came through it.

"Oh, good, you're back!" she said, as she reached the last stair.

"Hiya – wow, you look lovely, what's the occasion?" Will looked admiringly at his wife.

"I'm going up town with Jon and Anna and some of the people from Keller House, remember?"

"Oh. Oh, yeah. I forgot about that." Will's face dropped and he placed his work bag by the stairs. Things had been strained of late. Amy could not believe the progression of her life – at the same trajectory as her career was going up, her personal life was going down. Will said nothing further and made his way through to the kitchen. Amy frowned and followed him.

"You said you were OK with me going, are you not OK?" she said, as she caught up with him. He was putting the kettle on, his back to her. She stood there waiting for his response. He stopped what he was doing and placed his hands on the counter. He heaved a big sigh.

"Would it make any difference if I wasn't OK with it?" He turned to face her.

Amy knew Will was struggling with her success, ever since her book was published. Especially as the plot had laid their personal life bare. She had no idea it would be as popular as it had become and, thus, she was in strong demand – events, press, a whole new circle of friends and acquaintances. Will had always been a private, reserved person, so this new-found attention did not sit well. It was Amy's turn to sigh. She loved Will, but his resistance to her career was becoming stultifying. Up until now, she had mollified his negativity with reassurances, but since he had discovered she had written yet another book that her publisher had picked up, he had reached a new low. Her career as a writer was not a whim, it was, in fact, just kicking off.

Amy put her hands on her hips. "You resent my success, don't you?"

"No! Of course I don't. I'm pleased for you. I'm proud of you. It's just…"

"What? What then?" she pressed.

Will sighed again. "You have this whole new life now. I'm just not sure it has room in it for me."

"That's ridiculous."

"Is it? You've seen Jon and Anna more this month than you've seen me."

"Well, you've been away for work too, so don't lay that entirely at my door. Jon and Anna are fellow authors, with the same publishing house, I'm bound to see them a lot."

Will muttered something inaudibly.

"What did you say?"

"I said 'cronies'."

Amy turned away, folding her arms. She could feel her temper bubbling to the surface. "You know what your problem is? You're out of your depth. Intellectually. When was the last time you read a book? Apart from a plane manual or the AAIB monthly bulletin?"

"Thanks for that." He stormed out of the kitchen. Amy closed her eyes and regretted her invective.

"I'm sorry, that was really bitchy." She followed him into the lounge.

"Do you not understand why I find it hard? You secretly wrote a book I had no idea you were writing, with us in it, about you having an affair. I work in a very serious and sometimes sensitive profession, and I have not lived it down. As soon as people realise, that's all they can talk about." He rubbed his brow. Amy hated that she had caused him pain.

That seemed to be happening a lot lately. Just as she was about to reply, the doorbell sounded.

"Go. Go with your friends," Will said, curmudgeonly.

"We can't go on like this."

"No." Will did not meet her eyes.

"Will you be up when I get back?"

"Will you be late?"

"Yes."

"Then, no."

Amy moved towards him to kiss him goodbye. He kissed her tenderly on the lips and immediately she was reminded of why to fight to keep this together – their love for each other.

"I'm sorry. I don't want to fight," Amy said.

"Me neither. Have a nice evening." Will hugged her. But the atmosphere remained stilted. She turned and made her way to the front door; Will followed her and watched her leave.

Her face lit up as she opened the door to Anna and they greeted each other with a hug and a kiss and left the house, but her heart was heavy.

"Hey, Amy, you OK?" Anna said, as they made their way to Jon's car.

"Yes. Just had a fight with Will, that's all."

Anna put her arm around her tightly. "Well, don't think on that now, try to enjoy the evening." She smiled as they got into the car together.

She greeted Jon with a kiss on each cheek and got in the back of the car.

"All set for your TV debut tomorrow, Ames?" Jon said.

"I am the perfect fifty-fifty mix of poise and trepidation." The mention of her TV interview made her woes slide away a little.

Jon chuckled. "Undoubtably."

They pulled away from Amy's house for the journey into the city. She put her troubles to one side in her mind and set her resolve to enjoy tonight. This was a big deal, a meal at The Ivy with her publishing house and her friends. The word *'cronies'* reared in her head, but she batted it away. This was her pre-launch dinner, before the release of her second book. The talk in the car had turned to literary subjects and Anna and Jon talked animatedly about femininity and masculinity in their respective works. Amy drifted off, uncharacteristically. Normally, she would be putting her two pennies-worth into the discussion; instead, she tapped into Twitter '#WrittenInTheStars', which was the title of her first book. As usual, there were many posts, some from women inspired to write their own romantic literature, some just appreciating her story. It always made her feel better to read these and it boosted her mood.

"What do you think, Amy?" Anna spoke to her from the passenger seat of the car.

"Sorry, I was miles away."

Anna tutted. "I was just saying to Jon about how difficult it is to write a strong female protagonist without her appearing like a bitch. Not like writing a male – always seen as the hero. That must resonate with you and your writing – dominance and balance of sexual prowess features in your book."

"Yes. Yes, it does. It is tricky to get it right. Much like life, really. Can a woman really have it all? A great career and a successful personal life as well? How is it that guys can do it and when we try something always suffers somehow?"

Anna looked back at her. "No woman should ever feel like she has to suffer personally because of her career success." She raised her eyebrows at Amy; Amy smiled and looked away.

"Of course, man came first," Jon quipped, with a wry grin, deliberately trying to provoke them.

"Probably the last time he did," Amy shot back. Jon and Anna laughed.

Jon parked the car and they walked to Covent Garden, chatting and laughing as they went into the fancy Art Deco restaurant. This was a far cry from her life four years ago. She never dreamed she would be here in a million years. Will was never one for this sort of fine dining – overpriced and silly small portions is what he would say. He liked good food, of course, but this was just too pretentious for him. Things had changed, Amy now earned far more money than he did; her career had overshadowed his for the first time. Perhaps this was why he was struggling with her success; he had said he was afraid she would feel she no longer needed him.

They made their way to the table where Amy, Anna and Jon's literary agent, plus three of the team from Keller House – their publishers – were already seated. They already had fancy-looking gin and tonic cocktails and Amy grabbed the gin menu. Tonight was not the night to fret about her personal maelstrom; tonight was about celebrating.

***

Amy got home just before two a.m. She made her way upstairs with a glass of water and, of course, Will was already asleep. She got herself into bed, but was buzzing from the evening she had had. She lay in the dark room staring up at the grainy ceiling, eyes wide open. She reached for her earphones and put some music on her phone. It had to be Sovereign X, the band that had started all this off, her heady, absorbing obsession with them. She wondered if her book had made its way into Zach Hayes' hands yet, something she had secretly hoped for since she had written it. Maybe an elaborate way of reaching out to him, but still. In the dead of the night, she lay fiddling with her earphones cable, thinking about the last few years.

She thought back to the time when she revealed her book to Will. He began by being bemused. He knew she had this itch for the band and their lead singer, ever since that time she had met them on the plane; he also knew she had agonised on the what if scenarios. But when he had read it, he had no idea how much she had taken it to heart. It unnerved him, she knew it, even though he never said. She had put their lives entirely into the story and had invented an affair. But surely, he could not be lugubrious about fiction? That's what she had always said to him. And in any case, it was just a hobby of hers, writing, it wouldn't go anywhere. Little did she know then that a top London publishing house would snap it up and turn it into a hugely successful novel. She closed her troubled mind off as much as she could, she needed her sleep – tomorrow was a big day.

***

"OK, be cool," Amy said to herself, waiting in the green room at the TV studio. She took a deep breath and held her new book tightly in her right hand. Her heart was beating fast, she did not like this sort of thing. She looked up to the ceiling. She had not had the best start to the day either – Will had been very quiet and cold that morning, and he had to work, so could not come with her to the interview. Amy was getting used to doing more and more things on her own, but it disappointed her.

Any moment now the runner would call her to go through to the studios.

"Amy, we need you now please, you are just about to be introduced by Jonathan."

"OK." She stood up and smoothed her leather trousers down. Why had she decided to wear such a ridiculously hot outfit for a television interview? She got her game face on and followed the runner down the hallway. The applause was more and more audible as she neared the bright lights and cameras. She waved to the audience as the presenter walked towards her to greet her with a kiss on each cheek.

"Amy, please sit down. Now, your book, *Written In The Stars* has become a nationwide sensation and there is talk, I understand, of a movie, right?"

"Yes, I had heard that talk too." She smiled.

"Did you have any idea the book would be so popular when you were writing it?"

"Of course not! I was recovering at home from an injury and I had so much time on my hands. I was inspired by something that happened to me when I was a flight attendant, and that was that. I typed and typed and here I am."

"What do you think about people saying it's a cross between *Notting Hill* and *Fifty Shades*?"

Amy smiled. "I can see why. Well, who am I to complain about that? Two huge successes."

"Now, let me go back to what you were just saying – the inspiration behind the book. Explain this to us, because I've heard about this and wondered if what I had heard was true."

Amy smiled and leaned towards him, "Well, what have you heard, Jonathan?"

"Well, the obvious thing is the fact that there would seem to be many aspects that could be autobiographical. Names, for example, are a real give-away," he said, sardonically.

Amy laughed. "Yes, that was one thing I insisted on with my publisher. And they say, write about what you know. What do I know better than my own life?"

"So, tell us the story of how it came about."

"Well, like many people, particularly girls I guess, I was obsessed with a popular band, then one flight I was working on, they were on the plane. I had a massive crush on the lead singer, but never got past pleasantries. I left the flight wondering what would have happened had I hit it off with him and we had met again under different circumstances – could we have had an affair? And then that was that, I wrote my book."

"Now, some of the love scenes are quite raunchy, are they autobiographical too?" He gave a sideways grin to the audience.

Amy leaned across and touched his knee. "I write about what I know, Jonathan," she repeated, suggestively. The audience whooped and Jonathan waved his cards theatrically in front of his face as if needing to cool down.

"And this is based on the American group, Sovereign X – again, names not changed for the book?"

"No. Bold as brass, aren't I?"

"Do you know if the band and, in particular, the lead singer, Zach, have any idea about the book?"

"I don't know, I mean the book has been big here, but I'm not sure about the States."

"So, you haven't met the band, since writing the book?"

"No! I think I would be quite embarrassed, to be honest."

"Well, Amy, we have a bit of a surprise for you. Here, just for this show, please show your appreciation for... Sovereign X!" He stood up, Amy's jaw dropped and she covered her face with her hands, her cheeks burning. She dared to look at the doorway she had just walked through and all five band members walked into the studio. Zach lifted his hand up to wave to the audience and they made their way to the sofa. Amy stood up, not sure what she should do with herself.

All that she had written, all those love scenes that had formulated in her mind after seeing them on the plane all that time ago. She had written this book, placed herself and her life in it – the playing out of a 'what if' scenario had she hit it off with the famous person she was infatuated by, what impact would it have on her and her life had it taken place? And then the ending, where she dumps him to go back to the love of her life, her real-life husband, Will. Using real names right now did not seem the best idea. How could she hide behind it all as artistic licence? But then again, when she had written the whole thing in the weeks she had been stuck at home after her real-life plane accident (in which her and Will's Cessna had had to make an emergency landing in high winds, and her foot had been crushed: another fact she had doctored slightly to include in the closing chapters of the book), she had no idea how popular her book would be. She was delighted just to get the damn thing published and for all her mates to buy a copy.

At the time, there was a tiny part of her that had hoped that by insisting on the real names being kept in, maybe a copy would fall into Zach Hayes' hands and he would be curious to meet her. But before she could reconsider the blatant autobiographical aspects, the book had exploded onto the download and reading charts in Britain and, it seemed, her success had been overnight. She watched Zach as they walked towards the sofa, her heart thumping, her real-life infatuation every bit as powerful as what she had written about.

One question burned in her chest – would he remember the encounter that started the whole thing in the first place, the time she served him on British Airways flight BA268 six or seven years ago? He kissed her on the cheek and shook her hand, as did the other members one by one. She sat back down as they sat, Zach next to her, so close, on her left. She flapped her hand in front of her face, aware that her cheeks were glowing. The presenter, Jonathan, was looking at her smiling.

She put her hand over her eyes. "I'm totally shocked. And totally speechless. And I am *never* speechless."

Jonathan laughed. She glanced sideways at Zach who was casually sitting back, his arm across the chair behind her, looking directly at her, an admiring smile on his face. The audience laughed at the blatant awkwardness. Amy just kept casting furtive side glances to Zach.

"Now, the big question I'm sure on everyone's minds, including yours, Amy, I imagine, is have you read the book, Zach?"

"Actually, I have. I enjoyed it. I'm looking forward to the movie and who might play me."

Amy put her face in her hands again. She giggled and Jonathan laughingly looked at her.

"I'm so embarrassed," she said, through laughs.

"I'm sorry, we have been so cruel springing this on you. But it does make for good TV, right?" he said to the audience. They all cheered. Amy could not bring herself to look at Zach and the interview continued only for a few more moments with a plug for her new book, before they cut to a commercial break. Jonathan stood up and shook Amy's hand.

"Well done, Amy, what a great sport."

"I'm still in shock, I think." She glanced to her left, but the band had quickly been moved away to set up the stage for a performance of their new single on the show.

They reappeared with their instruments. Amy watched as Zach put his guitar strap over his head and strummed a few chords. He adjusted the microphone and looked across at her. She turned away quickly and sat back on the sofa as the commercial break was coming to an end.

Jonathan introduced the band and the lights went down in the studio for the performance. Amy watched, maintaining her composure, ever conscious of the cameras still rolling. She could not hide the euphoria of the moment, to watch them perform – her joy was two-fold. Not only was she a massive fan, of epic, obsessive proportions, but it had been that obsession that had brought her so much personal success in the writing of her book. And here she was, a little famous herself, on the same sofa of the same chat show as them.

"This is for you, Amy," Zach said, pointing her way as he began the song, to cheers from the audience.

Her immortalisation of them in the book, seemed to have benefitted them in some way too, the interest in their last few songs was markedly more, this side of the Atlantic, since the success of her book.

After the show had finished, Amy made her way back to the green room to get her bag and jacket, checking her phone as she did. Her Twitter feed and Instagram account were going wild with comments from people, wowed by the surprise that had been sprung upon her, many of her fans asking her if she was going to try to make her fantasy book a reality and try it on with Zach. She smiled. She was married, she did not see the fruition of it, albeit that Will was struggling with her new-found fame and the fact that he himself had been immortalised in her book too; that so much of their real life and love was laid bare. She had ribbed him that at least her character ends up with his character in the end anyway, but he was such a private person and he was garnering a recognisable face in the wake of her exposure in the press. As she was scrolling through her extensive social media, she became aware of someone standing in the doorway.

"Knock, knock." She looked up, surprised to see Zach standing there.

"Hi," she said, coyly, feeling the flush rush up her neck and cheeks again. It was embarrassing enough meeting your idol, tenfold embarrassment when you have written a book about them. A book, it transpires, he has read.

"I guess I don't need to tell you how much I love you guys." She looked down. She flicked her hair away from her face and looked at him. Her heart made a gazelle-esque jump, she could not deny it. He was leaning on the door frame with his hands behind his back.

"I liked your book. Interesting read," he said, with a wry grin. She grinned back. Her embarrassment was maxed out. Strangely, that made it abate.

"Thanks." She so desperately wanted to ask him if he remembered her. She did not know how to start.

"I was wondering if you would sign this." Zach produced a copy of her new book and gestured it towards her. She looked at him, stunned. Surely, she should be asking for his autograph? She laughed, and he smiled too. "You weren't expecting that, were you?" He tilted his head at her.

"No." She looked him in the eyes, wondering if she would feel anything like what she had pondered on and written about for her alter ego. She was certainly attracted to him; he just smiled benignly. She grabbed a pen from the coffee table. This might be her only chance.

"You know, one thing I was wondering, and have done for some time. I want to ask you... do you remember meeting me on the plane all that time ago?" She knew it was a shot in the dark and having read her book, he could easily lie and say yes, to be polite. He paused.

"You know, we travel on a lot of planes..."

She looked down. "Sure. Of course."

It was just the sort of rebuttal she had imagined over and over again. She shook off the feeling of disappointment and tried not to look too crestfallen. She was aware, as she wrote a note in the front of the book, that he was still watching her face intently. She hesitantly looked up as she finished the note. There was something there, something had entered the room with him, an atmosphere, a frisson. She paused for a moment to put her finger on it. It was chemistry, unmistakable. He was attracted to her, she could feel it. She scribbled something more into the book. He moved into the room.

"There," she said, passing the book to him. He did not take it straight away. His eyes were narrowed and he was looking inquisitively at her. The corners of her mouth drew up into a smile.

"Intriguing subject matter. I'm looking forward to the next one."

"It's quite different." She still had the book, he was still not taking it. She felt the intensity of the situation mount.

"I do remember meeting you on the plane," he said, suddenly. "I remember you saying you wanted to be a writer." He smiled and took the book. "I'm glad you made it."

It was her turn to smile benignly. He was clearly just saying that to spare her feelings. "Thank you," she said graciously, hoping he would not open the cover of the book in front of her now.

"How could I forget that flight? I think anyone would remember a lap full of noodles." He put his free hand in his pocket and smiled, raising his eyebrows.

Amy shot a surprised look at him. Her heart rose into her throat. "You... you do remember... for real?" She had not included this detail in her book for two reasons: one was that if she ever found herself in the situation she was now faced with – she could test to see if Zach would *really* remember, and the second... well, no one really wants to publicise their own clumsiness, after a freak pocket of turbulence and the subsequent humiliation of spilling a dish all over the celebrity they admire the most. She coloured at the memory. But she could not feel anything other than a bizarre thrill at the position she now found herself in.

"You were so kooky. So sweet." His gaze never left hers. "I admire you, Amy. I actually read your book a few months ago, I didn't just read it to come on this show like you might be thinking. I've been watching your star rising from afar, utterly taken in by your openness about your admiration of us… of me." He paused. "I wasn't keen on the ending though," he said, flicking the front cover of the book in his hand. She watched him intently.

"No, I don't suppose you were. It's just fiction though." She was amazed at how easily she had slipped into flirting.

"How much like your heroine are you?"

She pursed her lips. "Quite a bit. How much like my hero are you?"

"Well, I definitely would not have let you go." He flicked his hair back; she smiled and licked her lips. "What about real life? What do you think would happen in reality?"

"I… well. I guess we'll never know." She leaned against the wall gauging his response. He leaned his shoulder on the wall facing her.

"Wanna find out?" She was dumbfounded by how forward he was. And it sent shivers down her spine that her fantasy story had led to this moment. "Can I have your phone number?"

She was here, now, in the cold light of day, facing the sort of dilemma that she had written about in her book. The only difference there was that the Amy in her book had not been married. She was.

She ran her fingers through her hair. "I… wow." She smiled and looked him directly in the eyes. She was more confident than the Amy in her book. She was much more on a level with him in real life now; successful, famous in her own right, if much more modestly, learning to deal with media attention. She moved nearer to him and opened the cover of the book, their eyes making contact. Under her message, she had already written her mobile phone number.

He laughed at her predetermined move. "OK. Talk about art imitating life."

"Life imitating art, you mean."

"I guess so."

He slowly took the pen from her hand, brushing his fingers with hers as he did. She looked at him, feeling a surge of electricity through her body. By the look on his face, he felt it too. He was watching her intently, desire and attraction lighting up his face. They maintained eye contact while he took her hand, then he wrote his number on the back of it. Amy couldn't believe how something so simple could be so sensual and she felt shivers through her body at every stroke of the pen. Her head, normally so focussed and certain, suddenly felt so messed up, and seized by a ravishing feeling of danger and desire – she put her heart and her life and her marriage on the line.

"What hotel are you staying at?" She capitalised on her opportunity.

"The Connaught. For two days." There was a glint in his eye.

"Wanna rewrite the ending?"

THE END